PENGUIN MODERN CLASSICS

*Unknown Soldiers*

Väinö Linna (1920–1992) was one of the most influential Finnish authors of the twentieth century. He shot to immediate literary fame with his third novel, *Tuntematon sotilas* (*Unknown Soldiers*), and consolidated his position with the trilogy *Täällä Pohjantähden alla* (*Under the North Star*).

Liesl Yamaguchi, a former Fulbright grantee to the University of Helsinki and subsequent Special Assistant and Adviser to the US Ambassador to Finland, is currently completing a dissertation in Comparative Literature at Princeton University.

# VÄINÖ LINNA

## *Unknown Soldiers*

Translated from the Finnish by Liesl Yamaguchi

PENGUIN BOOKS

PENGUIN CLASSICS

UK | USA | Canada | Ireland | Australia
India | New Zealand | South Africa

Penguin Books is part of the Penguin Random House group of companies
whose addresses can be found at global.penguinrandomhouse.com.

First published in Finnish as *Tuntematon sotilas* by Werner Söderström Corporation (WSOY)
Helsinki, Finland 1954
This translation first published in Penguin Classics 2015
Published in paperback 2016
Published by arrangement with Werner Söderström Ltd. (WSOY)
004

This translation is based on the 1954 printing with the exception of the passage on pp. 265–6
['Lahtinen paused for a moment' to 'Just tryin' to get this sled to move'], whose expansion
just after the first printing reflects the author's sole amendment to the published work.

The translation was supported by the American-Scandinavian Foundation,
Finnish Literature Exchange FILI and WSOY Literary Foundation.

Copyright © The Estate of Väinö Linna and WSOY
Translation and editorial matter copyright © Liesl Yamaguchi, 2015

The moral rights of the author and translator have been asserted

Set in Dante MT Std 12/14.75 pt
Typeset by Palimpsest Book Production Limited, Falkirk, Stirlingshire
Printed in Great Britain by Clays Ltd, St Ives plc

A CIP catalogue record for this book is available from the British Library

ISBN: 978-0-141-39365-0

www.greenpenguin.co.uk

# Contents

# Chapter One

As we all know, the Lord is almighty – he knows all and sees far. And so, one day, he let a forest fire burn a good swath of state land, laying waste to acres of the dry, pine forest around the town of Joensuu. The people did everything in their power to put a stop to his work, as they always did, but he burned the forest undeterred, just as far as it suited him. He had his own plans.

A certain colonel was the first to appreciate just how far the Almighty's gaze had extended. Chief of staff of an army corps at the time, he noticed that the fire had opened up first-rate sites for his returning men to set up camp. Finland's Winter War had ended: the war that was, of all wars up to then, the best – seeing as both sides won. The Finns, however, won a bit less, in that they were obliged to cede some land to their opponents and retreat behind a new border.

What was left of the troops was sent home, and a younger set was called up in replacement. And so the clearing found itself beset with a battalion of infantry. The older men set off in the warmth of the spring – in fur caps, coats, felt boots and thick, wool sweaters. They returned without any 'difficulties of reintegration'. First, a good, old-fashioned Finnish dousing – then, back to work. Were all of our sacrifices in vain? Well, that was a question reserved for people without spring planting to do – and those people might well wonder whether their sacrifices had been so terribly great after all.

For the most part, they were a solid crop. The spiritual difficulties of re-entry into civilian life? They couldn't afford to invent stumbling blocks like that. People in the winter of life may have souls, but a soldier has nothing of the kind. Anybody who had such a thing would have had it anaesthetized as quickly as possible. No, the deep-set eyes above their chapped, stubbly cheeks revealed only animals, sly and ferocious, trying to hang onto two things: their positions and their dear lives.

The younger troops assumed their ranks.

There they stood, bumbling into lines with a bit of difficulty: Mother Finland's chosen sacrifice to world history. Farmers in coarse, sturdy clothes – day-laborers in flimsy jackets, ties sticking out from underneath their cheap, milled collars – and even some clueless city slicker with a wool 'ulster' on, who has 'like, no idea what happened on the trip out here. Like, seriously, none.'

Mäkinen was a bit hesitant, at first. A bundle under his arm, he had his best clothes on and his last wood-chopping pay tucked into his pocket. He had a picture of the neighbors' daughter too. Mäkinen wasn't actually in love with the girl, any more than she was with him, but he'd heard that looking at girls' pictures was something you did in the army. They were just neighbors, having lived down the road from each other their whole blessed lives, but when he was leaving, Mäkinen had taken the picture, awkwardly half-joking, 'Remember to write!'

What was his relationship to the great tides of world history, ripples of which had reached his ears one way or another? Adolf was raising a ruckus. That much he knew. And he knew what a ruckus would mean, too. It had already happened, at the dances, that some 'chest-beater' would climb up onto a chair, yank the lamps from the ceiling, and roar, 'Everybody out, goddamn it!' Finns are fierce – and we didn't start this. It's our right. That was just what Mäkinen thought as well. And if anybody comes over here again, then by God, we'll meet iron with iron.

'*What greater honor than dying in battle, valiant guardian of your nation's land . . .*' That was how the Finnish schools tried to cultivate the chest-beating bravado into something a bit more respectable. The future looked brighter if you considered it from a developmental point of view. But ditties dreamed up by some hobbling old man weren't quite the thing to spark these men's imaginations. '*Back in old Hellas! I mean, way, way back, fellas, when there was no Finland, yet . . . alas . . .'*

Trumped-up tunes were fine for gents – the average Finnish male having none too high an opinion of whatever it is that knocks around in the mind of a gentleman. More to his taste were tales of men who jumped on tanks and banged iron bars down machine guns to knock them out of plumb. Those guys were more in line with the heroes from the stories he knew.

So, their Finnishness was ennobled. Duly cast into the model of patriotism. Truth be told, their spirit could not have been better suited to the task for which they'd been assembled.

A year went by. Barracks rose along the edges of the clearing, which itself had been leveled into a training area. There the men ran, shouted and gradually grew into a lazy lot of confirmed 'old-timers'. Mäkinen was a soldier now too – or would have to suffice. He hadn't turned out quite the way his makers had intended, but he would have to do. The gaping jaws of world history were waiting.

## II

The machine-gunners were training on a separate side of the clearing. The afternoon was sweltering, and the heat, combined with the meal they'd just eaten, made the men so sluggish that their drills became even more slack than usual. Even the drill leaders had been NCOs too long to have any of that sharpness of ambition about them. This was particularly true after they realized that a conscript with the rank of corporal could consider himself at the highest peak his military career was going to afford him. The officers lingering further off weren't particularly keen to back them up either, should they manage to muster up more than the minimum amount of effort required. Enthusiasm of that variety would be shot down immediately by murmurs of mutiny from the ranks.

'Stop screaming, you fucking war horse!'

Listless orders rang out through the clanging of the guns the men lifted and lowered, going through the motions of their even more listless pivots.

'Boys, this is it! What'cha gotta know in war is how to pivot. Just bust out one of these little doozies, and that'll clear everything right up. In the bag.'

'What's that fellow Rahikainen muttering over there? Shut your traps in the ranks!'

'Soon as you shut yours, pal . . .'

Suddenly, the drill sprang to life. Clangs sharpened and steps quickened and the officers loitering further off hurried briskly toward their platoons. Prompting all of this was a thin-blooded little man who had emerged from the barracks headquarters and was now heading for the training area. It was Captain Kaarna, formerly of the renowned Finnish Jaeger Battalion trained in Germany, and presently commander of the company. Fifty-something, clean-cut and straight as a ramrod, he cut a compelling figure, despite his small stature. The Captain was a swift and nimble fellow, but even so, something in his present step signaled exceptional urgency. Kaarna kept his eyes fixed on the company as he walked, as if, in his impatience, he might will himself to his destination. And so he stumbled on a burnt tree root, regaining his balance quickly, though not before sputtering, 'Yee-aach! Mother f—'

Turning around to look for the root, the Captain promptly tripped on another, this time only barely managing to remain upright. '*Whaaoah!* Son of a bitch!' All his bottled-up tension erupted in an impromptu soliloquy that fizzled out into series of disgruntled coughs. 'Achem. Hmm.'

Upon reaching the company, he paused for a deep breath. Then, sitting on each syllable, he yelled, his voice cracking mid-command: 'Ma-chiii-hi-iine Gu-nnaaars!'

The men turned to face the Captain, each soldier stiffening to attention. One guy turned the wrong way in a panic, and was correcting his error with bated breath when a new command rang out, much to his relief.

'At ease. Platoon leaders!'

The tension in the men's bodies went slack and the three officers started quickly toward the Captain. He awaited them impatiently, shuffling his feet as his restless eyes glanced back and forth between the sky and their approaching figures. They formed a line in front of him and stiffened to attention. Kaarna avoided looking at the First Platoon leader, Lieutenant Lammio. Lammio had a habit of raising his hand to the visor of his cap in a jerky, almost spastic manner that Kaarna found supremely irritating – particularly because, on top of everything else, Lammio curved his wrist, which was against regulations. Anyway, the Captain really couldn't stand the man himself. The Helsinki lieutenant was tall, thin-faced and possessed of a self-assured arrogance that severely tried Kaarna's patience – which was none too bountiful to begin with. Lammio was a career officer, and the Army Academy had spoiled him for good. He had picked up all sorts of mannered gestures there that really made the old captain grit his teeth. The sound of Lammio's voice alone was enough to prick the men's hostility, piercing the air with its shrill, pretentiously convoluted orders.

The Second Platoon leader was a young, conscripted ensign – a small-town, high-school graduate from the wealthier, western part of the country, trying to live up to some mythic ideal of the Winter War ensign by performing his duties with outlandish ceremony.

The Third Platoon leader was also an ensign, aged about thirty. Vilho Koskela was a country boy, hailing from a small farm in Häme, some hours north of Helsinki. Sturdily built, blond-haired and blue-eyed, he had a cleft chin and spoke so little that he had acquired the nickname 'Quiet Koski'. The men had heard rumors of his feats during the Winter War, though he himself had never spoken a word of it. All anybody knew was that near the end, he had been serving as a company commander, even though by rank he was only a sergeant. When the war ended, he had been sent into officer training, and he had remained in the army beyond his conscripted time at the pay grade of ensign. He spoke very little and was somewhat awkward in carrying out his duties, but he was very direct, so in the end he was able to manage his men as well as anybody else.

The Captain held him in high regard, and even now it seemed as if he were addressing Koskela personally, reducing the other two officers to mere onlookers. The company watched as the four officers' conversation dragged on, raising their hopes that a change of activity might be afoot. Finally, the consultation ended. The Captain went back to the barracks headquarters and the officers returned to their units. The company's spirits perked up considerably when the order rang out that all platoons were to march back to their barracks.

'I bet we're going swimming,' one guy whispered to the fellow next to him. The latter, well past entertaining the illusion that pleasant surprises were something that army life afforded, restricted himself to a half-hearted sneer.

Koskela marched his platoon to the front of the barracks. He stood awkwardly for a moment, as if uncertain how to begin. He was uncomfortable giving orders in general, and formulating commands was particularly difficult, because somehow or other he was embarrassed by the contrived formality army commanders used to say such simple things.

'Right. NCOs, there's some stuff you guys need to take care of. A transport's coming to move the battalion to a new location, so we need to pare down the equipment. Everybody take the clothes you've got on and put a change of underwear, foot flannels and your overcoat in your pack. Bread sacks and mess kits come too. And weapons, of course. Everything else goes into storage. Try to be quick about it. I'll be back as soon as I've packed my own stuff.'

The situation was so out of the ordinary that the first section leader ventured a question that was actually rather out of line. The assignment they'd received hadn't been accompanied by any indication of why it was to be carried out, so Corporal Hietanen, boldly assuming a 'just between us' sort of air, asked, 'So, uh, where are we headed? The depths of hell, I guess?'

Koskela glanced at the horizon and answered, 'I don't know. Those were the orders. I've got to get moving. You'd better hurry, too.'

6

So that was all the men were to know of their fate. That being the case, they can be held only so responsible for it. But, anyway, they were very excited. Some men even took the initiative and asked their squad leaders what needed to be done – a rare occurrence indeed. Hietanen sat down at the table and drew up a list of the equipment to be taken along, which cut down on the chaos considerably. The Corporal was from the southwest part of the country around Turku, and in Koskela's absence he was the eldest in the platoon. His great voice boomed out over the others as he took charge of the preparations, setting time in his amusingly staccato Turku accent. He was a breezy, easy-going fellow – young, with a powerful build; and he had managed to garner some sort of authority within the platoon, mainly thanks to his imposing strength.

'The guys said the runner reported that the company secretary said that they're sending us to garrison Joensuu,' a self-important voice called out.

Hietanen was all too familiar with these rumors, which hope spawned now and again, and replied mockingly, 'Well, I heard from the drivers that this whole battalion here's being sent to garrison Helsinki! We're gonna trade in all these old rags for new, and we're all gonna get riding breeches into the bargain. That's what I heard. Oh, I hear all sorts of things.'

The second squad leader, Corporal Lahtinen, was kneeling on the floor, tying up his pack. He was a big guy from northern Häme with evident communist sympathies. He was leaning over his pack, muttering, 'There's gonna be a stink, boys. You'll see. That nutcase in Germany'll take off first, and then our idiot big-shots'll hoof it after him. Might as well be written on the wall, the way he's been yabbering on about it.'

Lahtinen looked around apprehensively, his mouth twisted into an anxious knot. Then he continued, 'Well, we'll just see how things work out for him. They sure aren't gonna to run out of ammunition over there' – his head tilted ever so slightly east – 'and they've got mines lying in wait on all those roads, too.'

'Ah, and there my Katyusha lies waiting for me, too!' grinned

Private Rahikainen, the unconcerned, perennial truant from North Karelia.

'Nah, listen guys,' Hietanen spoke up. 'I bet I know. We're just going to build fortifications along the border. The stuffed shirts are scared that if they join up with the Germans, the Russians'll drop in again—'

'But what would the Russians want here?' Lahtinen cut in, unconvinced. 'Far as I know they've never attacked anybody. But Herr Fritz and his buddies are already here.'

'Just passing through on leave!' somebody said.

'On leave!' The sharp accent of Lahtinen's voice revealed an untold reservoir of fury and disdain that sparked an all-out uproar. 'About as "on leave" as the Russians down there in our seaside hotels in Hanko! Just renting the place, uh-huh. Right! Like the ones in Viipuri. Vyborg, my ass. Stop defending them, for Christ's sake.'

Any attempt at defense was obviously hopeless, and even Lahtinen's 'Well, we'll just see!' was drowned out by the din. They didn't really think the question was as momentous as all that, but the clamoring might well have continued indefinitely had it not been cut short by Hietanen's deafening roar of 'Attention!'

The Captain stepped into the barracks. 'As you were, as you were, it's all right. Everyone taken care of?' The Captain strode swiftly about the room, inspecting the men's equipment as he said, 'Swap any broken equipment for new. If you have any civilian clothes, pack them up and smack a home address on them. The quartermaster will be responsible for taking care of them from there. Don't bring any unnecessary extra gear like writing pads and that kind of stuff. You know what it says on a boy scout's belt? "Be prepared." Be prepared! All right, all right, let's go.'

'Oh, but Captain, sir! Not the writing pads, please. The ladies won't oblige if we don't lay on the love songs.'

The men choked back their laughter at Rahikainen's plea, all the more outrageous for having been addressed directly to the Captain. But even the corners of Kaarna's lips betrayed the trace of a dry smile as he said, 'Well, well. Listen to this. Listen to this man! Won't oblige, he says. Naaw . . . nah. If she takes after her mother, she will, and if she takes after her father, she'll downright beg you for it. All right, let me see. Those boots – trade 'em in for new ones. They won't last the march . . . hee, hee. Lay on the love songs. So that's what it is. Well, well. This boy's going to conquer the ladies with his pen . . . his pen, he says! Hietanen! The NCOs appear to have taken advantage of their friendly relations with weapons supply to get some shoddy rifles for themselves. Well, that's one way to get out of cleaning and greasing your gun barrels . . . sneaky business . . . sneaky business. But if anyone in the platoon is still hanging on to one of those, have him go and trade it in immediately. Is that clear? OK, all right. With his pen, he says. Hmm. Ha! Well. Lah-dee-dah . . . da-dee-dum-dada.'

The whole time, the Captain's sharp eyes had been surveying the men's gear. The running monologue and constant humming were typical of his general mode of operation – outlets for his excess energy.

Without even standing at attention, the first squad leader, Corporal Lehto, suddenly asked, 'Captain, sir, I'm not a boy scout, so I don't know what we're supposed to be prepared for. It's not war, is it?'

'Nooo . . . no . . .' The Captain kept his composure. 'You don't go to war just like that. The war's pretty far off. All the way in the Balkans.'

'Captain, sir,' Rahikainen piped up, 'it seems to move pretty quick these days! You know . . . uh, "Blitzkrieg", so to speak.'

Kaarna looked at Rahikainen and laughed. 'Well, if it comes, it comes! War comes, you fight!'

'Oh, we'll fight all right. And once we get started, there's no telling how far we'll go.'

'That's the way, that's the way!' Private Salo, the guy from Ostrobothnia, was eager to chip in a word.

A ripple of disdain flashed across the Captain's face. Salo's ingratiating zeal clearly nauseated him, but his voice remained businesslike as he turned to Lehto. 'By the way. It seems you may have to do without that coffee.'

'Makes no difference to me,' Lehto replied flatly.

Lehto had taken on a position of trust with the Captain, having recently moved the latter's family into a new apartment in town. The lady of the house hadn't been able to offer him the customary coffee during the move, so Lehto had been promised it at some later date. This corporal from the outskirts of the working-class town of Tampere had taken a rather curious route to becoming the Captain's favorite – namely, by returning late from leave. Lehto had been without his parents since he was a little boy, and so was accustomed to fending for himself. There was something shady, even sinister about him, and the others all sensed it, though they wouldn't have been able to put it into words. They were all about the same age, but Lehto seemed older. His terse, surly manner never betrayed the slightest hint of warmth, and he became visibly irritated when confronted with sentimental situations. Homeland, family, faith, the Glorious Finnish Army and anything at all that smacked of 'spirituality' – Lehto had one swift answer to all of it: 'Cut the crap! Let's see who's got cash. Who's playing?'

As a civilian he'd ridden shotgun for a truck driver, but beyond that no one had managed to squeeze any information out of him about his previous life. Marches and other heavy-duty exercises never seemed to tire him. His face alone would take on a stony cast, and his thin-lipped mouth would stretch tight into an almost savage expression.

He'd been a full week late returning from leave, and in response to the Captain's questioning, he had replied flatly, 'Didn't feel like it.'

'Feel like it!' Kaarna fairly trembled with rage. 'Are you aware of the consequences?'

'I know the Disciplinary Code, Captain, sir.'

The Captain paused for a moment, staring out of the window. He tapped his fingers on the corner of the table and finally said quietly, 'If that's the road you want to take, you'd better be prepared to see it to the end. A man can take his own will for the law only on the condition that he forfeit all rights. You set yourself outside the tribe, outside of its jurisdiction, and you are an outlaw.'

For just one moment the Captain had tested Lehto's willpower. But Lehto's eyes were level with the Captain's, cold and expressionless. His gaze entertained not the slightest distraction – no diversions, no evasion.

'At its extreme, it means your life is always on the table. Do you think you would play with those stakes, if this incident had escalated to those dimensions? Now we're just talking about a couple of weeks' confinement, which is nothing. But if push came to shove, and it was your will against that of the army with every security it offers you at stake, do you think you'd hold your ground?'

Lehto hadn't actually looked at it from so high a vantage point. In his mind it was more of a private affair. 'Long as they don't torture you before they kill you,' he replied, 'then why not?'

'Fine. If that's how it is, listen: everything great that man has ever done has depended on that conviction. There's no use wasting it on petty insubordination. Strength and determination come to nothing if you squander them on just being defiant – they lose all their value, and then they just look ridiculous. I have no ethical right to punish you, only a right conferred by power. You ask nothing, so you owe nothing. I don't think your position is any more incorrect than my use of power. But if you waste your energy on stunts like this, I will consider you a fool. Aim higher. Every man's got a shot in this game – it's a battle of wills and the field is wide open. But winning is not easy, and it requires more intelligence than you've just demonstrated. Just being able to muddle through trivial incidents as they come up isn't going to cut it. You need a broader field of vision. Find it.'

A brief silence ensued before the Captain shook himself back to reality and said, 'Very well. You're dismissed.'

No disciplinary measures were taken, but Lehto was entrusted with various private tasks instead, including this whole moving business. And one evening, for no apparent reason, the Captain said in passing, 'It's never too late to start studying, you know. There's always more worth knowing. Start with history.'

The suggestion bore no fruit. Lehto didn't acquire any books, but the men did learn that the Captain himself read voraciously.

Otherwise, Lehto passed the test Kaarna's favors presented. His attitude toward the Captain himself remained gruff and non-committal, but his work was always meticulously and carefully done.

'Makes no difference to me,' he said flatly, tossing his pack onto the bed as if the Captain weren't there at all.

'Right, right. So it goes,' the Captain replied, matching the Corporal's work-a-day nonchalance. And with that, he resumed his game face, calling out, 'Hurry up, then!' and strode swiftly from the barracks.

## III

The exhortation was unnecessary. The men were already heading out. Where to they did not know, but that was what made it exciting – not to mention the truck transport, which meant that there would be no onerous foot-march to kill their mood. Truck transport, in the Finnish army! What on earth could such extravagance possibly foretell? It seemed wildly out of keeping with the whole enterprise.

They lugged their blankets and mattresses to the storeroom, where chaos reigned as never before. The quartermaster was beside himself. Corporal Mäkilä hailed from Laihia, a town renowned as Finland's stingiest – and he had not been raised there for nothing. Thriftiness was Mäkilä's passion – to such a degree that the term 'pathological' would not have been out of place, had the men been aware of such fine psychological distinctions. He kept the shelves in impeccable order, stocked with all the finest equipment, unmarred by any worn-out items – which he distributed to the company. He even spent his free time in the storeroom, checking the inventory against his account book over and over again. An ongoing feud prevailed between Mäkilä and the company. The men coming to trade in their equipment made their clamoring demands, only to be met with Mäkilä's low-voiced – and thus, all the more stubborn – refusal, which he typically checked only upon receiving express orders from the Captain. The most excruciating moments of his military career were those in which he was obliged to stand by and watch, turning red and clearing his throat, as the officers cherry-picked the best equipment for themselves, enjoying the privilege of their rank. A low muttering would emanate from the storeroom for a long time after such an incident, and any man who dared enter would be met with a reception even more offputting than usual.

Unlike most quartermasters, Mäkilä dressed himself in the shabbiest garments to be found in the storeroom. He was quick to point to his own scarecrowesque attire as grounds for his refusal. 'Of course, everyone wants to walk around dressed like a brigadier general. But we have to make do with what's left, when the actual officers keep snatching everything right out of my hands. You all want riding breeches and patent-leather boots, but then where will they be when you actually need them?'

Such 'actual need' as would induce Mäkilä to surrender gear voluntarily was not likely ever to arise. As the son of a big farm-owner in Laihia, Mäkilä often received packages from home, which he would furtively sneak off to the storeroom so he wouldn't have to share them. Once the mail arrived so late that Mäkilä had already undressed for bed. His package was dispatched to the corporals' barracks, putting him in a tight spot. He didn't dare get dressed again to take the package away, but if he kept it in the barracks he would be forced to share its contents. Mäkilä fended off the men temporarily by mumbling something about sharing things in the morning, and hid the package under his pillow.

That night, a cautious rustling of paper began to issue from Mäkilä's bed, prompting the lights to flood back on as Hietanen's voice boomed through the barracks, 'Guys, wake up! Mäkilä's sharing his package!'

Suspecting that Mäkilä might try to pull something during the night, the others had organized a rota to stand watch, just in case – and now they descended upon the package's luckless owner by the dozen. Mäkilä sat on his bed, blinking his eyes and gripping his package to his chest, concealing it beneath the corner of his felt blanket. No physical blows were dealt, but every possible psychological pressure was applied in full. All in vain, however – for, as Mäkilä assured them, 'It's just clothes. There's nothing to eat but a couple of rye crackers. And those aren't even worth trying to divide up. It's just the underwear I wrote home for – there's nothing to eat.'

Not so much as a crumb made it into the men's clutches, and for weeks afterwards their jeering and abuse fell on Mäkilä's deaf ears.

The men did recognize that Mäkilä had his merits, however. The machine-gunners faced none of the usual supply-chain thievery that usually diverted chunks of the soldiers' spartan rations to a circle of insiders, and this was due solely to the fact that Mäkilä was scrupulously honest in performing his duties. Once, one of the squad leaders from Mäkilä's barracks had appealed to his sense of camaraderie to try to get something from the storeroom, but that turned out to be a mistake. Mäkilä just stared at the ceiling, going red, blinking his eyes and clearing his throat in his typical fashion. Then he indignantly declared, 'You should be aware that all rations are shared on the mess hall table. The provisions I receive from the battalion are set according to company headcount, and I weigh them on scales and divide them up for meals. The only way to get extra food in the army is by stealing.'

The company's unexpected departure presented a severe trial for Mäkilä. It pained him to watch the men detailed to help him carelessly rolling up blankets and mattresses into unruly bundles, but his book-keeping prevented him from getting mixed up in the matter. It was equally distressing for him to watch men dumping their equipment all over the floor in their impatience to be off.

'There's all the gear for Old Lady Rahikainen's boy! Gimme a receipt, now, huh?'

Mäkilä was beet-red. Beet-red and clearing his throat. And it says a lot that this man, who had never sworn in his life, who clasped his hands in prayer furtively under the table at meals so the others wouldn't see, now sputtered, 'My God, what a sorry state of affairs this world is in! Sure, just drop your gear wherever you want, like a dog drops shit. Nobody gets a receipt until I've taken an inventory!'

Just then a fellow from the Third Platoon walked in, the guy the Captain had ordered to trade in his boots. He was turned away, and so had to fetch Hietanen to come and back him up. Hietanen had already managed to get himself into a card game, and so, annoyed at the interruption, he hurried to the doorway and hollered, 'Boots for Salonen on the double! Cap'n's orders.'

'I do not have time to give out boots. And that Cap'n gives orders as if we were in America, where there's more stuff than anybody needs. Just go crying to your Cap'n and he'll order me to give out whatever it is you're hankering after!'

Now Hietanen was hacked off, too. 'Jesus! It will never cease to amaze me how you hoard all that garbage back there. How in the hell anybody can love those ratty, tatty rags so goddamn much is beyond me. Some pretty, affectionate girl, well, sure, I can understand that just fine, but Christ! Plain old rags? Nah, you got me on that one, I'm stumped. Pre-tty damn strange if you ask me. Just thinking about it makes me feel like somebody dropped an anvil on my head.'

Even Mäkilä's patience had its limits. He stammered for a moment before the words came. 'Take it all. Take whatever you want. Here, clear the place out. Call over the whole platoon and deck yourselves out. We're clean out of those spurs with the nice clink, but we'll divvy up the best we've got.'

'Look, I don't need any jingle bells, but I am taking boots for Salonen. Those, grab those ones there. Just swap your old ones and let's go.'

Salonen exchanged his boots and they left, but Hietanen was so tickled with amusement at the whole situation, and particularly his victory, that he couldn't resist hollering from the door, 'Don't you give up hope, now! There's enough ratty tatty rags to go around!'

Mäkilä moved a pair of gloves onto a different shelf and seized a pile of mattresses, then lowered it back down to the ground. His voice cracked as he said bitterly, sulking, 'Just take a-anything you need. It's not worth keeping track of anything around here any-more. Call in the whole battalion so they can stock up on riding breeches – and seam-stripes, too. The machine-gunners are going to set out dressed like real gentlemen. Just got to dig up some of those patent-leather boots . . .'

One of the men opted to take Mäkilä's speech at face value and, pulling a new shirt out of the bundle, started taking off his old one. Mäkilä watched for a moment, racking his brain for the most vindictive possible punishment. His shrill voice cracked as he screamed, 'Ge-et down!'

Mäkilä had always avoided taking any kind of managerial stance in relation to the men, and was even fairly embarrassed whenever he had to give them orders. His outburst was, therefore, all the more jarring, and the stunned man cowered in obedience. Then he scrambled to his feet and slipped in behind the others, trying to save face by muttering, 'Now the son of a bitch has lost it completely!'

From that point on, the distribution of equipment went more smoothly, however. Mäkilä seemed to suffer at least a few pangs of conscience, and proceeded somewhat shame-faced. He even took the initiative to give some men new items when he saw the state their equipment was in. Wordlessly, he passed out gear, clearing his throat quietly as splotches of red burned on his cheeks.

At last all the gear was packed and loaded into carts. Mäkilä followed the carts toward the battalion, his account book under his arm. As they were leaving, the driver offered him a ride, but Mäkilä turned him down, saying with an insinuation the driver pretended not to grasp, 'Horses are just fine for transporting equipment. There is no need to start transporting legs good enough for walking.'

The uneven cart tracks through the sandy forest were riddled with roots and potholes, and a deep one jolted the cart to a complete stop. The driver slapped his reins and shouted, 'C'mon! Goddamn it . . . git!'

Mäkilä raised his arm in disapproval, cleared his throat and offered the driver a word of advice. 'You should use the reins to direct the horse. It is not difficult to avoid the potholes if you just pull a little on the lines.'

'Damn it! . . . This way . . .'

The horse braced itself, leaned into its harness, and yanked the wheel loose. The journey continued across the burnt clearing, the tall pine trunks along its rim already reddish in the sinking sun.

## IV

Preparations for departure were underway in the barracks headquarters as well. The bed in the Captain's room had been stripped, and the last, yellowed shreds of the paper shades had been tossed into the fire. The orderly and the company secretary had already packed the archives into a wooden crate and were now loading up their own packs. These gentlemen could take along whatever they wanted, not having to worry about the strain the weight would put on their shoulders. The company secretary had packed 'parade boots' and a pair of civilian slacks. He was a curious creature, in a way – a real quirk of nature. A child of the people, but excessively refined; he was a bit feminine and spoke with a sort of lisp. He had a long cigarette-holder as well, which he used to smoke North State cigarettes, imported from America. Only the best would do.

Coffee was brewing on the stove over the crackling waste paper. A rough-hewn, wooden table sat beneath the window. The Captain was seated beside it, gazing out. He twirled a pencil in his slim, sinewy fingers. A faint smile flickered at the corners of his mouth as he noticed Master Sergeant Korsumäki slowly making his way down the path to the office. Korsumäki had been a master sergeant with the Border Patrol before being transferred to the company on account of his age. A '36 field cap sat on his head, perfectly straight, pressing down slightly over his eyes so that the top of the cap just covered the smooth crown of his head. He wore carded-wool trousers and tall army boots, and the red-on-gray stripes of his thick, wool socks peeked out over their tops. The Master Sergeant moved slowly, scanning the ground around him as he walked. Then, spotting a wooden stick on the ground, he bent down, picked it up, and stuck it in the crook of his elbow with two sticks that were already there.

Soon his soft footfalls reached the porch, and he walked over to the stove, the three sticks still in the crook of his arm. Setting the wood on the fire, he lamented, 'There's bits of firewood strewn all along the paths. Funny how these things work. We're like a pack of spoiled brats out here. Nobody would stand for this kind of wastefulness at home, but out here we all act like it doesn't matter at all.'

He lifted the lid off the coffee pot, saw that the coffee wasn't ready, and sat down at the table opposite the Captain. He took off his cap and ran his fingers through his hair. Then, glancing at the phone, he asked, 'Any word on the convoy?'

The Captain roused himself from his silence and quickly resumed his customary rapid retort. 'No, no. Nothing at all. They don't even know themselves. I told them it was one hell of a way to run an army. You'd think they could at least keep us informed. Strange how we can't even get a straight answer about where the convoy is. They say there's some large-scale reorganizing going on higher up. I think it means new troops. It looks like the rumors of mobilization may be true. They're forming divisions. We'll be the seed for one of them. The other two regiments will come out of the reserves . . . Orderlyyy . . . the kettle . . .'

They fell silent as the orderly made up the coffee and returned to the porch, where he and the company secretary were packing their bags. Then the Master Sergeant resumed, somewhat dejectedly, 'That means war.'

'I don't know. I'd say it depends on Germany. Theoretically it depends on three parties: Germany, Russia and ourselves. Germany could attack Russia – and I don't doubt for a second that she will – and demand that we enter the war. The importance of the Murmansk railway supports that possibility. On the other hand, Russia might try to simplify matters by taking us out right away, or at least moving the war onto our territory. She's hardly going to sit back and wait for us to decide whether we want to let this opportunity pass us by or not. Then there's a third possibility, which is that we might not let this opportunity pass us by. To hell with the peace agreement. We're going to have to take sides one way or the other, and anyone can see which way it's going to go.'

'Of course. It's just a question of how it's all going to play out for us.'

'Afraid we're in for a whipping?' The Captain gave a short laugh and then continued, 'We'll never have another opportunity like this. As far as I'm concerned, we should go for a bold offensive. Justice has always followed the sword of the victor. As it will now. The losers are in the wrong. But take whatever position you like, one thing is clear. Our fate is bound to Germany's success. And that's why it's our job to do everything we can to make sure the Germans succeed. The way I see it, central Europe is the center of power, and Finland's fate hinges upon the degree of force it exerts at any given moment. German pressure is directed outwards, and when it's strong, eastern power declines. If it weakens, then everything along the peripheries draws in toward the center and we're snuffed out in the process. That's just how it is – strange as it may seem from our usual perspective on things, by which we consider France and England our friends, when in truth they're our worst enemies. Their defeat is Germany's victory, and Germany's victory is also our victory. If we're defeated, then we're six feet under and that's the end of it, but the thing to do now is hit Russia with everything we've got and take her out – preferably permanently.'

The Master Sergeant stared at the floor and said, 'So I should keep my family where they are.'

The Captain realized that Korsumäki hadn't been following his train of thought in the least, but had been preoccupied with his own affairs the whole time. Age and the Winter War had stripped the Sergeant of all idealism – assuming he'd had any to begin with – and so, with a sigh, he thought of the suffering and hardship to come, which he had already known intimately once before. Kaarna could appreciate Korsumäki's frame of mind, though it was utterly foreign to him personally. He hoped there would be a war. More than that, he hoped it would be a tough war. His career demanded it. He had had to leave the army some twenty years earlier, as a lieutenant, after having taken part in the controversial campaign in the Olonets. That, anybody could guess, was the reason he maintained a permanent state of war between himself and his superiors, even now. For his men he had not a mean word, but even the battalion commander was liable to be given hell. Kaarna was a difficult subordinate, no question – exceptionally talented and smart as a whip. He didn't hide his light under a bushel either, but shone it ruthlessly upon any issue that provoked controversy. Despite his superior rank and position, even the Major had difficulty holding his own against the man who, on top of everything else, had enough medals to outweigh a two-pound sack of potatoes. He had been promoted to captain during the Winter War and commanded his own battalion. Then he'd remained in the service yet again when the war was over, but only as a company commander, demobilization having freed up too many majors and lieutenant colonels for the higher command positions. Even now, he still wasn't going to get a battalion. Not even an infantry company! And what use were machine-gunners, least of all in an offensive attack? Well, death and duty would weed out the ranks, and his turn would come. His whole body itched for a chance to exercise its prowess. He had taken on death's challenge enough times to know that he could face it down. It was as if the world war had reignited all his drive and ambition, making them flare up with new life. And he was patriotic, besides. He cultivated the sentiment actively because it fired him up with vigor and a desire for action.

Whole and powerful – that was him. His gaze betrayed none of the soul's weaker points, vulnerabilities that might bring him to his knees.

The Master Sergeant called to the orderly to pour more coffee and the Captain resumed where they'd left off. 'Yes, better leave your family where they are. We won't be turning back. It's not like last time. By the way, the supply vehicles will only meet up with the company once we reach our destination. They have to load them up first. And the supply train isn't assigned just to the company, it's arranged in conjunction with the whole battalion.'

Well, that's a relief, the Master Sergeant thought. So we don't have to worry about that. 'But this smells a heck of a lot like war. Whole lot of hurry up and wait.'

The Captain laughed. 'That's it all right. It'll be time to head out pretty soon. Say, whatever happened to supper? Or did they take the field kitchen in advance? Oh well, that's their business.'

They drank their coffee in silence. The Master Sergeant was lost in thought, gazing out at the porch, where the company secretary was combing his hair. The man was making faces at himself in the mirror, adjusting its distance from his head as he pressed down on his wavy hair. The Master Sergeant sighed, as if to expel his rather melancholy state of mind, and said, 'Takes all sorts.'

Kaarna gave a dry, cutting laugh and said, 'The history of the world's made up of all kinds of deeds. Some fellow in Berlin may be looking at a map of Russia and laying plans. This guy here, he's combing his hair. But he comes along for the ride, too.'

The Captain set his cup on the table and, trying to cheer up the Sergeant, said confidently, 'Well, we're all in this together. All in for the long haul, wherever the devil it takes us. So it goes . . . Hmm . . . hmm . . . dum-dee-dum. Orderly! Fetch some razor blades from the canteen, will you? Get a bunch of packs. Pick up some bread rolls with the rest of the money – you can finish the coffee . . . Ah-ha. Moment I leave that damn phone, it rings . . . hmmm . . . hmm.'

## V

The local branch of the Lotta Svärd, the women's auxiliary, held a nightly canteen in one of the empty barracks. It was crammed with soldiers when the orderly arrived. The place sold coffee mixed with substitute, rock-hard bread rolls, tobacco, razors, envelopes and notepads. The notepads featured a stylized drawing of a soldier on the front. There he stood: helmeted, creases running down the front of his trousers, the blue cross of the Finnish flag billowing in the background. Some fantasy image or other. Just never, under any circumstances, reality. Reality was crowding around the canteen counter in a sort of mob, shouting, 'Damn it! Don't push in, you dickhead! Go to the back of the line!'

There was not a creased trouser-leg in sight. One guy had brown hand-me-downs from the charitable nation of England, somebody else had civilian trousers, somebody else, gray military slacks. The only articles of clothing they had been uniformly issued with were a cap, a light button-down shirt, and a belt.

There was just one Lotta behind the counter. The men were cracking jokes up and down the line – whatever jokes anybody happened to know, as they had to attract her attention somehow. Of course, they knew none of them stood much of a chance with Lieutenant Lammio sitting over at the end of the counter. But Rahikainen was one of those guys who refuse to recognize any opportunity as hopeless, on principle. He strutted up to the counter and said gallantly, 'Now, what does the pretty girl have for Rahikainen today? Before we must part for ever! Ah, well. Cuppa coffee, of course. And a bread roll.'

'Tonight we're selling as many rolls as you want. We're closing down the canteen.'

'So that's how it is. War's comin', huh? Signs of it in the air. Before we only got one per cup. What grave misfortune awaits us! I may never look into this little lady's beautiful eyes again.'

The Lotta flushed with pleasure and glanced at Lammio, who was sitting at the end of the counter. Because it was for him – the radiance emanating from her. Even the flicker Rahikainen had sparked. Lammio was irritated at Rahikainen's gallantry. First, for the general reason that he couldn't stand the presence of another rooster on the roof, and second, because he had already arranged to profit by this particular Lotta's presence in the barracks. Who knew when he'd see a woman again? And there wasn't enough time to make it to the city. But if the convoy was slow enough coming, he could see this Lotta home and try his luck.

There was, of course, a clear division separating the Helsinki lieutenant from the North Karelian private, which was indeed so great that Lammio was not concerned, even if he knew Rahikainen to be a ladies' man, and a successful one. Rahikainen was a tall, handsome fellow, well built, with a curly mop, a rich singing voice, and an everlasting motor-mouth that typically ran on empty. The last was Rahikainen's primary vehicle for advancing his cause, but this time he hit a wall.

'Finish your business so the others can have a chance, please.' Lammio was suddenly very concerned on behalf of the other men in line, though he himself had dawdled for no less than twenty minutes making his own purchases. Rahikainen, however, was not the born-yesterday type. You couldn't scare him with stripes and buttons, and Lammio's power did not extend so far as to govern his canteen purchasing practices.

'Oh, but Lieutenant, sir, let's not be too hasty. If we've got a long trip ahead of us, we'd better have some provisions. How much of that tobacco am I allowed?'

'How much would you like?'

'Let's say that pack there. And toss in about ten of those bread rolls.' Rahikainen paid slowly and made a few more passes at the girl before being supplanted by the next fellow in line. Gathering up his purchases, he moved out of the way and found a seat at the table by the door, where some guys from the Third Platoon were already seated. Seeing as the Lotta was the communal center of attention, Rahikainen's little enterprise had not gone unnoticed.

'Looks like that girl ain't gonna be the mother of your children,' Hietanen smirked. 'Need a few more pins on your collar.'

'I don't have any need for her services at the moment.'

'Now you're just tellin' whoppers. Guy like you – why I'll take you out to our neck of the woods and use you as a stud if you make it out of this alive!'

Just then the orderly came in to announce that the convoy would arrive at ten o'clock. For Lammio, the announcement meant the possibility that his hopes would be realized, but for the rest of them it just meant more waiting around. The canteen closed and Lammio set off with the Lotta, walking her bicycle. The men wandered back to the barracks, their excitement at departure souring.

'What are they dawdling for? What kind of numbskulls do they have up there running this show? We're not really going to just keep milling around the empty barracks, are we?'

The bed frames sat in their spots, empty. The beds and the narrow spaces between them had grown familiar to the men, and the blue-stained boards seemed strangely dreary now that they had been stripped bare. An inscription had already appeared at the head of one of the beds: 'This bed belonged to Pentti Niemi, who slept here during his service to the Finnish army and departed 16 June 1941 for an unknown destination. Recruit, rookie, FNG: when you come near this bed, take your boots off, because this bed was a sacred spot to some guy once.'

# VI

They were blessed, however, before departure. Since there was time, the battalion's chaplain came round to hold evening prayer services in each of the companies. The duty officer rounded up the men, and this time both the officers and the utilities platoon took part as well.

The Captain stood a little way off, awaiting his cue, and the Master Sergeant followed at the tail end of the company, looking very grave. The duty officer wasn't sure whom he was supposed to cue to bring the company, since the officers' presence eliminated the possibility of the Master Sergeant's serving this role. Koskela was the oldest officer present, but he was just walking along at the head of his platoon, and clearly had no intention of getting involved. Luckily, just then Lammio rushed onto the scene. His plans had been seriously thwarted. He had been pinning his hopes on this Lotta, knowing that she was a country girl, but this very fact had turned out to be the cause of his downfall.

Lammio took over the company from the duty officer and presented it to the Captain. Kaarna had observed Lammio's entrance but averted his gaze. He had no patience with men who went absent without leave, officers included, and it was even more irritating in this case because it was Lammio. Keeping his voice low, so that the company would not hear, the Captain murmured, 'The company is on alert, which means no absences are permitted. As far as I know, the Lieutenant is still a member of the company.'

'Yes I am, Captain, sir.'

'Well then. Assume your position.'

The scolding didn't ruffle Lammio in the least. He walked calmly to the head of his platoon. The haughty expression of his face was just slightly stronger than usual, reinforced by the stiff flair of his nostrils. It was his typical response to any and all criticisms directed his way.

The Captain was pacing back and forth in front of the company. He muttered something to himself and kept glancing at his watch. Once he stopped, turned to the company and said, 'OK. Now we should . . . Well, no, no, let's not.'

Resuming his pacing, he reasoned with himself, 'There's no need. It'll work out without . . . hmm . . . hmmm . . .'

The chaplain came across the clearing on his bicycle.

'The crow has landed,' Rahikainen whispered, as the others suppressed their smiles. 'The crow' was their nickname for the chaplain. It drew its inspiration from the fact that the chaplain was a frail, dark-skinned, narrow-shouldered type. A prime target for tuberculosis bacteria.

The Captain's orders rang out. The men removed their caps, allowing their bristly hair to stick out in whatever direction it pleased. Or directions, rather, as even within just one head there seemed to be aspirations in several directions.

The minister began the hymn in his thin, tinny little voice, to which the men contributed a vague sort of moo that gradually developed into singing: '*forrr . . . truuuss . . . is . . . aar . . . Go . . . od . . .*'

Faces were stiff, brows knitted, eyes dull and squinting. Bearing no sentiments of devotion whatsoever, the men paid their respects to their god looking rather dismal and cross. Hietanen furrowed his brows and choked out some noises, though his singing skills were a little questionable. Lehto stood mute, his thin lips firmly shut. It was as if he had been turned to stone, and would have preferred to get through the whole hymn without having to hear a word of it. But next to the Master Sergeant, a clear, beautiful voice was ringing out from Mäkilä's mouth. The quiet man had no equal when it came to hymn-singing. He opened up his whole soul, and its strength seemed to lift him up into the clear twilight.

'Let us pray.'

In so far as it was possible, the men's expressions grew even angrier. They looked as though they were just about ready to eat somebody alive. The minister tried to deepen his voice to make it sound more powerful. 'O Lord, God of nations. You who hold our fate in Your hands. May You turn Your face to us and have mercy upon us, for You are our refuge. Let Your will be done, for Your vision exceeds our humble understanding. If You send us trials, it is no more than we deserve, but we pray to You: strengthen our souls with Your power, so that we may withstand Your trials. Help us to fulfill our duties in Your name, to our families and to our homeland. Give us the strength to make even the greatest sacrifices, for it is in Your name that Your chosen people move toward their destiny. Fill our souls with the same steadfast courage and the same, burning spirit of patriotism that our brothers felt as they faced their deaths – our fallen heroes, who now sleep in the cemeteries of soldiers. This is all we ask of You. Bless these men in all that they do, in whatever may lie before them. Bless all the people of our nation and make us one. May You open our hearts to Your will, that we may travel the path of righteousness.'

Then the chaplain read the Lord's Blessing, his voice returning to normal, as he had exhausted his fervor in the three identical services he'd already given in the battalion's infantry companies. After the blessing, he struck up one last, short hymn, and then the service was over.

The Captain allowed the company a break, and the men began wandering around aimlessly. Rahikainen lumbered along, shoving his hands in his pockets as he said, 'Ye-ees, what a sermon! How in the world does that spindly little man drone on so damn long? Did you hear the horrible things that guy said? We're headed for the cemeteries, boys! My neck-hairs are still standing on end from the threats that chump made.'

'I thought that guy did purty good,' Salo said.

They stayed outside with their packs and weapons. Some men gathered in little groups to play cards or tell stories, and the others just loitered around with nothing to do. Ten o'clock came and went, revealing the meaninglessness of the appointed hour. The convoy didn't arrive.

Hietanen was lying on his back with his pack for a pillow and singing. It was a bit of a funny song, as it didn't really have a tune, and the lyrics were sort of all over the place too. He just improvised, belting out:

> Dum-daddy lumbadee politty lumbadee
> dum-daddy politty politty lumbadee . . .

As he sang, he looked up at the pale blue sky, which had darkened just enough to offset one, powerful star. Then, interrupting his song, he burst out: 'Nah, I have to say, those stars are pre-tty far out there. It seems like they're real close and all, but when you start thinking about it, you realize that the distance between you and them is pre-tty damn far, and you can't even conceive of it the same way you normally look at things. And the thing that's really got me stumped is what in the world anybody does with 'em. Seems like they're totally pointless, if you ask me. Who needs 'em? Nobody.'

'They do create some light, though.' Corporal Lahtinen was sticking a needle back into the side of his cap, having just finished sewing back on a shirt button that was coming loose. He'd been focusing intently on his task, and had just tossed off his comment in passing, but Hietanen was vehemently intent on the issue and burst out, 'Light! Sunlight and moonlight, sure, I can understand that just fine, but what does this kind of light do? Nothing! I think that if I'd have been God, I wouldn't have made all these stars. And if I could,

I'd get rid of the lot of them. What are you supposed to make of things that don't do anything?'

Lahtinen's needle was now firmly in place, leaving him free to consider the matter. He glanced around carefully and spoke in a low, slightly hesitant voice, as if preparing in advance for opposition from the others. 'No-o, they weren't made by God. That's just talk. That's what they teach you in school, even though they know it's a lie. He didn't create people, either. They were born in the sea. People are made out of carbon and other things. The simple man is kept in ignorance so he'll be more submissive to the capitalists. That's all there is to it.'

Hietanen laughed, 'Yeah, I get that, but I don't believe it. Carbon! You gone soft or something? That sounds pre-tty strange if you ask me. How the hell could a normal human being be born in the sea? Just being underwater half a minute's enough to finish you off. And there ain't a speck of carbon in my body. Muscles and bones, that's what people are made out of. Anybody can tell you that. I don't know anything about capitalists. If my old man dies before I do, I get twenty-three and a half acres of real shitty land. I'm that much of a capitalist. Don't think I'm particularly submissive, though – let whatever capitalist you want come up to the edge of our field. I'll just walk right over with my hands in my pockets and give him a good, long spit. That's what I'd do.'

Lahtinen spoke again quietly, earnest as ever, which suited him really – he who never took anything lightly. Assessing the loneliness of his position all too well, he was a little uncomfortable. He certainly didn't want to get into a fight, but he couldn't just drop the issue, so he said in his defense, 'You can be underwater, if you have gills. Man began as a fish. Even the capitalist scientist has recognized that.'

Now Hietanen wasn't laughing anymore. He sat up and looked straight at Lahtinen, his eyes wide, blazing with astonishment. 'Hey guys, listen to this! Listen to what our boy Yrjö has to say! Well, I'll be damned. Now you've really started it. Listen, guys! I guess I'm a perch, 'cause I've got stooped shoulders. Come chew on this, guys

... Gills ... Look, I've never read anything but the Turku newspaper once in a while since I finished school – painfully – but I still know better than to believe that. So I'm a perch! A carbon perch ... Pre-tty strange if you ask me.'

Hietanen was on a roll. And he was whipping himself up into an even greater tizzy. He glanced around, looking for others to confirm his astonishment, but no one had taken any interest in their conversation except Private Vanhala, the only guy lying nearby. He was lying silently, but he had been following the debate and was quivering with suppressed laughter. Vanhala was a quiet, chubby fellow, who rarely took part in conversation, though it was clear that he would happily have done so. When he did cut in on occasion, he would instantly start struggling for words and turn red, glancing around at the others, embarrassed by his difficulties. He had followed Hietanen and Lahtinen's argument with a smile dancing in his eyes, laughing to himself, repeating: 'Fi-ish ... heehee ... fi-ish ... Hietanen is a pe-erch ... heeheehee ...'

Lahtinen's face had withdrawn into a sullen expression. You could tell from his tone of voice that he didn't want to argue any more – though, of course, he knew how things really were. 'It's Nature that creates,' he said. 'That's just how it is ... Everything else is hogwash. Sure, rich people know what tune to sing, soon as any question about their purse-strings comes up. That's what that spindly crow was just harping on about. We got it all wrapped up in one go just now. Give us the strength to defend the moneybags of capitalism! I mean, if this homeland had left them as poor as it's left me, I don't think they'd care for it any more than I do. And I wouldn't give up so much as an old foot rag for it. Well, whatever, let's move on, but we'll just see how things pan out ... There are enough fellows over there to fight us, that's for sure.'

Vanhala hesitated a moment. Then he said, 'But one Finn's a match for ten Russkis. Heehee.'

'Mmm ... Sure. And what do we do when they send round the eleventh?'

Hietanen, who had no interest in the political question, only the purely theological one, turned the conversation back around to its previous topic. 'Look, I'm no Doctor of Philosophy, but my reasoning says the world couldn't just pop up all by itself. I'm sure about that. I don't believe in any of that supernatural stuff. How could something be born by itself, without anybody making it? God has to exist. But I have to say, he sure did do a lot of work for nothing. We don't need all those stars. I've thought that a bunch of times. I can't see any use in having things like ants and frogs in the world. They are totally useless if you ask me. Just like bedbugs and cockroaches.'

Vanhala could scarcely contain his giggles, and his whole body quivered as he gasped, 'And lice!'

No sooner had he said it than he blushed and went straight-faced. But then he noticed Hietanen's approval, and his round face broke into a broad grin and his body started quivering again. Hietanen pounced, continuing to rattle off his evidence. 'You said it! Who needs lice eating away at him? Nobody. And then you gotta feed the goddamn pests somehow! On top of everything else. Yeah, I know old people say frogs keep the well-water clean, but I don't buy that at all. That's just batty. Who the hell wants to drink frog eggs?'

'And tadpoles! Heehee.' Now Vanhala was feeling so self-assured that he stopped blushing and downright shone when Hietanen concurred straight away, 'Exactly!'

Hietanen lay back down on the ground, brushing the conversation aside, but not without concluding, finally, 'I don't believe in any of that supernatural stuff. But I still say there's a whole lot of unnecessary junk in this world.'

This final point prompted him to tack on another. 'To hell with all of it.'

Then he drew a deep breath of fresh air into his lungs, as if he wanted to blow out the whole pointless train of thought, and began to sing. He just sort of wove the words together as they came to mind, making up a tune to fit the song that went:

> I watched as the boat sailed
> past the window on the smooth River Aura.
> Farewell, yea, I say sail well
> as you steam off down that smooth River Aura.
> No, pony, pony! Don't poop on your cart beams,
> tomorrow is market day.
> Babadaba trot soft lalala
> for tomorrow is market day.

Several of the men wandered further off to write letters, driven by some vague foreboding of what fate held in store. Others tried to sleep, and a few gathered around card games, murmuring now and again. 'Couple of whores. You tried to pull a fast one, you old cheat. Stop grumbling and get to it! Pot limit. Three shorties and a jack high. You got a pair a kings over there, don't you? Written all over your face.'

Dusk began to settle over the burnt clearing. The warmth of the day still hovered, so the men could lie outside, gazing up into the depths of the twilit sky that seemed to conceal within it both the past and all that was to come. The rumble of trains drifted over from the railroad tracks as singing, shouts and the occasional order rang out through the camp.

## VII

The next pointless alarm came sometime around midnight. The men had already started shivering from the cold, and murmurs of discontent were rumbling here and there. They set in for another wait, until at about one o'clock the duty officer came to put the company on alert. Boisterous with excitement, the men got into formation. They were bursting with that thrilling sensation probably familiar to all troops heading off to war. True, these men weren't entirely sure it was war they were heading off to, but over the course of the night, a rumor to that effect had taken hold throughout the company. And when Lammio called them to attention, their heels clicked more crisply than usual, and even their pivots betrayed a model precision. And what was the cause of this sudden verve and enthusiasm? May those who wonder why the world goes to war find an answer to that!

They set off toward the other side of the burnt clearing, where there was a path leading to the main road, which would take you just about anywhere. East to Lake Onega and the Svir River, for example – amongst other places. And why not further, if the men had it in them?

The First Company commander, Captain Helminen, had been put in charge of the transport. He issued orders to the officers as he walked. Captain Kaarna arrived after his company and immediately began quarreling with Helminen, as if holding him personally responsible. 'Should be! The convoy should be on its way! Remarkable, how it continually should be coming. When is it actually coming, then? This is the third time we've been called to alert and I'm afraid this one's a washout, too. Where is the convoy and what is it driving? A convoy can't just disappear.'

'I don't know,' Helminen replied defensively. 'The Commander said they drove the Second Battalion to the border during the night, or rather, late in the evening. So maybe they're still out there. Otherwise, there was just one artillery transport that passed. Supposedly, those guys weren't regular troops – so mobilization is underway.'

'Mm . . . sure, sure. Looks that way. Well, we've also been mobilized since yesterday. So who knows? Maybe by tomorrow we'll actually be mobile.'

Kaarna set off toward his company and said to the men, 'Well, boys, looks like you're going to learn how to wait. Don't get worked up, now. Take advantage of every opportunity you can to get some rest. Coats on, packs for pillows. Get some sleep.'

'Learn to wait? Oh, we got that down already. Year and a half now we been waiting to go back to being civilians.'

Rahikainen hadn't meant that for the Captain's ears. The Captain caught it, however, though he didn't bother to address it. He just laughed and gazed sidelong at Rahikainen. The men wrapped themselves in their coats and tried to sleep. The cold kept them awake, and they cursed the whole system through their chattering teeth. The 'gentlemen officers' could hear snippets here and there – a Finnish private can be pretty cutting when the mood strikes him. The men were hungry, too, though that was by no means exceptional. They'd been hungry since they'd joined the army, and some of them probably well before that. Malnutrition had not yet disappeared from Finland – not in the least. There were still pockets here and there that provided entirely favorable conditions for it to flourish. Certainly the doctors the military had called in to examine the recruits were aware of it. The human stock comprising the infantry bore weaknesses that were the clear product of malnutrition.

Besides being cold and hungry, the men were also sleep-deprived – so, of the four components we might say encapsulate the essence of war, fear was the only thing missing.

Time passed. The summer sky grew lighter, and the edge of the dawn began to glow red in the east. At four o'clock the companies were called together and the march back to the barracks began. The officers let the men grumble in peace. 'Stroke of genius from our esteemed officers! Just another piss alarm, boys! Practice for the war, right. Sweat saves blood – so every time they mess with us it's a goddamn "exercise". Hurry up so you can come and loll around on some clumpy grass!'

The company hadn't even reached the barracks when an orderly pedaled up behind them on his bicycle. 'Come back, come back, the convoy's coming!'

'About, face! March!'

The murmurs fell silent. Now they were sure departure was imminent. That was how everything happened in the army. They were also sure that a mad rush would set in now, just because the occasion seemed to call for it.

Dusty vehicles began to wobble into view just as the company reached the roadside. A dust-covered master sergeant on a motorbike led the convoy, circling round as the vehicles followed suit, pulling up in a line. The tired drivers took no notice whatsoever of the loading, their bloodshot eyes sinking shut as they dozed off over their steering wheels.

'Machine-gunners, lighten your water weight,' Kaarna called out to his company. The men smiled, but the Captain said, almost irritated, 'Yeah yeah. There's nothing to laugh about. It's a long drive.' He offered himself as an example. Once he had taken care of his business, he jiggled himself dry, buttoned up his trousers and said, looking at the sky, 'A beautiful day is about to dawn. A great start! A really great start! What a brilliant, red glow . . . Mmm. Into the vehicles by platoon!'

'How the hell's a platoon supposed to fit in that?' One of the soldiers stared in disbelief, but only until he realized that stalling would mean a bad spot, at which point he dived in with the others. Koskela pressed his thumbs under his belt and looked on silently as the men crammed into the vehicles. He knew the human cargo would organize itself into the best possible configuration, so he left the men to their own devices.

'Quit shoving, will you? Say, where do we put the packs and guns, huh?' Having cut the line and seized a prime spot by the wall of the cab, Rahikainen was now demanding more space.

His constant cheating and corner-cutting had earned him a place of special disrepute with Hietanen, who shouted, 'Pretty sure you can sit on your pack with your gun in your lap just like everybody else.'

'Sit on my pack? Why, my writing pad'll get crushed!' There was no way Rahikainen would have sat on the bare floor of the truck, but he was hoping his ruse might win him more space for later use.

'Jesus! We're not gonna start making separate space for the bags on account of your stationery supplies,' said Hietanen.

'Well, excuse me. I'll be happy to put it under me, if it disturbs your soul so greatly.'

'It doesn't disturb my soul in the least, but Salo and Vanhala's rears won't fit in the truck if you don't sit on your damn pack!'

Gradually they all situated themselves as comfortably as they could. Koskela got into the cab and the platoon sat waiting for the last ten minutes. They were in a hurry.

'Well, looks like we're stuck here. Might as well enjoy the chance to sit in a vehicle for once. The Finnish army doesn't pay for this kind of thing too often. The higher-ups must've got some wires crossed. You know, some people get things turned around from time to time, but somehow those clowns always do.'

The guy leading the convoy drove away from the truck, dragging his feet on the ground. Somewhere within the trucks a voice cried out, 'Ready!'

The Master Sergeant, who was from Savo – where else, with those absurdly rolled Rs – called back, 'All rrrrrrighty, boys! Keep a hundred and fifty yards between the vehicles so the dust can settle in between.'

The first vehicle started off. The transmission screeched and the motor groaned: *ay yai yai yai* . . .

The Third Platoon's truck shook and rumbled off in turn. The men bounced down the uneven road to the rhythm of the potholes as the vehicle pitched this way and that. Their spirits rose, as if shaken loose by the lurching of the truck. Some shouts emerged from the convoy, and somewhere in the truck somebody had already burst into song: *'On the heath a little bloom called Erika . . .'*

'So long, camp!' somebody yelled from the Third Platoon's truck, and others chimed in, 'So long, barracks!' 'The old troops are headin' out!'

Hietanen had already forgotten his recent exchange with Rahikainen. Drunk with excitement at their chaotic departure, he outdid them all and launched into a full-on speech. Rising to stand, he steadied himself on Lehto's shoulder, gesturing extravagantly with his free hand as he said, 'One last goodbye to you, burnt clearing. Farewell, you old sweat-sucking swamp! The old boys are off and we salute you! You, whose surface our boots have messed up with so many footprints. You give the next round of rookies hell, now, all right? The old guard's rootin' for ya!'

Cheers from the other vehicles joined in his hurrah, as did his own men. But Rahikainen just grumbled irritably, 'Of course they drive us off at night. Not one little lady by the side of the road to see us off.'

The truck turned onto the main road, into the dust cloud floating in the wake of the preceding vehicles. The drone of the trucks emanated from its midst, accompanied by strains of the old school songs, *'What happiness greater than taking up arms, protecting the land of our birth . . .'*

Glints of the clear morning shone between the trees lining the road, gilding the dust cloud with gold as loads of excited young men drove through, one after the other.

# Chapter Two

## I

A little-used road, or actually just a couple of faint tracks turning off into the forest, wound their way through the spruce grove. The men had pitched their tents beside the tracks and were now idling and milling about. They had dug out little fire pits in front of each tent, and now their mess kits hung above them, dangling from the ends of poles.

They'd pitched the tents the night before, and a strange serious-ness had descended for a moment when the duty officer came through the tents announcing, 'Keep it down. The border's only about a mile off.'

They got used to the idea fairly quickly, but a perceptible gravity settled over them. They roamed about playing cards all day, having nothing better to do, but among them some men just sat silently, lost in thought, staring into the campfires. When they spoke, it was at half-volume, though the precaution felt slightly absurd, since the dry cracks their axes made chopping firewood carried for miles.

A good two weeks had passed since the battalion had left the burnt clearing. Stiff and dusty, they had unloaded and set up camp along the side of the road. Here, it had gradually been confirmed that this was the real deal. Magazines were loaded up, units were configured for war, and all activity was geared toward preparing for combat. Then they heard that Germany had made a 'pre-emptive strike on Russia', thus initiating the fighting. 'That nutcase over there took off,' as Lahtinen had put it, and now they were just await-ing the order to 'hoof it after him'. The others didn't see things as Lahtinen did, however. On the contrary – they saw things quite the other way around. Germany was tying up the Russian troops so that it would be easy for the Finns to launch an attack on the entirety of the Soviet Union. So great is the power of megalomania.

The previous evening, they had marched to this spot near the border, turned off onto the forest path and set up camp beside it.

The machine-gunners' command tent was just beside the road. Crawling out of its door flap came the NCO battle-runner, Corporal Mielonen. 'If anybody wants to hear the news, come on over! Afterwards some government secretary's gonna give a speech. Tell the others, too, in case anybody wants to hear.'

The two tents belonging to the Third Platoon were situated right next to the command post, so the Captain could keep himself entertained listening to the men's chatter. He was feeling particularly fond of Hietanen today, though he had always liked him, being an admirer of anyone energetic and direct. Hietanen's gusto kept the men's spirits up, and prevented them from getting too depressed – which was why Hietanen, rather than Lehto, served as deputy platoon leader. The Captain knew Lehto was a capable corporal, but he had no ability to exert a positive influence on the other men. He operated in a vacuum. An off-putting tension set him apart from everything. Hietanen's easy spontaneity, on the other hand, tethered him to the other men, so he was perfectly positioned to influence them with his behavior. The Captain, being a good judge of character, was also aware that Hietanen would be invaluable in a combat situation.

'I'll come and listen to the news, but I couldn't care less about those government secretaries. I just don't care what those buzzards jabber on about. Can't even do anything about the goddamn mosquitoes.'

At this the Captain laughed. 'We need guys like that. Absolutely, absolutely. Just can't let this baptism of fire go awry. We need this operation to succeed.'

More than once over the course of the day, the Captain had surveyed the map, which was folded at the ready beneath the celluloid map-case cover. 'Somewhere around there. That's where the Third Platoon will be baptized.'

They knew the enemy's first line of defense lay just behind the border – with outposts before that. Those would have to be overcome, and then when the Second Battalion launched a frontal attack, their battalion would strike from the side and take control of the service road. There was just one dicey spot – that exposed swamp, which the Third Company would have to cross in its attack. Koskela's platoon would back it up, with his own command post bringing up the rear. The rear! The Captain's position irked him no end. Company commander of a bunch of machine-gunners – what was that? Director of Social Life. God damn it! Well, it wouldn't last long. He could already sniff a battalion heading his way. Come to think of it, who was to prevent him from putting his command post even in front of the line . . . ? Well, so it goes . . . Hmm . . . dum-dee-dum.

Mielonen's voice rang out from somewhere near the other tents. At the same time Private Salo spoke up as well. 'We're comin', we're comin'! Come listen to the radio, boys! The news is about to come on and the Secretary's speakin'.'

The men gradually began to gather around the command tent. The faint music wafting from it grew louder as somebody turned up the volume on the radio inside. Then the music stopped and the news began:

'The air force of the Soviet Union has continued to bomb several counties within Finnish territory. The damage, however, has been limited. Shelling targeted at Finnish territory has continued at multiple points along the border, and in some locations our troops have repulsed minor attacks launched by enemy patrols.'

Then came the announcement from the Führer's Headquarters: 'Our advance on the Eastern Front continues. Several heavily armed tank formations have already penetrated . . .'

A crackly voice read off the names of some cities, places of which the men had but the vaguest of notions, at best. Some Churchill and some Roosevelt guy had said something that, for whatever reason, was supposed to be very important. Then it was announced that one of their own government secretaries would give a speech.

'Who is it?' somebody asked Mielonen in a low voice. But the latter answered, 'I don't know. They'll say it soon. I don't know any of the government officials. Somebody over there's spoutin' hot air.'

Mielonen was from Savo, somewhere just past Kuopio. He was a little young and self-important, but he was fairly sensible. When assembling the command group, the Captain had selected him as its leader, which further elevated Mielonen's sense of importance. 'The Captain and I arranged it,' he was wont to explain. And to the queries the men directed to him, he would respond with an all-knowing air, 'Well, obviously that's where it should be taken. Where else?'

Even he didn't know anything about government secretaries, though. 'That rrriffraff?'

The speech started after the news broadcast. First there was a quiet rustling of paper, then a low whisper and a small cough.

'My fellow Finns. Without any prior declaration of war, the armed forces of the Soviet Union have launched repeated attacks in violation of the Finnish border. Our defense forces have put down each of these attacks, but refrained from transgressing onto Soviet territory. Because of these continuing violations of our neutrality, the administration considers Finland and the Soviet Union to be in a state of war . . .'

More detailed information about the border violations followed, as well as a special report on the government's response. Finally, the Secretary shifted into sentimental gear, warming the hearts of the Finnish people:

'Great changes in the political landscape have once again presented us with a great trial. For the second time in a short while, the men of Finland are being called upon to defend their families and their homeland. We have desired nothing but peace: the peace to build this nation and to develop it toward ever greater prosperity. But our enemy's thirst for power has not permitted us that opportunity. War is never something that we wish for, but we want even less the renunciation of our freedom and our independence. As in the darkest days of the Winter War, the people of Finland will stand united in the struggle to defend our freedom. Our army, tried and true, stands at the nation's border, guided by the leadership of Marshal Mannerheim, and is prepared to strike back at every attack. And this time, we are not alone. The great German army has already dealt devastating blows upon our common enemy. Our faith in ultimate victory is unshakeable. So, trusting in the justice of our position, we enter into battle in the name of all we hold sacred, and all we hold dear . . .'

'Hey, guys! They're bringing out the cannons . . .'

From behind a bend in the road they could hear the snorting of horses and voices urging them on: 'C'mon now. Whatta ya nibblin' at . . . Git!'

The first cannon came into view. It was a three-incher, pulled by a team of frothy, sweaty horses. The guys on horseback were slapping their animals, trying to coax them up the slope, and the cannon was lurching so badly on the miserable road that all the baggage tied to it kept rolling all over the place.

The men transporting the cannons were reservists, many of whom were old men. They tried to help the horses along by pushing the cannons, but the horses' speed was such that they actually just ended up pulling the men. Rushing along at the rear was one small, older reservist. Streams of sweat had drawn stripes down his dust-covered face, his visor sat askew between one eye and his ear, and his belt was sagging under the weight of his heavy bags of ammunition. His shirt had bunched up over his belt, and the couple of buttons he'd left open revealed a thick, flannel undershirt bearing the mark 'Int. 40'. His trousers were too long for him, and because he didn't have any boots – only leather shoes – he had tucked the bottoms of the legs into his socks. So the ankles of his socks, which were held up with safety-pins, were a bit overstuffed. When the team of horses picked up the pace at the base of the hill, he stumbled after them in a desperate half-run, too fixated on his hopeless pursuit to so much as glance around him.

The evening sunlight filtered through the spruce trees onto the road, striking the swarms of insects hovering above it and dispersing as the cannons drove through. Even in the somber darkness of the spruce grove, the summer evening's calm beauty was palpable. The moss glistened green in the falling light, and the metal cannons flashed in the shafts of sun that filtered through the branches.

Wheels rattled, horses snorted, men shouted and the Secretary spoke:

'. . . courageous men of Finland. We were born free, we have lived in freedom, and we will stand with our heads held high against anyone who desires to wrest that freedom from us. Our path is clear, and we know it well. The great deeds of our fathers have paved the way that lies before us; that is the precious legacy they have left us.'

The old reservist ran panting behind his cannon. The machine-gunners standing on the side of the road had ceased listening to the Secretary, and were staring in wonder at the cannons instead. There was something grand in their approach – in spite of the desperate old man, who aroused pity in many of them.

'They really shouldn't be sending guys like that out here,' somebody muttered. But Private Salo had fallen completely under the spell of the three-incher, which in truth was something of a vintage model. His cigarette hung from the corner of his mouth as manfully he shoved his hands in his pockets, boasting, 'Take a look at those guns, boys. Won't take long to clear out the neighbors when these babies start to blow.'

The developments on the Eastern Front had shaken up Lahtinen's righteous convictions somewhat. He looked uneasy when the others questioned him on such topics, and he now sheathed even his critiques in a mantle of goodwill. He still tried to rein in the others when their zealousness verged on the excessive, though. And so, in response to Salo's speech, he said, 'Humph. Herrings are a little slim for a Christmas dinner. Rumor has it they've got some of that stuff over on the other side, too. I mean, if we can push back the neighbors that easy, well, swell. But I'm afraid anything we send over's gonna come right back at us. And how.'

'I dunno what kinda weapons they got. But it don't look like they got much down there at Bialystok. Seems like they're havin' a purty rough time, but I dunno. We'll see how it goes.'

'Yeah, well, of course it's like that when somebody blindsides you ... look, I'm just saying you oughtta cool it ... it's like you're asking for it ... and things aren't always going quite the way they say they are ...'

'I dunno. I heard they had to tie our Ostrobothnian boys to the trees to keep them from heading over here before they was supposed to ... Our neighbors are gonna see what you get for picking a fight with somebody smaller than you. Just like in the Winter War.'

The argument was cut short by a rumbling starting up a little way off.

'They're driving to the positions over there. Things are gonna get cookin', boys.'

They glanced around at one another, trying to avoid eye contact. Then they returned to the campfires in silence. The card players were still at it. 'Lintu's dealing. Can we bet cigarettes? I'm out of cash. Yeah, that's fine. Ach! One over, goddamn it.'

Everything was in order, but some men were still fiddling around needlessly with their equipment. Silence didn't really suit them just then, as it was too easy to fill up with the fantastic visions they were trying not to think about. Half-unconsciously, the men were mentally preparing themselves for what was to come. They stayed up late that night. Bits of information trickled in from here and there, always compounding their sense of gravity. Some reserve regiments had set up camp along the side of the main road. Somebody knew about the massive amount of artillery that was standing at the ready in the depots. Some group had sent a patrol across the border and returned two men short.

'Let 'em do what they want. I'm gettin' some sleep.' Hietanen pulled his coat up around his ears and the others followed suit.

## II

'Wake up, guys! It's started!'

A nervous excitement stirred in the tent. The men grabbed

whichever belts and caps their hands touched first. Everybody was rushing to get out, and some guys even had their packs on already.

They heard a few isolated cannon blasts off to the right, where the main road was. A dull thud boomed somewhere behind the border, and a few moments later a shell went off. The men listened in silence. The night forest was quiet, save for the occasional twitter of an early bird high in a spruce tree. The pale, summer night gave the men's faces a blue-white cast. Even their breathing was quiet and cautious. Finally, somebody broke the silence, whispering, 'Cannon fire.'

'Cannons.'

'Headed for the road.'

'Aim's pretty far off still. Can't even hear the whistle.'

'If it turns just a little, though, it'll be right here.'

The last remark was ill-considered. Some of the men stirred restlessly. Several fumbled with their shovels. Ensign Koskela emerged from the command tent. The soldier who carried the first machine gun's ammunition, Private Riitaoja, approached him anxiously. His eyes darted furtively about as he mumbled quietly to Koskela, 'Ensign, sir. If they turn, are they gonna strike?'

Koskela reflected for a moment before responding to the question posed by this boy from central Finland. He didn't quite grasp what he was getting at, however, as he then asked, 'Turn what?'

'The c-c-c-cannons. They're shooting toward the road. But if they turn, will they strike?'

'Oh! No, no. They're just shooting toward the road to stir things up. They won't shoot randomly into the forest.'

Riitaoja broke into a childish smile. The sudden release of tension in his body was so great that his very eyes danced, and he said lightly, 'Yessir, Ensign, sir! That's what I was thinking, too. They wouldn't shoot into the forest. They don't even know we're here. They think we're just rabbits or something.'

Koskela's presence dispelled the others' nervousness too.

'The cannons are already singing out there!' Hietanen smiled to Koskela, and Vanhala sniggered to himself, 'Singing . . . heehee! Cannons sing. But bullets just ring. Heehee!'

'Of course they're making a racket over there,' Koskela said. 'The guys drove the trucks up too close. Just asking for a nosebleed for no reason. OK, departure's in half an hour. We go with the Third Company. And one more thing. Strap two ammo boxes together with a belt. That way you can wear them around your neck. So your hands don't go numb holding 'em, I mean.'

Koskela fell silent, but the men sensed, correctly, that he hadn't quite finished. He cleared his throat for a moment, then swallowed before beginning again. 'So. I, uh, guess I should explain a few things. I mean, since I've been out there before. There's not really much to it, but you want to stay calm. Hurry when the moment comes, but otherwise rushing around just makes for a lot of dumb dickheads, like they say. Getting yourself all worked up won't help, but that doesn't mean you should rush in and hand 'em everything you've got, either. They'll be happy to take it the moment you let 'em. Aim for the belt buckles, that's the best way to settle things. Just remember, they're no different from other people. They bow to bullets, just like everybody else.'

Private Sihvonen, who hailed from the same part of North Karelia as Rahikainen – but managed to be his living antithesis – said, gesticulating nervously, 'Stay calm, stay calm. Rushing around makes for dumb dickheads. That's for sure. Best to stay calm.'

'OK. Tents down and into the vehicles.'

They collapsed the tents, rolled them up and carried them off to the carts. The supply train was sitting a little way off, and Mäkilä was roaming about in the dim light, taking one last inventory before departure. The men bringing the tents asked him when the next mealtime would be, to which Mäkilä responded, 'All in good time. We're just on the normal schedule, there are no extra portions.'

Master Sergeant Korsumäki was also up and, to the men's bewildered surprise, the old man, who'd always been so withdrawn before, now chimed in kindly, 'Maybe we could spare a little bread for these boys to stick in their pockets.'

Mäkilä gave one rye cracker to each of the men who'd carried the tents, advising them the whole time not to tell the others. 'Right, sure, why not? Because I can't make bread out of pine cones, that's why not!'

The men concealed their booty in their pockets: one half of a dried-out rye roll the size of your palm. They were hungry, but they had the future to consider too.

In unusually short order, everybody was ready for departure. The machine-gun teams kept hoisting the guns and gun mounts up on their shoulders, as if they needed to get used to their weight, having the first shift. The scouts and ammunition carriers belted up the cartridge boxes according to Koskela's instructions. Each of the machine-gun leaders carried a back-up gun barrel, a box of ammunition and a water container. And so the pack animals were ready to set out on their journey across hundreds of miles. The journey would be shorter for some, of course, but nobody wasted a moment's thought on that.

The infantry companies set off, each one followed by a platoon of machine-gunners. The First and Second Platoons vanished into the dark spruce grove as commands sounded low beneath the clatter of their gear.

Koskela's whisper cut through the rustling march of the Third Platoon. 'Double file. To the road.'

Once the group had settled into formation, a message rippled down the line from one man to the next: 'Head out.'

The infantry company they were trailing hollered furtive greetings in their direction, hissing at half-volume, 'Welcome to Camp Finland! We're a little low on wheat, but chaff we have in spades.'

They passed the artillery battery they'd seen on its way out earlier that evening and saw that the cannons were now fully manned. The men kept their voices low, shielding their cigarettes with their hands. A bit further down the road, they turned off into a dark spruce forest. The cannon fire they'd heard to the south had already died down, but somehow silence felt even more oppressive.

They advanced slowly. They made several stops along the way, and the men breathed heavily, listening anxiously to the silence of the night and the pounding of their own hearts.

'Ha . . . alt.'

The company got itself into formation. The submachine-gunners situated themselves as scouts twenty paces or so out in front, and the machine-gunners split up into squads, holding further back at about the same distance. Then the Company Commander's battle-runner arrived with an announcement. 'Border directly ahead. Silence imperative. First Platoon's got a patrol out on the border. Don't shoot without asking the password.'

'What was it again?'

'Striker. Lightning.'

'Quiet! You don't want those assholes to hear you!'

The murmurs fell silent. A few of the men started smoking – the ones who still had cigarettes, that is. For several days now they'd been suffering from a serious tobacco shortage, as the cigarette rations hadn't been distributed, so you couldn't get cigarettes anywhere.

Rahikainen had some, thanks to his swaggering escapades back at the canteen. He'd already made a pretty penny out of his bread rolls, and now he was vending cigarettes by the piece at outrageous prices. Many of the men were living on their meager army wages, so the luxury of buying was restricted to the wealthy. When one of these lucky souls tossed away a tiny cigarette butt, others would pounce on it immediately and stuff it into a cigarette-holder, blowing on their singed fingers. You could still get something out of it, if you smoked it in the grubby holder.

One guy tried to buy on credit, promising to settle up on the next payday, but Rahikainen wasn't interested. 'Who knows who'll still be here by the time the next payday rolls around? Who's gonna be responsible for settlin' up then?'

'Me.' Koskela cleared his throat and said rather hurriedly, 'I haven't got any money either, but if something happens, you can take my binoculars. They belong to me, not the army, and you could easily sell them to make up the difference. You won't have any trouble finding a buyer around here, that's for sure.'

'Well, I believe that . . . yeah, sure . . . I didn't mean . . . I mean, it's not about the money.' Rahikainen sounded half-ashamed, half-hurt, but in any case he shared the cigarettes.

Every one of them had taken note of the fact that Koskela had broken rank in his exchange with Rahikainen, getting involved as if the two men were equals, rather than private and officer. And from then on, Koskela interacted with all of them that way. At first the men found it strange, and many of them struggled to treat him the same way in return. None of them ever really managed to pull it off convincingly. It was a rare phenomenon in this regiment of conscripts, in which the officers were constantly trying to maintain their so-called status, even in wartime. Of course, many officers did maintain their superior status across all units, though it was hardly by means of pretentious standoffishness that they commanded the men's respect. The marked gesture on Koskela's part was not without effect, however. Just his presence was enough to calm his men's nerves, as he seemed somehow closer to them. He was the one they trusted to resolve all the questions the future promised to pose.

They heard low voices and the dry sputtering of engines coming from somewhere behind them. It was Kaarna, shadowed by Mielonen, close on his heels.

'All right, all right. Quiet down, boys. We're going to get the rabbit. We've already got him surrounded. Where's Autio?'

'Over by the Second Platoon.'

'Right, right, sure, sure. Hietanen, what kind of troops do we have here?

'The finest machine-gunners in the nation, Captain, sir.'

'Right, right, that's the way, that's the way.'

It was an old question, to which there was only one answer. Kaarna habitually held his own company to be just a cut above the rest. He didn't really care whether this belief corresponded to reality or not – he was just aware of what healthy self-confidence can do. He knew, of course, that machine guns were dwindling in significance, at least in offensive combat operations, but he encouraged his men to take pride in their weapons anyway. Also, the man was like a rock when it came to defending his company. Officers from other companies had best refrain from coming to him with any complaints about his men. Some cadet had tried it once, when somebody or other failed to salute. Kaarna replied coldly that his men certainly never failed to salute, therefore the cadet must be mistaken. 'On top of which, it seems that the cadet's own stance demonstrates rather poor form. Why don't you go practice it a couple more times?'

The man in question was duly punished, but the cadet made sure to give Kaarna a wide berth after that.

All these kinds of things that Kaarna did stuck in the minds of his men, so even now his words brought smiles to their all-too-grim faces. 'A man who bears the unbounded admiration of his men' is the phrase often applied to some officer or other. It has a slightly nauseating ring, besides which it's false, since no cradle yet has rocked such an officer as could inspire the unbounded admiration of a Finnish private. But Kaarna's relationship to his men was exceptional. 'Won't find another one quite like that son of a bitch. Real bird of prey,' the men would say. The relationship was anything but equal, however. There was no question who was calling the shots. It was just Kaarna's direct, fair and absolutely straightforward manner that made an impression on the men.

There were smiles on their faces as they watched him leave, heading off in search of the Third Company commander, Lieutenant Autio.

'You'll see, boys. Wherever it is that things get cracking, that man's command post won't be far off,' somebody said, and the others murmured in agreement. Kaarna and Mielonen set off, one after the other, with Mielonen issuing instructions regarding their direction, which he presumed to have a better sense of than the Captain. Their conversations generally consisted of a string of little disputes, as Mielonen did not hesitate to issue commands and voice his opinions, even on questions of strategy. The Captain was happy to let the Corporal do this, though he would never have taken it from a major. He squabbled with Mielonen to pass the time and did as he liked, regardless, though he had nothing against Mielonen's suggestions. The

Corporal was a sensible fellow, which was something. The Captain didn't trust Mielonen's sense of direction, though, and said, 'No-o-o, Mielonen. Follow the eye of experience. The Russkis are over there.'

'I don't think so. Not so far from the front. The command post, I mean.'

Kaarna and Mielonen's murmuring faded away and silence reigned, until suddenly it was shattered.

'Holy Christ!'

'Everybody down!'

The leafy undergrowth rustled and weapons clanged as the men frantically dropped to the ground. Behind them, as if just behind their ears, there came a series of deafening artillery explosions. *Ba-boom. Boom. Boom.*

A sharp, piercing whistle soared over the treetops, and the men clung to the ground with their eyes opened wide. Then more explosions came, more randomly now, and again the air was filled with hissing. Somewhere far behind the border they could hear faint thuds.

Koskela, who was sitting on a mound of grass, called out, 'Get up, guys! It's our own guns. And try to keep those boxes from rattling so goddamn much.'

They clambered to their feet, grateful that the embarrassment was communal. Only Lehto hadn't moved a muscle. He was just sitting right where he had been, a thin, slightly contemptuous smile on his face. Soon Hietanen pulled himself together as well, as did another machine-gun leader, Private Määttä, a shortish guy from the northern town of Kainuu, not far from the eastern border.

Vanhala had sunk down to the ground rather languidly, following the others' lead. And now, the corners of his eyes crinkling with his smile all the while, he was the last to rise. 'The booming voice of authority! Heehee,' he whispered to his neighbor. He didn't even blush this time, though it certainly took some daring to start cracking jokes when the others were taking the incident so seriously.

Riitaoja, on the other hand, was slow to recover, and Sihvonen blustered, 'Of course. It's our own guns. Getting all jumpy over that! Clear as day that that was our guns. Stupid to get all worked up.' He himself was the one who had plunged to the ground with the most terrific clatter, however.

The battery fell silent, but the men's uneasiness was slow to recede. The leader of the rifle platoon in front of them was pacing back and forth restlessly in front of his men. He was speaking to them in an offhand sort of way, but you could tell from the stiffness in his voice and the unevenness of his breath that his heart was racing. He strode over to Koskela and said, with a contrived gruffness, 'Well, Koski, let's pull out all the stops! Autio promised me two of your guns.'

'We'll see when we get there,' Koskela replied briefly, and the Ensign returned to his men, making a personal note that Koskela was not the man to turn to when you wanted someone to chat with. The machine-gunners were somewhat acquainted with this blond-haired, slightly precocious ensign as well. Kariluoto, they'd heard his name was. Back in the burnt clearing he'd comported himself with a bit too much machismo, and the men's sharp instincts made it impossible for them to take him seriously. The Ensign was happy to curse like a sailor, but it was painfully obvious that it was all just some sort of misguided idea of manliness. Coarseness didn't suit the well-spoken, high-born fellow in the least. No wonder the other men grunted rather contemptuously, 'Talks about the goods almost as if he'd had a feel himself.'

They waited quietly for half an hour, until, finally, rippling down the line from the right, the command came: 'Move out!'

Their gray shadows moved silently through the dusky forest toward the border. The submachine-gunners stole out in front. They stared unblinking through the trees, hearts racing and hands gripping their weapons so tightly their knuckles went white. Before them lay the border: an open stretch hacked out of the forest with a double barbed-wire fence running down the length of it. They kicked down the fence amidst an ear-splitting screech of metal. Then they slipped through the gaps, save for Hietanen, who got carried away and started kicking at one of the fence posts, snarling,

'Oh for Chrissakes! Open the roads, open the goddamn roads all the way to the skies!'

'For God's sake, keep it down,' Koskela warned, and Hietanen abandoned his effort, but not without muttering, 'All these goddamn posts here, in the middle of the woods! I wouldn't stand for it.'

They proceeded cautiously. They expected gunfire from behind every tree, every shrub. But nothing came. Not even when they crossed a small, open meadow, which they assumed the enemy must be waiting behind. The meadow widened on the left, where it met up with a small, open field that had a gray house sitting near its edge. The border ran right beside the house, which was on the Finnish side, and several men appeared to be standing around it. They recognized them as guys from the Second Battalion, the one that was supposed to advance toward the road.

Then they saw a skittish horse start jumping about, and several men began chasing after it, trying to get it under control. One company from the Second Battalion, it seems, had decided to take tea before the departure, but because they were running late, the driver had driven the field kitchen all the way up to the border to save time. The Battalion Commander, his nervousness further exacerbated by the delay their gathering had caused, arrived on the scene, bellowing, 'Good Lord, man! Get that kitchen the hell out of here! What in God's name do you think you're doing?'

The man panicked and started tugging at his horse, which promptly bolted off completely. With the men's help, he finally captured the horse and led it away. The men from the First Battalion, who watched from behind the clearing, would never have thought to connect the scene they'd witnessed with the rumor that circulated later, according to which the Second Battalion had sent their field kitchen to spearhead their advance across the border, just for the hell of it. The rumor snowballed and spread widely. The Battalion Commander came to be known as 'Madcap Karl' and the story stuck to him. Young officers who had been sufficiently far off from the scene of the event said, 'That's just Karl's way. That's him through and through.' Many of them had never seen Karl himself, but they spoke of him as if they were close personal acquaintances. Before long, one of these officers' mothers was telling her friends how her son and some Madcap Karl, along with several officers, had been the first to drive across the border with a field kitchen. The enemy had mistaken the contraption for a tank and hightailed it out of there without firing a shot.

In reality, Karl was angry as a bear with a bullet in his back as he ordered the kitchen to be driven back from the front lines. The men couldn't seem to get themselves properly organized into squads. The companies blundered about in utter chaos and, in his disgruntled exasperation, Karl mixed up the chain of command and started issuing orders directly to the platoons instead of to the company commanders.

The First Battalion was waiting with bated breath. The sun had risen and the men were sprawled out on the damp grass, warming themselves in its rays. The mosquitoes buzzed and an airplane drone came from somewhere further off, but besides that it was perfectly silent.

Finally, the men saw the others moving away from the little house. They prepared to set out themselves, but no orders came. Then, suddenly, they went stiff, listening and looking at one another. A string of submachine-gun shots rang out on their left. The sudden staccato was quickly followed by the clatter of more weapons. The rattle of light machine guns echoed through the forest, and then a machine gun hammered out a long string of shots. The men listened, silent.

'The whole belt in one go,' somebody observed.

'Whole belt.'

'Some guy's already going cold over there.'

For the first time they heard the ricochet of a stray bullet: *Voo . . . phiew.*

'Somebody over there's taking a beating.'

'Why are we staying here?' Sihvonen exclaimed. 'They might still turn this way.'

'Don't worry,' Koskela replied calmly, brushing the mosquitoes from his face with an alder branch. 'There's nothing over there but some outpost – at most. You'll get your chance to smell burnt gunpowder, don't worry.'

The firing died down, and they waited. Then they started off, but the shooting started up again on the left, and they stopped again.

'This is pointless,' somebody said. 'Something's wrong.'

'Nothing's wrong. This is war. In a few days you'll understand,' Koskela said.

By five o'clock in the afternoon they had advanced a mile or so. The firing on their left was continuous now. The Second Battalion, they realized, must have reached the enemy positions.

## III

The swamp lay in front of them. Behind it rose a wooded ridge. A few dwarf pines trees grew in the swamp, and the men tried to peek between them to the edge of the forest opposite. They couldn't make out anything significant, but they knew the enemy was over there, regardless. The term 'enemy' is a bit misleading, actually, as none of them bore any particular enmity toward anybody just then. They were too nervous for that.

The Third Company commander, Lieutenant Autio, came up to Ensign Kariluoto's platoon from behind. Autio was a regular officer – a calm, young fellow with a resolute face, generally reputed to be a good leader. Kariluoto was trying to keep calm, despite the fact that he couldn't understand anything Autio was saying.

'The artillery will send a bombardment out in front of the Second Battalion. Mortars, too. As soon as it's over, we go in – don't wait for a separate command. Do not let up at any point, as you want to make it in one go. Under no circumstances is anyone to lie down under fire. Koskela, you set up both your machine guns for support if the advance gets stuck, but only then. We want to escape notice as long as possible. They know we're around, of course, but we should try to take them by surprise, regardless. I'll be directly behind the Second Platoon. Anything unclear?'

'No . . . I've got it. Just keep your fingers crossed.'

Autio left, and Kariluoto reviewed mixed-up bits of his instructions in his head. 'No one lies down under fire . . . take them by surprise . . .'

Koskela was speaking to his own men. 'Keep close behind the guys in front of you, and if the line stops, get into position immediately. And remember, you can't hesitate in opening fire. And don't all bunch up behind the guns. There should just be one guy shooting and one guy helping him.'

'Got it . . . Yup, we've got it.' They all nodded their heads, though none of them had the faintest idea what this 'opening fire' actually entailed. They all knew how to shoot a gun, but nobody knew how he would hold up in the face of one. For the first time in their lives, they would be put to the test. Loading a belt and pulling a trigger were simple enough, but facing down death was harder – and that was the thought that was writhing about in their minds, making their earnest faces twist into vaguely comical contortions.

They heard the opening shots ring out from behind the border. It was the same artillery battery that had frightened them during the night, accompanied now by even deeper booms from further behind. Vicious whistles pierced the air and then the ground shook with the jarring force of the explosions. In between you could hear the weak coughs of bursting hand grenades.

When the barrage fell silent, an intense clanging of infantry fire started up, and a long, sustained cry rose up from the din.

'Second Battalion's attacking,' somebody whispered low, his voice choking with nervousness.

Ensign Kariluoto was lying crouched behind a grass-covered mound. Gasping for breath, he repeated over and over again the line that had been hammered into his head: '*What greater honor . . . what greater honor . . .*' He didn't dare finish the phrase: '*than dying in battle*', so he just kept repeating the opening over and over again.

The platoon beside them set off. Kariluoto rose and called out stiffly, 'Fourth Platoon, advance!'

He forced himself to start moving forward and the men followed. They hadn't got very far when they began to hear whistling plinks and rustles in the dwarf pines.

*Piew, piew . . . piewpiew.*

Angry little gusts sent them diving to the ground. Kariluoto ran a few steps further on, then ducked behind a small rise in the swampland. Breathlessly he yelled, 'Advance! Don't stop . . . No one is to lie down under fire . . . take them by surprise . . .'

No one got up, and even Kariluoto stayed where he was, his will shaken. It was as if he'd been paralyzed. He grasped from his surroundings that the entire company was under fire, and that his platoon was lying under cover in the uneven terrain. A petrifying thought wound its way insidiously through his consciousness: I can't do it . . . I can't get my men to advance . . . I've done exactly what Autio said not to . . .

'Machine guns into position.' Koskela was on his knees behind a pine, pistol in hand. The men lay further back. Not until they heard Koskela's command did they set up the machine guns. Seeing that Koskela was kneeling, Lehto rose up onto his knees as well and, a tightness in his voice, ordered, 'Move it, guys. Load the belts. Fast.'

Once Koskela saw that the guns were ready to go, he called out, 'Shoot for their nuts!'

'Shoot for their nuts!' Hietanen repeated, and Lehto and Lahtinen joined in, 'Shoot for their nuts!' The guy shooting Lehto's team's gun, Private Kaukonen, called out nervously after them, 'Shoot for their nuts!' and pulled the trigger. Lahtinen's gun was already hacking away. Määttä was shooting it, calmly and deliberately, his face utterly blank.

The weapon shook in Kaukonen's hands and he watched, through eyes stinging with sweat, how the sight skipped along the rim of the forest as the belt jerked in rapidly from the feeder. His nostrils felt as though they were burning with the nauseating stench of grease and gunpowder.

Their own fire kept them from hearing the crackling amidst the pines. Nicks in the trees already shone white where the bark had been torn off.

Suddenly a shell from some kind of direct-fire weapon exploded into a tree, and a low, inaugural blast sounded from the opposite edge of the forest.

'Anti-tank gun. Shit!' Koskela crouched to the ground. He wondered for just a moment if he should take over command of the platoon, but decided against it. He could imagine the panic the young ensign was in, and he knew he'd have to conquer it himself.

The machine-gun belt ran out. Vanhala, who was feeding the gun, yelled back, 'Ammo! Hurry!'

Riitaoja, lying under cover beside the boxes of ammunition, didn't move a muscle. His eyes were terribly round, and his face twisted into a strangely contorted grin at Vanhala's shout.

'Give me a belt!' Lehto called out as well, but Riitaoja scarcely noticed. Lehto bounded over, tossed Vanhala a belt and, seething with rage, hissed at Riitaoja, 'You shit-eating pansy. I'm going to beat you into this swamp.'

Riitaoja blinked his eyes in terror, but said nothing. Trembling, he crouched into his hollow and Lehto crawled back to the gun.

'Let him be,' Koskela said, having observed Riitaoja's terror. Lehto grunted back offhandedly, 'I guess everybody here's scared, but you'd think he could lift a finger.'

As if determined to prove he was everything Riitaoja was not, Lehto rose to his knees and began shooting at the forest's edge. Randomly, like everybody else, since none of them had caught so much as a glimpse of the enemy.

Two men approached the swamp – Kaarna and Mielonen. Mielonen was walking several steps behind, saying, 'Captain, sir. They're using the anti-tank rrrifle.'

'No. It's a tank.'

'You think?'

'Yes, yes, of course. You could tell from the sound of it.'

'Rrreally? A tank on rrroads like this?'

'Yeah, yeah, it's not impossible.'

'I wouldn't be too sure.'

'Sure, sure, you can never be too sure, but anyway it's a tank. But hey! Looks like we're going to get a bumper crop of berries this year. What with all these blossoms.'

They made it to the swamp and Kaarna pounced immediately. 'What's going on here? What's this? Look here, you boys have made a mess of this whole thing. Ay-ay-ay! Boys, boys, this isn't how you fight a war. Noo-oo-oo. Fighting like this isn't going to get you anywhere. Now, we're going to pull ourselves together and cross this little swamp. The others are already at the enemy positions.'

The men raised their heads. Kariluoto's head, on the other hand, sank even lower. The bitterness of shame had completely paralyzed him. Kaarna stepped right beside him and said in a collegial tone, 'Give it another go, Ensign. They'll take off all right.'

Then the Captain took a deep breath. He stepped forward, straight as a ramrod. Only a slight shudder flickered across his cheekbones as he stepped forward, turned slightly to the side, like a man facing into a blizzard. His voice cracked as he bellowed, *'Cut them down, Kaleva!'*

A blast went off. The men realized Kaarna and Mielonen had collapsed to the ground. Mielonen rose immediately, however, and bounded over to the Captain, who was lying motionless, his body strangely contorted. Mielonen knelt beside him and yelled, his voice trembling, 'First aid, first aid . . . hurry . . . he's losing blood . . . Captain, tell me if I hurt you . . . Here, it'll be better if I turn you this way.'

Carefully he rolled the Captain onto his back, and the men saw that one of his legs was twisting unnaturally to the side. The direct-fire gun had struck him squarely in the hip. His ripped trouser-leg held the limb in a little, but aside from that it was completely torn off. Mielonen was beside himself, repeating, 'They got my arm, too . . . I'm hurt . . . medics . . . where are those bastards hiding?'

A couple of medics arrived and tried with trembling hands to help Mielonen bind the Captain's wounds. It was hopeless, however.

'Let's get him to the aid station . . . his hand's still moving . . . he's alive.'

Kaarna looked at Mielonen. His eyes were cloudy, but there was no lack of consciousness in his gaze. Mielonen couldn't understand what the Captain meant, as he whispered, stammering, 'O-oul-ld. An . . . old . . . man . . . already . . .' Then, with an unexpected sharpness, he said, 'Say what you will . . . it's a tank all right . . . motherfucker . . . sure is.'

His hand twitched for a moment, then his mouth hung open and his eyes rolled upwards. Mielonen understood that the end had come. They lifted the body onto the stretcher and Mielonen covered it with his overcoat. The arduous journey to the rear began.

## IV

The realization that the Captain had collapsed stunned Kariluoto. A lump formed in his throat and tears welled up in his eyes. He felt strangled by a sense of irrevocable defeat. 'Advance, advance,' he commanded himself, but his body refused to obey. The school refrain pounded through his panicked consciousness, *'Black and defamed be for ever the name . . . of the troops who in battle enraged . . . watch their elders fall before them . . .'*

His hands mangled the stems of the wild hemlock. He heard the medics' yelling and tried to get up. Images rose up from somewhere in the dark recesses of his soul. His mother and father, bragging about him to their friends. Buddies he'd celebrated with when the war broke out. Finland would have her due . . . And then he remembered Sirkka. The thought nearly broke him.

Not ten seconds had passed since Kaarna's death. Now Kariluoto got up and heard his own unbridled scream, *'Cut them down, Kaleva!* Advance! Shoot for their nuts. Charge!'

He saw Koskela running beside him, yelling, 'C'mon guys, keep in contact!'

Private Ukkola was running on the other side, screaming like a madman with his gun tucked under his arm and his mouth foaming. 'Ahhh-ahh! Baaa-staaards!'

A wild rage for victory flooded through Kariluoto. He emptied his pistol into the edge of the swamp, wishing in his fury that he could get into hand-to-hand combat. He hadn't even noticed that the fire coming from the opposite edge of the forest had stopped. Nor did he look back when one of the guys with the light machine guns wobbled to his knees, hands grasping his stomach, screaming, 'Help! Help me!'

The cry was drowned out by the men's shouts and the clanging of the submachine guns. Hietanen followed close on Koskela's heels, yelling, 'Let the bastards have it, boys!'

The machine-gunners were panting heavily, staggering under the weight of their heavy equipment. Vanhala kept repeating, breathlessly, 'Let 'em have it! Let 'em have it!' as he struggled forward with the gun stand on his shoulder. Riitaoja, however, just cowered in his hollow, gaping at everything and grasping nothing.

They found the enemy positions deserted. Kariluoto spotted just one brown uniform darting behind the bushes. Lahtinen caught up with the firing line in time to take a shot at him, but missed. The men were panting. Several of them threw themselves to the ground, and somebody called out frantically, 'Ensign, sir, Jaakko was hit . . . Ensign, sir, Jaakko Vuorela's still back there.'

'Two men from the group go back and help,' Kariluoto called out. 'All the others, keep on advancing. Don't stop. The road's straight ahead. We press on until we reach it.'

His wild rage had subsided and exhilaration now surged up in its place. He strode forward briskly, upright, urging his men onward. Before them lay the road – the same one they had turned off into the forest that morning. Everything was quiet to their left, but to the right they still heard intense firing in the First Company's sector. An engine rumbled above the din. A tank tread lay imprinted on the road, and in the forest they could see sheets of moss that had been uprooted by a turning vehicle.

They paused on the road. The clamor on the right died down as the enemy turned into the forest to circumvent the First Company's roadblock. Only now did they have time to think about what had happened.

'We lost the Captain and Mielonen.'

'Not Mielonen. I saw him run to help the Captain.'

'Whew, that was something! Machine gun's still red hot. Feel!'

'Not a single Russki down,' Hietanen said. 'Not one. I watched while we were shooting.'

Koskela used his shirtsleeve to wipe off the sweaty leather band inside his cap, then said, staring at the ground, 'They got Kaarna with a tank . . . The man just went and got himself killed.'

At the time, the men weren't able to understand Koskela's reckoning, and his face quickly resumed its usual reserve, but he remained silent all evening, staring vaguely at nothing in particular.

'They didn't say the Captain wouldn't make it,' one guy whispered, his voice low, but somebody else dismissed the idea as impossible. 'Don't be ridiculous. Looked pretty clear from the way his leg was hanging off.'

Ensign Kariluoto was pacing back and forth along the road. He couldn't keep still. His blond hair was blowing about wildly above his beaming face, as he'd taken off his cap and tucked it under his belt. It was as if this surge of self-confidence within him demanded that he be bareheaded. A cap would have interfered, somehow, with the roaring winds of victory ringing in his ears, unheard by the others. Lieutenant Autio came up on his left, and Kariluoto rushed over to meet him.

'Good job, boys. That was a solid start,' Autio said, though it sounded more like an obligatory greeting than actual praise, as Autio was not one to get overly emotional. 'So, how'd it feel?'

'Quite all right, once we got going. I didn't think there was any way I'd get them moving at first . . . But Kaarna . . .'

'I heard.'

Autio's expression remained unchanged. He had already been through the Winter War, and so had quite a bit of experience.

'I wasn't aware that the tank was there, or I would have given you the anti-tank rifle. But in any case, many thanks. You're off to a good start. Any casualties?

'Vuorela. Light machine-gunner. I sent two men back to help, when the medics took Kaarna.'

It was not until he was talking with Autio that Kariluoto remembered the first part of the attack. His face flushed, and he diverted his gaze. But as soon as Autio started talking about the tank, Kariluoto seized on the notion. It was that damn tank! Hell . . . what was a man supposed to do with his bare hands up against that? Then Kariluoto's spirits began to rise, and his shame lifted. He was so happy to be liberated of its weight that he started singing Kaarna's praises to Autio.

'He was too good a man to die. Far too good for death, that man.'

'True,' Autio kicked at a rock. 'Though no one life is any more valuable than any other, really. But that one went too cheap, it's true. Well, you'll get used to that . . . Lammio will take over as company commander, of course.'

Autio turned to leave, then said, 'The Third Battalion will take the lead as soon as the terrain's been scoured. We'll camp here. The tents and the kitchens are right behind the Third Battalion.'

## V

Kariluoto returned to his men. 'If only they hadn't had that damn tank!'

His spirits perked up again. He forgot about the fact that they had all taken the tank for an anti-tank gun; he just took refuge in the fact that there was nothing anyone could do with his bare hands up against a tank. And, after a couple of minutes, he was firmly convinced that this was the sole reason he had taken cover in the swamp: because you can't fight a tank without any anti-tank guns.

Once again, he was the vigorous ensign who had drilled his men back in the burnt clearing. He even thought of Sirkka, and felt a powerful wave of masculinity pervade his being. Sirkka was sacred to him. Kariluoto's relationship with the girl had begun with such refinement that, indeed, there was nothing to stand in the way of their potential union. And at this very moment, that question, too, was settled. He would marry her, and when he did, it would be as captain of the army of the Greater Finland – if not as major! He would enroll at the Army Academy at the first opportunity. Yes, that's how it would be. No law school for him.

Kariluoto could already see himself as a young career officer. He was still quite childish, in a way, full of fantasies he would have been embarrassed to acknowledge as his own.

He took a couple of boxes of cigarettes out of his map case and called out cheerfully, 'Come and get a smoke! Cigarettes for every man with a mouth to smoke 'em in. Bursche, come, pass 'em round.' (This word 'Bursche' had emerged directly from his thoughts about the Army Academy. Some legacy from the 'Iron-fisted German army', with its high command and lowly gophers, called 'Burschen'. The word in itself wasn't so bad, as it basically just meant 'boy', but the class-ridden mentality wrapped up in it certainly was. So much so that now, even this pure-minded youth appeared to have been infected by it. There was an antidote to prevent the spread of this particular affliction, however – war.)

A peculiar traveling party was approaching the swamp. Two men were carrying a third, who was bound with three belts to a birch trunk that somebody had sawed off with his hand-knife. A fourth man tottered along behind, staggering beneath the weight of his baggage. The last was Riitaoja. The man bound to the pole was Vuorela, and the two men carrying him were the ones who had been sent back to help.

'How'd it go?'

Between gasps, the guy in front managed to choke out, 'Jaakko's done for.'

They hadn't even been able to bind his wound, because Vuorela, who'd been shot in the stomach, had writhed so violently in his death throes. The two of them had nearly broken down in tears of despair as they tried to calm him, but Vuorela hadn't even been able to recognize them. Then they had prepared the birch pole and bound him to it. They had come across Riitaoja on their way through the swamp and made him carry their packs.

Riitaoja's absence had been noticed, but no one had gone out to search for him, because somebody had seen him lying unharmed in his little nook back at the edge of the swamp.

The men lowered their burden to the ground. With all his recent emotions still stirred up in his mind, Kariluoto said, rather too ceremoniously, 'Well, men, Vuorela is the first to go. Are any of you from the same area?'

'Other side of the same county, but I didn't know him as a civilian. He was from somewhere out in the country.'

'Very well, I'll write . . . One ought to say a few words, I think.' Kariluoto's sentiment was sincere, even if his phrases were all lifted from something he'd read. The men looked at the body in a state of anguish. Vuorela's shirt was stained with blood around his stomach. The wet swamp had washed the leather soles of his shoes clean, and it made the men slightly sick to see his ankles tied together with a belt around the pole. There was a second belt around the center of his body, and a third around his neck. The worst was his face. His dirty, suntanned skin gleamed with a yellowish hue. His gums were contorted into a gruesome smile. A few of the men felt sick and turned away.

'Take him to the side of the road.'

They were relieved when Vuorela had been carried away. Now the machine-gunners' attention turned to Riitaoja. He was standing awkwardly off to the side, grinning with embarrassment. Nobody had the heart to say anything, save Lehto, who gave him the evil eye and snorted at him in contempt.

Somewhere, at the back of their minds, they were all dimly aware that Riitaoja's terror had not been an isolated phenomenon by any means – fear was just exceptionally visible in his case. Even the call to attack, that rang so handsomely in their memories now, had aroused only terror in them then, followed by the rage they had summoned to suppress it. Nobody felt like boasting. And besides, tomorrow would bring a new day. They had heard rumors of some 'bunker line', which was supposedly just a little way out in front of where they were. But there was no point in dwelling on that now. Tents and potato soup were on their way, and there was plenty of time before the morning.


# VI

'Hey, there's one guy curled up over here, at least.'

'Where?'

'Here, in the bushes. It's an officer. Got badges on his lapels.'

They gathered around to look. A Russian lieutenant lay face-down in the juniper bushes. His body was strangely contorted, just as Vuorela's had been, but the sight didn't affect them the same way. They were just curious.

'Look! The guy dragged himself a long way. Still got mud under his nails.'

'Doesn't seem like those guys do much looking out for one another. Leaving him here to crawl back by himself.'

'Guy was tough. Dragged himself ten yards just with his arms.'

They looked on solemnly until Rahikainen tapped his gun barrel on the dead man's helmet and said, 'Yoo-hoo! 'Scuse me, 'sit cold down there in Russki hell?'

Vanhala looked around at the others, but so few of them were smiling that he choked down his laughter.

Rahikainen stooped down and started cutting off the Lieutenant's badges. 'These babies are mine.'

'Give me one, too.'

'I don't think so! There aren't enough on this little stooge to pass 'em round to everybody. That'll hafta wait until we knock off some of the big cheeses.'

The others were a bit dismayed, but the red badges had already disappeared into Rahikainen's wallet. 'You let me know whose bullet brought this guy down, and I'll hand over the booty. Otherwise, you can just lay off.'

No heir apparent appeared, so Rahikainen kept the badges. But the men had overcome their initial tentativeness. One guy took the belt – a fine, new officer's belt. They turned the man's pockets inside out and found a leather bag containing a toothbrush, a set of nail files and a flask of cologne.

Hietanen gamely flicked the cologne onto their dirty sweaters, making them all shriek with laughter like little kids. One guy swung his hips from side to side, puckered his lips and called out, 'Get in line, boys! Two hundred marks a pop!'

Another fellow used his filthy hands to splash cologne on his face. 'Discover this distinctive perfume! All the biggest stars are wearing *Mouson Lavendel!*'

They divvied up all the nail files too, though admittedly their fingernails were the least of their concerns. The dirt mostly came off on its own if you let it get thick enough.

'Here's his wallet.'

'It's got an ID. With a photo. And there's his birth date. Born in '16. Four years older than we are.'

'Hey look, rubles!'

'Those are chervonets. They're worth ten rubles each.'

'But what's it say there, huh? On the copper coin? Koneek, koneek. Why, that's just chicken scratch. Who can read that?'

'It means kopek.'

'Whatever you say, pal. Still looks like chicken scratch.'

Troops were marching by along the road. It was the Third Battalion, heading out to relieve the First Company on the front line.

'Have a good rest, guys, so we don't leave you in the dust tomorrow!' somebody shouted from the ranks.

'You just make sure you don't end up heading back this way.'

There were silent men too. Somebody mumbled anxiously, 'How far are their positions from here?'

'Keep moving! You'll get there, don't worry.'

They left the dead man in the bushes. And there he remained, Lieutenant Boris Braskanov, born Vologda, 6 May 1916: face-down, with neither belt nor badge of rank, and his pockets inside out.

The supply vehicles arrived. The men got their tents and food. The machine-gunners gathered together again, inquiring about one another's losses. The First Platoon had lost one man, but the others had escaped without casualties. Kaarna's death touched many of them, and they all considered it a great loss. If for no other reason than it meant that Lammio would probably be their new commander.

They exchanged impressions as they ate. Lahtinen was a little irritable, but somehow or other even he was interested. He trotted out his old position with an air of consternation. 'Looks like we won't exactly be parading to the Urals, after all. I mean, the air's pretty thick with lead, that's all I'm sayin'. Be interesting to see just how long we hold out.'

Then a deep-seated amusement rose in his voice as he added, 'But man, the thing that made me laugh – damndest thing of all was when our neighbor went and hightailed it into those juniper bushes like a scared rabbit! I chased after him and took a shot at him, but I didn't manage to get him – what with this shitty excuse for a gun.'

Ensign Kariluoto wrote three letters that night. But first he raked over the day's events with the other platoon leaders . . . Then I bawled out . . . come on, boys! C'mon, you bastards . . . thought my days were over for a moment there . . . good guy, that son of a bitch . . . fearless guy. I threw this hand grenade . . . the MG commander . . . fierce old guy, good God. Luostarinen, from the First Company . . . two officers on day one.

Kariluoto then wrote to Vuorela's family:

. . . for this news has surely reached you by now. Allow me to share the burden of your heavy grief. I wish you to know that he was one of my finest men; and it is a great blow to me, as well, that he should be the first to go. Our nation's lot is hard; and so our sacrifices are very great. But even so – we must endure. I say this so that you will have the consolation of knowing, even in your grief, that our suffering is a sacrifice to the highest and most honorable of human causes: the freedom of our land and our people. And now, as the chains of Karelia are breaking, and Finland stands before a new dawn, may you hear, even in your grief, your son's proud voice rising from the fray, *'O, dear Finlandia . . .'*

To his own mother and father, he wrote:

. . . I am proud of my mission. I have decided once and for all that I will pursue a career as an officer. Just now, every other career looks meaningless to me. Soon, we will see Karelia free once more. And from her deepest despair, Finland will rise up to fulfill her manifest destiny. Today, in one short instant, I experienced so much. I understood definitively, today, that my life belongs not to me, but to Finland. I do not deceive myself; I know it will not be easy, but I see a straight road lying out clearly before me, and I will strive with everything I have to see it to the end. I acquired a deep debt today to a certain Jaeger captain, who showed me how to keep on to the end with one's head held high. The sight of him showed me the standard that we must all strive to meet. After such a baptism of fire, one hardly uses grand phrases, but as I said: I know my duty now, and already everything is much easier . . .

But in reality, Kariluoto was bowled over with emotion, baptism of fire or not. He and his family had always lived in an atmosphere of high patriotism, but even so, his letters had never risen to quite such ceremonious heights before.

He wrote to Sirkka:

. . . today I feel I can speak of something that might be difficult at other times. I think you know what I mean. I confess, I did not have the courage to bring it up the last time I saw you. Today, my timidity makes me smile. What children we all are before we are forced to take honest stock of ourselves! So I speak, even if I am not entirely sure of your answer, whatever it may be. As difficult as your refusal would be, I will strive to fulfill my duty, regardless. Today I stand indebted before all those who have already fulfilled theirs . . .

Vanhala was on night-watch guarding the camp. He circulated around, glancing at the tents, the corners of his eyes crinkled with his smile. 'Yoo-hoo! 'Scuse me, 'sit cold down there in Russki hell?'

Rahikainen's words had made him laugh, and now that he was alone, he laughed with abandon, not having to worry about what the others might think. He listened unflinchingly as an artillery battery opened fire, sending shells howling over the encampment. A terrified face popped out from one of the tent flaps, but relaxed when the man caught sight of Vanhala's smile.

The sun had set. A low mist rose from the swamp and darkness fell over the spruce grove. The booming of cannons came frequently from the north and the south. Somewhere a pistol shot pierced through the air, and a slow-firing Russian machine gun hammered back in response.

A horse-cart drove down the road. It was coming from the front lines, carrying four bodies wrapped in tent tarps. The First Company's dead.

# Chapter Three

## I

The men sat on the roadside and waited, chewing on the bread they'd saved. Gunshots rang out now and again from the front lines. Airplane engines rumbled in the distance, paused, then started up again, accelerating into a querulous whine, occasionally punctuated by the chatter of machine guns.

'Air combat,' somebody said, trying to make out the planes overhead.

'Let 'em fight,' somebody else said dismissively, with the unimpressed air of the combat veteran. Vanhala sniggered to himself and then finally burst out, 'Our boys – battling sons of the air!'

Ensign Kariluoto was pacing back and forth along the road. He had posted his letters straight away the previous evening, so he couldn't get them back this morning, unfortunately. Steadied by a good night's sleep, he suspected that the letters might have been a little too grandiose, and he would have liked to have revised them, had the mail not been picked up already. For the moment, however, he had forgotten all about them. He joked boisterously with his men, determined to put any jitters about the upcoming combat out of his mind. He was overplaying it and it showed – but anyway, it helped. Thinking about their next attack had made him restless again. He wasn't entirely sure that the humiliations of the previous day wouldn't repeat themselves. What if his moment of personal conquest had just been a one-off? But no. No, no, that would not happen again. Never again.

Lieutenant Lammio came up behind them. A disgruntled Mielonen trailed a few paces after. The change in company commander had hit him hardest of all. No more of the Captain's familiar humming and rambling on, not to mention the squabbling, which was certainly out of the question now. Now, commands came in shrill, hyper-correct contortions, whose every pretentiously crossed 't' made the men wince.

Lammio had no particular business being there, seeing as the machine-gunners had been split up into platoons and attached to individual infantry companies. He was just strutting about for his own amusement, flexing his muscles and enjoying his new position. As soon as he was out of earshot, Rahikainen snorted, 'So now they've landed us with that peacock. It's just a wonder he didn't ask us to salute.'

Private Määttä took a drag on his cigarette and murmured, 'He can ask whatever he wants. Don't mean we're gonna do it. My flipper's feeling pretty heavy these days.'

It was a startling outburst, as up to then Määttä had been the most compliant and obedient of men, never uttering so much as a word of complaint. In the previous day's attack, every one of them had taken note of his calm, downright cold-blooded bravery. They had also noticed that he never requested a rotation in carrying equipment. It was as if the little guy could haul a machine gun indefinitely. Shifts would stretch out longer when it was his turn to carry, since it was only after a long battle with his conscience that the next guy would finally say, 'All right, hand it over.'

'Sure, if you want,' Määttä would reply. 'Or I can just keep it.'

Määttä was smoking his cigarette in long, slow drags. There was no mistaking his words. They sensed that instinctively. His wasn't just the usual talking big while backs were turned. What they couldn't understand was where this sudden defiance had appeared from. In truth, the matter was simple: this quiet guy, whose reticence tended to relegate him to the fringes of things, had realized that he could stand his ground just as well as anybody else when the chips were down. Death had failed to impress him – and there's nothing worse than that.

'My flipper's feelin' pretty heavy, too,' Rahikainen chimed in.

The morning sun was hot. The men were glum and worn out.

Can't the Third Battalion advance? . . . We're gonna have to open the road again ourselves . . . of course we are . . . no news there.

Booms began echoing from the enemy side. They dragged themselves up to a seated position and listened. The rumbling lasted three, four, five seconds, and then: *hoo-ee!*

The first shell crashed down on the roadside just in front of them. 'Get down!' The order was pointless, as every one of them was already trembling in a ditch somewhere on the side of the road. All thoughts were banished and their heads pounded as they waited for their worst fears to be realized. The ground shook and blasts of air kept pressing their clothes against their bodies. Shrapnel whirred through the air, dropping to the ground with rocks and clods of earth. It lasted scarcely two minutes. When the echo of the last explosion had died away, a frantic scream pierced the silence. 'Stretchers! Bring the stretchers! Medics!'

Two medics came running from behind, carrying a stretcher. Somebody was lying on the road bank out in front of them trying to get up. 'Aargh . . . yeow . . . help me . . .'

A couple of men were kneeling beside the wounded. 'Shh, shh, stop crying, stop crying,' they kept repeating frantically. The man's scream was so gut-wrenching that they lost their heads entirely and couldn't even manage to help him. His shoulders were badly torn up. The medics started binding his wounds, struggling against the man's frenzied thrashing. He tried to yank himself upright and yelled, 'Help . . . shoot me, somebody! Ah . . . ow . . . you goddamn pansies! Somebody shoot, damn it!'

'Ylitalo's dead.' A pale-faced man was coming toward them from further down the road, holding his bleeding arm. 'Could you guys bandage this?'

The overwrought medics were in a panic. One was struggling to keep the wounded guy from thrashing about, while the other was trying to bandage him as best he could. Their words came rushing out all at once. 'How – we can't do everything all at once! Where the hell is the head medic? Scaredy-cat son-of-a-bitch is hiding and we're supposed to be all over the goddamn place.'

The man sat down on the bank of the road. A resolute expression fell over his pale face as he said, 'Stop whining like a two-year-old, for fuck's sake. I can wrap this myself. Ylitalo over there in that ditch's got half his brains blown out.'

The air was still thick with smoke and dust. 'Scatter!' Kariluoto yelled. 'Don't bunch up all together!' His face was pale, but a resolute gleam lit up his eyes. In the brunt of the attack, he had lifted his head, just to test himself – and it had risen easily. He felt the same victorious feeling wash over him that he had felt after the previous day's attack. It didn't have the same wild abandon this time, though, as Ylitalo was one of his men, as were both of the wounded.

Lahtinen crawled out of his ditch. 'To the Urals, huh, boys? Well, by all means, why don't you strike up the band!'

'You know that chorus even in your sleep, don't you?' Hietanen was irritated. 'Of all the goddamn lies. Sure, just listen to a shell to hear if it's coming close. Hell of a whopper that is! Biggest goddamn lie I ever heard. It doesn't make any noise at all. Nothing! Just *thwamp!* when it blows up on the side of the road. Pre-tty curious if you ask me. They said out on the Western Front you could hear 'em in time to get down. Well, I'll tell you straight out that those guys have never heard a shell over there if that's the case. Maybe they've got something else.'

Määttä took a drag on his cigarette. 'The thing's gonna blow up just the same whether it makes a noise or not.'

Lammio arrived. 'Scatter! Did you not hear the command?'

'Oh, shut the fuck up, asshole,' Rahikainen muttered from his ditch. Just then the enemy artillery started rumbling again and a thump shook the ground as the men dived for cover. Lammio hadn't moved a muscle. Neither had Koskela, who was still sitting perfectly still. 'They're over us, guys.'

Lehto, Määttä and Hietanen pulled themselves together quickly. The bombs whistled overhead and exploded far behind them.

'Whistling bad news for our artillery battery,' somebody observed.

Lammio stood on the road and screeched, 'All of you men had better start believing what you are told. That round could just as easily have struck here.'

His lack of fear made the men hate him all the more, depriving them as it did of the opportunity to despise him. Rahikainen even whispered again, 'Quit whining, you little bugger.'

Riitaoja was still lying in his ditch, face pressed to the ground. He was like a terrified child. Lucky for him, ambition did not figure amongst his concerns. Neither did any conception of 'homeland', so he was at liberty to be just as terrified as he liked.

'Why don't you make some more noise?' Sihvonen muttered. 'Holler and wave your arms around, why don't you? That way those binoculars over in that observation tower'll spot you right away and be sure to shoot all our guts out. And we'll just stand here like a bull's-eye. That's right. Nothing but goddamn blockheads running this show.'

The injured guy had fallen unconscious. Two medics drenched in sweat carried him back on the stretcher. The fellow with the injured arm had refused to let the medic bandage his wound after he'd finished with the other man, snarling angrily, 'Gi-git . . .'

'Hey, hey,' the nervous medic said. 'I popped out about twenty years ago and I'm not goin' back in . . . Look, bandage it yourself, if you like. It's not like I want to.'

The man walked off, waving his good arm and calling out, 'So long, boys! This fellow here is headed home on leave.' He was happy. Not only because of the leave, but also because he knew that later that night, somebody in a tent would say, 'Tough son-of-a-bitch, that Rantanen guy. Whew! My God!'

'Move out!'

They got up. They practically marched on one other's heels they were so eager to get away. Ylitalo's head was covered, but some liquid from his canned pork was dripping from his bread sack, as a shard of shrapnel had punctured his emergency rations as well.

## II

'Enemy directly ahead, behind a barricade about three hundred yards out. Two armed bunkers reported back there, at least. Artillery opens fire for five minutes. Mortars join two minutes after that. H-hour is at 10.48.' Kariluoto kept his voice low.

The men listened, looking at the barricade visible between the trees. It ran along a rather steep slope and stretched for tens of yards. They couldn't see any barbed wire, though. Reconnaissance missions carried out earlier had determined that there were several machine-gun nests in dugouts behind the barricade. Two fell in the sector assigned to Kariluoto's platoon.

A scout about a dozen yards out in front of them whispered hoarsely, 'Movement behind the barricade. Shall I give it a shot?'

'Absolutely not. Everyone still.'

Off to the right, the artillery observer was speaking into his radio. 'Esa speaking. Esa here. Masa, do you read me? Masa, do you read me? Over, over.'

The artillery observer's low voice sounded as if it were reciting a strange incantation. The men's anxiety mounted, as his call meant that all hell was about to break loose. The forest was damp with morning dew and humming with the buzzing of mosquitoes. The spiderwebs hanging in the low blueberry bushes clung to their hands unpleasantly as blood pounded through their wrists. Squad leaders whispered final instructions. The men tightened their belts and put their cartridges into their pockets where they'd be easy to reach.

'Hand grenades at the ready. Who's got the satchel charges?'

'Here's one. Two . . . Should I launch them?'

'No, absolutely not.'

The artillery observer was muttering figures into his radio. Nervous explosions went off on their left, here and there, in the Second Company's sector. The enemy could scent an attack.

It was 10.43. Behind them it seemed like the whole world was being torn to pieces. Shrill cannons, low-booming howitzer fire, and the rolling thunder of the heavy artillery came thumping on one another's heels as if they were racing. The men clung to the ground as the shower of shells sailed over them, sounding like a clattering train. Their bodies bounced and shook along with the movements of the earth beneath them. Smoke, earth, rocks and wood came pouring down from behind the barricade. Flames flared up in the gray whirl.

'Jesus! Can a person survive that?' A pale face rose to watch.

'And now it's your turn, buddy,' another voice murmured low, with vindictive pleasure.

'They've overshot a little,' Koskela said, kneeling to look up the hill.

Kariluoto's watch ticked. 10.44 ... 45 ... 46 ... 47 ... 'Forty-seven ... keep them under fire as you move out ... use the barricade to your advantage ... if I get scared, just shoot me ... we're going all-out ...'

10.47. Kariluoto waited conscientiously until his watch showed 48 minutes exactly, and just at that moment the last shell sailed overhead.

'Fourth Platoon, advance!'

Kariluoto dashed quickly toward the barricade, keeping low to the ground. The men followed. The scout darted out in front of all of them. Enemy mortars whistled overhead and exploded behind them.

'Advance! Advance!' the men urged one another on.

Fighting was already in full swing in the neighboring sector. The scout's submachine gun rattled away and returning fire hammered straight back. The air whistled and whined, pounded and boomed.

'All right men, let 'er rip!' Kariluoto leapt forward. He gritted his teeth and hollered, 'Move out! Mow them down ... the bastards ... now we're going to shove you bastards right back where you came from ... Asia for the Asians ...' Kariluoto stoked the flames of his anger to keep his courage up. Maybe it helped him – in any case, he advanced ever further, despite the angry whizzes nearly grazing his eyebrows.

'Yeeessss, men ...'

Because the platoon was still advancing at a crouch, taking cover only now and then, he was hoping to advance directly into a charge, which would settle the whole thing quickly.

Just then, the scout dropped his submachine gun and fell to his knees, pressing his cap to his face. Blood seeped between his fingers. 'My head . . . it got me in the head . . . my eyebrow's torn up . . .'

'Can you manage by yourself?'

'Yeah, I think so . . . it's not fatal . . . can't be dangerous . . . a head wound kills instantly if it's fatal . . . but I'm still here . . . so it's not an emergency . . .' The man was dazed by the blow and kept repeating this thought that had sprung into his mind, which in itself was perfectly correct.

He started to make his way back on all fours as the others continued to advance, though the sight of his injury had prompted several of them to take cover. The barricaded slope lay in front of them. An unbroken stream of infantry fire was coming out from behind it, but the fervor of the fire far exceeded its threat. It basically went straight over them.

About halfway up the slope, however, it began to be more effective. The men pressed themselves low to the ground. Some darted from cover to cover and some crawled, but several were already trapped in the line of fire. Kariluoto was four or five yards out in front of his men. He was crawling on all fours, yelling constantly, 'Advance, men . . . ! Let 'em have it!'

Then somebody yelled, 'Watch out for the bars of soap!'

'Huh?'

'The soap. Hanging from the logs. It's TNT.'

'The barricade's mined. Watch out for the wires.'

The barricade was hung with little TNT explosives that looked remarkably like bars of soap. They weren't terribly dangerous, so long as you weren't right next to them when they went off, since without shells they were basically just pressure explosives.

'Dismantle them. Be careful!'

They didn't have any sappers, but somehow or other they had enough training to manage situations like this, which they were supposed to navigate on their own. The sappers were with the neighboring company, as it was the one tasked with spearheading the attack.

The men were wary of touching the wires. The advance came to a halt.

'We're stuck.'

'What kind of sucker's gonna touch that?'

'They don't do anything. They're harmless.' Kariluoto detached one of the wires, emboldening the men around him to follow his lead.

*Bam!*

'Get anyone?'

'Nope. Just the world gettin' a word in.'

Kariluoto rose to a squat. 'Try to keep clear of the rest. Let's crawl from here.'

The clamor intensified. It billowed in waves on the right, then on the left. Men screamed out orders and calls to charge. Shells whizzed overhead in both directions as the artilleries battled it out. Bullets whistled, ricochets whined. They began to hear screams of 'Stre-e-e-tch-ers!' from the neighboring platoon's sector.

The barricade provided them with some cover, as did the boulders and hollows in the terrain. The enemy machine guns weren't just firing off bursts, but whole belts, hammering from one end straight through to the other. The uproar of battle continued as far as the men could make out above the blasts of their own fire. The regiment was attacking the bunker line. And from further off on the right, they could hear the clatter of a neighboring regiment's attack.

The air trembled as booms echoed through the summer morning. Thousands of gun barrels glowed with heat, thousands of hands loaded and fired, and thousands of men crawled and dashed their way forward, body and soul gripped with anxiety. And in that same anxious grip, thousands of others fended them off, staunchly defending their posts to the bitter end. Tens, hundreds died; hundreds were wounded; there were displays of fear, and there were displays of spectacular bravery. For more than a year, a great proportion of the Finnish people had been quietly awaiting their moment of revenge, fists clenched in their pockets. There was real force behind the attack.

But there was real force behind the defense, too. It was clear to

Kariluoto that leading a charge in the face of this fire would mean the end of his platoon, even if he could convince the men to attempt it. They were crawling slowly.

'Fucking artillery! It's no help at all,' somebody gasped.

Kariluoto was desperate. He could sense that the attack was losing its edge. But the thought unleashed a powerful wave of his former drive. Fear lurked in the depths of his soul. Strained, tottering on the brink of despair, he suppressed it, and little by little his will won the upper hand, and he was able to get his anxiety under control. 'Crawl forward! Take turns firing. Take advantage of the terrain. Squad leaders. Get your guys together and advance in squads, half the guys cover while the other half advance. Give an example for the others to follow!'

Kariluoto was already nearly ten yards out in front of the others. The nearest squad leader ordered his men to fire and rose to make a run for it. He had just come into line with Kariluoto when his sprint was cut short. The man rolled onto his back. A blue hole lay between his eyes, right in the center of his forehead. His hand fumbled for the button of his collar and went stiff, his mouth gasping for air a few times, like a fish out of water.

'Tyynelä!'

No answer. Kariluoto crawled over and confirmed that the man was dead. Just then a bullet tore a hole through his own cap.

'Rekomaa, take the second squad.'

A man from the second squad, Tyynelä's coffee buddy and closest friend, was endeavoring to aim his gun. The sight was blurry. His eyes smarted with tears and sweat. In a choked-up voice, wavering with anger – an anger directed at Kariluoto – he muttered, 'Example, example. There's Tyynelä's example.'

They advanced a few more yards, but Tyynelä's death had taken a toll on the men.

'I'm hit!' Somebody started crawling back on all fours.

'Medics!'

A minute later, nineteen bullets raked the body of some guy who was crawling. They counted the bullets later, at the aid station.

Kariluoto had a hole in his holster now, too, as well as his cap. He was taut with nervous exhaustion, but he refused to let up. No sooner would the platoon catch up with him than he would start advancing again. Private Ukkola, the guy who had run beside him the previous day, was following close behind him now. Each of them threw a hand grenade, but both fell hopelessly short. Four or five enemy grenades came thudding down in response, though they, too, fell too far off to be effective.

Kariluoto heard someone calling out his name and, spotting Autio lying behind him, crawled over.

'Can't you get any further?' Autio asked.

'I've tried everything.' Kariluoto's voice was angry, but not in a defensive way – more despairing. He tried to spit, but the pitiful drop dried up on his lips. His mouth was horribly dry. He wiped his sleeve across his lips and caught a bitter, crushed worm in his mouth. 'Lost three men and my best squad leader. The barricade's mined and the lead's coming down like rain. It'll be the death of the whole platoon . . . but if you think . . . I mean, personally I'm ready . . .'

'No . . . no. None of that . . . The whole battalion's stuck. The Second Company's got heavy losses . . . Two platoon leaders. And from my men, Lilius is out of the game. Took it in the shoulder. I notified the Commander of the situation, but he ordered us to keep at it.'

'Can we soften them up again?'

'We'll never get another attack launched if we pull back now . . . If you make it, you know . . . look, I won't mince words. You make it through, today's your day.'

Autio knew Kariluoto and his plans to pursue a career as an officer – which was why he was applying every possible psychological pressure. He knew that, of all the platoon leaders, Kariluoto was the one who, despite his weaknesses, would have the hardest time saying, 'I can't make it any further.'

'I'll do what I can . . . if I can just get the guys to move.'

'Give it a shot. It's not obligatory. It's just that it would be pretty rough having to turn back now, after all these casualties.'

Autio returned to his men and Kariluoto crawled back to the head of his platoon, which was still exchanging fire. The shooting had died down a little. Every last one of the men would have fiercely denied that it had taken them a full hour and a half to advance these sixty-odd yards. The men were already getting tired. Their lips were parched with thirst. Several were already lying down apathetically behind boulders.

The peat-covered enemy bunker was already clearly visible. Continuous fire streamed out from its black openings. There was another one a little ways off to the left. After that, the line turned a corner and the Second Company's sector began. There, men had been ordered out of the ranks to assist the medics. Spearheading the attack had cost them many men. The platoon leaders had taken the brunt of it, and two of them were already dead. To make matters worse, the Second Platoon had lost its deputy platoon leader just after its leader.

When the platoon leader fell, the ambitious corporal had envisioned taking over his duties, which would send him straight to the top. 'All right, boys, this is it!' He managed to sprint four steps as a platoon leader before a spray of light-machine-gun fire cut short his dreams of promotion for evermore.

In the protected area, there were eleven bodies and eighteen wounded. And more kept arriving. The stretchers were sticky with blood. The head medic rushed about amidst a sea of wails and moans. 'How am I ever going to get all of these back? Pretty soon half the company's going to be carrying the other half.'

The men had reached the end of their tether. They were cursing and yelling at one another, 'Shut up . . . pick up the fucking stretcher or I'll just drag him!'


## III


Koskela and the first section had had almost nothing to do since the fighting began. The machine guns couldn't be brought in for support until they were closer to the bunkers. Koskela could see that it wouldn't pay to carry such easy prey into the fighting unless they could run the guns straight into reasonable range of the bunkers. This made some of the men happy, but some of them felt uneasy standing around idly while the others were engaged in such heavy fighting. They hadn't been hardened against that sort of thing yet, as this was their first real battle. When Koskela saw that the men had stopped before the bunkers, he decided the moment had come.

And so they had their first taste of the miserable task of all machine-gunners. 'It's easy shit, running in behind?' the infantry guys would sometimes ask. The easy life didn't come cheap, however, and they paid for it in the tens of pounds of equipment they had to lug. It was hard to take cover with the equipment, so they tried to slither up the slope on their sides, dragging the gun-stands, but the going was excruciating. Koskela sent Hietanen off with Lahtinen's machine gun to attack one bunker, and he himself took Lehto's to the other.

The worst part was that, when you were bogged down with those contraptions, it was hard to stop anywhere you wouldn't be seen. But, finally, the sweaty ordeal was over, and they were just behind the infantry.

'Get into position!'

Panting, cursing and urging one another on, they lugged the gun to a small depression shielded by a fallen birch. Vanhala pulled the heavy gun-stand into the ditch. Kaukonen fixed the gun to it. Koskela and Kariluoto agreed that the machine gun would fire at the openings in the bunker, providing some cover for Kariluoto and his men to try to get into the trench.

'Shoot for the mouths of the bunker!' Koskela commanded, and Kaukonen started shooting.

Kariluoto rose to a crouch: 'My platoon: advance!' The side of the fallen birch crackled beside him, obliging him to press low to the ground again.

Vanhala smiled, in the middle of everything, and said, 'Those fellows are out to kill us over there. Guys can't take a joke.'

'Feed the belts!' Lehto called curtly, sending Vanhala cowering into silence.

'You got it, Kaukonen. Aim's good.'

Kaukonen glowed at these words of praise and lifted his head to see better, but quickly ducked back down again. Kariluoto crawled off.

Several of the men tried to follow, but their venture was cut short when one of the light machine-gunners fell and the guy helping him was wounded in the same burst. A bullet had gone through his throat, which now wheezed grotesquely, its broken whine draining the men of their last shreds of willpower. The gruesome sights were starting to overwhelm them. It was too much to take all at once.

'They're sending us out to be killed for nothing,' a voice came from somewhere. 'Where are those fucking fancy-pants hiding?'

'Shut up and adva-h-ance!' Kariluoto's angry voice wavered on the brink of sobs as he screamed. He knew 'fancy-pants' couldn't be referring to him, since he had been out in front of his men the whole time, but he still felt as if he had been insulted. Koskela crawled beside him and said, 'Let it go. You'll get yourself killed for nothing . . . you won't get 'em to move that way . . . you'll just get yourself killed, and for nothing.'

'What am I supposed to do? What else is there to be done? We have to try to advance somehow. Either they come or they don't . . . but I for one am not stopping.'

'I know a trick. We could try to get one guy up close with a satchel charge. It'd work better if some of the others could help him out with some fire. Tiny little movement like that might go unnoticed. If you get the whole platoon to charge, it will cost us several men no matter what.'

'I'll try it myself.'

'Won't work. I'm going.'

'But I should be the one . . . This is my mission, not yours. In any case, a machine-gunner's not supposed to take the lead.' Kariluoto was dismayed. Koskela's suggestion struck him as insulting, and in the same blow it seemed to confirm that he had failed.

Koskela could feel himself getting irritated at this excessive touchiness and egotism, as he himself had never set much store by such things. Nonetheless he replied calmly, 'It won't work that way. Somebody's got to get the men to advance and that's your job. Otherwise there's no point.'

Kariluoto realized Koskela was right and ordered his men to bring over the satchel charges. The men had been lugging them along to the right of the formation, and Koskela started binding two of the nine-pound charges together with some wire.

'Eighteen pounds. You think you can make it with all that?'

No answer. Koskela was running his mouth down the twisted wire to clamp it tight. Finally the satchel charge was ready.

'Lehto. You keep that rooster crowing non-stop soon as I head out. And the same goes for Kariluoto's guys. Just don't shoot me.'

Koskela examined the terrain closely. The men, for their part, just watched him. Quiet Koski's heading in.

Kariluoto was beginning to have doubts. His mind was suddenly overcome with fear that Koskela would be shot down in his mission, or that the satchel charge would have no effect, in which case Koskela would also be shot. That would make two men lost on his account. Kaarna's death returned to him now as something that had been his fault.

'What if the charge doesn't have any effect?' he asked, hesitating. 'Maybe I should just try again without . . .'

Koskela was no longer looking at Kariluoto. His eyes were fixed on the terrain and his mind was focused on the task before him, as he said, almost in passing, 'There's nothing over there but a layer of logs and mud. Eighteen pounds oughtta do something to it. Anyway, it buys you the time you need.' He set out, dragging the satchel charges at his side.

'Watch out for Koskela and fire!' Kariluoto ordered. He had definitely decided to attack immediately – alone if need be – if Koskela was killed, just as he would in the event that he was able to throw the satchel charges. The men accelerated their fire until they were shooting at maximum capacity. The machine gun chattered and rattled.

The water boiled trying to cool the gun, and Kaukonen lifted his head to try to better direct the stream of fire. At just that moment a heavy sigh burst from his mouth – 'Aa–aah!' and his head hit the handle as it slumped over the machine gun.

'Kaukonen!' Vanhala yelled, half asking, half trying to attract the others' attention.

Lehto went pale, but resolutely took hold of Kaukonen's body, lifted it to the side, took hold of the handle, and started shooting. He spotted a man's upper body swing into view from the enemy trench and throw a hand grenade in Koskela's direction. He turned the machine gun in the same blink of an eye and watched his fire strike its target. 'Koskela . . . watch out,' he hollered, and then with cruel glee he muttered, 'Got him.'

The hand grenade went off several yards from Koskela. He lost his cap and hair was flying wildly above his face. He yelled backwards, 'Just keep shooting like hell, I'm gonna try to get closer.'

He inched his way forward, darting from one bit of cover to the next. The tall grass helped, as did the fact that the barricade had been set too close to the enemy positions. There was a boulder he could crouch behind about a dozen yards from the bunker. Holding their breath, the men firing realized that if he managed to make it behind that boulder, victory was theirs. And when Koskela made it, they watched how he calmly settled his body into position. Then he pulled the fuse and, like a flash of lightning, shot up and swung round, and the charge was flying. It happened so quickly that the men hardly knew how Koskela had thrown it. The moment he rose, the satchel charge was already airborne, and scarcely had it left his hands than he was lying behind the boulder again, hands over his ears.

A few dozen nearby voices screamed at the top of their lungs as the charge exploded directly on the roof of the bunker. The end of a log stuck out of the smoke.

'Charge!' Kariluoto dashed forward and his men immediately followed.

'The Russkis are running . . . take 'em down, men!'

'Over there . . . shoot! They're pulling out. Don't let them get away.'

Kariluoto was already in the trench, launching a stream of hand grenades into the mouth of the bunker. Ukkola's submachine gun purred through cartridges, following them up. The platoon was already in the trench, and the men, drunk with excitement, had begun to overrun it, which was not difficult, seeing as the stunned enemy soldiers had already started to abandon it.

Kariluoto sent a message to Autio requesting a reserve platoon be dispatched on the double to help sweep the positions in front of the Second Company. He sent his platoon out in front of their own company, while one machine gun and one infantry squad went to secure the opposite direction. The defense disintegrated quickly. The neighboring platoon was already in the trench and the fleeing enemy troops were falling along the edge of the forest as they ran for cover.

The squad sent to reinforce the Second Company observed that the enemy had abandoned the second bunker as well, and so started securing it for themselves. The Jaeger platoon Autio had sent from his battalion arrived from the rear and continued the sweep of enemy positions.

Koskela sat on the ground, blinking his eyes and shaking the dirt from his hair. Lehto was on his knees in front of him, bursting, 'Ho-ly shit! Ho-ly shiiiit! What a stunt!'

'What?'

'What a stunt!'

'I won't be able to hear anything for a little while. It's happened to me before. Same thing happened back at Lemetti . . . But woof, what a blast! Go with Kariluoto. I'm gonna wait here for a bit, till these flaps open up a little. It's kind of rough out there when you can't hear anything . . .'


IV


Bodies were strewn about the trench, many with their pockets already flipped inside out.

'Look guys, insignia.'

'Wow, that revolver's a Nagant . . .'

'It's mine. I saw it first.'

'Guys, stop scrounging. Keep moving.' The machine-gunners went back to see Kaukonen's body. The medics already had it on a stretcher.

'Where did it hit?'

'Went in through his cheek. Came out the back of his neck.'

'Better to go quick.' Lehto's voice had an almost cruel pleasure in it.

'So ends the war for the Kaukonen boy,' Rahikainen said, and even he seemed solemn, though the deaths of the others didn't interest him much.

'Let's get moving. We'll be left behind.'

In truth, they just wanted to get away from the body as quickly as possible, as they'd known the guy for more than a year, after all. The fighting of just moments ago still held them in its grip, but even so it felt strange to contemplate this yellowish face. One eye had fallen shut, but the other was bulging out, glassy and empty.

'You guys go. I'll be right there,' Lehto said as he headed off to the rear.

'Riitaoja.'

A man appeared from the bushes and stood at attention. 'C-c-c-corporal, sir,' Riitaoja obediently replied, like a new recruit, smiling an idiotic smile.

'You motherfucking piece of shit! What are you grinning at?'

'I'm not grinning, C-c-c-corporal, sir.' Riitaoja's smile disappeared, and his terrified eyes started darting about furtively, though he was still standing stiffly at attention.

'C-c-c-corporal, sir! C-c-c-corporal, sir!' Lehto mimicked him furiously. 'You're not going to get out of this by calling me "sir". Fuck, I'd make hash out of you – if it was worth it.'

Riitaoja took a few steps backward and stuttered, his voice wavering: 'It scares me, C-c-c-corporal, sir. When it whistles. That noise it makes.'

'Oh wah-wah, you miserable piece of shit!' Lehto was furious and disgusted, but he stopped bullying the poor wretch. He despised Riitaoja's fear as he despised all weakness – just as he had despised all discussions of anything 'spiritual' back in the barracks. He didn't even know why, as the question had never crossed his mind. He just had this feeling and he responded accordingly. It certainly wasn't out of any obligation as squad leader or supervisor that he came back to punish Riitaoja, as Lehto couldn't have cared less who performed his duties and who didn't. At most he might have forced the others into submission on some point or other just because he couldn't stand anything that went against his will.

'You go to the road and you get two cases of ammo from the trucks. Then you come back with the medics from the Third Company. They're carrying the bodies to the roadside. You're such a worthless fool you won't know how to get anywhere otherwise. And don't you dare just mess around here hiding.'

'Yessir, C-c-c-corporal, sir.'

Relieved, Riitaoja flew off toward the rear, and Lehto hurried after the company. As he was about to cross the trench, he spotted a mess kit lying on the ground, half-filled with bread-and-water mush. Beside it lay a dark-haired, slant-eyed corpse. The attack had obviously caught the guy in the middle of a meal. At first Lehto started to jump over the trench, but then he lowered himself into it and kicked the mess kit, sending mush flying into the dead guy's face. Then he gave a cruel laugh and left.

He met up with the company advancing through the forest. The other section had joined back up with them, as Lahtinen's machine gun was there too. It hadn't actually been of any use, since by the time they had reached the enemy positions, the defense had already collapsed.

Hietanen was feeling blissfully carefree, fired up with the elation of victory, and smoking some horrible Russian mahorka as he chattered away. 'Well, that was one bloody day, boys. How's it go, that song they taught us in school? *"When Lapua's glorious day was done, von Döbeln rode to see the brave ranks had been sadly thinned . . ."* Or was it a poem or something like that?'

'Oh, please. Nothin' glorious 'bout this day. I'm thirsty as hell and there's not a sip of water to be had anywhere.'

'Urho Hietanen, poet extraordinaire! *"The brave ranks had been sadly thinned . . ."* God damn this bread bag! It keeps slipping down and whacking me in the gut.'

The others poked good-spirited fun at Hietanen's poetic efforts, which cracked them all up, Vanhala in particular. The tiniest thing was enough to make them all burst out laughing. The drone of death had been ringing in their ears for the past three hours – and yet here they were, still alive. That was reason enough to smile. Hietanen did not appreciate being the butt of the joke, however, and said irritably, 'Yeah, yeah. That's what they taught us in school all right. Why in the world I remember it so well is beyond me. I've certainly got better things to do than memorize shit some fool made up off the top of his head. All that stuff's a big waste of time if you ask me.'

'Quiet! Open field just ahead,' the scout yelled from out front as he threw himself to the ground.

'Houses. It's a village.'

'What village?'

'Dangerville, of course. All the villages round here're dangerville to us.'

'And this one, too. Everybody down!'

*Ta-ta-ta. Phiew phiew phiew.*

'There they are again, the little fuckers.'

'Shut up!'

'Cover!'

They heard the rumble of the first shot from the enemy side. Koskela crouched down as he saw the men throwing themselves to the ground, as he still couldn't hear anything. The forest shook as shells exploded behind them. Faces were anxious, eyes fearful of what was to come.

'Shouldn't it be our turn to go into reserve now? We're the ones who broke through the line. The others were all off somewhere just hanging out.'

'Dream on. Our esteemed officers've got medals to earn.'

'Machine guns in front! Hurry! Enemy on the right.'

The sight almost took their breath away. On the right, the field sloped down to a small pond. Some forty Russians had emerged from the forest and were calmly heading toward the village, entirely unsuspecting. They were clearly unaware of what was going on. The men quickly set the machine guns at the ready.

'Get them in your sights. But let the machine guns start,' said Kariluoto. Burning with excitement, he grabbed a gun from one of the men, saying, 'Give me a rifle, too . . . pistol won't reach.'

The enemy hadn't noticed anything yet. Lehto settled himself at the gun to shoot, aiming at the densest part of the group. The flesh of his cheeks moved as if he were eating. Calm and expressionless, Määttä aimed the second machine gun.

'All right, men. Drop the needle. *Valse triste*,' Kariluoto said, registering the horror of the situation, despite his excitement.

The enemy group fell to the ground. Some men crawled into ditches, but about ten of them immediately fell motionless in the tall sedge. Unfortunately for them, the ditches faced toward the oncoming fire, and soon cries of despair pierced the air, even through the rattling of the guns.

'Good, that's the way.'

'Done deal.'

'I definitely got at least two.'

'Listen to 'em howl!'

'Give 'em some more, that'll put 'em out of their misery.'

The guy Kariluoto had taken the gun from tugged on the sleeve of the fellow next to him. 'Let me get one. Give it here. Lemme get at least one. Damn ensign took my gun.'

'Stop pulling on me! I'm trying to aim.'

'C'mon, lemme get one of 'em, too. I haven't gotten any.'

'Get your own gun . . . I'm gettin' that crawler over there.'

Lehto was focused and firing away. He called out to Määttä and, as always happened when he was excited, his voice rose into a falsetto that would eventually break into a piercing scream. 'The bottom of the ditches, Määttä! Rake the bottom of those ditches. One at a time.'

'Well, what does it look like I'm doing?' Määttä was talking to himself. He loaded a new belt and took aim, squinting his eye strangely. When he aimed, he basically squeezed one eye so tight that it seemed like his cheek was right on top of his eye.

The firing died down. A few stray shots rang out and then they heard a voice moan something from the field, which sounded to their ears like a word: 'Va saaa . . . va . . . saaa.'

Only then did they realize that they had been under continual fire from the village. Wild with excitement, one guy rose up on his knees shouting, 'I got at least four for sure! Almost got the fif—'

A bullet struck. The others heard it clearly, followed by the man's weak cry, right in its wake.

'Medics!'

'It's no use. He's done for.'

Faces grave, they crawled to cover and grimly answered fire.

## V

A deluge of explosives descended upon the village. Six-inchers shook the ground. The roof of some hay barn went catapulting into the air.

'Are we attacking?'

'Of course. Everybody quiet!'

When the barrage was over, they were surprised to hear the crashing of combat coming from behind the village, but any wondering about what it might be was cut short as Kariluoto shouted, 'Advance!'

They received only weak fire in response. It wasn't a question of an organized opposition line, but rather the remnants of the village's local defense forces, fighting for their existence with neither direction nor organization. They were cornered behind the village, trying to retreat through the trees in a scattered swarm. Heavy fighting had been taking place behind the village all day, as the Second Battalion had penetrated through to the main road that morning, racking up enemy positions as it made its way through the back-woods. The din of their own fighting had prevented the men in the First Battalion from hearing anything of it.

As they neared the closest building, they saw a courtyard with a team of horses that had been shot, a destroyed field kitchen and a grenade launcher, beside which lay several bodies.

A few men appeared in the village square, advancing at a crouch. Then a string of pistol shots rang out from here and there, ending the lives of at least a few unlucky souls. The clean up was under-way.

Autio's runner met up with Kariluoto's platoon and notified them that the Second Battalion was behind the village, so they should be careful not to shoot their own men. The news broke the tension, as it meant that things were beginning to improve. Many men disappeared in search of booty, and the officers had their hands full trying to get even a few of the men to scour the terrain that hadn't yet been searched.

Rahikainen staggered out of one of the buildings with a huge sack on his back.

'What did you find?'

'Sugar. Whole blocks the size of your fist.'

'Gimme a little.'

'Gimme, gimme. No sooner do I find something and go get it than I got the whole regiment on my back. This here's for me and my squad. The rest of you can go find your own sugar.'

'What's up?' Koskela asked, looking interested but just sort of gawking since he still couldn't really hear when people spoke softly.

'Bag full of sugar,' Hietanen yelled into Koskela's ear. 'But he's only sharing with his own squad.'

'Well, the way it goes is basically that you're not allowed to scrounge. So these don't really belong to anybody. So, just keep your mouths shut and eat quietly. In any case they have to be shared amongst the whole platoon.'

'Well, okey-doke! But I'm not luggin' this whole thing around by my—'

Rahikainen's sentence was cut short as he and his sack thumped to the ground. As did the others. A stream of light-machine-gun fire whistled over them.

'Little bugger's tryin' to get his share, too.' Rahikainen raised his head behind his sack. 'There, he's runnin' over there. Disappeared into that thicket.'

There was a low willow thicket growing out of the stony field of rubble, with mounds of haystacks rotting along its edge.

'Don't shoot! Let's take him prisoner.'

They dispersed into a half-circle around the thicket. 'Make sure he doesn't escape.'

'*Rookee veer!* Hands up!'

A shower of submachine-gun fire answered back.

'*Idzii surdaa! Idzii surdaa!* Come out! We'll give you some sugar. *Tovarisch, idzii surdaa!*'

The thicket was quiet. Then they started hearing noises, which, dumbfounded, they realized were sobs. The men looked at one another. Somebody burst out, an unnatural harshness in his voice, 'Give it to 'im. Even the goddamn devil couldn't listen to that.'

Bolts clicked and weapons rose, but just then a hand grenade thumped in the thicket.

'Who threw that?'

'Nobody.'

'He blew himself up, guys.'

'Good God!' somebody said in shock. Cautiously, they approached the thicket.

'There he is. Guts all splayed out. Blew up right under his gut.'

Some of them lingered, but most of them went straight back to the village, stealing a furtive backward glance or two as they left.

'Nice image.'

'War's brutal.'

'—and fighting the cavalry's futile.'

'*When Lapua's glorious day was done, von Döbeln rode to see the brave ranks had been sadly thinned . . .*'

'Got something to chew on there, have you?' Hietanen said, petulantly. 'All right, now stop gawking at the guts and get going! We need to get in contact with the Second Battalion. I'll carry the sugar.'

They scoured the edge of the village. Here and there a shot would go off somewhere, as the enemy were still refusing to give themselves up. Even in this hopeless state of affairs, they just kept trying to shoot, almost without even aiming, blasting away desperately to the end, in whatever direction. These desperate deeds garnered not one word of admiration from the men. When somebody commented on them, Salo said, 'They're scared. Wouldn't you be, if you knew they were going to shoot your relatives if you surrendered?'

'Yeah, that's obviously the case,' Sihvonen confirmed.

The others weren't at all sure about this theory, but in any case they didn't start any arguments over it.

Behind the village, they heard somebody cry, 'Don't shoot! We're Finns.'

'What unit?'

'Fourth Company.'

The men were lying on the ground, silent and morose. They'd been having a pretty rough time of it the whole day, resisting the enemy's breakaway attempts as well as its efforts to get reinforcements in from the rear. Even the end of the fighting hadn't raised their spirits – they just responded irritably to the others' questioning.

'Did you guys break through the main road?'

'Yup.'

'How'd you get up to the road?'

'Uh, from the roadside.'

'We broke through the bunker line.'

'That so.'

'Nearly one in three guys knocked off.'

'Well, thank lady luck you made it through. No use crowing

about dead guys round here. We got ours over there, lined up by the root of that spruce. The wounded've been lying there since morning. Can't do anything for 'em but stick needles in their arms.'

'Got any bread?'

'Nope.'

'Neither do we.'

'What's Sarge got in his sack there?'

'Nothing.'

'Nothing? You scrounged something. I can see it.'

'Wouldja listen to this guy? First he asks and then he says that he knows. If a guy says he knows something, then why's he gotta ask? Pre-tty strange if you ask me.'

'Oh spare yourself, Sarge.'

'I'm pretty pleased I was spared, now that you mention it! And if you keep askin' for it, it might be more than I can say for you!' Hietanen was wound up and the argument might well have continued if Kariluoto hadn't turned up.

'Whoa, whoa, there. What's to get all worked up about? Look, it's all over now. Food's on its way.'

'Well, Jesus! What's he pickin' a fight for, then? What'd I ever do to him?'

The two men parted ways, joining the others as they began bunching into groups. Now that the danger was past, their spirits revived quickly, and soon they were even chatting about the more comical aspects of the day's events. Hardly anybody was thinking about the guys who had fallen. They were just happy they were still alive themselves.

When the platoons assembled on the road, Kariluoto said to Koskela, 'I still haven't had a chance to thank you. You defused that whole situation back there. We'd have been dead in the water if it hadn't been for that maneuver of yours.'

'Time was it'd be called mischief.' A flattered smile flashed across Koskela's face, but he banished it quickly and resumed a serious air as he said, 'Well, anyway, it was your platoon that did the work today. Good guys. Wouldn't have taken 'em for first-timers.'

Now it was Kariluoto who smiled with pleasure – and he was in no hurry to wipe it off his face. Koskela's thank you meant more to him than the others could possibly have understood. In the past two days, Kariluoto had developed a sort of inferiority complex toward this quiet ensign, whom he, like many of the other officers, had previously written off as rather clumsy and lackluster. Now Kariluoto could afford to recognize the man's merits – for although Koskela's satchel-charge stunt had been most decisive in saving the day, Kariluoto's own charge on the bunkers was not far behind. Kariluoto had led his platoon into hand-to-hand combat, which for him sufficed as definitive proof that he was up to the tasks he'd been called to.

Full to bursting, he set off toward his men, congratulating them as soon as he arrived. 'Men, remember this: we are the ones who made the breakthrough for the battalion today. Good old Platoon Four here ran the show. And Ukkola, that was some first-rate work you did with the second squad's submachine gun. You keep it up just like that from here on out.'

The men were pleased. They stopped whispering snidely amongst themselves about the Ensign's posturing. Kariluoto had gained a foothold in the minds of his men. That fellow's not half bad when it comes down to it. Yeah, but he's still got some of that cock-a-doodle-doo about him. Look! Look how he swaggers when he walks!

# VI

The field kitchen was distributing pea soup. The soup was no worse than usual, but somehow or other the men had understood that this meal was to be a victory celebration of sorts, so the sight of pea skins floating along on that dishwater-gray surface made them rather bitter. Famished as they were, they had rejoiced in their victory and the knowledge that soon they would get to eat in peace – so the half-raw pea soup hit like a ton of bricks. The cook received curses in exchange for each bowl he ladled out.

'You'd think that with a whole day they could have cooked it till it's done,' Rahikainen moaned, staring into his mess bowl. 'I've got one little pea looking for a friend, but alas, his efforts are in vain.'

Mäkilä, standing next to the field kitchen, coughed and said, 'All the peas that are supposed to be in there are in there. And it's a kind of pea that doesn't get soft.'

'Oh please, pea soup gets soft if you shove some firewood under it.' Hietanen angrily snatched his bowl out from under the ladle.

'It's not worth mouthing off about it. Look, we're all in the same boat here. The artillery and the mortars haven't stopped pounding all day. And the First Company lost their cook.' The fellow dishing out the soup defended himself staunchly, but his efforts only earned him more abuse.

'Well, why the hell did they choose the First Company? They should have come to us!'

Vanhala alone kept his mouth shut. Meekly, he requested just a little more: 'Maybe just a little of the broth?'

The cook appreciated Vanhala's conciliatory attitude in the midst of the general fury and uproar, and so topped up his bowl, scraping the ladle against the bottom of the pot. Vanhala struggled to suppress his smile as he scuttled off to enjoy his bounty in solitude.

Even Lammio's arrival didn't put a stop to the heckling until he announced, 'Anyone who finds the provisions unsatisfactory is welcome to do without. Eating is not mandatory.'

The chaos died down, but a low murmur rumbled on, asserting the general discontent. 'If that guy turns up on the line, he's dead. If they don't get him from out front, I'm gettin' him from behind.'

'Now if you could just stretch your neck out for me . . .'

'Little bastard crowing like he was somebody. Fuckin' beanpole. That man's like bait squirming on a hook and yet he goes mouthing off like a big shot.'

A mysterious rustling was emanating from the Third Platoon. They had retreated into a dense clump of alder trees to divide up the sugar. Hietanen was counting out the lumps into piles.

'Guys, let's make a rule that if somebody gets knocked off before he has a chance to eat his sugar, then the group divides up equally whatever he's got left. Then we won't have to fight over it,' Lahtinen suggested.

Grunts of consent sounded above the quiet crunching and grinding of teeth.

'They're not gonna send us into any more scuffles for a long time. We've done that bit already,' somebody said.

'Don't be so sure,' Lahtinen said. 'Nobody got off easy today. The whole world was shaking as far as my ear could hear. And I don't know if you saw what kind of shape the guys from the Second Battalion were in.'

Lahtinen was always ready to chip in with his sobering two cents lest the general happiness get out of hand. It wasn't that he wanted to trivialize the men's accomplishments exactly, it was just habit that made him feel obliged to take things down a notch.

'If they don't come out even, I get whatever's left,' Rahikainen said. 'Since I'm the one who found the bag, see.'

'Wasn't there anything else there, where you found it?'

'Couple of carcasses and a bag full of cabbages. But what'cha gonna do with cabbages? Take too long to cook.'

'Man, if only there'd been some flour and butter, we could have made pancakes.'

'Yeah. With jam.'

'Lay off, lay off, wouldja? You guys are killin' me.'

Then they started rolling cigarettes with the mahorka they'd scrounged from the dead enemy soldiers' pockets. They lay out on the grass and shot the breeze. It seemed as if the whole world was at peace, as if the war didn't exist at all. The landscape around the village had been left to run wild, and it was beautiful. Several shades of wildflowers had sprung up in the uncultivated fields, and the smell of the coarse grass was pungent. The men drew in deep breaths of the crisp, evening air. Wide stretches of clouds spread across the sky as it faded into dusk. Rain was in the air.

'Hey, guys! Lottas!'

'And the Commander!'

The Battalion Commander was coming down the road, accompanied by an aide and two Lottas. They had taken a tour of the battlefield, and the aide had taken some pictures of the Lottas posing beside the captured mortars. They had gone to see some fallen Russians, and the Lottas, shuddering at the corpses, had said, 'Ugh, how dreadful!'

'Oh, how terrible!' they had exclaimed, seeing the fallen man whose brain had been partially torn out of his head by a piece of shrapnel.

'Dear Lord, what pain those boys must be in!' they had said to one another as they watched the ambulances drive the Second Battalion's wounded off to the field hospital.

'There was no time to take care of all of this beforehand,' the Commander apologized. 'The Second Battalion was encircled itself after cutting off the road.'

'Oh, war is so terrible!' Lotta Raili Kotilainen reminded herself that, as a woman, she was more or less obliged to make some such sympathetic remark. Truth be told, she was so happy that any feeling of pity on her part was quite superficial. For the duration of their tour, her interest had been directed toward the aide, who was a very handsome and upstanding officer indeed – quite cultivated. He even spoke four languages.

Was he *the* one? This Raili Kotilainen had had a dream, which led her to join up as a front-line Lotta, a role that was connected to some image of the mythic Lotta heroine conjured up by the Winter War, some dim-witted foreign journalists, and the patriotism of a countryside telephone operator with five years of secondary education.

'The German advance has been astoundingly swift,' the aide said, remembering the news broadcast. 'Even the most wishful thinkers hardly dared hope for so much.'

'Wishful thinkers, no. But careful calculators, yes. German military leadership has one golden tradition: it does not hope, it calculates. Russia has just one crucial asset: the apathetic endurance of a donkey. But the value of plain stamina is decreasing as war is becoming increasingly technological in nature. And when it comes to technical prowess, no one can compete with the Germans.' The Battalion Commander, Major Sarastie, enjoyed talking about war and war operations 'scientifically'. He had read quite a bit of military literature, and his own sympathies aligned, quite traditionally, with the Germans. But this scientific orientation genuinely suited him, and you really could see a spark light up in him on occasions like this. He tended to make sense of things by taking small incidents and abstracting from them to formulate maxims.

Major Sarastie was a very tall man. His stride bore the ungainly awkwardness typical of men of his stature. His neck was ruddy with health and vigor, as was his face. He carried a stripped willow branch that he was continually whacking against the leg of his boot.

The machine-gunners were lying about by the roadside, averting their eyes so as to avoid having to salute. They hadn't yet mastered the art of ignoring the obligation altogether.

But the Major paused and asked, 'Have you men had something to eat?'

'Yes, we have, Major, sir,' Salo responded, rising to attention.

The Major knew perfectly well that the men had eaten, but a commander had to make some kind of affable inquiry on a night like this. He had spent the entire day in a state of nervous anxiety, receiving nothing from the battlefield but one piece of unpromising news after the next. The number of casualties had soared and the enemy line remained unbroken. All in all, the day had stripped the battalion's ranks of over a hundred men, and it would have been a formidable casualty count to report, were he not now striding down the main road of the village. But there he strode, and, somehow or other, could say he was in the best of spirits. He felt as if some life force had doubled within him, compounding all his capacities and making him downright impatient to set off on a new assignment. A good-natured benevolence rang in his voice as he addressed the men – 'Strapping bundles of Finnish ferocity'.

'Ah, good. And do you men have anything to smoke?'

'Yes, we do, Major, sir,' Salo responded again, but Hietanen cut in, 'We're rolling mahorka.'

'Ah, I see. How's it taste?'

'Like home-grown tobacco, Major, sir. Tastes the same everywhere.'

'Yes, indeed. Well, have a good rest. You'll need all the strength you've got.'

'Would you take a look at those hips?' Rahikainen said. 'Ah, the treasures stored up in those pistons ... but what's a private supposed to do about it, huh? Boys, there you see the sweetest goods in the world, packed up into five feet and three little inches. And yet Rahikainen here's just left to eat his heart out. There's another thing they've got divvied up all wrong. Some guys got more'n they need and others got nothin' at all.'

'Light field mattress, 1918 model,' somebody said.

'If I was a general, I'd set up a girly house for those little ladies,' Rahikainen mused, 'and pass out tickets on payday.'

The idea caught Rahikainen's interest, and he said almost seriously, 'You could do good business with those tickets, actually.'

'Ha, ha, ha, Rahikainen doing business with those tickets? You mean, buying 'em all up? Pretty sure you'd never see him selling those off.'

Riitaoja had also turned up to eat, lugging his ammunition boxes. He blushed and smiled his childish smile. 'There are bodies by the side of the road at the aid station. K-k-k-kaukonen's there with the others. There are dozens from the Second C-c-c-company. The minister was breaking off the ID tags. Death tags. Some horses were killed in a blast. And lots of boys from the utilities staff. But one of the wounded guys k-k-k-kept screaming, over and over, "Forgive me ... Forgive me." He k-k-k-kept saying it again and again, muttering ugly things in between.'

Lehto turned away from Riitaoja in disgust, but the others looked at him indulgently. His childishness was disarming.

'What kinds of ugly things?' Rahikainen asked.

'I wouldn't dare to say.'

'If a dying guy can say it, why can't you?'

'Jesus fucking C-c-c-christ, go to fucking hell.'

Riitaoja flushed with embarrassment as soon as the words left his mouth, but Rahikainen just shrugged nonchalantly, 'Probably figured if he was headed south it'd be nice to have some company.'

'You shouldn't talk that way. The medics were almost c-c-c-crying.'

'Crying's not gonna help anybody round here. Better just man up and push on like hell. It's pretty rough when horses are getting popped off, the ground's shaking, and fences are all being torn down.'

At that, Mielonen arrived, yelling, 'Everybody rrready!'

'Ready for what?'

'To move out, to move out.'

'Move out where? Where are we going?'

'To attack, to attack. Where do you think? Back home?'

'No, goddamn it! Is this the only battalion in the Finnish army?'

'It's not our turn.'

'We've done our share. Let the other guys go. What about the reserve regiments, the ones that were all along the roadside?'

'I don't command the rrregiments. I'm just a miserable corporal. But these are the orders from up top.'

'That Major must be looking for a promotion. Goddamn giraffe. I bet he asked if we could take the lead again.'

Hietanen was as irritated as any of them, but his position as deputy platoon leader obliged him to try to help out one way or another. He hadn't thought about what to say at all, but a keen instinct brought the words right to his lips. He turned the whole thing into a kind of game, knowing that would be the quickest way out. 'Prepare to die on behalf of your home, your faith and your homeland! Packs on your backs, men! *"Once more the Finnish bear lives on, he lifts his claw and strikes."*'

'*"When Lapua's glorious day was done, von Döbeln rode to see the brave ranks had been sadly thinned,"*' Vanhala giggled, lifting his pack over his shoulder. Lehto's group was silent, observing that their leader had tossed his rifle over his shoulder without saying a word. They could tell they had better keep their mouths shut. Hietanen caught sight of a fellow here and there smiling at his charade, so he continued, 'Sure, just like Döbeln if that's what you want! C'mon, what's wrong with you guys? Your bread bags are full of sugar. We are Finland's young heroes! They've promised to write songs about us for the generations to come! Yes, onwards we march – to eternity if necessary!'

'You must want another stripe really badly.'

'And why not? Every man here has been hankering after them for days now.'

'To the road, double file!'

The whole sky was hidden behind the clouds. Cannon fire boomed somewhere far off, and flames flared up along the horizon. The first drops of rain were already beginning to fall. The road crunched beneath hundreds of feet as the ranks filed off into the thickening darkness.

# Chapter Four

## I

'Watch your intervals . . . Do we have contact on the left?'

'What?'

'Do you have contact on the left?'

'Yeah, they're stumbling along over there all right.'

Panting, puffing, cursing and tripping, the two extended lines advanced through the dark forest. The somber spruce grove and low-hanging rainclouds made the night even darker. Water sloshed in the men's boots. Their wet, scratchy clothing clung to their skin, steaming with body heat. Dizzy with hunger and exhaustion, each man stared fixedly ahead at the gray ghost stumbling along in front of him. He thought neither of where he was coming from nor of where he was going. He had no information on the latter point, anyway. With each step, he concentrated all his efforts on surveying the terrain: step on that moss hump, there's a pothole over there, keep clear of the shrubs.

The noise of battle was rumbling somewhere further off, but he paid no attention. He just nurtured the hope that the submachine gun of the scout out in front of him would not start rattling. That the enemy was far away and heading even further. All the way to hell, ideally. Otherwise, he consoled himself with visions of a road opening up before them, with tents and a field kitchen assembled beside it, awaiting their arrival.

Had it really only been twenty-four hours since they'd left the village?

They had pushed the enemy out of its positions the night before. They didn't have much information about the skirmish that had taken place under cover of darkness. Firing, whistling bullets, muzzle flashes. Somebody had called out for medics, but it wasn't until the following morning that they learned it was Virtanen, a fellow from the neighboring platoon. 'Oh, that Virtanen guy.'

They had also come across a few dead enemy soldiers and stripped them of their badges, despite the darkness and the rain. They had advanced over the course of the day, stopping frequently, ignorant of the general situation. A few men were lost in an artillery and mortar barrage. Around mid-morning the day before, they finally received some food. Experience had already taught them that they could have absolutely no certainty when the next opportunity to eat would be, so they broke their bread in half: this one I eat and this one I save.

Then they would start picking at the piece they intended to save a little at a time, finally wondering, 'Well, what's the use in keepin' that, anyway?' And then they would ask, 'Does anybody have any bread? I'll trade half a cigarette.'

'Nope. Did yesterday, but it's all eaten up.'

'Haven't got any bread left, but I haven't got so much of that soul-crushing hunger, either!'

It was one of their better jokes.

They'd lost their sugar to the rain. They had scraped the wet, crumbling gunk from the bottoms of their bread bags and eaten it, but their hunger remained.

In the evening, they had turned off the main road and pressed into the dark forest, trudging onwards with no idea where they were being taken or why.

'Do we have contact?'

'Rotate!'

'But that shift was shorter than the one I just had carrying.'

'That's a lie.'

'Who the hell can carry this thing?'

'Quit whining all the time! You wimps! Here, give me the gunstand.'

It was Lehto.

One guy used his shoulder to push a spruce branch out of his way. It whacked the guy behind him directly in the eyes.

'Watch what you're doing, asshole!'

'Why don't you look where you're going and shut up?'

'Oh, come off it!'

The verbal jousting never led to any serious brawls, or even real rifts between the men. As soon as the cause of the spat disappeared, and the strain and nervous tension passed, it was as if nothing had ever happened.

No one ever launched any of these invectives at Koskela. This was because he never took any rotations out, but carried one machine gun or other the whole time, to lighten the rotations for the others. Somebody had protested at the start, as a matter of formality, but they were all happy about it. Not to be outdone, Lehto insisted on carrying the whole time as well, just like Koskela.

'Where's the second machine gun? I'm supposed to take that one now,' Koskela said.

'Määttä has it.'

'So where's Määttä?'

'Määttääää!'

'He was walking right there just a second ago.'

'Keep moving . . . can't search now.'

'Of course Määttä's lost! With all you guys avoiding him so you won't have to carry his gun!' Hietanen exploded.

'Shove it. Every man here's carried it,' Sihvonen hissed irritably.

*Prrrrrrrr . . .*

A long, sharp string of submachine-gun fire cut the conversation short.

They dropped to their knees. Bodies trembling and hearts pounding.

'What's over there?'

'A Russki, of course.'

'Bullet's already nicked that tree.'

'Get the machine guns into position.'

They lugged the weapons down the line. The second machine gun was missing and Lahtinen was about to set off in search of Määttä. Being a fairly conscientious leader, he considered himself at fault for the fact that Määttä had gone missing from his team.

But Koskela stopped him. 'You won't be able to find him searching in a dark forest like this. He'll be able to find his way from the sound of the firing.'

Enemy fire flew out of the darkness, striking here and there, and the men answered fire just as haphazardly.

'As far as I know,' Koskela whispered, 'we're supposed to be securing things from this side. We might be waiting here a while. Let's rotate taking half-hour shifts on guard so the others can relax behind. It'll be a little nicer that way.'

It was a welcome suggestion. The guards were assigned and the others gathered further back at the base of a few large firs. Water dripped from the branches. Bracken and blueberry twigs dripped water onto their already soaking-wet boots. Pale splotches had already appeared in the sky, and the men could make out each other's faces in the dim light. They weren't pretty. Blank, expressionless eyes stared out of dirty, stubbly faces, quivering with anguished creases around the corners of their mouths. Was it really only the fourth day of war now dawning?

They wrapped themselves in their overcoats, but the cold still kept them awake. Whenever the firing grew more intense, they would get to their feet with a start and look at one another inquisitively, but as soon as the fire died down they would sink back to the ground, the anxious look in their eyes extinguished.

The rain let up and the sky grew brighter. A gust of wind shook droplets of water down from the branches. Their wet clothes collected debris from the decades of pine needles carpeting the base of the fir trees. A bird broke hesitatingly into song and artillery fire boomed somewhere further off.

Rahikainen leaned against the trunk of a tree, staring at his sopping-wet boots and squirting the water around between his toes. He started crooning in his rich, gentle voice:

> Up in the sky there's no dyin'
> no need for cryin', no dark of night . . .

Generally speaking, the men were not very tolerant of singing or whistling when they were worn out and ready to aim their ill will at any available target, but this time they let Rahikainen sing in peace. They were happy to listen, as his voice was easy on the ears. Lehto put a stop to Rahikainen's singing, however, glancing at his watch, which he'd won in a card game. 'Go relieve Salo and Vanhala.'

''Sit my turn already?'

'Yep.'

'Well, hell's bells. Whatta ya know? Without me this army'd never reach Moscow.' Displeased, he threw his gun over his shoulder and headed toward the guard posts with Sihvonen. Their steps had hardly died out when a rustling came from the forest. The men grabbed their guns and listened.

'Stop! Password?'

'Can't remember. But I got the day before yesterday's if you want that one.'

'You Määttä?'

'That's me. You the machine-gunners?'

'That's us. Yeah, that's Määttä all right. And with the machine gun, too. Welcome to Camp Finland!'

Everybody was glad to see Määttä back, though they hadn't been overly concerned about his absence, as they knew he could look after himself. He arrived soaked to the bone, but just as calm as ever. He looked around, silently taking stock of the situation, as he tried to manage without asking questions. The questions came from the others.

'Where have you been?'

'Lost.'

'How'd you find us?'

'Guessed from the shooting.' Määttä sat down at the base of a fir and started taking off his shoes. He wrung out his drenched boot flannels and said offhandedly to Koskela, as if in passing, 'Seems to be some Russkis over there in that forest. Might be reason to send word upstream. We'd better keep an eye out, too.'

'Where?'

'Over that direction. Half-mile, mile maybe. Hard to say.'

'How many?'

'I saw about a dozen or so.'

Koskela dispatched a runner to send word, but the runner came right back, saying that the Second Company was supposed to scour the terrain in that direction. That calmed them a little, but they still kept their weapons close. As their anxiety eased, their hunger mounted, and the conversation slipped back into its old grooves.

'Would you boys believe it? I'm hungry.'

'Now, where could that hunger possibly be coming from? When we ate just yesterday morning! But would you guys believe it, I'm freezing and soaking wet?'

'No, but would anybody believe that I'd happily go back to being a civilian?'

'Civilian! All I'm asking for is a slice of bread. And we can't even get that.'

'How long do those stuffed shirts think a deep-forest warrior can last out here on these rations?' Vanhala asked.

Lahtinen was maybe the most wound up of all of them, and muttered with biting disdain, 'Think? They don't think. They know. They've counted the calories, or whatever the hell it is that's supposed to be in the stuff you eat. Go complain about being hungry and they'll go and wave some kind of form in front of you that proves you could not possibly be hungry. And besides, who's gonna dare complain about it? Don't you remember what they did to Isoaho?'

Lahtinen was referring to a certain guy from the First Company who had stepped forward once at the main inspection to complain about the lack of food when the General asked if there were any concerns. It had gotten the man into such a stew that he nearly went out of his mind. They weighed him two, three times a day, dragged him from one medical exam to the next, and made such a laughing stock out of him that he deeply regretted ever having opened his mouth. He suffered the typical fate of the Messiah, in other words. For the complaint had not been personal – they had all put him up to it – he had merely been the bravest in taking up the common cause. They all remembered the ordeal, which had been designed to demonstrate to them all that a private has no rights whatsoever, and that even those he is theoretically granted can be easily disposed of.

Hietanen tapped his palms on his wet knees and said, 'I don't know the first thing about calories. My gut's just telling me that whatever they are, they're pre-tty scarce.'

'Hm . . . Yeah, maybe they're telling you. But do you think those bourgeois gentlemen up there can understand your rumbling stomach? This nation's guts have been rumbling so damn long those guys have forgotten what that sound even means. Especially since their own bellies are full.'

Lahtinen was just a die-hard proletarian, but Hietanen burst out laughing and said, 'Hey, I got it! Aren't there some kinda actors who make it sound like their stomachs are talking? Let's train ourselves, guys! Then every time we're all out there in front of the officers, see, we'll have all our bellies belch out, "Brehhhd!"'

Vanhala was literally shaking with laughter. Lahtinen's lesson for the day was drowned out once again, just as it had been thousands of times before. And right there a limit appeared – drawing a line between griping and any actual idea of rebellion. They were all ready to howl in protest and jeer at their country and its 'stuffed shirts' however they wanted – but if somebody tried to steer the sneering into something that smacked of an agenda, they would drown him out with roars of laughter. There was a degree of seriousness that remained off-limits, that lay behind a line the men would not transgress. It was the very same aversion that made them avoid that particular type of patriotism that bears even the tiniest glimmer of mania. 'Fuckin' fanatic' was their preferred term for the welfare officer guilty of this particular sin.

Vanhala was laughing so hard that he shook for a good while before gasping out, 'Our deep-forest warriors' bellies appear to be rumbling, heehee! What would the stuffed shirts say to that?'

Lahtinen descended into the irritable funk these encounters inevitably left him in. But this time he was so annoyed that he picked it up again, rather than sulking in silence. 'What would they say? They'd stick you in solitary confinement and give you the New Testament to read! If not *The Tales of Ensign Stål*! There's a hell of a hunger story for you. I mean, it's all this same glorification of hunger. It's like our cultural heritage, hunger. And the bourgeois gentlemen up there would like this nation to believe it's a very sacred thing. This army's been fighting half-dead with hunger for six, seven hundred years straight, with all its bald asses peeking out between their rags. First I thought we had to make some sort of story for the Swedes, something to warm their spirits and all, and now I guess it's our own upper crust that needs it. Wealthy old men and their wives need that kind of stuff. Gives 'em a reason to squeeze out a tear or two. They even like the fact that there are poor people! Otherwise, who would they help and cheer up out of their own goodness and decency? Same way that if we had bread and clothes, we couldn't possibly be heroes! What kind of a hero is that?'

'Starving to death in sub-zero climes is the path to victory, hee-heehee. A Finnish warrior on the hunt and a Suomi submachine gun is a terrifying combination. Heeheehee!'

The bantering stopped short as they turned to Lehto in astonishment. He had opened his emergency ration tin and was using his knife to lever the better part of its contents out of the can.

'Don't you know that's not allowed?' Hietanen said.

A thin, dry smile flashed across Lehto's lips. 'So's killing. Fifth Command, wasn't it? Can of food's a pretty minor offense when there's skulls busting open all over the place.'

The others turned to Koskela, as if waiting for him to take a stance that would resolve this dilemma so that they could follow suit. Koskela had been listening to the men in silence. They amused him greatly, though his amusement never revealed itself beyond the subtle crinkles at the corners of his eyes. His face remained stiff and expressionless, with just a trace of a smile hovering in and around his eyes. He felt a certain revulsion all of a sudden, when the men turned to him awaiting his judgement. In the first place, he had no desire to make other people's decisions for them, generally speaking, and in the second place, he sort of despised the men for not being able to just take their rations and eat them. He diverted his gaze and said rather abruptly, 'Far as I'm concerned it's fine. We can't get much hungrier than we are now. It's after twenty-four hours that the edge wears off and you go kind of numb, right? So sure, this is the emergency the rations are meant for, anyway.'

He realized that his reasoning was incoherent, and he knew the men were no less aware of it, but somehow it still sort of veiled the event in his shadow, making the rest of them feel less like they were going against orders.

A general feeding frenzy began, and although he personally would have endured his hunger, Koskela joined in with the others for precisely this same reason. His action legitimated theirs.

A broad smile spread across Hietanen's face as he dug his fingers into the canned pork and shoveled it into his mouth. They all lit up with the familiar, mischievous joy that comes of breaking the rules, which in Hietanen overflowed into the grandiloquent declaration, 'I've fought on a lot of battlefields, but I've never seen gluttony like this before!'

They smoked the mahorka to top off their meal, and a feeling of contentment settled over them. Määttä picked at his teeth with a match. Somebody asked for more details about his adventure, and the feeling of well-being induced him to talk about it at greater length than he normally would have. He burped first, then, slowly, he started to speak. 'Bastards nearly got me back there.'

'How'd you get lost?'

'I was just going around some bushes. Seemed to me the line was turning right, so I thought I'd just cut straight through, but then there I was standing all alone in the middle of a dark forest. Only way I can figure it out is that the company must have turned left. And I just went straight.'

'And you saw Russkis.'

'Well, I heard some rustling and decided to go see who was over there. 'Bout a dozen of their big shots were all crouching down, and I'd already yelled out 'Hey guys!' before I realized they all had helmets on. They asked something, but I can't make head or tail of those foreign languages. Didn't have much to say back to 'em, either. I just made a run for it. They fired after me, but I zigzagged and they missed.'

'Shit, guys. We better keep it down. The bushes are crawling with Russkis.'

'Bushkis! Heehee,' Vanhala giggled, thus coining right there in their group the term that would become so widely used.

## II

Määttä's story set them on their guard and then, to crown it, Koskela whispered, 'Get down!'

He pulled his pistol from its holster and signaled to the men. 'Somebody's moving.'

They loaded their guns and cautiously clicked the bolts shut. The guns turned in the direction Koskela had indicated. 'Get in formation! Advance quietly!'

They darted from tree to tree. Each twig that snapped underfoot felt like an explosion, and would prompt one's neighbor to shake his head angrily. Then a shot rang out.

Vanhala was firing. 'Vanhala's shooting!' rippled down the line.

'What's over there?'

'Somebody's running.'

A brown-clad man was making a dash for a tree. He tripped and fell to the ground, but recovered and kept running.

'*Rookee veer!* Hands up!'

The Russian emerged from behind the tree, his arms raised. He glanced from man to man and took a few steps toward them. His filthy face was exceedingly pale, and a dreadful trembling shook his body. His eyes darted from one man to the next as he scanned those closest to him, but you could tell from the expression in his eyes that he was too focused on some strenuous internal effort to actually see anything. His intense, anxious shaking and darting eyes laid bare his whole mental state. He was clearly terrified at the sight of the raised guns pointed in his direction. He awaited death with each step, but hoped, at the same time, that it would not come.

'Check the bushes! Case he's got friends with him.'

There were no others to be found, however, so they gathered around the captive, who was growing discernibly calmer. He stood with his trembling arms raised, trying to force some kind of distorted smile. The smile intuitively sought the humans behind the soldiers. It was as if he wanted to say, 'Don't hurt me. Let's smile and be friends. I'm smiling, see? Just as if we happened to be meeting in peacetime.'

The man was maybe in his thirties. His face bore traces of long suffering and heavy exertion. He wore a moss-brown shirt and the same color trousers, the knees of which had been reinforced with triangular patches. Below them he wore black legwarmers and leather shoes.

'His belt's made out of cloth.'

'Even the superpower's gear is looking a little ragged.'

'Got any comrades with you? *Tovarisch?*'

The prisoner shook his head.

'*Tovarisch, tovarisch.* Understand? *Ponimai?* Are there any others? No *ponimai?*'

'*Nyet tovarisch,*' the man mumbled indistinctly.

'Got any weapons in your pockets? *Vintovka plakkar?* In here, in here, any *vintovka?*'

'Don't ask, check!' Lehto started patting down the prisoner's pockets. He found a hand grenade in his breast pocket. 'Hey bud, what you doing with this little guy?'

'He could have blown himself up and taken us with him.'

'He's not one of those guys. You can tell just by looking at his head,' Koskela said. 'The guys who pull those stunts are different. And of course he's got a hand grenade on him – we all do.'

'What do we do with him?'

'Take him to the command post, I guess,' Koskela said, looking around inquiringly at the men. 'Who wants to go?'

'I'll take him,' Lehto said. 'This way!' He signaled the direction to the prisoner, who hesitated as if he was afraid he'd misunderstood, then started walking. Lehto followed behind with his rifle under his arm, and the others began heading back, keeping an even sharper lookout. Lehto and the prisoner had just disappeared from view when a gunshot rang out from the same direction. Then came a desperate, wrenching death cry, followed by another shot. The men rushed to the site. The prisoner lay face-down on the ground and Lehto was yanking an empty cartridge from his gun.

'What did he do?'

'Died.' Lehto's lips were stretched into a thin line.

'Did he try to get away?'

'Yep.'

Koskela looked at Lehto out of the corner of his eye. His voice was not really accusatory, it was more evasive as he said, 'You didn't have to do that. He wasn't one of those guys.'

'Damned if I'm going to sort 'em out.' Lehto laughed his cutting laugh, the same laugh that had always evoked a certain revulsion in them.

'You shot him in the back. He didn't try to run anywhere.' Hietanen seemed pretty worked up. The desperate scream had upset him, and because experiences immediately cut to the quick with him, more so than with any of the others, the prisoner's pleading smile had already managed to stir up his sympathy. The man really was a human being to him, not just some creature that had been regarded as a concept so it could be killed without any pangs of conscience.

Lehto flew into a rage. 'From the back!' he snarled viciously. 'Better that than from the front. Ends quicker that way. Go on, why don't you snivel over the bastard, for fuck's sake. Read him "Our Father".'

Riitaoja turned away, trembling. He couldn't look at the body, which had two bullet holes between the shoulders. Hietanen turned his back to Lehto, and said, 'Shoot, shoot, for all I care. I'm not the court martial. But that man had been damn well scared enough.'

'Yeah, but that don't mean we gotta whimper over him,' Salo said, with contrived machismo.

'What's all the fuss about, then?' Lahtinen asked, looking rather contemptuously at the lot of them. 'One man pulls the trigger over there, a grenade lands on somebody else dozens of miles away, and there's nothing you can do about any of it. But we're gentlemen, huh? We don't shoot guys who aren't armed. Ha! Those bourgeois officers are just trying to put some kind of noble seal on killing. War is senseless enough all by itself without us adding all kinds of rules about courtesy and politeness.'

'OK, OK. Let's head back.' For the first time, they detected a note of irritation in Koskela's voice. His gait was a bit stiffer than usual, too. Some of them figured it was Lehto who had irritated him, and others assumed it was Lahtinen, but in truth it was all of them. The event and its aftermath had stirred up feelings in Koskela he thought he had buried beneath the snowdrifts of the Winter War. He had tried to forget about death – his own or anybody else's – and to maintain a certain tranquility. This tranquility was dear to him, and he was angry now that it had been upset. Nothing had been quite brutal enough to desensitize him to the insanity of war. He fought, and he fought better than countless others, but each despicable deed and show of pride in killing awakened the judge in him. He had tried to fulfill his duty, blocking out its insanity, and now this equilibrium had been upset – which was why he was walking jerkily several yards in front of his men. But soon his heaving breath evened out. He calmed down. The lingering shock of the experience fell away and Koskela was his former self once more. The baseness of what Lehto had done had affected him most deeply of all of them, probably – but after a few minutes, it ceased to trouble him. And so, one more incident receded into the past. Nobody learned anything from it, and everybody, by forgetting, condoned it.

Their spirits remained low for quite a while, however. Lehto was sullen and quick to glare back defiantly at anybody who happened to catch his eye. He set off to relieve the guys on guard duty, their shift having gone over-time because of the disturbance. An occasional bullet would emerge from the forest here and there, but Lehto stayed standing behind the machine gun, smoking his mahorka in long, furious drags. Kariluoto ordered him to take cover, but Lehto just flashed him a contemptuous, thin-lipped sneer.

Rahikainen returned from guard duty with Sihvonen. 'You boys ate your emergency rations while we were on guard!'

'Well, why don't eat yours too?'

'Oh, I already ate 'em back on the other side of the border.'

'Shoulda guessed.'

'Well, why didn't you guess, then? You boys shot that Russki.'

'Wasn't the first.'

'Oh, I'm not keepin' count. Just makin' small talk with ya.'

'You should have seen how scared that guy was,' Hietanen insisted. In his mind, the prisoner's fear had established the degree of humanity with which he should have been treated. The amount of pity they owed him was determined by the amount of fear he demonstrated, in other words. A natural response from a child of nature.

'They're afraid we'll shoot 'em if they give themselves up,' Salo explained.

'Well, you shot him, didn't you? The guy wasn't scared for nothin'!' Rahikainen shouted over in passing, digging his sugar out of his gas mask. 'You boys are all out of sugar, aren'tcha? I rigged up a storage method to keep mine dry.'

Salo's comment had set some of the others laughing as its comedy dawned on them. Salo's simple-mindedness wasn't news to anybody, of course, as it was clear that he, more than any of them, had swallowed the national curriculum hook, line and sinker. This instance struck them as particularly amusing, though. Even Salo perceived it, and started protesting defensively, 'Well, it's not like we poke their eyes out and chop their tongues off! And Lehto said he tried to make a break for it. When that happens, you're allowed to shoot. The Code of Military Justice gives you permission.'

The duty guard walked by shouting, 'The infantry is moving out! Get ready to head out!'

'Whistles in your pockets!' Koskela said as he headed into position. And so the men followed suit, leaving their new impressions to pile up on top of the old, with one more inoculation against humanity down.

## III

The rain clouds dispersed into ever fainter strands. The gray morning gave way to radiance as sunlight pierced through the clouds. Droplets glistened in the wet forest, and even if the grass drenched the men's trousers up to the knee, it was still nice to walk. Their damp clothing began to dry in the warmth of the sun, and the crisp summer morning washed away the heavy mood of the rainy night.

Stray shots rang out now and again, and then an engine rumbled somewhere out in front of them.

'We're coming to a road, guys.'

'*Rookee veer, idzii surdaa!* Come out!'

A man emerged from the bushes, a white rag in his hand. Others followed behind him – about twenty men in all. They belonged to the same wandering, lost detachment as the men Määttä had seen and as the prisoner Lehto had shot. Nobody really knew what was going on, but the men understood that something decisive must have taken place if these prisoners were surrendering. The enemy was scattered, and the artillery fire had moved during the night and now seemed to be firing from somewhere far out in front of them.

Then they spotted the main road. They approached it with caution, but quickly confirmed that it presented no danger. The morning sun had already dried out the road's surface, which had been torn up by tank treads. They had barely made it to the road when a fleet of cyclists appeared, on their way from the border.

'Unit?'

'Jaeger Battalion. Neighbors far off?'

'Got about twenty of them in the bushes over there.'

'Don't get smart with me. Where's your company commander?'

The helmeted Jaeger lieutenant stepped off his bicycle. He was an extremely militaristic-looking fellow, in his helmet and rolled-up shirt sleeves, with his submachine gun slung around his neck. His men were just the same. They evidently imagined themselves to be some sort of elite unit, and they clearly did not belong to the tattered ranks of the infantry.

Kariluoto hurried over. Eagerly, he greeted the visiting officer, 'How do you do? Where are you gentlemen headed?'

'Lake Onega. Next stop's Loimola. Are you the company commander? I was told I would find units from your regiment here and was ordered to make contact.'

'No, I'm not. That's Autio, over there with the Second Platoon, round the bend in the road.'

Kariluoto was in a splendid mood. He felt some sort of unfounded camaraderie with this lieutenant, though the man was a total stranger. This morning had brought Kariluoto one of the most glorious moments of his life. He had realized that their breakthrough was a fact, and that now they were preparing to advance into Karelia. He chatted on eagerly, pumping the Lieutenant for every possible bit of information, brimming with such excitement that he failed to note the man's seriousness. The Lieutenant, preoccupied with his upcoming mission, said little, but that didn't stop Kariluoto from trying to inject some of his own enthusiasm into the man.

The Jaegers were leaning on their bicycles, eyeing the infantrymen loitering along the roadside.

Rahikainen headed over to test the waters. 'So you boys haven't got any field kitchen, huh?'

'How's that?'

'Each guy just carries one pot on his head, I mean.'

'Don't you have helmets?'

'No, we don't. Nothin' but hunger here. Don't suppose you boys got any bread, do ya?'

'A little. They distributed some dry rations last night.'

Rahikainen reached for his wallet. 'How much would you give me for one of these badges?'

The Jaeger shoved his hand into his pocket. He pulled out a fistful of red stars, asking, 'What do you think we are, rookies?'

'Well, would ya look at that. I didn't have the time to gather up many of those. I had to do some fightin' in between. But these here are officers' badges. What would you give for 'em?'

'I've got some of those, too. Triangular kind.'

'That's just a puny NCO badge.'

'OK, let's trade. Two triangles for one rectangle.'

'You crazy? What's an NCO compared to an officer? But here, you can gimme three crackers to make up the difference.'

'You can have two.'

'Show me what kind they are.'

The Jaeger rummaged around in his bread bag for the rye crackers.

'Those are the thin ones,' Rahikainen sniffed, with the air of one who has lost interest in the whole deal. 'Three of those. Nothin' doing for anythin' less.'

'OK, hand it over.'

They wrapped up the deal and Rahikainen looked down at his crackers as if he regretted it. 'Dandy badge gone awful cheap . . . But, oh well, let it be. Got these anyway.'

They asked about one another's experiences fighting, despite their exhaustion.

'Whereabouts you fellows been?'

'We've been round over there. Broke through the bunker line.'

'There were bunkers along this road, too.'

'I bet there were. Russians are pretty handy with their shovels. Ten scoops in the air and another on the spade.'

Lahtinen sat up on the bank of the ditch, watching the Jaegers out of the corner of his eye, as if scanning to see what their response would be as he said, 'Yeah, there's been talk about the misery of the Russian people. But just about every Russian we've met we've had to chase down to his hole to kill. I mean, they're a tough lot, that's all I'm sayin'. . . At least against us they have been,' he continued, as if to pre-empt any possible objections from the Jaegers before they could even launch them. The Jaegers didn't take issue with anything he said, though. It was Rahikainen who jumped in, combining his urge to brag in front of the Jaegers with his desire to mock Lahtinen's over-earnest idealism, saying, 'Well, it'd be nothin' if we only had to kill 'em once. But there's some we've had to kill a couple of times! That's how tough those boys are. A cat's got nine lives, so they say. Though I wouldn't guarantee it, mind you.'

The Jaegers joined in the banter as well. They joked and laughed, and even gave the others some of their rye crackers for free. They could spare them, having just received several days' rations. The sunny morning revived all of their spirits. A handful of days had already taught them to seize the pleasure of a few minutes' pause on a fresh summer morning. When any hour might be your last, you learned to be grateful for even the minutes.

When the Lieutenant returned and ordered his men back onto their bikes, the Jaegers grew serious again. The joking stopped, and the men, adjusting their gear, awaited the command to set out; though as soon as they received their next break, they would kick back and laugh again, just as they had here.

'All right. Onward!'

'Get going, then! And mind we don't catch up with you just behind the next bend in the road.'

They took off, and more came down the road to follow them. Bicycle units, tanks, motorized artillery.

Kariluoto was mesmerized. Just like German Storm Troops! Why weren't we assigned helmets too? he wondered. How stern and masculine their faces look in them! Kariluoto did realize, on the other hand, that even if they had been assigned helmets, the men would have cast them off into the forest last night at the latest. Indeed, he was proud to be a Finnish officer, an officer of the greatest army in the world – but it had its downsides too. This army had no military bite. These Jaegers were a slight exception, but even his unit was getting quite a bit sloppier. And the reserve regiments were particularly bad. The beckoning, sunlit road to Eastern Karelia was right there. But where were the rigid ranks of iron-clad Storm Troopers? That was what Kariluoto was yearning for this morning, in his overblown fervor. He would have liked to have seized upon the momentum of their opening success by thrusting forward with bold, thundering troops, who would look as if they were cast out of steel as they drove past, singing '*The call to arms . . . has sounded for the final time! And we're prepared . . . to head into the fray!*'

But no, there were no Storm Troops. There was nothing but a circus of scruffy wisecrackers, scrounging for food like a pack of homeless people. They were cursing and griping and wagging their tongues, desecrating every last sacred thing. They even had the gall to mock the noble and dignified manner in which the Marshal issued his Orders of the Day. They were almost like communists. They downed their emergency rations at the first pangs of hunger, and when they felt like singing, it was not 'Die Fahne hoch' but some rowdy rendition of 'Korhola Girls' that rang out from the ranks. And less inspiring, if more illustrative, were the names they gave themselves, such as 'the pack', 'the gang', 'the herd', 'the shit-shebang', 'the loony platoon' and 'the desperadoes'.

Then infantrymen began trickling down the road. New units kept streaming through the breach in the Russians' defensive line. You could tell from the look of the reservists marching in their ranks that Finland was really giving this everything she had. There were work-worn, hunchbacked guys with pained expressions on their faces, struggling to keep up. Kariluoto noticed them, but he didn't find them depressing. On the contrary. '*Now every man has taken up arms.*' Wasn't that just how the song went? '*All who are able are wielding their swords!*'

Kariluoto no longer wrote to the families of men who died in his platoon. The combat of the last few days had made him grow up somehow, stripping him of many a superfluous gesture. But this morning he was overcome with his former idealism once more. He straightened up his thin, boyish frame, smoothed his shirt, and strode off toward his platoon. His step was brisk, despite his fatigue.

Jalmari Lahti, a day laborer, was walking down the road, his unshaven face creased with pain and exhaustion. He wasn't even bitter anymore. He had just settled into a state of hopeless dejection. The ditch job wasn't finished. Sure, old man Kantala had promised to settle up with the missus, but it'd be nothing short of a miracle if that man forked out the sum he owed for the work that was already done. And how would they get the hay out of the ditch? Who's going to cut it, he wondered? How will they find a man to do it, assuming there's a man left to be found? And here I've taken eighty marks that I don't really need. And borrowed a pound of butter from our neighbor for the provisions. Well, that can be paid back when the cow gives birth. The boys'll be some help, at least – but then, which of the youngsters is actually big enough to be of any use? The eldest was already enlisted. He was a Jaeger, pedaling his bicycle around just these parts, heading toward Lake Ladoga. Or so Papa Jallu thought. Actually, the boy had ceased to be a Jaeger two hours earlier, and his bicycle was a mess of metal coils. A tank had shot him down from behind a bend in the road. But, at the moment, Jallu still imagined that he had this son, his eldest, who was serving in the army's youngest division, while he, Jallu, was serving in its oldest. He tried to pick up his pace, noticing that all the men around him belonged to the platoon behind his. He was afraid he wouldn't be able to keep up with the others. Jallu could feel his old back pain starting to set in again.

The Storm Troops advanced.

## IV

The First Battalion cut through the passing troops to meet up with their regiment, which was advancing down a different road. It felt strange to find the regiment out in front of them, at a fork in the road a few miles out. They'd been fighting for three days without the faintest idea what was going on beyond their immediate surroundings. Now they heard vague rumors that the enemy lines had been broken, and that the Jaegers and the division next to theirs had already penetrated far into enemy territory very early that morning. They were happy, as it seemed they might be allowed some time off the line as a reward for the relentless campaign of the past three days. When they glimpsed their own field kitchen coming toward them, their elation was almost as great as Kariluoto's had been as he watched the Jaegers streaming by, ready to drive back the enemy.

'What've we got?'

'Pulp porridge.'

'Fucking hell!'

'Pulp porridge' was a kind of mush made of whole-grain wheat pulp, which the men hated with particular fervor, but which unfortunately composed a solid portion of their diet. Once again, Mäkilä and the kitchen staff had to bear the brunt of the men's anger at the poverty of their homeland and the inefficiency of its primitive provisions department. Their outcry was so obscene that Master Sergeant Korsumäki nearly lost his temper. He did understand their resentment, though, and so began consoling them that plans for organizing cigarette sales had finally gotten the go-ahead. And that they would be getting increased wages now, just like the reservists, starting from the date of mobilization.

'Well, swell! So we'll get to play cards,' Hietanen said, sprinkling saccharine over his porridge. 'I guess we'll stay in reserve. They oughtta be able to manage with that endless stream of guys they're sending out here.'

'Humph. They'll shove us out in front again soon as things heat up. You'll see,' Lahtinen replied. 'That's always why they keep the good units in reserve.'

'Naw ... so we really are a good unit then, huh? Well, I'll be damned!'

'Humph. Well, there aren't actually any *good* units ... what I mean is, we're young and we'll go wherever the hell some blockhead orders us. I mean, those reservists aren't going to go just anywhere. And I have to say, if we're in as desperate shape as it seems from the look of those fellows back there, I don't think we have any business setting out to build some kind of superpower. They've rounded up every last man whose mouth can still melt butter.'

'But look, pal, all you hafta do is choke down mush! Who needs to melt butter?' Rahikainen exclaimed.

'Well, there's some prisoners over there. Why don't you go take a look? Real live heroes. There, by the side of the road. Those guys aren't looking so hot, either,' Sihvonen said, gesturing toward the prisoners.

Salo went one better, pointing out, 'Their belts look like they're made of thresher straps. And they've got strips of torn-up black bags tied on as gaiters. Plus, they're enlisted by force.'

Lahtinen stretched out on his back. 'I don't know about that. I mean, sure, so long as everything is going well. But you don't fight with belts. What I mean is, they're a tough lot, that's all I'm sayin'. And judging from the way they kill, I wouldn't be too sure anybody's forcing them.'

'Maybe you oughtta change sides, Yrjö-boy!' said Hietanen, laughing mischievously. 'If I took all this as hard as you do, why, I sure wouldn't be here yapping about it. I'd go over to the other side and give us hell! But Lahtinen is a radical. He wants to give everybody land and money. So that nobody has to work, just keep his health. So much for the radical. But gee whiz, am I clever or what? I even know all about radicals!'

'Yeah, or if Lahtinen is just fanatical! Heehee,' Vanhala hesitated cautiously for a second, then burst into giggles. He won the day. The other men began to laugh, rolling their mahorka in newspaper as Lahtinen angrily turned his back on them.

Even with their ravenous hunger, the men were so disgusted by the porridge that they left plenty for the prisoners to eat. The latter were sitting huddled in a group, taking turns to eat since they didn't have enough cutlery. The ones awaiting their turn looked on hungrily as the others ate. A group of curious onlookers had gathered around them.

'Look at them down that porridge,' somebody said.

'They've been starved,' explained Salo, who had also come over to gawk at the Russians.

One of the young, blond prisoners started to smile and suddenly said in Finnish, 'Ah! Three days with no vood.'

'Do you speak Finnish?'

'Ah! Of course. Pure Vinnish. I'm Ingrian. From Rääpyvä, near Leningrad.'

'How do you know Finnish?'

'How could I not know Vinnish? My mother hardly spoke a word of Russian.'

The men barraged the prisoner with more questions than he could answer. He gestured wildly as he explained how his company had been split up, and how some sub-lieutenant had gathered together some of the men and assembled them into a unit, which he planned to lead through the forest to the road. But they had been drawn into some fighting during the night, and the sub-lieutenant had been killed, so they surrendered, having no idea where the rest of their units even were.

'But weren't the Ingrians sent to work camps in Siberia?'

'What vor? We didn't do anything.'

'Is living in Russia better than living in Finland?'

'Ah! How would I know? I have never lived in Vinland.'

'Have you seen Stalin?'

The man stretched his arms wide. Then he said something in Russian to the others. The prisoners nodded, looking sly, and then one struck the ground with a stone and repeated, 'Stalin, Stalin!' pointing at the spot on the ground. The Ingrian exclaimed, 'Go give it to them! We were vorced into the army.'

The prisoners' clumsy ruse didn't fool anybody, except maybe Salo. Somebody asked what names the Russians had for Finns, and the Ingrian hesitated for a moment before he laughed, '*Tsuhna*', which made the other prisoners laugh too. Vanhala was shaking with laughter as well, shuffling his feet as if he couldn't stand still he was so amused. He whispered the name to himself over and over, eyeing his companions as if trying to determine how it suited them: '*Suhna, suhna*, heeheeheehee . . .'

When the prisoners realized the name could be laughed at so easily, they went wild, gleefully pumping their heads and chanting, '*Tsuhna, tsuhna!*'

'Russki, Russki,' Rahikainen joined in, coming toward the group, pumping his head in time.

The men were so gratified at the idea of staying in reserve that they couldn't bring themselves to go to bed straight away, no matter how exhausted they were. 'We've got plenty of time for that.'

The blow was all the more devastating, then, when Mielonen

appeared, walking through the camp and calling out, 'Get rrready to head out! Make sure your feet are well wrapped! Gonna be a long march.'

'Stop screeching, damn it!'

'Somebody shoot that screaming son-of-a-bitch.'

'To the road, double file!'

'Route step, march!'

# Chapter Five

They marched. A second, third, fourth day. They were glorious midsummer days. The gardens of the Karelian villages they passed through were overgrown with wild grass. The air shimmered with a bluish haze that occasionally vibrated with the faint sounds of cannon fire and plane engines somewhere to the south. An aerial battle was taking place up there in the endless blue, though from the ground the dull chattering of machine guns sounded more like an army of croaking frogs.

'Those are our boys,' an officer said, watching the planes speed off into the horizon. 'Shielding our army from attack . . . I bet our neighbors over there aren't celebrating now the way they were in the Winter War.'

The men no longer cared about the Winter War, however – any more than they cared about this one. Their feet were covered in pus-filled blisters and they were exhausted and irritated, trudging on with little thought of anything going on around them. The first day they'd been buoyed up by some sort of delight in the fact of advancing. But the strain of the march had sapped their spirits quickly.

This army had a style all its own. It's possible that other armies of the world resembled it while in flight or retreat, but certainly not at any other time. In this army, it was all the same – advance or retreat. They lumbered along in a disjointed herd. The companies would assemble in rows in the morning when they set out for the day's march, but within the first hour they would drift into smaller groups, plodding along as they pleased, requesting no instructions and ignoring any that might be on offer. Rifles dangled and swung from side to side. One guy tiptoed barefoot through the grass beside the road, his boots slung over his shoulder and the hems of his long johns dragging through the dirt. Another guy was bare-chested, sunbathing as he walked, carrying all his gear bundled up under his arm. The first day, one fellow carried a mildewy suitcase over his shoulder, dangling from the end of a pole. The suitcase contained items scrounged from various houses: a glass jar and a worn-out pair of women's shoes (never know when you might need 'em!).

By the second day, however, the suitcase had already flown, literally, by the wayside, which had become the receptacle of even essential belongings. The gas masks were rounded up, as too many of them would have been tossed aside otherwise. The men scrounged for food wherever they got so much as a whiff of it. One village had had a pig kolkhoz, whose livestock were now running free in the hills, the collective farm having been disbanded. A light machine gun, it turns out, is very effective in a pig-hunt, but only the companies marching in front had a chance to take advantage of the bounty, as the pigs were quickly rounded up and taken to safety.

Some of the villages had been inhabited. Arbors framed their alleyways, and ornaments made out of moss and stone popped up here and there.

'What's with all the decorations?'

'They must have had some kind of harvest festival. I've heard folk dancing is really popular around here.'

'All kinds of trumped-up shit out there in this world.'

Their bitterness let fly at every possible pretext. Trucks drove by transporting laughing officers and Lottas. A comet tail of staff, canteens, laundries, field hospitals, and everything else trailed after the troops. The men jeered at the vehicles as they passed, hurling such obscene expletives at Finland's proud Lottas that the overexcited auntie Lottas back in the local parish would have died of a collective heart attack had they been within earshot. The passing general's car provoked such a virulent spate of swearing that an onlooker would have thought the army only about a day away from all-out mutiny.

'Sure, just spray that dust in the infantry's eyes, asshole! Funny how the gas shortage doesn't matter a shit when the boss feels like taking his field whore out for a spin. Who the hell is whistling over there? Shut up! We got our hands full enough over here without you hissing on top of everything else.'

Village after village slipped by. Columns of men cut across Karelia, streaming down every road to Lake Ladoga. Dust clouds rose underfoot, blending into the blue smoke of countless forest fires, and the sun glowed red and hot through the haze. Somewhere, further off, where shoe soles weren't pocked with holes and collarbones weren't chafed raw beneath carrying straps, exultation was at its height: Finland was marching forward.

## II

Lehto, Määttä and Rahikainen did not march. They disappeared from the ranks each morning and reappeared at the camp each night from somewhere further down the convoy. They didn't offer much of an explanation as to where they'd spent their time, but anybody could guess, even without an explanation. Each night they brought something to eat, however, and when they shared it with the others like good Christians, no one pressed the issue of their apparently effortless march.

One evening Rahikainen was more chipper than usual. 'Lehto over there's got butter and flour in his pack. Anybody for hotcakes?'

'For real?'

'Show 'em.'

'Good Lord! Guys!'

'Quick, boys, get the campfire going!'

Their exhaustion was forgotten. They fried up the pancakes in a mess tin and devoured them in the quiet, summer twilight. The sun was sinking in a red globe behind the forests of the Karelian borderlands and a dusky haze softened the contours of the landscape.

'Don't wolf them down all at once! Those didn't come cheap. I had to trade eight times before I managed to get my hands on 'em. I had a bottle of booze at one point and I didn't even drink it.'

'You'd have drunk it if I'd have let you,' Lehto said, establishing who was to thank for the outing's results, which the whole platoon was now enjoying.

The march started up again.

'OK. Better get going again, huh?' Koskela rose and tossed his pack over his shoulder. Grunting and cursing, the men slowly got up out of the ditch where they'd been lying with their feet propped up on a muddy bank. Using their rifles as walking sticks, they hobbled along the first couple of steps until their legs could handle bolder strides.

Koskela seemed to be immune to fatigue. His shoulders swung steadily in front of his men, mile after mile. 'Train yourself to walk properly,' he had instructed them. 'Don't get all tense and rigid. You should have a kind of loose, easy step, like a tramp. That lax, sort of vagabond walk saves the most energy. Your leg has to move from the hip.'

Vanhala's gait was stiff, but despite his stiffness and his chubbiness he withstood the marching and exhaustion pretty well. And his good spirits never flagged, not even for a moment, despite the prevailing atmosphere of annoyance. His eyes had a smile in them that was ready for anything. Once he looked as if he had suddenly remembered something. Then he gazed around for a long time, looking at all the men marching, and finally he burst into an explosion of giggles, shouting, '*Suhnas* on the March!'

A few angry glares silenced him, but he continued chuckling with pleasure at his own joke. He looked at the men shuffling along – faces grimy and covered in dust, expressions dour, caps and shirts dangling from gun barrels, trouser-legs hanging down over the tops of their boots.

'*Suhnas* March off to War!' he giggled to himself, tickled at the startling discrepancy between the high, overblown patriotism surrounding the Finnish soldier and his actual existence. The Information Bureau pamphlets, amongst other things, provided

Vanhala with an endless source of amusement. By now he had amassed a stockpile of official terminology from whatever pamphlets had fallen into his hands: 'our boys', 'our deep-forest warriors', 'our fearless fighters', 'the blazing will of the nation's defense'. He would toss in these sayings now and again, whenever an opportunity presented itself, though he had to restrain himself somewhat during the marches, as there was a limit to what the men would tolerate.

Riitaoja marched at the very back of the group, silent but childishly happy that they weren't under fire. He would gladly have marched from eternity to eternity and withstood the strain of endless marching rather than hear those angry squeals whistling in his ears, announcing death in search of its prey.

On the fifth day of the march, toward evening, they noticed that the road began to look less trampled on. Before long it dwindled into nothing more than a path, and just about then a long swath hacked out of the forest opened up before them.

'Guys, the old border.'

The event revived their spirits somewhat. Hietanen, standing in the middle of the clearing, took one big leap and said, 'Aaand now! The Hietanen boy stands on foreign soil!'

'We're in Russia now, boys,' Salo said.

Lahtinen hobbled over irritably, glaring at the others out of the corner of his eye and muttering, 'So we are. And here our rights end. By which I mean, from this point on, we're a pack of bandits. Just so you know.'

'Bandits, bandits!' Sihvonen snarled angrily. 'So we're bandits when we cross borders? And when other people move them, they're just protecting their nation's security . . . ? Bandits, bandits . . . huh-huh.' He gave a few bitter snorts, not so much because he was in a political passion as because he had sand in his shoe and couldn't stop to get it out without falling too far behind.

Hietanen looked around and said congenially, 'Doesn't seem like there's a whole lot for a pack of bandits to steal around here. Even the road got a whole lot worse all of a sudden. Woods look the same, though . . . Hey . . . hey, guys. We've marched across Karelian song country! Isn't it somewhere around here that those old boys and biddies sang all kinds of folk songs and dirges? I heard something like that somewhere or other. Though I wonder what in the world a dirge is anyway. Crying and singing at the same time? I watched some old biddies at a funeral once try to chant and cry at the same time, but nothing much came outta that. Nothing but some sorta whiny screeching.'

'Seems like we might have reason to sing a dirge or two ourselves around here.' Lahtinen took a swig of warmish water from his canteen and continued, 'I mean, I guess they're gonna dig in pretty good now that we've crossed over onto their side. Before they were, like, sure, go ahead and take Karelia if it means that much to you – look, we'll give it to you. But we'll just see how things go once we're in there. I mean, you shouldn't go poking a bear in its den, that's all I'm sayin'.'

'Well, it's different if you got a gun,' said Salo. 'Even we're not going in with spears to fight them this time.'

'Humph . . . you and your guns . . . Guns aren't gonna to be much help . . .'

'There's a lot of troops in front of us,' Hietanen said. 'They won't send us back out to the line right away.'

'Look boys, we don't even know, our job might end right here,' Salo broke in. 'The fellows over there was sayin' they told the reservists it'll take three weeks and then we'll be heading back in time to make hay. And it's already been two.'

'Ha, ha, ha,' Lahtinen laughed with bitter contempt. 'Where'd you get that? *The Daily Bullshitter*? The officers made that rumor up to get the reservists to cross the old border. Oh, they know how to do it all right. Gonna build that Greater Finland. Got their heads so hot they got steam coming out their noses.'

'*Suhna* Superpower in the Making! Heehee. And they're off! Our forest warriors show the world what Finnish spirit can do. With our valiant Lottas standing by our boys. Heehee . . .'

'Humph . . . Tell you what . . .'

The lift they'd felt upon crossing the border died away, and they trudged on in silence. Astonishingly, the march ended earlier than usual, however, and they set up camp in a thicket of saplings along the banks of a creek. As soon as they'd eaten, they hurried to soak their feet in the cold creek water. Some men even splashed around trying to swim, though the water barely reached their knees. Cannons boomed somewhere out in front of them, mingling occasionally with the faint, far-off chatter of machine guns.

'There it is again, boys. They're waiting for us.'

'Of course they are. We're about to go open the road.' Sihvonen was standing in the creek with his trouser-legs rolled up, washing his foot-rags. 'But hey, look, the peacock's headed this way. I wonder what he wants over here.'

Lieutenant Lammio stepped off the main road toward their encampment. He had already managed to get cleaned up and don a fresh uniform. Knowing that the regiment would still be on break for a while, he had decided to take advantage of this time by redressing the declining discipline of his company. The Lieutenant was possessed of a principle, which he had fashioned for himself by drawing upon his vast store of stupidity, as well as his many character flaws. The principle was: strict discipline and systematic militarism. He established the necessity of this principle for himself via such thoughts as: discipline is the backbone of the army, and the will of the leader can affect men only through that spine of discipline that runs down the center of the group. This reasoning wasn't something that Lammio had dreamt up on his own, it just happened to offer a position that suited his needs. His ideal soldier was an officer who, well-groomed and white-gloved, led his unit with a cold, proud bravery. His men would feel a humble admiration toward him and obey him out of sheer respect. Such an officer would himself demonstrate unfailing compliance with the demands of military discipline. Lammio did grant his exalted being one reprieve in this regard, however, particularly while he was still young: after a few drinks, he might ride his horse right into some restaurant or other and order two glasses of champagne – one for

himself, and one for the horse. He would get a confinement, naturally, but the Commander would clap him on the shoulder with a
knowing smile and say, 'Well, you know the rules . . . But what a
devil . . . what a devil!'

The Division Management headquarters were nearby, and there
were some 'feisty little Lottas' over there – which explained the
white collar Lammio had fixed to the neck of his shirt.

He stopped and tapped his index finger on the stem of his bone
cigarette-holder, dumping out the ash before beginning to speak
in his shrill voice: 'A-hem. The Master Sergeant will be arriving to
distribute your daily allowance, so everyone is to remain within
the camp area. In any case, absence without official leave is, of
course, prohibited. You are to assemble in work groups with your
comrades-in-arms to wash your shirts in the creek. Then you are
to cut your hair and shave. If I see unkempt men at noon tomorrow, additional housekeeping diversions will be devised for those
parties. And one more item. Just because we are now at war does
not mean that discipline has been relaxed. I observed some notable
lapses during the march, and I intend to root them out immediately.
The company looked more like a band of vagrants than an army
unit. That kind of pig-headed, battle-hardened mentality will not be
tolerated. This regiment has already proven instrumental in the
army corps' war operations, earning a reputation on the basis of its
first combat situation. Each man here is to take that reputation as
his own and conduct himself accordingly. Remember, this is not the
Rajamäki Regiment, nor the Friday Fishing Club. This is an elite
troop of the Finnish army. And may I remind you that the upper
management is located not far from where we stand, so should the
company's conduct provoke any criticism, I have plenty of means
available to me to get things back in line. I hope my meaning is not
lost on any of you. To your assignments.'

Hietanen was sitting on a rock on the creek bank, dangling his
feet in the water. He'd been watching the others during Lammio's
speech, looking at them one at a time, and when Lammio finally fell
silent, he said, 'I trust that all of you heard this very important

speech. I only hope you are capable of understanding what it means.'

Hietanen turned with affected solemnity toward Lahtinen, as if demanding his opinion. Lahtinen responded bitingly, 'The German model, that's what it means. And above all, it means that that nutcase has lost the one smidgin of sense he had. Wasn't much to begin with, but now even that's gone.'

'Laundry. Heehee . . . Our boys are taking a break from the fighting to wash their shirts. Our forest warriors demonstrate the diverse range of their capabilities . . .' Vanhala chuckled, then suddenly went stiff and said, 'Guys.'

They all looked in the direction he was facing and saw one of the big trucks stop on the main road to let Lehto, Määttä and Rahikainen jump off.

'Oh Jesus! Now they're in for it!' Hietanen said and began waving his arms to get their attention. He couldn't yell, but he waved and gestured to try to alert them to the danger, whispering over and over again, 'Guys, go! Go to the other side! Go through the woods! No, not straight ahead into the wolf's mouth . . . you bumbling idiots . . . oh, for Chrissakes . . . biggest goddamn idiots in tarnation!'

The trio realized their danger too late. In the past they had always driven a way beyond the camp and then made their way back through the forest, but habit had made them careless, and now here they were, standing before Lammio with cardboard boxes under their arms.

Lammio paused for dramatic effect and then asked, 'On whose authority were you riding in that vehicle?'

'Our authority,' Lehto replied. Seeing as there was no saving them now, he figured it didn't really matter what anybody said and decided to be his usual surly self.

'What is in those boxes? Show me.'

Nobody made a move to open the boxes, and only when he realized that the others weren't going to say anything did Rahikainen venture, 'Oh! Well, these here are some crackers and, uh . . . jelly.'

'Tell me where you stole them from!'

With a look of pure innocence, Rahikainen shifted his feet and started to explain, as if it were the most natural thing in the world, 'Oh, we haven't stolen any of this! Some of the guys at the field storehouse back there by the roadside are from my home town, and they just gave us this stuff. We didn't steal it.'

'You're lying. Furthermore, you have no right to take more than your allotted rations from the government's food supply. Do you pretend you were not aware that those men had no right to give you provisions?'

Rahikainen kept playing dumb. 'Oh, I guess that could be – that they didn't have any right to do it. I don't know anythin' about their management. When they offered us stuff we hadn't even asked for, I just assumed they knew what they were doin'.'

'Don't start giving me excuses. Are you really so stupid as to think I would fall for that kind of . . . And Lehto, am I to believe that even you were unaware that absence without official leave during a march is prohibited?'

'Nah. I knew.'

'The insolence! You all think very highly of yourselves. Do you know what would happen if I were to hand your case over to the court martial? You'd be stripped of your ranks and sent out to hoe swampland. How would you feel about that?'

'Doesn't seem like it's worth a lieutenant's time to ask my opinion. Seems like a lieutenant ought be able to figure out something like that all by himself.' Lehto was in a mood – such a mood that he would have happily turned himself over to be hacked to pieces rather than humble himself before Lammio. Lammio's tone of voice and condescending self-importance rankled him to the depths of his soul, and from that moment on, Lehto hated Lammio with a dark and unrelenting hatred. He had regarded him with cold disdain before, but now, as he clenched his teeth, it was only Lammio's complete inability to understand anybody that protected him from perceiving what had transpired.

'What are you saying?' Lammio was on the verge of screaming, but then he remembered that his ideal officer would never do such a thing – he would be cool, meticulous, *comme il faut* – so he put on his most official voice and called out, 'Ensign Koskela!'

'Yee-up.' Koskela emerged from the tent, and Lammio started dictating in a voice that insinuated to Koskela as to everyone else that he was a bad officer, incapable of maintaining discipline in his platoon. 'Punishment for Corporal Lehto and Privates Määttä and Rahikainen issued as follows: twenty-four hours in close confinement. The punishment is modified under the circumstances into two hours' standing at attention with full machine-gun equipment and field packs, fully loaded – to be carried out upon the start of the next hour. Offence: unwarranted absence from march formation, misappropriation of provisions, and, for Lehto, inappropriate conduct toward a superior. Do I make myself clear?'

'Yeah, sure.' Koskela crawled back into the tent. Undeterred, Lammio continued shouting after him, 'The stolen foodstuffs are to be turned over to Mäkilä, to be handled in the provisions unit of the First Battalion.'

Lammio took his leave and the three delinquents slunk into their tent. Lehto threw himself on the ground and said darkly, 'So the way it's going to go is, I'm not standing.'

Koskela looked pained. He stood for a long time clearing his throat and finally said, 'Yeah, uh, I don't want to get mixed up in this thing, but it would be simplest if you guys could just do it.'

'I'm not afraid of a little snot like him . . . Let 'em pin me to the wall if they want.' Lehto clenched his teeth. 'For a moment there we were pretty close to putting him in the hospital and me in the clink.'

Koskela rummaged around in his pack. 'Right, well, this isn't really about fear at all. It's just the path of least resistance, I mean.'

'Well, I can stand for a couple of hours, but I'm not putting anything in my pack. And I'm just saying that if that snotty little jackass doesn't keep his distance, he's gonna get it in the jaw and then what will be will be.'

'I don't care about the pack. Just that you have it on.' Koskela seemed to relax a bit. Then he said, 'But the stuff has to go to Mäkilä.'

'You don't mean we're gonna have to give it all back!' Rahikainen exclaimed. 'If he was stupid enough not to check how much is in here, we can just put some in the boxes and eat the rest. I held my breath half an hour waiting to make a dash for these, and the duty guard nearly took a crack at me. I'm not gonna stand there for two hours for nothin'.'

So that was how they did it. They sent about a third of the food to Mäkilä and divvied up the rest. Koskela turned a blind eye to the proceedings, but refrained from taking his share. When they stepped out of the tent for a moment, Lehto turned to the others and said, 'If it didn't put Koskela in such a fix, I wouldn't stand for two hours. Let 'em put a gun to my head, I still wouldn't do it. Huh huh. Let 'em send six hundred strong! What are they going to do?'

### III

The Master Sergeant doled out their pay. The men gathered around card games accordingly, as the pay was more than usual this time, having just been raised to the new scale. The three delinquents received their money first so that they could hurry off to take their punishment. This punishment gave Korsumäki a good laugh, and he smiled contentedly as he told the boys, 'Well, at least you'll hang on to your dough two hours longer than usual.'

The company secretary recorded the payments in his ledger. He was carefully groomed and combed, looking just as much the dandy as he had back in the burnt clearing. Rahikainen looked at him for a moment, thinking, and then took out Lieutenant Braskanov's nail file and started buffing up his nails.

'Nifty little gadget. But who's got the time to file his nails out here? I'd trade this for a pack of cigarettes, if anybody needs a nail file.'

'Let me see.' The secretary inspected the file with great interest and said, after he'd thought it over for a moment, 'I'll give you a pack.'

'Deal. I'm lettin' it go awful cheap, but then, I don't need it myself. Haven't got time for that sort of thing.'

Others who had ended up with items from the Lieutenant's nail-care set offered to trade them with the secretary, but none of them got more than a few cigarettes out of him.

Hietanen had been appointed to oversee the punishment, and so was urging Rahikainen to get a move on. The others were already on their way and Rahikainen trailed after them, dragging his gun behind him and chattering away contentedly, 'I bet our gentleman neighbor wouldn't have guessed how valuable his gadgets would be in the hands of the right fellow! Everything I touch turns to gold. That must be some kind of gift from on high. How else would you explain . . . But all righty, here we go, gotta go stand with the guns over our shoulders, even if we're the ones who risked our necks gettin' grub for the group.'

Hietanen led them a little way from the camp, as they weren't exactly planning to carry out the orders to a T. The guilty trio shuffled themselves into a line.

'But you're the one who oughtta stand in the middle, since you're the squad leader and the biggest bandit,' Määttä said to Lehto.

'Looks just like Golgotha, the three of you standing there,' Hietanen said as he sat down on a rock to smoke. 'Just stand there a little while. We're not gonna hang around here the full two hours. The peacock went to go check out the Lottas in the staff headquarters, I'm sure of that, and Koskela'll head to bed soon.'

'Okey-doke. But what kind of Jesus does our corporal here think he is, standing there in the middle? You're the one who got us into this whole mess in the first place. Leading us poor, innocent soldiers astray from the path of military discipline.'

They stood at something vaguely resembling attention. They rested the butts of their rifles on their belts so they could keep them upright without having to carry their whole weight. Hietanen had some good tips to offer, for while he generally respected authority, he had lost his temper once as a new recruit, lashing out at some corporal who'd made the mistake of being too insolent with him and twisting the guy's nose between his fingers so hard that the cartilage squeaked. The affair had resulted in some similar standing exercises for Hietanen.

The charade had been underway for about half an hour when they started to hear a low drone coming from the sky. The sound grew louder and pretty soon they could make out black spots getting bigger and bigger.

'Bombers.'

'Could they be ours?'

'Coming from the east. Though we could have planes coming from that direction, too. Oh wait, hang on, guys . . . one, two, three, four . . . Holy bejesus. Eighteen . . . we haven't got a fleet anywhere near that big. Wait, more . . . nine fighter planes covering their tail . . .'

The drone grew louder. The engines sounded like organs plodding out a monotonous beat: *voo voo voo voo.*

'It's the enemy . . . the anti-aircraft guns are firing.'

They began to hear the light clatter of the anti-aircraft guns somewhere further off, but the red streaks of light from the shots fell far behind the enemy planes.

'Headed this way.'

Shouts came from the camp. 'Danger overhead! Take cover!'

Koskela emerged from the tent, looked at the approaching planes and shouted to Hietanen, 'Stop with the guys' punishment and get under cover!'

'Get in the woods, guys!' Hietanen said to the others, but Lehto stood right where he was and said fiercely, 'I'm not going anywhere. I'm standing out my sentence.'

Hietanen grinned, thinking the comment was a joke, but then he realized Lehto was not joking.

'Don't you go nutty on us now!' Rahikainen exclaimed, looking uneasily at the approaching planes.

Lehto cracked a cruel smile. Without so much as a glance at the planes, he said with pointed detachment, 'Anybody who is scared is free to go. I'm not leaving.'

'Well, I guess I can stay here too,' Määttä said, putting Rahikainen in a tight spot. He was not exactly the stuff heroes are made of, and he certainly was not one to behave irrationally, and yet, blinking anxiously at the planes all the while, he said, 'Well, all righty, let 'em blast us up into the tree branches, then. I'm not gonna be the one to say no.'

'Don't you all go batty now! What's the point of this?' Hietanen glanced back and forth between the approaching menace and the standing men.

'Ask the peacock,' Lehto said. 'Wasn't my idea.'

'I guess you think I'm such an idiot I can't see what you're angling at. You wanna tell everybody the guard ran scared, but you stayed . . . Well, if you're not leaving, I'm not leaving. Let 'em send down bombs and old biddies on bobsleighs . . . but look! I can see the shells dropping! Jesus Christ, that'll put a stop to the creekside laundry!'

The powerful roar of tens of engines set the air vibrating. The planes flashed in the evening sunlight as bombs dropped distinctly beneath them. Out in front of them, shells were already exploding. Smoke rose and columns of earth spewed up over the tree tops.

'Those ones are for us! There they go.'

The fleet was upon them. The last, six-plane formation was not yet overhead, but they knew that the bombs it had dropped would hit the ground the same moment the planes themselves flew over. A piercing whistle cut through the air.

'Stay where you are . . . Do not move!' Lehto yelled. His face had gone entirely white, but his expression remained stiff and resolute. As the bombs' whistle grew louder, Rahikainen ducked his head in between his shoulders and said, 'And now . . . we die.'

When the first explosions went off behind the road, Rahikainen huddled down in a squat. The others remained standing, however. Then came a series of powerful thumps whose air pressure nearly leveled them. The closest bomb was still a safe distance away, however – over between the tents, one of which collapsed into a heap. Rahikainen was face-flat on the ground when it exploded, but he scrambled quickly to his feet so the others wouldn't notice that he had succumbed in the heat of the moment. Their faces were pale and taut, but as soon as they realized that the last bomb had exploded, and that they were still standing there – intact – smiles stretched wide across their lips. This would be news.

But their smiles fell. The fighter planes started sowing lead over the field the bombs had plowed open, and a garbled wailing was coming from somewhere near the tents. 'Somebody, help me! What's happened to me? Oh, ahh ... oh Jesus, help me ... So this is how it ends ... help me ... what's wrong with me?'

The wailing was drowned out by the sputtering and screeching of engines. Lehto's face grew taut as he said to the others, 'Through to the end, boys ... through to the end ... we're staying here ...'

Actually, they weren't in any great danger, as the fighter planes had targeted the edge of the main road, which was a little way off.

'Somebody's hit, guys! We'd better go and help,' Hietanen said, but Lehto refused.

'Well, I'm going, damn it!' Hietanen said and darted off toward the tents at a crouch. Rahikainen and Määttä started to follow, but Lehto cut in prohibitively, 'There's no reason to go! Let's see it through. Hietanen can manage whatever needs to be done on his own. And there goes Koskela, too, and the medics are coming down the road.'

The others decided to stay, as the last fighter plane had already vanished and there were already several men running toward the tents.

'Who is it?' Rahikainen wondered. 'Sounded like Salonen ... No, hell no. You!' He turned to Lehto. 'You're the one who got me into this mess ... and it's not going to happen again.'

Lehto gave a strange, deep laugh. He was so pleased that he nearly softened, for a moment. He knew he'd had his revenge. No, there was nothing they could do to him. They couldn't concoct anything worse than death, and death he could cope with well enough.

Rahikainen acted as if the attack hadn't frightened him in the least. He was already back to cracking jokes with his customary panache. 'Let's see what grade Liberty Cross we get when the

peacock hears what heroes we are! And Hietanen oughtta get one
of the oak-leaf pins for sticking around so long, even though he
wasn't one of the crooks like the rest of us.'

When the guys in the camp had recognized the planes as Russian, they had abandoned their card games and laundry. Koskela
ordered everyone to take cover in the forest, and a few of them ran
like mad as far as they could, but some stayed by the tents because
somebody shouted, 'They never hit the tents since that's where
they're aiming!'

After distributing the men's pay, Master Sergeant Korsumäki had
stuck around to chat with Koskela, so he was still in the camp when
the planes flew over. Koskela ordered him to take cover in the forest
with himself and the others, but Korsumäki had stayed by the tents.
He lay in a ditch beside a mound of grass, holding his hands over his
ears. He'd stuck the empty cigarette-holder in his mouth so it would
stay open and protect his eardrums.

The earth heaved beneath him and when the explosions grew
near, he felt something fall and strike his shoulders, knocking him
unconscious. As he came to, he realized he was on his knees. Everything felt incomprehensible. Only when he heard groaning and saw
a man lying on the ground did he realize what had happened, and
that he himself had been injured too. A heavy drowsiness swept
over his body, but he didn't feel any pain. He rose to his feet and
took a few halting steps forward. His entire being flooded with
agony. 'I can't . . . I can't . . . I got it bad.'

In a confused blur, he remembered fearing death the entire time
he had been at war, waiting for it . . . So this was how it happened.
'It's over . . . I can't go on.'

The ground swayed and his eyes dimmed, and consciousness had
left him by the time the fighter planes raked his body with machine-
gun fire. The last sounds to escape his mouth were a sob and a
helpless whimper. 'Stop . . . stop . . . let me live.'

Koskela and Hietanen arrived on the scene simultaneously, just
as the medics were arriving from the road. There was nothing to be
done. Korsumäki was already dead, and the other guy who had

been injured had lost consciousness. It was in fact Salonen, just as Rahikainen had guessed – the same Salonen for whom Hietanen had convinced Mäkilä to hand over new boots before their departure. One of his hands was torn off entirely, and his heartbeat was scarcely perceptible by the time the medic took his pulse.

The men began to gather round. Even the company secretary came rushing over, repeating over and over like a madman, 'I was right there! If I had stayed with the Master Sergeant . . . it's just like being on the front lines, even if I am staff!'

He was so worked up that even he himself didn't understand the stream of speech pouring out of his mouth, in which the words 'right there' and 'front lines' shot out over and over in quick succession.

Hietanen was feeling rattled and jittery from all that had happened, and finally he exploded angrily, 'To hell with your goddamn chatter!'

The secretary straightened his shirt, smoothed his hair, set his cap on his head, and kept overflowing with verbiage. Hietanen checked Salonen's pulse, then picked up his cap from where it had fallen, used it to flick away some debris and said, 'You can stop bandaging. It's over.'

They lifted the body onto a stretcher, and the men's shock manifested itself in an eagerness to help take care of everything. Somebody carefully picked up the severed hand and placed it beside the body.

'Set him in good . . .'

'His leg's kind of . . .'

'Somebody press his eyelids down a little . . .'

Their careful attentions revealed the awe in which they held death, and for no apparent reason even their voices dropped almost to whispers. The medics carried Salonen away and Korsumäki lay awaiting his turn. They set the Master Sergeant's fallen cap back on his head, though not too firmly, nor quite as straight as it had always been before. They noticed a tear in the corner of the Master Sergeant's eye. Perhaps it had welled up there in the final seconds, as he realized that he was dying. The old man's limp body had melted into a helpless sob as he understood that the end had come. There was something touchingly elderly about his corpse, which the men perceived as well. It was probably just his thick, patterned wool socks, whose homey quality brought to mind the old people who generally wore them.

There was a third body lying on the ground beneath the collapsed tent. It was Private Kaivonen from the fourth squad. He still had three crumpled 100-mark notes and five playing cards clenched in his fist.

'What are they?'

'Four aces and a lady.'

'Good Lord.'

'Rough game. I'd have bet my spot in heaven on that hand.'

'Guess those devils must have had a joker.'

They were perfectly serious. No one smiled; they expressed their astonishment with perfect gravity, as if they were reading the Lord's Prayer. But as soon as the bodies were carried away, the heavy atmosphere began to lift. They tried to be even more chipper than usual, making careless declarations like, 'Boys've gone and left us for the cemetery sector!' 'Only hurts once . . .' 'Can't lose any more than the life ya got.'

They lamented the Master Sergeant's fate a while longer. Now nobody had the smallest grievance with him and he had even become quite popular since the fighting had begun, particularly after the men observed his cold conduct toward Lammio, everyone's enemy. They knew that the Master Sergeant could have obtained a transfer away from the front as soon as mobilization came, but that he had refused to do so. 'Death had to come all the way out here looking for the old man.'

The three bandits were still standing at attention at the edge of the forest. Only once the dead had been carried away did it occur to Koskela to turn his attention to them and ask Hietanen, 'Those three still standing over there?'

'They stood over there through the whole bombing. Wouldn't leave, even though I ordered 'em to.'

Koskela laughed and ordered the culprits to come away, but they asked to stay and carry out their punishment to its completion.

'Well, whatever suits you,' Koskela chuckled, amused. He was quick to see the comedy in the whole ordeal, with all its nuances, and it tickled him. Lammio needed a lesson, and Koskela was more than happy to hand him one. Although Lammio put precious little store by other people, even he was careful never to attack Koskela directly. Koskela still felt a certain aversion toward him, though, and he was also sensible enough to see that Lammio's every move poisoned the men's spirits.

When the two hours were up, the trio returned to their tent. Lehto was silent, but his cruel smile kept flickering across his face. '"You'd better be prepared to see it to the end." That's what Kaarna told me once. That old man knew what he was talking about and he lived up to his word. But that snotty little jackass just needs a good fist in the face. And I might just keep it there till Christmas. With one good, extra twist on Christmas Eve.'

Rahikainen was bragging about his heroic feats, never mind about the squatting in the middle. 'No use kowtowin' before death. A fellow'd get his neck all whacked out of shape if he kept noddin' every time things started heating up! Well, anyway, now that the old accounts are settled, we can start in on some new ones tomorrow. If we're gonna get on here, we're gonna hafta go about making some acquisitions. Koskela, you're gonna hafta cover up our operations, cause we're not about to start goin' hungry round here.'

'That cloud the bomb made is pretty high up there.' That was what had interested Määttä.

## IV

Their break stretched on for a surprisingly long time. Lammio's 'return to discipline' had no effect whatsoever, as orders came down from on high, instructing the officers to avoid putting any unnecessary strain upon the men. Rahikainen's threat of sneaking more rations was realized as well, and Koskela even agreed to use all the powers of his position to assist in the operation. He knew perfectly well that Rahikainen was stealing the provisions from somewhere, but he also knew that the men were genuinely suffering from lack of nourishment. One serving could keep a man's strength up – just – but it was far from sufficient for a growing adolescent stomach, which would start eating up its owner's body instead and make him emaciated. Koskela also knew that the men in charge of provisions were hardly denying themselves the privilege of sneaking more than their allotted rations, so he privately hoped Rahikainen would succeed in his venture and appointed him as his interim runner to replace the fallen Salonen. In truth, from that point onward, Koskela ceased to have a special runner because he didn't need one, but he kept Rahikainen in the position because it permitted him the greatest freedom of mobility. Rahikainen's standard reply from then on, whenever anybody took an interest in his comings and goings, was, 'Errand for Ensign Koskela!'

News of the machine-gunners' famous punishment had spread throughout the regiment, transforming as it went, of course, into a rumor of fantastic proportions. Even the Commander took an interest in the event, stopping on one of his rounds through the camp to ask Lehto, 'Were you the one who took the punishment over there?'

'Me and a couple others, Major, sir.'

Sarastie smiled benevolently. 'Well, well. Next time you start adventuring, you might want to be a little more careful. Playing hooky is all well and good, but you can't let yourself get caught.'

As he was leaving, he explained to his aide, mostly to demonstrate the sharpness of his psychological eye, 'Even from up here where I stand, anyone can see that every last inch of that man is made out of steel. He just has that typical Finnish hatred of having anyone over him. That kind of energy and grit are worth their weight in gold. Lammio's just squandered them. It seems that his hold on things generally isn't quite up to the demands of the current situation. I've observed as much, but it's hard to get him to understand these types of things, as capable an officer as he is otherwise. I remember Kaarna talked about this guy Lehto once and proposed him for officer training. The basis for his argument was entirely accurate – that the man's character was extremely valuable, but that placed under authority he would just revolt, whereas if they put him in a position commensurate with his skill level, he would be extremely successful.'

'Indeed,' the aide replied. 'This event clearly demonstrates how aggression operates. If it is suppressed, it is spoiled and transforms into a spirit of revolt. Correctly handled, it can be cultivated upwards for the benefit of society.'

'Precisely. This is what each social community needs to know in order to function properly. Just think how many men with this kind of anger, which gnaws away at society itself, could be directed upwards, for the greater good.' The Major fell silent in such a way that imposed silence upon his aide as well. An intense, inward-looking gaze lit up Sarastie's eyes. He looked as if he must be thinking wise thoughts. In truth he wasn't thinking anything at all, he was just feeling pleased with his recent speech and the depth of his insight. Sarastie was not willing to grant that the ideal officer was this kind of 'daredevil' type who was merely effective in carrying out his missions. He was of the opinion that you had to be able to consider the world a bit more broadly too. Take him, for example. His thoughts didn't circle around in the conventional grooves that suited a battalion commander. He had read a great deal of military history and he was able to conceive of the war within a larger framework. Then his thoughts turned to the decorations ceremony to be held that evening, which pleased him, as he was to be awarded a Liberty Cross.

The battalion did indeed gather that evening for the investiture of decorations. The Regiment Commander had arrived personally to distribute the medals.

First, he inspected the battalion, looking each man in the eye as if he were trying to pierce straight through him. One of the great skills the army can provide is that which enables a person, whom one might otherwise consider perfectly sensible, to carry out this kind of exercise without laughing. To walk up and down the ranks with furrowed brows, staring the people down, and taking in the grave, disheveled faces staring back in return, each struggling to express the very surliest aspects of its owner's personality.

Then the Colonel gave a speech. He tried to infuse his voice with a certain tone of camaraderie, and to speak in a way that was both elegant and masculine at the same time. 'Men! Now, at my first opportunity to see you all gathered together since the outbreak of the war, I would like to thank each and every one of you for the work you have done. I do not need to read off your accomplishments, for you know them yourselves; and one day they will be known everywhere. You have been confronted with daunting tasks, and you have carried them out superbly. The regiment has already made its proud and distinguished mark in the glorious pages of Finland's military history. And I am convinced that you will continue to fill its covers with new and equally brilliant chapters. I thank each and every one of you for the readiness and bravery you have demonstrated in your service to this shared cause so dear to all of us. The admiration and esteem of our friends, and the fear of our enemies, provide testaments to the Finnish man's capacity to take up arms in the defense of his home and the safety of his family. And so we continue on. Our task is to ensure the security and independence of our nation, and we will keep our swords drawn as long as necessary in the fulfillment of that duty.

'I have been charged with the task of distributing tokens of the nation's gratitude: medals of distinguished service awarded in recognition of those who have had the opportunity to serve with exceptional distinction.'

Names followed. The officers received Liberty Crosses and the NCOs and privates got Liberty Medals. Each man went up to receive his decoration from the hands of the Colonel, along with congratulations. Some of them took their time walking up, soaking up every last moment in the limelight, but most scurried up and back at a sort of half-run, as if embarrassed to be receiving a prize for something they didn't realize they had done. They could not have been more Finnish in the disparaging attitude they all took toward the proceedings. Shitty little trinkets.

The trinkets were trivial, of course, particularly in the minds of those to whom they were not conferred. The strangest thing about the whole business, though, was that it did not seem to dawn on a single one of them that what they were honoring was the best killers. Not even the battalion chaplain, who led the closing prayer. This last went rather dismally, as the Colonel's presence gave the chaplain stage fright and banished whatever pitiful trace of oratorical skill he might have possessed.

All sorts of curiosities emerged from that man's mouth: about how the devil's henchmen were going to be crushed with the help of God and the German army; and about how many of their comrades had already borne the heavy burden of sacrifice before the altar of the nation's success.

They sang the hymns and returned to their tents. They gossiped over the decorations, and the guys who had been passed over pointed out how many of their undeserving compatriots had received a medal. Koskela had been awarded a Fourth-Class Liberty Cross, and Hietanen, Lehto, Määttä and Lahtinen had each received a Second-Class Liberty Medal.

Rahikainen cracked a joke about some decoration or other, prompting Lehto to throw his own medal at his feet.

'Take it, if you want one so much. I don't go for shiny stuff.'

'Aw, I couldn't do that to a pal! 'Sides, neither do I.'

So that was where Lehto's medal stayed. Lahtinen looked at his and muttered, 'They're really bribing us with stripy colored ribbons? I'm not killing anybody for that. Don't want to be killed for one, either. I'll shoot like hell if somebody shoots at me, but I don't jump for bronze lumps and ribbons.'

Määttä flipped his over, studying it carefully on both sides. After he'd looked it over for a while, he showed the others what had caught his interest. '"Awarded for valor", it says. The other bit must mean the same thing in Swedish. *"För tapperhet"* it's got scratched in there. But what's that supposed to mean, "valor"? Can't make head or tail of that.'

'It means, the deep-forest warrior has no fear except the fear of God. He removes his cap for nothing save the church and the courtroom. It signals the conviction and fearlessness of the Finnish hero . . . Heeheeheehee!'

'Oh. Well, that clears it up. Of all the . . . I thought it was something important since they put it on there in lots of languages.' Määttä genuinely despised his medal. He pinned it so it dangled from one of the straps of his pack, and later it fell off and disappeared somewhere along the road.

The distribution of decorations made them suspect that their break would be over shortly, and Lahtinen summed up the general sentiment when he declared, 'They don't give these ribbons out for free, boys. Won't be long before they send us off somewhere where we'll be paying dearly for them.'

It was August already. The summer was heavy with all the produce the sun had sired. Light greens deepened and the whole landscape brimmed with overripeness, indicating that the glory of its summer youth was gone. The last few nights, having had some respite, the men had been able to admire the magnificent moonlight. Many childish letters were scribbled on such nights. The camp guards wandered about in the moonlight, dreaming of women – naked, usually. And the shouts issuing from the tents typically went something like, 'They keep harping on about how small the nation is and how small the army is, but then they don't give us any leave!'

'If I had a couple of weeks' leave, the Class of '41 would be massive. They would not want for recruits. Guaranteed.'

'Shut up and let a fellow sleep, wouldja? . . . Go bang your elbow against some rock out there and it'll calm down all right.' Hietanen's protest didn't by any means put a stop to their fantasizing, however. More and more attractive visions of their upcoming leave came drifting into view, visions which, while highly unlikely to reach fruition in the majority of cases, still made each man feel like quite the lady conqueror.

The whole business came to an abrupt halt as the tent flap opened and a face popped in, its two sharp eyes darting quickly about. 'Which tent the bosses in round here?'

The question rolled out in the rapid-fire clip of the Karelian isthmus as its speaker's penetrating eyes surveyed the tent's interior.

'There's one there,' somebody gestured toward Koskela.

'It'ssa company commander I want. Guess you're a platoon leader?'

They pointed the man toward the command tent and he left. He had a buddy with him, too, and one after the other they walked over to Lammio's tent. Lammio was sitting in the back, listening to the radio. The two of them crawled into the tent on all fours.

'Ah-hah. Guess this here'ssa company commander. We're your reinforcements. Guess'sa Major called'da say we'd be comin'. This here's our orders, both of 'em.'

Lammio looked the two men over in the weak light of the oil lamp. 'Indeed . . . well. You're a corporal?'

''Ndeed I am. Earned me some stripes in'na Winner War. Not too sure what for, though. Ain't done nothin' bad to nobody . . . but hey, lissen here, Lieutenant, you just sign us up in'na same squad, same platoon at least, all right? We're neighbors, see, made it through the whole Winner War together.'

Lammio was offended. 'You will do well to remember that this is not a reserve regiment. We are not in the habit of instructing our superiors to "Lissen here". Nor do we tolerate exceptions, as they encourage a relaxing of discipline amongst the conscripts.'

The man looked at Lammio out of the corner of his eye. A tiny, almost imperceptible smile flickered at the corners of his mouth as he said, 'Aw, I see! So that's how it is. Well, now, I didn't know nothin' 'bout that. Two a us here, we're just reservists, see.'

His voice had taken on a penitent, beg-your-pardon sort of air, but he forgot it quickly as he barreled on at his usual clip. 'But lissen here, ahem, ahmmean, Lieutenant, sir, you just make sure me 'n' Suslin' here stays in'na same group, all right?'

'Who?'

'Suslin'.'

'What is your name?'

'Sus. Private Sus's m'name.'

'So, "Susi" then. And your name?'

'Rokka here, yessirree. First name Antero. Been called Antti m'hole life, though, and I even say it m'self.'

'So it is Corporal Rokka, then. We do not have any squad leader positions available at the moment, so you will commence as deputy leader in one of the squads. You can join the Third Platoon. Address yourselves to Ensign Koskela. He will assign you your positions within the platoon as necessary. Is that clear?'

'Yee-ess indeedee, clear as a bell! Now if you could just let us know where'da find this fella Koskela, we'll be all set.'

Lammio was a little thrown by these continual orders issued by an inferior, and not entirely certain how to handle them. They seemed to belong so naturally to this man's whole persona that even Lammio hesitated in making a fuss, however contrary to regulations his conduct may have been and indeed was.

He pointed the men toward the Third Platoon's tents and Rokka said, 'Oh we already stopped in'nere! C'mon Suslin'.'

They walked one after the other, the quiet Susi speaking now and again as he followed Rokka. 'Stickler for the rules, that fella. If there's any more like him I'm not sure we're gonna git on so well round here, Antti.'

'It'll work out all right, always does! Don't you worry, Suslin'. That fella's awful young, see. I guess all a bosses round here's career fellas, so a course they're pretty militaristic. But we'll git on same way we always have. Or whadda you thinkin'?'

'We'll git on,' Susling agreed, and the issue was settled.

A small chaos ensued as the two of them scuttled into Koskela's tent. It was as if the whole tent was suddenly filled up by one man, with Susi seeming but a shadow of his chatty companion.

'Happened upon just the right spot first time round! Company boss said'da go over'n join Koskela's fellas. You must be Koskela then. Boss said we oughdda introduce ourselves and you'd figger out what to do with us. We're your replacements, see. I'm Rokka and this fella here's my buddy Suslin'. But where're we gonna find a place to sleep? Well, guess there's a lil' space here. C'mere Suslin'. Over here. Just squish this stuff over a lil' bit, you with those buckets for boots. Here, kick that bag a lil' closer this way! Say, why you still got your boots on anyway? 'Spectin' an alarm? OK, that'll do. Suslin', you use your coat for a blanket, might git cold overnight. Signs of it in'na air, see. Lord only knows, but just in case. All right, we sleep here. Goddamn it! Well 'at's no good. There's a rock under there. Look, lookit dat! Stuck good and deep right there in'na ground, ain't comin' up neither. Lemme move over a lil' more this way. There. That's good now. Plenty a space for that rock to sit'ter self down anywhere else, but no, she's just gotta cram'mer self in right there. Well, guess that's how it goes the world over, don't it. Suslin', if you're hungry there's still some crackers in'na pack. I'm gonna fall clear asleep soon . . . Hey lissen, Ensign! You know what time we're headin' out?'

'Seems likely we'll head out early, if they're sending us reinforcements.'

'Could mean'nat. Guess you must a lost some fellas for 'em to be sendin' us out here.'

'A few. Bombing just took a couple. You guys stick with the first squad from now on, OK? Then we'll see if we start needing you more somewhere else.'

'Don't matter where you stick us long as we stick together. We're neighbors, see.'

Finally, the man fell silent and dropped off to sleep. Somebody was still asking him something, but no further reply came.

'He drops off kinda quick,' Susi explained.


## V


The next morning they were roused by a chattering Rokka, who had already been up Lord knows how long. 'Tea, fellas! I took some mess bowls and fetched it from the kitchen. You all know which one's yours. Lissen, Ensign! We're headin' out today. I went checkin' up on things over there and they've already got gear for the whole battalion packed up on'na carts. That means we'll be headin' out soon for sure. Say, you fellas's all pretty young. Me and Suslin' here's both over thirty. Got wives and kids, too.'

'None of us's hitched,' Hietanen said. 'We're, uh, Finland's junior heroes.'

'Well, we're heroes, too, me and Suslin'! But, goollord! Lissen'na that cannon fire. Well, that's where we're headin' real soon.'

'Have you guys been out on the front before?' Koskela asked.

'In'na Winner War. We had our jitters out down in Taipale. Kannas's where we come from. Got our goddamn farms stolen. Got out with our lives, though! Course they took a couple a cracks at those too. We'll see if they git on any better this time round. It's Kannas where I wanna fight. I got some things a settle up with the neighbors round there, see. Ain't got no damn business round these parts.'

'It doesn't matter where we fight,' Salo said. 'There's cabins up for the taking all the way to Smolensk.'

'I don't know nothin' 'bout Smolensk. Seems like we're makin' those Fritzis out as some kinda gift from God. They're makin' it through all right, but I saw some of 'em on my way out here and those fellas click their heels too goddamn much 'fyask me. That ain't how you git things done. But anyway, that ain't our business. Europe can go to hell far as we're concerned. We just take Karelia and go home.'

'I don't know,' Hietanen said. 'If we were thirty million, we could take a crack at the whole world too – 'cause we'd hold all the cards.'

'Deep-Forest Warrior Takes Charge. Heeheehee!' Vanhala giggled.

Rokka started gathering his belongings into a pile, making up a tune as he went.

> Mmbadedar-dee dah-dee dar . . . tell 'em
> we hold all the cards . . . mmba dee dah-dee dar
> 'cause we'd hold all the cards . . .

'Start gittin' your things together fellas, we're pushin' off soon . . .'

Right from the start Rokka seemed to belong – he never acted like a newcomer in a strange group, bashful for a while before acclimatizing to the particular spirit of the crew. Rokka was pretty much domineering right from the get-go. The others weren't really offended by it, sensing that beneath this man's brazen self-assurance lay the goods to back it up. He was certainly confident of their as-yet unannounced departure and acted accordingly. And indeed, when Mielonen came down the road twenty minutes later yelling, 'Get rrready to move out! Take down the tents! Departure in one hour!' he did not miss the opportunity to say, 'See? And what did I tell you all?'

Mielonen's announcement didn't provoke the usual round of commentary, however, since they all more or less recognized that their time was up.

And so they left. They marched rather gloomily toward the rumble of cannon fire. Little by little they slipped back into the mind-frame of the front, that curious state of mind governed – sometimes clearly, sometimes more obscurely – by death. The booming of cannons solidified into something real again. Men came toward them from the opposite direction, carrying guys from the preceding battalion who had been killed or wounded trying to penetrate the enemy artillery blockade.

Lucky for them there was a break in the firing, during which they were able to get through. As they neared the front, they turned off the road and set up camp in the forest behind the front line. They whiled away the entire day there, trying to guess what their assignment would be and listening to the faint fire coming from the positions down on the riverbank about half a mile in front of them.

Sometime before midnight, Rokka, who'd been wandering off somewhere unknown to them for quite some while, arrived, announcing, 'They're gonna make amphibians out of us this time, fellas! They're haulin' pontoons and storm boats over there.'

'Straight into the piss we go.'

'Aw, c'mon, fellas. It's just water.'

'Guys, we're crossing the river in cutters.'

'Yeah, I bet we are. Nothing but the best for the hero brigade.' Sihvonen was bitter.

'Seems'a me the job'ssa same wherever they dump you. What'ssa difference if you're on land or water? Death's pretty much the same wherever it nabs you, 'fyask me. Everbody thinks those pilot fellas're some kinda heroes, but I don't really see what difference it makes how high up you are when death shoots you down.'

'Don't talk about death!' Hietanen exclaimed in mock horror, shivering with fear. 'You're gonna make me wet my pants over here.'

'Well, just make sure you don't leak all over the rest of us.' Rokka sat down on the grass and started chomping on his rye crackers. He looked around for a second as if searching for a target upon which to unleash all his excess energy. Spotting Kariluoto's platoon a way off to the side, he yelled, 'Hey you, Ensign! Lissen!'

Kariluoto turned to Rokka in wonder and asked, 'What's the problem?'

'We're crossin'na crick soon!'

'Yes, I know.'

'Well, 'at's all.' Rokka waved him off and turned toward Koskela. 'Heya, Koskela, lissen here, how we gonna organize this here crossin'? Sh'we put the guns in'na boats or are we gonna set up some kinda firin' positions on'na bank?'

'They'll give us instructions soon enough. Probably both ways, I guess.'

'That's what I was thinkin', too. Few fellas take the boats and the rest set up on'na banks and give it all they got. Tricks a the trade, huh? I always said you gotta be tricky in a war. The Russians, see, they woulda taken our positions tons a times in'na Winner War if they'da just thought up a few good tricks. But they just kept at it straight on, straight on, so acourse not a damn thing came outta that. Gotta think about what it is you're doin' all'a time. Goes for each man just the same's for each unit. 'S'called strategy . . . Let's have a lil' shut-eye now, huh, fellas? Never know when you're gonna git another chance to sleep.'

Rokka crashed immediately, but the others had trouble falling asleep. Now that they had rested, their anxiety and dread of the coming events overpowered any drowsiness. Their egos got a little boost from the reservists on the side of the road, whom they could overhear murmuring, 'The guys on active duty are coming. Now things are really gonna heat up.'

Generally speaking, they considered themselves superior to the reserve units, and the officers capitalized on this fact, saying things like, 'All right men, let's show them how we see unwelcome visitors to the door.'

An innate want of action had resurfaced in some of the men after their long period of rest, so most of them didn't even need to be woken up when the order came for the companies to move out. They split into squads a little way from the riverbank, where the sappers who were manning the bridge had already dragged the storm boats. There they received their assignment. Half of the Third Platoon would stay on the bank and maintain fire. The other half would back up Kariluoto's platoon, which was to lead the charge.

Each squad was assigned a storm boat and the men then decided on the best routes to get to the other side. They set the machine guns into the bows, which they were supposed to shoot from, although Rokka protested that the effort was pointless, since the river was too narrow for them to fire more than a couple of rounds. And thus began the vicious verbal volley between Rokka and Lammio that would carry on just as long as the war did.

Lammio forbade Rokka from evaluating his orders, prompting Rokka to reply, 'Well, you can see for yourself it ain't no use puttin' machine guns in'nere, my fine friend! Slows you down when you git ashore and gotta disassemble the thing.'

'Listen, Corporal. I am not your "fine friend", I am your commander, and you will do as I order.'

'Yeah-huh. Well, at least we ain't gonna put the whole gun-stand in there, too.'

Lammio didn't respond, but as soon as Rokka had scurried off, he issued precisely the same command as if it were his idea. 'Load only the guns into the bows, no gun-stands. One belt should be more or less sufficient to get you across.'

Rokka, stationed at Lahtinen's machine gun, said, 'Lemme at 'er, huh? I'm just sittin' round like a bum over here. And anyway, you shot last time.'

'Fine by me,' Lahtinen said. 'I don't care who shoots. Don't think Määttä minds, either. Do you?'

'Fine by me . . .'

At four o'clock they were ordered into position. The men stood beside their boats. They tried to steel their minds against the persistent onslaught of images of machine-gun fire puncturing the sides of their boats and killing them. They tried to determine whether it would be possible to swim holding a machine gun and came to the conclusion that it would not.

Kariluoto's anxious face rose from behind the first boat. 'Keep it down! Not a word unless it's absolutely necessary.' The command had scarcely left his mouth when the world exploded behind them. *Whee-ee-ee . . .*

Intense, heavy shelling tore up the earth on the opposite shore. After it had gone on for about five minutes, they started dragging the boats down to the bank. The shells had blanketed the far shore in such heavy smoke that somebody muttered in relief, 'They'll have to aim by ear through that.'

'Advance!'

The storm-boat drivers started up the engines and the men began pushing the boats into the river.

'Everybody in!'

The propellers sank into the water and the boats started for the opposite shore.

The next echelon of guys was already approaching the river. Weak, random shots came from behind the smokescreen, hurting no one.

Rokka lay in the bow of the second squad's boat and shot into the smoke. He hadn't made it very far down the belt before the bow scratched against the bank and the men jumped ashore. It was there that the first man fell. One of the sappers slipped on a rock and fell into the water, which began to billow red all around him. The scare prompted some of the men to dive for cover on the slopes along the bank, but Kariluoto forced them on. Rokka helped, having already started to make his way through the smoke with the machine gun over his shoulder, yelling, 'Now'ssa time to git a move on! They'll recover soon and then we're cooked. 'Member, fellas, we got water behind us.'

They climbed up the meadowy bank in the smoke as the enemy fired from above. Kariluoto called to his men continually to make sure they were close, as their visibility was still limited, though the smoke was already beginning to clear up. Rokka ran beside him, panting, 'Hey, Ensign! Lissen here! Don't let your fellas dawdle in'na daisies back there! We gotta steamroll 'em! Keep up the pace! That's what we did at Kelja, sent 'em scurryin' with just the same trick.'

The enemy positions were set up along the rim of the forest. The smokescreen had already dissipated so much that it ceased to offer any protection, and one guy from Kariluoto's platoon took a fatal bullet. The others threw themselves to the ground and answered fire, and Koskela ordered the machine guns into position to counter the enemy's automatic weapons. The command was superfluous as far as the second gun was concerned, as Rokka was already shooting without the gun-stand, resting the gun barrel on the stump of a tree. Määttä remained standing nonchalantly as he fed the belt, determined to show this Rokka character that he didn't have a monopoly on courage.

'Over there, the bastards . . . Look! See . . . ? Machine gun 'hinda logs.' Rokka had spotted three heads behind a machine gun, but at just the same moment they had spotted him, and a hail of bullets whizzed by their ears. Two of the bullets tore through Lahtinen's coat, which was sticking up in a bundle on his back as he pressed to the ground beside the gun. Rokka aimed the sight with speed and precision. Two heads fell. The third sank on top of the machine gun and the gun fell silent.

Kariluoto ordered his men to charge, and when Rokka heard the command, he handed the machine gun to Määttä, saying hurriedly, 'Here, you take it . . . I'm goin' in with the infantry fellas . . . somebody over there said charge . . .'

The enemy had abandoned a length of trench in front of them, or rather its defenders had all been shot down. Kariluoto leapt into the trench and a few of his men followed. Rokka raced after them and snatched Kariluoto's submachine gun right out of his hands before the latter could even think to protest, saying in passing, 'Gimme that . . . here, you take these hand grenades . . . now ain't that a beauty! . . . mighty scarce in'na Winner War . . .'

Rokka raced off past him, and it all happened so naturally that Kariluoto just did as he was told without a second thought. There wasn't any time to wonder over this lively, chattering man dashing in a low crouch along the edge of the trench. Kariluoto gathered up hand grenades from his men as they came up behind him, and when they reached a bend in the trench, Rokka would order him to throw a grenade up over behind it.

'Soon's it goes off, I'll go in and take care a the moppin' up. Let's do one more round at the next bend. That oughdda take care of it . . . don't you think?'

Kariluoto threw a grenade and as soon as it had exploded Rokka dashed around the corner. Two fallen enemy soldiers lay in the trench, and a third was pointing his gun at Rokka. He was dead before he had a chance to think of shooting, though.

'Don't you aim at me, ol' man! That'ssa way to git yourself killed . . . this fella here's speedy . . .'

Three enemy soldiers went down at the next corner. Rokka's aim was swift and sharp. He called out instructions the whole time, which the others instinctively followed. Even Kariluoto didn't so much as notice that Rokka had taken over his platoon. He just kept throwing hand grenades on command, marveling at the unfailing speed and accuracy of this man running out in front of him. Rokka's mode of operation was fundamentally practical. His fearlessness meant he could keep a cool head and think without falling prey to panic, and he knew that the enemy would be helpless so long as they pressed onward relentlessly, without pause. As long as the enemy soldiers were under continual fire, they couldn't launch any hand grenades themselves, and Rokka's submachine gun took care of the rest, shooting decisively, though not hastily, and striking precisely where needed.

The Second Company, which had made the crossing behind them, now caught up on the right and easily took up the enemy positions, Kariluoto's platoon having already advanced far down the trench and paralyzed its defense. Kariluoto's men returned just as the platoon to the left of the Second Company was catching up to them. Part of the Third Company circled around, attacking from the opposite direction, or rather, just taking over the enemy positions, as a general flight was already underway. Koskela's machine-gunners were out in front securing the battalion's victory, with the exception of Rahikainen, who was in the back, securing his personal stockpile of insignia scrounged from dead Russian soldiers.

Kariluoto hurried over to Rokka in excitement. 'What's your name?'

'Rokka here. First name Antero. Already all signed up with another ensign, though.'

'No, no, I was just curious. That was some top-notch work you did in that push through the trench.' Kariluoto was so excited that it hadn't even occurred to him to be irritated with Rokka for giving him orders.

Rokka wiped his sweat with his cap and laughed. He had a peculiar way of looking at other people. He never looked anybody straight in the eye, but rather looked slightly sideways, out of the corner of his eye, which would flash with a sly twinkle more often than not. In general, his speech also had something about it that made it seem as if it were all half meaningless – except when he started lecturing pedantically on some topic or other. He answered Kariluoto's praise with his typical lightheartedness, laughing, 'Don't you start praisin' me, Ensign. You think I'm some kinda daredevil, don't you?'

Then he stopped laughing, pointed his finger and started lecturing Kariluoto in a tone so schoolteacherly it sounded humorous coming from the mouth of such an animated man. 'Lissen here, Ensign! You're a young fella and you still got some idea 'bout bein'na hero. You wanna go out and do heroic deeds. Now me, I don't give a damn 'bout none a that. You go where you gotta go when'na situation calls for it, and otherwise you keep low. In'nat attack back there you got yourself up and pushed on as a example to the others. That's good – but make sure you check what the situation is before you go doin'nat kinda thing. We ain't out here to die, we're out here to kill. You keep your eyes peeled, always. That's called offensive strategy. You go. They shoot at you. You run without lookin' and those damn fellas'll pop you off straight away. No – you look for cover, you see who's shootin', and you act fast but not hasty. Aim quick, aim sharp and shoot first. One second ahead's all you need. That's all there is to it.'

Then it was as if Rokka suddenly realized he was being unnecessarily serious and pedantic, and he followed up his speech with a wry laugh and said, 'Anyway, I can't seem to work up a fright in this here war. This's all child's play compared'da what we had out in Taipale. Suslin' over there, he can tell you how we hadda lie in'na ice in between'na dead bodies and how all'a fellas went bonkers, and how we hadda drag half of 'em back dead every night. That'ssa way it was all right . . . But hey, I'm gonna go see what kind of chump that fella is, one who tried at me with his machine gun.'

Rokka took off toward the machine-gun position and came upon Rahikainen, busily taking stock of his loot. 'What the hell you gonna do with those?'

'Turn a profit on 'em.'

'Where you plan on findin' buyers?'

'Bums in the back.'

'Well, whadda ya know. Hey, where'd those two fellas fall? Oops, there they are, lyin' on'na bottom a their trench. I wondered if I oughdda shoot the whole belt, but when those two fellas sunk down behind . . . Here's the one took a shot at me. Young fella. Poor kid. Well, you pick a fight with me and that'ssa way it goes. But let's git movin' . . . others's gonna leave us behind. Ain't changed, sound a bullet makes. Same ol' whistle.'

They resumed their advance. The machine-gunners held Rokka in such a degree of esteem that it went far beyond envy. It helped that Rokka himself seemed to think it all perfectly natural and demanded no particular recognition. At the moment he was just pestering Susling to take better care of himself. 'Quit rushin' around like that! We'll make it to Kannas all right, there ain't no need for all'at. But hey! Lissen, grab that tent tarp from the fellas that went down over there. Shucks, that'll make us a dandy blanket. Autumn rains gonna start up pretty soon.'

# Chapter Six

## I

From that point on, the fighting was more or less continuous until they reached Petroskoi. The Karelian Army had launched its second offensive, and they were under constant fire all along the rough country roads leading from the border to Lake Onega. They didn't know anything of the Karelian Army, however, much less the phases of its offensives. Each man knew his regiment number, but even a 'division' was a pretty hazy concept to most of them, not to mention an 'army corps' or an 'army'. Once in a while they would catch a glimpse of a general in a passing car, looking like a picture out of their 'Private's Handbook', and wonder, 'What the hell is that guy doin' all the way out here?' Generals belonged to a whole other world. In their world, there was nothing but misery, hunger, danger and exhaustion, and a group of guys who became your buddies – one or the other of whom would vanish from time to time, never to return.

On they lumbered, mile after mile, 'decimating the opposition with expertly designed maneuvers engineered to disrupt enemy communication lines'. And for this, their highest commanders received medals of the greatest distinction.

Continuous cannon fire rumbled as far as they could hear to the north and the south, and aerial battles were being played out overhead. Sometimes they would pause to watch a plane fall to the ground, flaming like a torch.

They were always hoping the advance would speed up once they'd driven the enemy back from some position, but to no avail. Every couple of miles brought new resistance. They grew increasingly quiet and irritable with each day that passed. Petty squabbles broke out constantly. Eyes sank deeper into their sockets, cheekbones grew more pronounced and, within a few weeks, lines carved their way into their smooth, boyish faces. Rahikainen stopped scavenging badges. Bread and tent tarps were in higher demand.

The relationship between Koskela and his platoon grew ever closer. The quiet ensign had attained such an unassailable position in the minds of his men that all he had to do was hint at what needed to be done and it would be taken care of. In combat he was silent, tireless, shrewd and calculating. As a result, his platoon escaped with very few casualties. Not once did he send the guns into a dangerous combat situation where they couldn't be of any use, and in situations where they could be effective, he accompanied them personally, guiding the others. But above all, the men felt he was one of their own because he was just like any one of them. When he was off-duty, no one would have been able to say he was an officer without checking his badges, so naturally did he blend in with his men, right down to the detail.

Lehto's moods grew ever darker. Once a grenade exploded beside him, but he escaped unharmed. He went deaf for a little while, and was, indeed, still deaf when he proceeded to shoot a wounded enemy soldier, saying that he couldn't take the man's moaning any longer. No one took much notice of the incident. They were soldiers now. Once, retreating from some hill, they had to leave a wounded guy behind. When they retook the hill, they found him stripped to his underwear, a deep bayonet gash in his side. In retaliation, one of the submachine-gunners from Kariluoto's platoon casually took aim at three of the Russians who had surrendered, shooting them down without even removing his gun from under his arm. Two days later that man met his own end when a grenade landed squarely upon him, cleaving his body in two. Death had ceased to be a moral issue.

Rokka seemed to be enjoying the war. He showed no signs of fatigue – on the contrary, he buoyed the others up with his excess energy. His reputation spread, but the officers were obliged to recognize that this man was not at all the model soldier he might have seemed. He demonstrated no respect for military hierarchy whatsoever. An officer with a rank sufficiently lofty to prevent Rokka from telling him to 'Lissen here!' had yet to be seen. As a fighter, he was evidently brilliant, a cool-headed killer – and it often happened that he would take off on his own with the submachine-gunners, in between his turns behind the machine gun. 'Hand-to-hand's a kinda military domain you don' git'ta see much of in a machine-gun out-fit, see. I wanna give it a whirl, see what it's all about.'

Vanhala increasingly overcame his bashfulness. His comments were already frequently spot-on. Moreover, he proved himself to be a reliable guy, and Lehto took him on as something of a right-hand man, which further solidified his credibility.

Each in his own way, the men were transformed by the response the slaughter drew out of them. The strong grew stronger; the weak faltered further under the strain. Riitaoja began to babble incomprehensibly and Lehto demanded a replacement, but the request was turned down. No man was excused from his butchering duties.

Little by little, Ensign Kariluoto had developed into one of the battalion's best platoon leaders. Autio gave him all the toughest assignments, and Kariluoto, for his part, tried to take Koskela with him whenever possible. Generally, Koskela did accompany him, or rather, accompanied the machine guns detailed to support his platoon, as he generally took the hardest missions himself. The relationship between the two officers was exceptional in all it comprised. Kariluoto tended to take his cues from Koskela's moods, and Koskela delicately tried to avoid being forced into any sort of role as psychological leader. He knew that every time Kariluoto boldly threw himself into the line of fire while he was watching, he was doing it to make up for that moment back in the swamp when he had taken cover, unable to lead the advance. It was as if the young man wanted to redeem himself with these courageous acts, to free himself from the shame of the memory and regain his self-respect.

And this is precisely what happened, in reality. With each new obstacle that confronted him, Kariluoto repeated his command over and over to himself: Fourth Platoon, advance! and his voice grew more assured every time. And every time he shoved the feeling of weakness deeper into the recesses of his chest. And so

Kariluoto came to be counted beside Koskela, Autio and Lammio as one of the battalion's bravest officers.

His idealism underwent a change as well. The irrational waves of emotion gave way to a firm sense of duty. He became a favorite within his platoon before long too. The men had never hated him, but they had considered him somewhat immature on account of his over-zealousness. Now the brave among them saw it as their duty to live up to him, and the weaker demonstrated their respect in other ways.

One day he received a profound shock that made a decisive impression on him. He had a volunteer battle-runner, a boy a couple of years younger than the rest of them. The kid was generally quite brave, if only out of childish fearlessness, as he didn't always understand just how close to death he was – luckily for him.

The enemy was defending some hill more relentlessly than usual. They were cast back from the slope four times, and it was there that the battalion lost the greatest number of men in one operation. Kariluoto's platoon was reduced to a couple of squads. The third machine-gun team from Koskela's platoon fell in a heap behind the weapon, one after the other, with the sole exception of the ammunition-bearer. Kariluoto pressed on desperately. The command to cut unnecessary losses had already been issued, but he still thought he might be able to succeed in the charge. Capturing even the smallest bit of the end of the trench would mean victory, and he planned to carry out the mission with just a few of his best men so as to avoid casualties.

He convinced a few guys to go with him, but they didn't make it to the trench. Instead, the battle-runner took a bullet in the stomach as he was throwing a hand grenade, and the venture stopped short. Kariluoto dragged the wounded boy to cover behind a rock. He was in severe pain, as an exploding bullet had torn his stomach to shreds. Kariluoto himself moaned at the horror of the sight as he tried to bind the boy's wounds. He just said gently, 'Don't move . . . It'll hurt more. The stretcher'll be right here. Hang on. They've had a lot to carry today.'

The boy's mouth foamed with blood. 'It's death that's coming . . .

not a stretcher. I'm going to Father . . . oh! It hurts . . . ah . . . ahhh
. . . It's burning . . .'

Kariluoto was crying. 'You aren't going to die . . . Stay calm . . . The
stretchers will be here soon and they'll operate at the field hospital . . .'

The boy was overcome with a child's fear of death. He struggled
to move and Kariluoto had to hold him down.

'Ensign . . . you pray . . . I can't . . . remember . . . it's burning . . .
I'm dying . . .'

Kariluoto was in such a state of shock he didn't know what to do.
In his panic, he didn't even register that he was praying, he just tried
to appease the boy, murmuring, 'Our Father . . . who art in heaven
. . . Hallowed be thy name . . .'

The boy moved his blood-stained lips, 'Our . . . Father . . . Our
Father . . .' Then he struggled violently a couple of times trying to
raise himself up, lifting his back off the ground. His face went blue
and his body stiffened. Kariluoto swept his cap over the boy's eyes
and crawled back to his men.

He wrote another letter. Not since Vuorela's death had he done
such a thing.

> . . . you, that my words are meaningless to you, and can do nothing
> to relieve you of your grief. In sorrow, each of us is alone, and it is
> alone that we must redeem each moment from fear and death. We
> must not sanctify the sadness our losses bring, but rather endure,
> with all the strength of our will. I am writing to you because I am
> the one who ordered him to the spot where he fell – I am not at
> fault, but I am aware of my responsibility. That is why I am writing:
> because I do not want to shirk this responsibility, but to take it on as
> my burden to bear, for great as it may be, greater still is the cause for
> which he, and all the rest of us, have come here . . .

Kariluoto wasn't ashamed of his letter this time. Instead, he was
sickened by the stupid, naïve, patriotic phrases in the letters he
received from home.

Days turned to weeks. Time no longer held any meaning for
them. They lost track of the days. Once in a while somebody would

say, 'Isn't it Sunday today?' and somebody else would think for a second and say, 'Shit – yeah, it is.' Periods of time appeared in their calendars as follows: the time the platoon lost six guys, the shitty encirclement, the alarm at the crack of dawn by the railroad embankment, the annihilation of the vehicle column, the mad dash, the run-in with the assault tanks.

The nights were beginning to get dark now. It rained frequently, and you could feel autumn in the air. They occupied tiny Karelian villages whose residents had been evacuated. Those who had stayed behind looked on them with a submissiveness that seemed somehow suspect. Behind the troops there trailed pastors and cultural counselors dispatched to begin assimilation efforts amongst the Karelians, but the men had nothing to do with any of that.

They just hoped for food and rest, both of which were in short supply. Once they seized a field kitchen full of freshly prepared cabbage soup.

'Don't touch it. It could be poisoned.'

Rokka scooped himself a bowl. 'You all are actin' like children. Here we got shells an' bullets whizzin' non-stop and you fellas are worried 'bout a lil' poison?'

Rokka ate, and when he showed no signs of poisoning, the others ate too. Lahtinen praised the soup to high heaven, comparing it to the meals from their own field kitchen. 'These past thirty years now we been hearing about how everybody over here on these communal farms was gonna start dying of starvation, but it looks to me like the kolkhoz boys got something to eat after all. We'll just see how all this turns out in the end.'

'Well, who knows?' Rokka said, licking his spoon and looking sly. 'Things's lookin' pretty bad, it's true. There is one bright side, though. Those poor devils lost some mighty fine soup. And that there's a sure victory for us. Lissen, you take another bowl, just to seal things up.'

Even Lahtinen laughed at that – and their spirits were a bit brighter as they set off. But then Hietanen started whistling.

Hietanen's whistling always had the same devastating effect on them, regardless of the situation, as it was truly dreadful, but our boy Urho just carried on whistling away. Once in a while he would issue harsh judgements of communism on the basis of the poorly maintained Eastern Karelian roads. Lahtinen often found himself hard pressed to defend it in light of the half-rotting buildings, the shoddy newsprint, and the inhabitants' ragged clothing.

On the other hand, they had to admit that its defenders seemed pretty attached to it. They died at their posts, behind great heaps of ammunition cartridges.

Barrages rumbled, automatic weapons rattled. Man after man died, each in his own way. Somewhere a sprint was cut short mid-race. Somewhere else a weapon slipped from arms gone limp and a head lurched down upon it. Some died moaning and begging for mercy, others cursing and gritting their teeth.

Somebody lay behind a rock waiting for death, brave and calm to the end.

Mile after mile was bought on these men's backs: miles of muddy, Eastern Karelian road, winding toward Petroskoi.

## II

Smoke struggled up from the stovepipes into the gray drizzle. Howitzers rumbled by, and an ammunition column clanged noisily down the muddy road. The racket didn't disturb the men sleeping in the tents, however. They'd been sleeping like the dead for fifteen hours and showed no signs of stirring anytime soon.

Rahikainen was on fire-watch. He passed the time playing poker by himself, pulling two separate hands of cards and murmuring back and forth, 'What'cha got? Three whores. Well, that ain't bad at all . . .' He tossed one hand angrily back on the deck. He glanced at the time and, seeing that his shift was finally almost up, hurried to wake Hietanen.

'Hey! Get up and watch the fire.' He poked and prodded Hietanen for a long time, until at last he got him to sit up. Hietanen groped around, entirely disorientated, pushing his hair out of his eyes.

'Go stand guard by the fire. It's your turn.'

'Yeah,' Hietanen said compliantly as he sank back into bed, blissfully ignorant of whatever it was he was being asked to do. Rahikainen relaunched his campaign.

'No, no, no you don't, you're gonna go stand watch by the fire.' Rahikainen was fired up by his own desire to sleep, so Hietanen would have to be roused, come hell or high water.

'What?'

'Fire-watch.'

'Aw, shit. Firewood still holding out?'

'Well, why wouldn't it be? And in nice little logs, too. Rahikainen the Patriot here chopped wood. Just like a real war horse.'

'Well, let's hope they give you a medal for it. Jesus, it feels good to sleep. How long did we go without rest?'

'Three days.'

Rahikainen crawled over to his bed and said as he dropped off to sleep, 'Artillery got hit with some shells minute ago. Probably made a few more heroes. Heard some shoutin' anyway. I'd be happy to do a round in artillery myself. Word is those guys get bigger rations. Might have been able to get some off of somebody over there, if I'd a had it in me to go that far. But I'm pretty beat.'

Hietanen looked out of the tent. Three wrecked tanks were lying on the main road and a few dead Russians lay by the wayside. That was where yesterday's counter-attack had ended. Hietanen pulled up his trouser-leg to check on the small wound in his thigh. It already showed promising signs of healing. One of the mangled tanks now out on the road had fired a shell right next to Hietanen, and a shard had lodged itself in his thigh. He had burned a safety pin with a match to kill off the bacteria and used it to carve out the shard, which was now wrapped in paper and tucked in his wallet.

He pulled his trouser-leg back down, dug the shard out of his wallet and considered it thoughtfully. 'This world's got everything all right. Put a hell of a lot of work into making that thing, and then they send it shooting along through the woods. And they don't even know how to shoot it! War's a pretty crazy business, that's for sure. All pre-tty strange if you ask me.'

Then he tossed some more wood onto the fire and sat dozing before the stove. The artillery kept rumbling by, and cracks of infantry fire rang out from the front line. Another regiment had been marched out there yesterday, when they had been ordered to stand down. Hietanen listened to the shooting and started dozing off. Machine guns hammered out intermittent bursts: *pa, pa, pa, pa, pa*. There was a light machine gun firing off solo rounds, and Hietanen figured it was probably Russian, since the sound of the shot had a different quality when you heard it from the front end of the barrel. *Pa-koo-pa-koo-pa-koo*.

Hietanen's head jerked up with a start. He was afraid he would fall asleep if he stayed beside the stove, so he threw his coat over his shoulders and crawled out of the tent. He checked on the other squad's fire and then, bored, started wandering around the encampment. A gray, misty rain drizzled from the low-hanging clouds. It cast a gray gloom over the whole, forested world and the war concealed inside it. Hidden in the trees, tens of thousands of men were fighting one another, and nothing but the clinks of combat revealed the existence of this life, and the death it portended. A horse-cart came down the road carrying a vat of soup – the driver huddled with his reins pulled in beneath his wet coat, which he had pulled up over his head like a hood. The horse's back and neck streamed with water as the rain pooled and collected into black streaks.

Mielonen approached from the direction of the command tent, prompting a familiar dread to rise up in Hietanen. Was their rest period up? Of course, Mielonen could be coming for some other reason than to order them to head out – so, Hietanen avoided the question, caught between hope and fear. What would he say? Hietanen was practically having heart palpitations he was so anxious. Was that mouth about to declare, 'Get rrready to head out!'? He calmed down slightly when he heard Mielonen's voice say, 'So, what's the Hietanen boy wandering around for?'

'Just sittin' here thinkin' war's a right miserable business. Hunger, cold, fear, sleep, and these lice-infested rags just to top it off.'

'Sounds about right. There's saunas in these villages, but no, always gotta be pressing onward. I was just asking that ambulance driver over there, and he said that the vehicles can barely keep up. Guys are going down all over the place now. Seems they're advancing down into the isthmus now, too, into Kannas.'

Whew, it's nothing, Hietanen thought, relieved at the conversational tone of Mielonen's banter. He was still afraid to ask straight out about departure, though. He was about to say something in response, but didn't manage to get it out before Mielonen continued, 'We're heading out, too. Go alert the Third Platoon, will you? I haven't got it in me to crawl in there and wake up Koskela.'

'You're joking.' Hietanen felt as if he'd been punched in the stomach.

'Nope. Sound the alarm!'

Blood rose to Hietanen's face. His first wave of anger was so powerful that he was deadly serious when he said, 'You motherfucking bastard. I ought to shoot you dead.'

'Down, boy. Shooting me's not gonna do anything. Gonna have to knock off some of the big boys for that.'

The angry outbursts that greeted Mielonen's calls to alert had long since ceased to offend him. He just hollered on as before, 'Machine-gunners, get rrready to head out!'

No other shout of that strength would have awakened the men just then, but this one did. As Mielonen made his way through the tents, yelling 'Wake up! Get rrready to head out!' faces emerged from the tent flaps, spewing curses so vile an onlooker would have thought Mielonen's calm indifference lunatic.

'Shut the fuck up, Savo!'

It was hardly the fault of his being from Savo that Mielonen had to wake the tired men, but the words 'Get ready to head out' were ones the men hated with a vengeance, rolled Rs or not. And, on hearing them, oh, how they hated Savo – apart from those who were themselves from Savo and thus obliged to demonstrate their anger in other ways.

A furious Hietanen stood between the tents, venting his anger by shouting, 'Third Platoon, wake up! You've slept too much already. Get up! Time to get up and show the people of the world what a terrifying creature the deep-forest warrior is. Up, fearsome lions of Finland! The ground is trembling and the cannons have already let fly. Put down your plow and take up your sabre! Time to add new pages to the glorious, the victorious, the downright staggering military history of Finland!'

Sleepy voices emerged from the tents. All the crown jewels in the arsenal of Finnish curses were trotted out in the service of the men's bitterness. For the ten-thousandth time, their medal-hunting officers had a chance to hear their glories sung.

'We're not going anywhere. Let's tell the bosses we demand at least three days' rest before we're going anywhere. That or they can take off by themselves if they want. Nothing to carry and orderlies looking after them. Ha! Assholes ought to try taking a load on their own backs, then they might understand how much a man can take. The strain on them is so much less than on us infantry guys that they think we can just keep going the way they can.'

Koskela packed up his things, and not without care. Nothing about him suggested that he considered this outburst a sign of insurgency – he seemed happy enough to let the men vent their anger in peace. Nature had somehow hit the bull's-eye in every aspect of this quiet ensign from the countryside. His education was limited to the basic elementary school curriculum, but his intelligence was keen and never failed to lead him to the best solution for any given situation. His intelligence was not dazzling in speed or agility – on the contrary, the blankness of Koskela's face might easily be interpreted as almost drowsiness at first glance – but it always cut straight to its target, and so managed to take care of everything it needed to. Now, for example, he knew perfectly well that when he tossed his pack on his back and left, the men would follow without further ado. But if he were to try to clamp down on their angry protests, in whatever way, the men's bitterness would just fester in the back of their minds, and far more dangerously. Furthermore, he wasn't pleased himself that their rest had been cut short. Exhaustion wasn't just unpleasant in itself, it was also dangerous, because it brought out this quarrelsome tenor in the men and caused unnecessary casualties. And this irritability in their operations would lead to even greater exhaustion. He didn't really feel he could say, though, whether it was an issue of necessity, or just poor management.

The grumbling continued, but Koskela foresaw that when the worst of the fury had died down, the situation would improve with the help of certain known individuals – Hietanen and Rokka, mainly. And, sure enough, Rokka started right in with his trivial chatter, sliding right into, 'Well, soldiers, let's git to it! Why's this job here gittin' you all so worked up? Fightin's a way to finish a war. Gotta head on outta here if we're gonna git anywhere. Who the hell wants'a dawdle around these backwoods for ever, anyway? C'mon fellas, mopin' time's done! There's some big towns up ahead, too, and Russian ladies a-waitin' for us to turn up, you hero-boys just wait and see.'

Rokka started swaying his shoulders and humming, looking mischievous. Vanhala melted completely and burst out laughing. And Hietanen comforted the rest of them by pointing out that when you were on the front line, at least you didn't have to dread when your rest period would be up. 'That's the upside.'

'There ain't no upside to this, turn the damn thing over and upside down as much as you please,' Rahikainen muttered flatly, angriest of them all.

Gradually they began to settle down, chatting idly to pass the time. Mäkilä called them to eat. He distributed three days' dry rations to each man, leading them to suspect that some kind of special mission awaited them.

'Don't eat it all at once. It'll have to last you three days,' Mäkilä warned.

'Have to last. Damn straight it'll last if you won't give us any more!'

'There isn't any more.'

'Then steal something!'

Mäkilä let the conversation drop, knowing that the men were just messing with him. Rahikainen put in a bid for new boots. 'These here ain't gonna make it to the Urals.'

'They're still in good shape.'

'Oh sure, they're in good shape. Just like our quartermaster's here. Excepting that I got this one toe here keeps tryin' to sneak a peek at the Greater Finland. Look!' Rahikainen covertly assisted his toe's sightseeing efforts, stepping on the binding where it joined the sole and raising his foot from the boot. Mäkilä was forced to hand over new boots.

The field kitchen was dishing out oatmeal mixed with some bluish and generally rotten-looking bits of meat.

'Yup. That's a horsey.' Hietanen removed a bit of chewed cartilage from his mouth. 'One of the gypsies', looks like. You can still see the whip-lash marks.'

'No complaints about the food, please. The meat is absolutely up to standard.'

It was the company's new master sergeant, First Sergeant Sinkkonen. He was on duty for the first time, having only just arrived. Following Korsumäki's death, Mäkilä had taken over the Master Sergeant's duties. Sinkkonen was a regular non-commissioned officer, over forty, and entirely incapable of relating to the men, from his first comment onward. He was dressed in full uniform, with a white collar setting off his neck, and tall, new boots on his feet, their tops folded over. His greeting to the men could not have been more tactless, and even Hietanen looked him over for a moment before saying, 'Well, who asked you? Who are you, anyway?'

'I'm the company's new master sergeant and I'd like to begin by pointing out that this perpetual complaining is beneath the dignity of a Finnish soldier. I'd say the food is quite good, under the circumstances.'

Lehto was sitting on a mound of grass, eating out of the lid of his mess kit. The mess kit itself was sitting on the ground beside him, and when Sinkkonen stepped near it, Lehto said flatly, 'Under the circumstances I'd say you'd better not kick over my tin.'

Sinkkonen's neck began to turn red, and grew increasingly

redder until Rahikainen said, 'Might be beneath our dignity, pal, but out here you better turn a blind eye to a thing or two. It is true, though, it ain't the horse's fault if he's got tough in his old age.'

For the first time in his life, this graying brat of the barracks realized that he commanded no authority whatsoever, and it shook the very foundations of his being. A misconception of his function had guided him through the entirety of his military career, and now it was backfiring. He was so shaken by the men's insolent mockery that all he could do was stutter, 'It has been said that the biggest whiners are the ones who turn out to be cowards in combat. The best men have performed their duties uncomplainingly.'

Rokka shook his spoon at Sinkkonen and said, 'Lissen here, Master Sarge! You got sumpin' real bad wrong with you. You crack jokes like they was serious. Out here a fella's gotta keep things light. We're all fellas with a sense a humor, see. Here, watch this!' Rokka stretched out his left arm as if he were holding a violin, and, using his spoon for bow, began to play as he sang:

> Fingerin'na fiddles! hiitulahaatuu
> Accordion'sa blowin' hilapatataa . . .

'Lissen! You hear that fiddle music? Lissen, why don't you join'na group! Let's make a orchestra. Here, grab that spoon there and keep beat on drums. And you got sticks over there, yeah, take 'em! Lissen . . . what, you ain't takin' nothin'? Spoilsport! This fella here's not playin'! We got a whole live show set up here, and he don't wanna play. Well, whadda ya know?'

Sinkkonen stalked off, but Vanhala was all set to start banging, so he and Rokka played together. Rahikainen joined in to complete the trio, improvising an instrument out of a comb and some wax paper.

'What kind of circus is this?' Lammio appeared behind them, almost as if he'd just popped up out of the ground. Vanhala put away his sticks in an embarrassed fluster. Rokka and Rahikainen stopped too, and Rokka said to Lammio, 'That new master sarge, see, he was so down we thought we might try to cheer a fella up with a lil' song. But he took off. Ain't much of a man for music, I guess.'

'Enough of your clowning around! The company is to be ready to march in one hour. Anyone who does not have a white handkerchief is to go collect a white piece of paper from the quartermaster. Squad leaders, make sure each man is taken care of. Move!'

This command was so unusual that nobody even knew how to joke about it.

'I bet I know where they're takin' us,' Rokka said. 'They're gonna press us deeper in'na forest overnight, and the handkerchiefs're so we can keep in contact.'

'Straight into the shit.'

'When are those goddamn Krauts gonna make it to Moscow?'

# III

Dusk was already falling. The rain continued and an autumn gloom reigned over the dark forest. Company after company turned off the main road, pressing into the forest in an extended formation.

'Big time, boys. Got the whole regiment lined up.'

Each man had attached a white handkerchief or piece of paper to his back. These were supposed to help them stay in contact in the darkness. They were ordered to keep conversation to a minimum. Smoking was prohibited entirely after nightfall. The sappers walking out front cut nicks into the trees to mark the direction the men were to follow, and set down log paths across streams and bogs. Soon the terrain changed into swampland, and remained so for a long time.

The men's loads were heavier than usual. They had twice the usual allocation of ammunition. The heaviest fell to the guys with the machine guns, mortars and anti-tank guns, as they had to carry the artillery on top of their own gear.

Mile after mile of the difficult journey slipped by in silence. The darkness thickened and their pace slowed. The first symptoms of exhaustion began to appear amongst the weakest. Their feet sank into the swamp's hidden potholes, and their tired bodies kept toppling over, unable to keep their balance. Panting for breath, the men would struggle to their feet and continue plodding on. Every now and again whispers would run through the line to confirm contact.

The head of the line had already trudged across miles of swampland by the time the tail end finally turned off the road. Three thousand men stretched out single-file across the swamp in the middle of the dark, foggy drizzle. The game was reckless and the stakes were high. And who was to guarantee that the line wouldn't break at some point? It was only as strong and shrewd as its weakest man. It might well happen that some guy would lose his way, leading those behind him who knows where. And it could also happen that, on top of everything else, that man would be afraid to send word of the break right away. The likelihood of a bottleneck and disintegration – and thus the possibility of failure – was great. And that was just the beginning. Awaiting them more than a dozen miles ahead was their destination: the junction of the enemy's main road and its rail line. It was into this lion's den that the regiment was supposed to elbow its way, alone, armed with the ammunition they held in their pockets, with no support, and nothing in the way of an umbilical cord but one phone line – which would certainly break before long.

The Regiment Commander used the phone frequently to make contact with the division. 'Point such and such. Southern tip of A. So far so good.'

'Status unchanged. No sign of any break in the line.'

The Commander walked along anxiously in his black raincoat, sucking on his moustache. At every moment he was expecting to hear shots from the head of the line, and for each moment of silence that passed he was grateful. It seemed impossible that the regiment would make it all the way to its destination unobserved, but nevertheless their odds improved with each mile they covered undetected. And what would happen if the dead-tired regiment did hit organized opposition? The Colonel hurried forward, then back to those behind, urging the men on. He was in desperate need of a cigarette, but hesitated to disobey his own orders. If he were to be caught, the situation would be embarrassing, to say the least. Sneaking off for a smoke didn't really befit a colonel and regiment commander, though there was no question this fellow had partaken of the pastime in days of yore.

By around midnight, a general fatigue had taken over. More than six miles lay behind them, and the men were faltering. There was a low murmur of groans, hisses and whispered curses, and somebody or other was constantly toppling over. Sometimes there were sobs mixed in amidst the curses. Mud squirted up as some man sank thigh-high into the swamp. Then this fellow, on his last legs, his will tottering at breaking point, would summon the last shreds of his strength and continue on. Each man stayed with the group. There was no need for discipline, homeland, honor, or a sense of duty. A force mightier than all of these whipped them onward. Death.

You couldn't fall behind, because that meant straying alone behind enemy lines – and thus certain annihilation. Ditching your ammunition or weapons would mean the same thing, even more certainly, as each man knew the price he would pay the next day. They left no gear behind. When they were allowed a break, they dropped to the ground right where they were. Oblivious to the wet and the cold, they lay in puddles in the swamp, panting for breath and collecting their strength for the next effort. Bit by bit, they devoured the little bread they had, but soon this source of pleasure, too, ran out for many. The hard rye crackers slipped into their mouths, neither nourishing nor satiating them.

Koskela carried four boxes of ammunition, having taken Salo's when the latter's strength had started giving out. Hietanen had Riitaoja's boxes, and Lehto carried the gun-stand the whole time, while Vanhala carried the gun. Lahtinen and Määttä carried these for the other machine gun, as Rokka was helping Sihvonen and Susling, both of whom were weaker than him.

Finally, Rahikainen was forced to take Riitaoja's rifle as well, as the man had reached the end of his tether. Even so, Rahikainen couldn't help muttering, 'Try to carry the clothes you've got on, OK, pal? My soldierly solidarity's got its limits.'

They were lying down on a break when three men approached them from behind. A cigarette glowed between the fingers of the man in front, and Hietanen noticed it. He personally was suffering acute withdrawal, which was the primary reason he exploded angrily, 'Don't you fucking know we're not allowed to smoke, ass-hole? You must be one hell of a big shot to smoke whenever you feel like it. Put it out! Now! It's our lives you're playing with, not just yours – which obviously isn't worth shit.'

The man put out his cigarette without a word, but the fellow next to him murmured rebukingly, 'Careful what you say – and to whom.'

'No, no, he was perfectly correct. I was just testing out how the command was being enforced. You did quite right. Name and company?'

'Corporal Hietanen, First Weapons Company, Colonel, sir.' Hiet-anen rose to his feet a little uneasily, recognizing the Regiment Commander, but calmed himself with the reassurance that he was in the right, after all. Even if it was just his craving for a cigarette that had made him jump on the Colonel for smoking.

'Well, Corporal Hietanen, keep up the good work.'

Then the Colonel turned to the rest of the men and asked, 'How are you boys making out?'

Salo struggled painfully to attention and tried to sound chipper as he responded, 'Very well, Colonel, sir.'

'Atta boy! That's Finnish endurance for you. The *"Blood of Vaasa trembles not, nor does Iron of Kauhava rust"*. The old Finnish way, boys. Nobody stands in the way of the mighty, not even the devil himself.' The Colonel turned away and Salo sank back into his puddle, trem-bling with exhaustion and feeling as much joy as his tired, depleted state would allow.

'So tell me, which one of those guys is the bigger tool?' Lahtinen whispered to Vanhala, who giggled with delight, 'Heehee . . . hee-hee. Ye-ess, the deep-forest soldier presses on! Fired up and ready to fight! Heeheehee.'

'Advance!'

The night was beginning to give way to a weak light. They could already make out one another's outlines: strange, monstrous phantoms staggering beneath their loads. Exhaustion began to recede into the shadows of their burgeoning anxiety, as they knew that by now the head of the line could not be far from the road. Messages urging them to be on their guard frequently rippled down the line. Every other man aimed right while the others aimed left, keeping watch in so far as was possible while still keeping an eye on the path and staying in contact.

Riitaoja fell and no longer had the strength to get up again. The others just walked past, but Lehto stopped beside him and yelled, 'Give me your pack and get up!'

'I c-c-c-can't go any further, C-c-c-corporal, sir.'

'Give me your pack when I tell you to and get up!'

'Over there.' Riitaoja began to cry, his sobs consuming the last shreds of his energy. He was entirely limp and incapable of doing anything. To make matters worse, he was so afraid of Lehto that he was trying to curl himself even deeper into the swamp. Riitaoja's sobbing brought Lehto to the point of rage. He kicked him, screaming in a hoarse whisper, 'I ought to shoot you, you little bastard! What I wouldn't give for the Russkis to take you off my hands. But no, you, you little pansy, you never get near enough to the action for that.'

'I c-c-c-can't keep going . . . Please don't hit me, C-c-c-corporal, sir . . . ahh . . . ahh . . .' In his panic, Riitaoja kept stuttering and calling Lehto 'sir', curling tighter into a ball to escape Lehto's blows. He groaned and cried out for Koskela, but the Ensign was walking far ahead at the head of the platoon. Unfamiliar men were already walking past. Each of them had his hands full just trying to keep up and so couldn't get involved, and anyway, the endless exertion had made them all apathetic. What did it matter what happened around them? One fellow did at least shout at Lehto as he passed, though the source of his fury and bitterness was as much the march as anything else. 'Don't kick the man, you fuckin' scumbag! I oughtta put a string of bullets through you!'

The man figured keeping his spot in the line was more important than getting involved, however, and so continued on without responding to Lehto, who yelled after him, his mouth foaming, 'Try your luck, asshole! We'll just see who the sun shines through.'

Whispers rippled down the line. 'Viipuri's been retaken . . . Pass it on . . . It was on the radio last night.'

'Viipuri's been retaken . . .'

'Viipuri's been retaken . . . Pass it on . . .'

'Viipuri's been retaken.'

Lehto grabbed hold of Riitaoja and yanked him upright. 'Now we march, you piece of shit,' he hissed, and started dragging the exhausted man supported in the crook of his arm. 'Viipuri's been retaken,' he whispered hoarsely forward. He forgot to change the tone of his voice, so the guy walking in front of him received the news in a furious hiss, as if Viipuri's retaking was the worst thing in the world that could have happened to Lehto.

'Viipuri's been retaken.'

'Viipuri's been retaken . . . pass it on.'

Lehto got Riitaoja up to speed and, shockingly enough, the latter managed to walk on his own again. There was no other option, as Lehto was walking menacingly behind him. 'You start lying down again and I'll take a stick and give you a beating you'll never forget. Of all the motherfucking pansies, I have to drag you along.'

Riitaoja had already been afraid of his squad leader during peacetime, even if, for the most part, it had just been the timidity of an overly meek private before his superior. He addressed Lehto as 'sir', even when the others had taken to responding to their leaders' commands with snarls of 'Shove it!' But in war his terror had altered. He feared the dark and violent nature of this man as if he were some sort of terrifying force that might crush him at any moment. True, Koskela had put Lehto under strict orders to stop abusing Riitaoja, but he wasn't always around, and besides, even Koskela understood Lehto's bitterness, seeing as Riitaoja not only left his duties to others, but also forced them to drag him along like a child. Riitaoja was also horrified by Lehto's bravery, and thought that because this madman seemed to have no regard for death at all, there was nothing to prevent him from killing him straight off. Not even understanding himself how he managed to put one foot in front of the other, he pressed on across the swamp, fearfully choking back his sobs of desperation.

Then they were given a break, but this time they could guess what was coming. The halt took place silently, with no command, and each man dropped to his knee, raising an arm to alert those behind. A sort of pile-up ensued, as the darkness prevented anybody from making out the signal prior to tripping over the guy in front of him.

'Road directly ahead. Eyes peeled, and stay calm.'

'Stay calm ... stay calm ...' Sihvonen repeated, but he was so restless that Lahtinen tried to urge him to calm down. 'Take it easy now, we'll be over there sticking our necks out soon enough. Ain't gonna be a walk in the park, I mean ... boys, tomorrow we're in for some fighting over there like we've never seen ...'

They stopped short as a gunshot rang out in front of them, and a submachine gun hammered back in response. *Brr ... brr ... brr ... brr.*

Then they set off, groping their way forward. The battalion split up, and the machine-gun platoons broke off and assembled behind their infantry companies. The Third Company fanned out to the left, the Second to the right, and the First set up in clusters behind them. Koskela divided the machine guns between the platoons, who set them in position. Lammio arrived with the order that one gun was to be moved further out to the left, where the Third Company's Second Platoon was advancing.

'Kariluoto, do you have contact over there?'

'No. My platoon's in reserve behind their First Platoon, and we have contact with them. And the First and Second Companies are in contact with each other.'

'Which of the guns wants to go? The second section's guns are already taken.' Koskela looked at Lehto and Lahtinen, who turned to look at each other. After a brief moment of silence, Lehto said, 'First'll go.'

'Short end of every goddamn stick,' Rahikainen muttered.

Lammio pulled out a map and pocket lamp. 'Come take a look.'

Koskela and Lehto knelt beside Lammio, pulling their coats up over their heads to study the map beneath the makeshift cover. 'The Second Platoon will assemble on the side of this meadow. Their objective is to advance to the main road, cut it off, and turn the front to the west. There is a path starting from the northernmost tip of the swamp that leads to the road, see? The platoon will advance along both sides of it. According to a patrol that went out, there should be some kind of barn in the meadow, but even without it it will be easy to find your way: two hundred yards out and to the left from here. You can't miss it. If the platoon has already left by the time you get there, follow the path to the road and you should find them there. It's about two hundred yards from the meadow to the road by way of the path. You could go through the First Platoon and follow the line along to the Second, but that would waste time, and besides, the First Platoon will already be under fire by that point. This is the safest and shortest way. Everything clear?'

'Yep. So it's Sarkola's platoon we're supposed to meet?'

'Precisely. If the side of the main road is manned, then we're in combat and you will easily find your way from the sound of the shooting. There's almost certainly something there, as we were observed on our way in. But nothing has been confirmed, so just keep your eyes peeled. There could be something or nothing. Look out for yourselves. On your way.'

'Hang on,' Lehto cut in. 'I'm not taking Riitaoja. Lahtinen can give me a man to replace him, he's got more men anyway.'

'True,' Koskela said. 'Lahtinen can give you one more man.'

'You can take Sihvonen.'

'Me! Of course.' Sihvonen was furious. He was displeased at the separate assignment, but beyond that he was offended, as obviously Lahtinen would hand over the member of the group he considered most expendable.

'Never mind the grumbling,' Lammio said. 'But Riitaoja will have to remain with the squad. If this shirking doesn't stop, I'll take whatever measures necessary to make it happen. A grown man ought to be able to pull himself together enough to serve as an ammunition-bearer.'

Riitaoja stood at attention and hastily gasped, ingratiatingly, 'I'm pulled together! I was just tired a moment ago . . .'

The poor man didn't know what he feared more – the enemy or Lammio – and he was so overcome with panic that he wasn't even ashamed at being scolded in public.

The first machine-gun team set off, and no sooner were they out of earshot than the bickering began.

'You! You goddamn war horse, you just had to offer us up, didn'tcha? Why don't you go by yourself if you want to! What the hell are we supposed to do when it's pitch dark out? They could be anywhere!'

As Rahikainen vented his anger, Lehto just walked on, every nerve on alert, muttering in passing, 'Keep your mouth shut and your eyes open.'

'Yeah, we'll just see what gets opened up out there. Do you hear that shooting on the right? They're already on the road. And there's a tank. What are we supposed to do without any anti-tank guns?'

'Shut up. There's the meadow and the barn. If we follow the edge of the meadow, we'll automatically hit the path . . . which should start from that hollow over there, if the map holds true.'

It was a bit brighter in the clearing than inside the forest, where it was just about pitch-black, and they started curving cautiously along its edge, soon coming upon the path to the road. But there was no sign of Ensign Sarkola's platoon. They heard some shooting off to the right, but according to Lammio's account of the situation, that would have to be in the First Platoon's sector.

'Let's turn back,' Rahikainen said.

'No, we're going to the road. Or didn't you hear the same command I did?'

'But if there's nobody over there—!' Rahikainen persisted. 'I don't believe half of what that peacock says. Who died and made him king anyway? Guy's full of it.'

'The layout seems right . . . and we are going.'

'Vanhala, let's you and me head back.'

'Let's all head back, all the way to Finland! We could just go home and tell them we got lost, heeheehee.'

'Fine, you sniggering bastard! You and that war horse can head off, the two of you.'

'Two little Finns off to conquer a tank! Heehee. That'll bring us stripes and medals by the bucket . . .' It wasn't clear whose side Vanhala was on, only that he was amused at how incensed Rahikainen was.

Lehto ordered them to shut up and follow. He released the safety catch on his gun and started groping his way though the pitch-black forest, creeping along parallel to the path. He navigated by watching for lighter spots between the branches, as pale channels of light shining down from the sky meant that the path was near. Mud oozed beneath his feet. The damp, dark forest was quiet.

Lehto was already nearly to the road, and he was beginning to doubt himself. Where was the Second Platoon? He paused and listened. The men following behind caught up.

'Let's turn back,' Rahikainen repeated.

Lehto's anxiety increased his irritation and he whispered angrily, 'Would you shut the fuck up? We have to at least locate our objective. I'm not giving that peacock the pleasure of seeing me turn back halfway through. I'm going to head out in front a little. If anything happens, get into positions and hold your ground. One of you can run for help. But remember, the others are on the road now, not back there where we left them.'

Lehto was off. For one moment a suffocating fear nearly choked him. What was out there in the still darkness? Why wasn't there any shooting, if their own guys were already over there? And why was there a tank rumbling so close on the right? His armpits were dripping with sweat, and his mind was fixated on this harrowing feeling that something was wrong. But when the thought of going back crept into his mind, his fear gave way to a strange, bitter rage. Never. Not ever. They would never get to see him turn back. 'They' was somewhat vague. It wasn't just Lammio, it was everything he'd been rebelling against since childhood. But then, what hadn't he been rebelling against? For him, there existed only enemies and extraneous people. He had hated people ever since the austerity years, as far as he could recall – since the time he had had to go to the Workers' Association Building in Tampere to fetch free pea soup in a rusty can, like a stray dog. He wasn't even cut out to join the communists – seeing as he couldn't stand having people anywhere near him. There were two men he'd felt some sort of respect for – Kaarna and Koskela – but even his regard for them was tinged with a certain proud disdain.

Tossing this anger around in his mind, he shifted his weight from one foot to the other, trying to see through the darkness and pricking his ears to make out even the faintest sounds in the night. The forest thinned, and he suspected he was a few yards from the main road. Just then, wafting through the damp, drizzly night air, a pungent smell came flooding through his nostrils – a smell he knew from Russian prisoners and fallen bodies. He raised his gun and was just stepping up to the side of the path when he heard a shout practically at his feet. He saw a bright muzzle flash, felt a crippling blast in his body, and fell to the ground with a weak cry.

# IV

When the enemy opened fire, Vanhala, Rahikainen and Sihvonen took cover beside the path. Riitaoja dropped his ammunition box and took off, running like a madman through the forest. Rahikainen had left the gun-stand by the path, but Vanhala still had the gun.

'Let's go, guys,' Sihvonen said. 'The attack's gonna start soon.'

'What happened to Lehto?' Vanhala's voice was serious this time.

'What happened? Did you hear that scream? We're not sticking around to get ourselves killed. I told you guys . . . but that loony had to go get himself killed.' Rahikainen started crawling back through the forest.

The enemy had stopped firing, but now the silence unnerved the men even more. The darkness seemed saturated with danger. The others were already making their retreat, but Vanhala whispered, 'What if he's just wounded? We should try to find out . . .'

'How you gonna find out? Look, even if he is alive, there's no way you'd be able to get him out that way . . . not from right under their noses . . . Nothing comes of that except the guys who go to fetch him end up stayin' out there too. And he himself ordered us to go back for help.'

'One man – but the others were supposed to remain in position . . . Where's the gun-stand?'

'I left it over there by the path . . . Goddamn dead-weight can stay there. Anyway, if we start dragging it off now they'll hear it and come and finish us off.'

'The officers might ask for it,' Vanhala said. He was in two minds. He could certainly keep his own fear under control, but he had a tougher time standing up to somebody else. Vanhala was not a leader, not by a long shot, but even so, leaving things as they were struck him as a little too inadequate. 'Here, you take the gun, I'll go get it.'

'OK, OK, knock yourself out,' Rahikainen said. 'I'm done tryin' to hold back the crazies tonight.'

Rahikainen and Sihvonen retreated further back, but Vanhala started crawling slowly alongside the path toward the gun-stand. He reached it without incident and began pulling it cautiously to the side. Naturally, it scraped against the only rock on the entire path, prompting some light machine guns to pepper the ground all around Vanhala. He heaved the gun-stand over his shoulder and clambered to cover with the others, abandoning any attempt at silence. And he was laughing as soon as he'd caught his breath. His success gave him the confidence to decide that he wouldn't just abandon Lehto, but would do something to set matters straight. There wasn't really much option besides yelling, however, so Vanhala just belted out, 'Lehtoo . . . oo!!!'

Light machine guns fired back angrily, but no other sound came.

'Jesus, pal, would you cool it? Maybe you better start believing he's done for. Why else would he be silent?'

'What was that rustling over there?' Sihvonen asked.

They listened, but nothing more remarkable came. The noise was enough to get them moving, however, and they made a hasty exit. There was something in Lehto's death that made them feel even more helpless than usual. They certainly weren't overly attached to their squad leader, but his bravery and ruthless, brute strength had given them a certain confidence in him. He had seemed sort of invincible, even to the enemy, making it seem to them as if even the Russians were powerless against him. And now a light machine gun aiming at nothing but a sound had taken him down. They had seen plenty of guys die by now, but the fact of Lehto's solitude made his death even more horrific. To be left back there, alone, in the darkness, before the enemy. They could still hear his quiet cry. It had struck them as a warning call, a shout of surprise and a whimper all at once.

They hadn't given Riitaoja a second thought this whole time, assuming he was lying in terror somewhere back behind them, by the side of the path. They called his name quietly as they headed back, but no response came. They scoured the edge of the meadow as well, and called out for some time.

'Where can that little fool have gone to?' Sihvonen wondered.

'He must have run back to the others,' Rahikainen figured. 'Anyway there's no point in trying to find one man in these swamps.'

Guided by the sounds of the firing, they made their way toward the road, taking a wide curve out to the right so they would be sure to hit it behind their front line.

## V

When Lehto first regained consciousness, all he knew was that he was in severe pain. Then darkness took mercy on him again. But the force of life within him was fierce and stubborn and, unwilling to surrender so easily, it woke him again. At first he couldn't remember anything; he had no idea where he was, nor what had happened to him. He felt a raging, burning pain somewhere around his chest and his stomach. Then he remembered walking along a path, which led him to the realization of where he was. Same path.

At the cost of severe pain, he ran his hands over his body. The area just below his chest was bloody, and his back felt similarly warm and wet. When he moved, it felt as if somebody were twisting a knife through his mid-section. He could feel nothing in his legs, and his whole lower body refused to move. Little by little he began to realize that his spine had been damaged and his legs were paralysed.

And then he also realized that this was the end.

He gave a quiet moan and lay for a moment in hopeless apathy.

For the first time in his life, for one brief moment, he gave in – but then, a fierce shooting pain wrenched him awake again. Even now, he didn't harbor any of that irrational hope of rescue people often cling to. Lehto looked upon his own situation with the same brutal clarity with which he looked upon everything else. He remembered his squad, but he didn't call for help straight away, as anybody else would have. He knew it would just drag out death's arrival, as he was sure that, in any case, he had no more than a few hours to live. On their way out across the swamp, they had talked about the injured, and what their fate would be on a campaign like this: to be doped up with morphine and left to the mercy of their own luck and the feeble prayers of that impoverished soul, the battalion chaplain.

When he determined that the upper portion of his stomach had been shot through with more than one bullet, Lehto was certain he was going to die. He was aware of some nearby enemy presence as well, since he could clearly make out some low coughing and whispering just across the main road. There was but one conclusion to be drawn from the situation, and Lehto reached it quickly: Where is my gun?

He groped around with his hands, but to no avail. The machine-gunners hadn't taken along any hand grenades on account of the extra ammunition, and he had already considered his hand-knife, but that seemed too difficult, especially when he considered what kind of botched job was likely to result from his present lack of strength. He kept groping. Even the smallest movement added to the already unbearable pain, and he lost consciousness again.

Upon waking, he found his strength had diminished further still, though the pain had not lessened. A plaintive moan tinged with some kind of sob tightened in his throat, and although he was sure that the others were no longer nearby, he spat the blood from his mouth and called out in a strangled voice, 'Vanhala . . .'

*Pa, pa, pa, pa, pa, pa, pa . . . pa, pa, pa, pa . . . pa, papa.*

'Rahikainen . . .'

*Pa, pa, pa, pa, pa, pa, pa, pa.*

'Vanhala, aa . . . aa . . .'

*Pa, pa, pa, pa, pa, pa, pa.*

The hail of bullets sailed overhead, as he was lying in a blind spot created by the bank beside the path. Had he thrown himself to the ground instantly upon hearing the enemy shout, it would have saved him. Now it just prolonged his agony. Gathering his forces, he managed to infuse his voice with all his previous rage as he yelled, 'Lower . . . aim lower . . . fucking cross-eyed bastards . . . aim lower!'

*Pa, pa, pa, pa, pa, pa, pa, pa, pa, pa.*

'First machine gun! Vanhala . . .'

*Pa, pa, pa, pa.*

'Are you motherfuckers deaf? Shoot here . . . down here . . . follow my voice . . . my gun . . . aaahh . . .'

*Pa, pa, pa, pa, pa, pa, pa, pa, pa, pa, pa, pa.*

In pain and fury, Lehto cried. It came out in a combination of curses and sobs, as if some wild animal were wheezing in pain. 'Aa . . . aah . . . hah . . . haa. Can't you motherfuckers kill anything? Toss a fucking hand grenade! Fu—'

*Pa, pa, pa, pa, pa.*

Lehto rolled onto his other side. The pain the movement brought on made his eyes black out, but just as they did he glimpsed something that restored his strength. Less than two yards away, the bolt of his gun was gleaming. His fall had sent it flying that far.

Now the painful journey began. It progressed no more than an inch at a time, as he dug his fingernails into the ground and dragged his paralyzed body forward. His nails bent back and his lips were in shreds, as he gnashed through them, biting down in pain. He fainted a couple of times, though each blackout lasted only a few seconds. He no longer had thoughts. There was nothing but that gleaming bolt, so close and yet so far away. He focused all efforts on that point, and finally the gun strap was in his hand. He pulled the weapon beside him. First he raised the gun barrel and set it in his mouth. Gritting his teeth, he bit down on the cold metal flecked with gunpowder, as if he were afraid somebody might still wrest it from his mouth. Then he twisted his neck so that the mouth of the gun pointed toward the roof of his mouth. Noiselessly, he eased his hand into the grip and curled his finger around the trigger. With no settling of accounts and not a shred of fear, he pulled it.

The shot frightened the enemy. A light machine gun rattled off a few rounds and a hand grenade thudded onto the road. Then all was quiet. And one more Finnish hero's story drew to a close.

## VI

Riitaoja crouched in a corner of the dilapidated barn in the meadow, sobbing softly and trying to muffle the sound of his sniffles. At first, the nearness of the building had been reassuring. At least it was made by human hands. In the middle of all this danger and darkness, it seemed to radiate the comforting presence of other people. But then its ominous silence grew downright terrifying. There might even be enemy soldiers in there. Tonight it seemed like ambushes lay in wait everywhere. And Lehto's cry. What in the world could have happened? What horrific force reigning over this darkness could have made that maniacal god make a sound like that?

As far as his crippling fear would allow, he steered his thoughts toward various scenarios of how he might get out of this situation. There were Finns in the direction of the crackling, but there was also Lammio. Yes – and he didn't have the ammunition cases. A rock and a hard place. The path was certain death. The whole first machine-gun team might be lying there dead.

A gentle gust of wind blew into a corner of the barn and rustled the hay. Riitaoja could endure it no longer. He walked quietly toward the path. If he could retrieve the cases of ammunition, he could go back and rejoin the others. He was only five minutes late, as Vanhala, Rahikainen and Sihvonen had just left the meadow's edge when he arrived.

The path stretched before him, dark and menacing. Sniffling and stopping frequently, Riitaoja advanced. In between, he called out the others' names. His legs did not want to obey. He had no idea how far it was from the meadow to the road, which was why he kept pausing every other second, expecting something terrible to happen.

Then he heard Lehto's voice out in front of him: 'Vanhala.'

When the light machine gun opened fire, Riitaoja threw himself to the ground and lay there trembling, unable to answer Lehto's cries. The shouts of Vanhala and Rahikainen's names misled him into thinking that they were over there too. Wild with panic, he didn't understand what was happening until he heard Lehto's terrifying cursing and moaning. Then, for a long time, silence reigned – the same silence in which Lehto was crawling toward his gun – and it gave Riitaoja the courage to crawl a short distance forward.

The shower Lehto's suicidal shot provoked crackled all around him. He rose in terror at the hand grenade's explosion and started sprinting toward the rear. Hysterically, he stammered, 'Don't shoot! Don't shoot! I didn't do anything!'

The bullet struck the back of his head, so he was spared the realization of the end.

# Chapter Seven

## I

The platoon Lehto's squad had been looking for hadn't flanked the
path to advance toward the road at all. As it turned out, it couldn't
spread out that far to the left without losing contact with the First
Platoon, which, for its part, was bound to other squads of the Battalion, so Ensign Sarkola had had to alter the command on his own
initiative and advance at a distance of one hundred yards to the right
of the path. He had sent word of the change and received the go-
ahead – which was perfectly understandable, since losing contact in
the dark would have been too risky.

As soon as Koskela had received word, he'd sent a runner to
inform Lehto. But the runner, fearful of the dark forest, had dawdled, and met up with the remaining members of the squad only
upon their return.

Koskela was kneeling in a ditch by the roadside, aiming into the
darkness in the direction of the rumbling of an enemy tank. Rahikainen crawled up behind him and said, 'Lehto's done for . . . And
we couldn't find anybody over there . . .'

Koskela glanced over his shoulder. Then he turned his head and
resumed staring out into the darkness. After a long silence he said,
as if only now realizing what had happened, 'Yeah . . . I mean, no.
There wasn't anybody over there.'

'There were some foreign chaps all right! Didn't seem too fond
of us, though.' Rahikainen was feeling slightly uneasy, and so spoke
with a rude defensiveness, as if in anticipation of the accusations to
come. He thought Koskela's silence seemed to imply some sort of
judgement, and so, acting insulted, he tried to make it clear in his
tone of voice that they were the ones who had been wronged. 'Well,

what did you expect? Of all the shitty places to send us . . . We were creeping along the path when those light machine guns just started cleaning up . . . took Lehto out straight away . . .'

'Yeah . . . body still over there?'

'Oh, it's over there all right. Right under their noses. We barely managed to get the machine gun out.'

'Where are the others?'

'They're over there in the back. But we don't know where Riit-aoja is. Didn't he come back here?'

'Haven't seen him.'

'He just disappeared back there. We searched for him and called out and all. But when we didn't hear anything, we figured he must've come back here.'

'He didn't come here, and we haven't sent any guys out searching for him, either. Rokka!'

'What'ssa trouble?' Rokka crawled down the ditch toward Koskela.

'Lehto's dead. You take charge of the first squad from here on out. Send Sihvonen back to his own squad and take Susi with you into the first.'

'Works for me. How'd he go?'

'Ran into the enemy.' Koskela was still staring out into the dark-ness as he mumbled, 'They shouldn't have been sent out straight. It would have been better to curve around through the First Platoon . . .'

'Well, there's two sorts a luck, see. You can have the good or the bad. Now that Lehto boy, he had the bad. But goddamn it, would that tank just drive a lil' closer! It's mined over there, see.'

'Get into position on the left. If it knows to avoid the mines, then just let it come and hold back the infantry.'

The main road had been cut off, and the enemy had instantly sent troops to the cut-off point. Under cover of darkness, both sides were preparing for action at daybreak, and any skirmishes in the meantime were just products of the men's nervousness. Rokka had taken over Lehto's squad, which was positioned on the side of the road. They were careful not to shoot, however, as the tank was rumbling out in front of them, firing occasional, random shots into the darkness.

'Now, don't waste your shots, fellas!' Rokka whispered. 'C'mere you lil' devil! Not too much, now ... just about three yards. Gaddamn it! Won't budge. Now either I'm goin' over there and tossin' a satchel charge on his roof, or – hey, he's movin', he's movin'! Hey fellas ... that's it ... now!'

The ground shook and flames lit up the night as the mine exploded beneath the tank treads. The men's tension erupted in a flurry of frantic shooting on both sides, and the fire blazed up wildly for a moment, before gradually receding into a low, steady burn. The low fire began to lick the sides of the tank, and soon it was engulfed in flames, glaring brightly through the early-morning darkness.

Rokka whispered in delight, 'You just drove yourself right on'na that mine! I didn't mean to order you around for real! I was just messin' with you, and you, you fool, you thought I was serious! A fella hears all kindsa things in this world, but that don't mean he's gotta believe everything he hears!'

'Shut up, pal. We don't know what else is coming.' Rahikainen still hadn't entirely recovered from his shock. Vanhala, on the other hand, was in a great mood. He preferred his new squad leader, as Lehto had been wont to spoil his fun all too often, with a terse 'Quit sniggering'. But Rokka kept up a pleasant chatter, and Vanhala thought the future under his leadership looked downright grand.

The tank chassis boomed and crackled as it burned, as the heat was beginning to make the ammunition explode. Rokka kept close watch to make sure no men tried to escape the flames, but they must have all lost consciousness when the mine went off, as nobody even tried to get out.

'Ol' fellas' butt-fuzz is burnin',' Rokka announced, concluding that by now it was too late for anybody to escape.

Vanhala lay beside the machine gun, fiddling with his belt and repeating Rokka's phrase, which had clearly struck his fancy. 'Buttfuzz ... heehee! ... Butt-fuzz.'

'Lissen, Vanhala, don't you giggle too much now. We're gonna be in for it ourselves in'na mornin'.'

They watched the fire. Reflections of the flames lit up their faces, making them gleam against the darkness. Rokka's eyes darted about furtively, like a cat's. He was in good spirits, as the tank's destruction meant a significant decrease in the danger awaiting them.

Susling watched the burning chassis in silence for a long time, and then he whispered, 'Hell of a way to go.'

'Now lissen here, Suslin'! Don't you start pityin' them! This ain't no Sunday school, you hear? Out here you're supposed'da kill, damn it. Like I always said, we ain't out here to die, we're out here to kill. Otherwise you ain't comin' out alive.'

Susling raised his gun to his cheek, sent a shot out into the darkness and said as he pulled out the cartridge, 'I wasn't talkin' 'bout that . . . Those fellas ain't out here all by their lonesome, neither. Seems a me I spotted sumpin' in'nat bush. But I guess it's empty.'

## II

The darkness gradually gave way to a gray, dismal morning. The rain had ceased, but its over-abundant moisture still reigned over the landscape. The branches of the spruce trees dripped with rain and their trunks surged up black against the pale dawn. The grass drenched the men's clothing. Each twig and leaf they brushed up against dropped a cold gush of rainwater onto them. Countless cobwebs hung between the shrubs and the tall grasses clung to their hands and faces.

The men shivered in their damp garments, trying to block out their misery, which gradually came to be drowned out by the knowledge that they would soon find themselves – yet again – experiencing that greatest of human anxieties: fear for their lives.

The enemy retreated backwards a little, as daybreak would have put them in a rather exposed position otherwise. This brought the men some relief, and the most gullible of them even wondered if

perhaps the enemy might decide to surrender the main road voluntarily. Lucky for them, they were ignorant of the general situation.
They did not know that the forest behind them was teeming with
enemy soldiers, nor that their phone line had been cut, which meant
that they were relying solely on a radio connection. They were also
unaware of the fact that the division heading toward the main road
had not been able to advance nearly far enough, so there was no
way the artillery would be able to offer them any support.

They had to try to spread out quickly over a wider sector, as the
ground they were covering was still too narrow. The battalion set
out, advancing down both sides of the road. When they reached the
spot where the path leading to the meadow turned off the main
road, they found Lehto and Riitaoja's bodies. Bit by bit they pieced
together the details of the drama. Lehto's mouth was smashed up
and the back of his head had been blasted off almost completely.

'Shot himself in the mouth. Looks like he was wounded pretty
bad. Three bullets right under the heart. Look, guys, look how he
dragged himself . . . his fingernails are totally torn up.'

'So Lehto is dead, huh?' Hietanen said, looking at Vanhala and
Rahikainen. Vanhala shifted his weight uneasily from one foot to
the other, looking embarrassed, but Rahikainen said curtly, 'I don't
know! We called and he didn't answer. Whatta you starin' at?'

'Seems pre-tty damn strange, if you ask me. Looks like we got a
real mystery on our hands, boys. Just like a real mystery play. Now,
how can a dead man shoot himself? Well, I'll be damned. I'll be so
goddamn damned that I don't even know how damned I am.'

'Well, damn you.' Rahikainen threw his gun savagely over his
shoulder.

Koskela looked at the bodies in silence. Then, to put the pointless
quarrel to rest, he said, 'Look, obviously he regained consciousness
later. Anyway, it's all the same now, whatever happened. What's for
sure in any case is that there's no way you could have gotten him
out of here. Whoever came to get him would have ended up lying
here too.' Then Koskela continued, as if to himself, 'Lucky it was
Lehto. Best man of any of us to endure a death like that.'

Riitaoja's body aroused further curiosity. The men who had set out with him insisted that he could not have been there when they left. Vanhala even showed them the spot where he'd retrieved the gun-stand, pointing out the traces its two front legs had left on the ground, which were still carved into the surface of the path where he'd dragged it away. Koskela seemed quite convinced that Riitaoja must have returned to the scene later. The others found the story pretty implausible, though, because in order for it to hold, Riitaoja's return would have had to have been voluntary.

They lifted the corpses onto the path and placed them side by side. Koskela removed the men's coats and spread them over the bodies. The gesture was unnecessary, of course, but somehow or other it was undeniably beautiful. It was like a blessing. The men did not want to talk about death. Their gaunt, worn-out faces just wore a strange gravity. Carefully, with a gentle deference, they slipped the ammunition from their comrades' pockets, as it wouldn't have done to let even one cartridge go to waste. Then they hurried after the advancing company.

Three hundred yards later, the battalion ran up against formidable enemy forces and took up its defensive positions. A massive tank rumbled into view from round a bend in the road, followed by a second. Under cover of the two vehicles, a sizeable fleet of infantrymen were gathering in groups, preparing to attack.

'Dig.'

'With what? Our fingernails?'

'What'd you guys do with your shovels? Well, now you'll see what you get for lightening your load. You might be best to head back to Koirinoja to find yours, Aromäki. I think that's about where I saw it flying by the wayside.'

The company's shovel strength tended to vary greatly. It would gradually increase during periods of heavy fighting, since the men scrounged equipment from dead enemy soldiers, but even a short break or slightly longer march would prompt them to send their shovels flying by the wayside. There were at least a few shovels left, however, and they were already in heavy use. The men without tried to dig themselves some kind of shelter using anything they had, which, in some cases, was indeed their bare fingernails. Self-delusion can always rise to the occasion, when called upon. They positioned themselves behind small rises in the terrain, set some rotting tree branches on top, and built up the structure with a few chunks of moss. A bullet could sail straight through even a thick tree trunk, it's true, but this shelter was really more for the soul than the body. A man felt a little more secure behind it.

The men were actually fairly calm and decisive. There was a sort of irrevocability about the situation that brought it about. Since there was no escaping the fix they were in, deciding how one felt about it was rather a straightforward matter.

Kariluoto and his platoon would defend the main road. The first and second machine-gun teams from Koskela's platoon would join them, setting up one on either side of the road. Kariluoto crawled down the line. His own chest felt hollow, but he urged the other men on nevertheless. 'Remember guys, nobody leaves his hole. Everyone stays put. No matter what.'

One of their own mortars shot off a pathetic barrage of their precious grenades. First, the men cursed its ineffectiveness, then the fact that it had been launched at all – for no sooner had it than the enemy started preparing to attack in what seemed to the men like an act of revenge for a few measly shells. When the first boom rang out in front of them, and the first grenades crashed down behind them, the men gave frightened, furious shouts of 'Motherfuckers! Now you've done it. See what that gets us!'

Shells crashed down behind them, the majority of them, luckily, having been launched too long. When the crashing died down, they began to catch glimpses of men in brown uniforms darting between the trees, and then, resonating over a terrifyingly broad expanse, there came a long, hair-raising cry of 'Uraa ... aaa ... raaa ... aaaaaaaa!!'

And then it started. A constant, unbroken clamor dulled the men's hearing. It was as if they were drunk on the rat-a-tat-tat of these endless, clattering waves that echoed endlessly through the

air. In their midst, voices rose and fell, bellowing, 'Uraaaaaa uraaaa
. . . aaaaa . . . aaaaa!!!'

The enemy tanks started to advance. They were evidently aware
that the anti-tank equipment had failed to reach the enemy troops
flanking them in the dense forest, as they drove boldly up to the
point where the Finnish sappers had mined the road, emptying their
ammunition supply as if they were on a firing range.

Panicked cries came from the line. 'Anti-tank rifle! Get the anti-
tank rifle!'

The men with the anti-tank rifle crawled closer, making their
way down the long ditch that ran beside the main road. On the
other side, the ensign who had mined the road tried to yell over the
shooting, 'It won't work! Hey! Guys! The rifle won't work on those
tanks. They're KVs . . .'

The men couldn't understand anything the Ensign was yelling
and kept advancing. Three of them advanced with the rifle while the
rest held further back down in the ditch. The anti-tank rifle managed
to fire off two inconsequential rounds. Then, like the judging eye of
God, the tank's main gun turned toward them. When the shot was
fired, the men and the rifle disappeared into a cloud of smoke. As the
cloud dispersed, three dismembered bodies came into view, a bent,
upturned gun barrel sticking up between them.

Cries of panic rang out from the line. 'Get the short-range weapons! . . . Hey, satchel charges! . . . We gotta hit 'em up close . . .'

They knew that as soon as the tank commander conquered his
fear and turned boldly off the road to advance alongside it, they
would be done for.

Already the enemy infantrymen were less than a hundred yards
off. A hunched man would suddenly appear out of the blue, darting
into view for a moment before disappearing under cover again, or
else falling mid-dash. The firing line's barrels were hot from shooting. Silent, dazed from the tension and the clanging, the men loaded
and shot, loaded and shot, and each time a hand grabbed a cartridge
from a pocket, a panicked mind writhed with the thought, 'Is that
all I have left . . . ?'

Here and there voices screamed, 'Mediiics . . .' and some guy shooting would notice that the weapon beside him had gone silent, then turn to see his neighbor lying still, his head sunk over the butt of his gun. But the man's attention would not rest there long. The noise of their own shooting prevented them from hearing anything else, so they didn't realize that the same clamor was underway in both the Second and Third Battalions' sectors. Nor had they exactly managed to keep track of what going on around them. With blanched, strained faces and hoarse voices screaming out warnings and commands, they fought, literally, for their lives.

The enemy forces were clearly piling up as they edged ever closer. Gradually, the fighting settled into a shoot-out. But both tanks were rumbling back and forth along the road as their opponents watched, hearts frozen in fear, waiting for them to turn off into the forest.

Hietanen was lying behind a rock on the left side of the road. Rahikainen lay a little way to his right, Rokka having taken all the other men from the machine gun off to join the firing line. There was a patch of juniper trees situated about a hundred yards in front of Hietanen, and he could glimpse some sort of frantic movement inside it. He suspected they were dragging a machine gun in there, and soon a crackling filled his ears, confirming this suspicion.

When the hail of bullets came down around them, Rahikainen ducked his head behind the rock and fired away, aiming his gun almost directly upwards. The senseless squandering of ammunition infuriated Hietanen, who, tense with anxiety over the situation, exploded, 'Aim, damn it! Don't shoot into the clouds! That juniper patch over there is crawling with men!'

Rahikainen shot, but his head stayed just where it was behind the rock. In Hietanen, as in many brave men, fear expressed itself in the form of a restless will to action, in light of which Rahikainen's hiding appeared all the more despicable. Hietanen was perfectly aware that destruction awaited them if they failed to stop the attack, as the enemy would have no trouble whatsoever steamrolling over a scattered mass of men. This fear threw him into a rage and he exploded, cursing,

'Jesus Christ! Stop wasting cartridges! They're not falling from the sky, you know!'

Rahikainen could feel his old aversion toward Hietanen surging up in him. He had hardly forgotten Hietanen's words beside Lehto's body, even if circumstances had now thrust them down another road. 'Don't you order me around, pal. Commander, my ass.'

'I'm at least commander enough to know that you oughtta aim. Shoot into those bushes! There's a machine gun in there with about as many jokers as can cram in there with it.'

Rahikainen ceremoniously lifted his head higher, shot and continued quarreling as he yanked the cartridge out of his gun. 'Shut up. Goddamn corporal. Shit's going to your head.'

Hietanen was so wound up that he was about to take a crack at Rahikainen, but just then the enemy started ramping up its fire, so he continued shooting. Nonetheless, he resumed yelling over the din, 'You shut up! Or I'll come over there and make you. You're some kind of guy – I don't even know what you are . . . What would I call you? You're like a . . . a limp rag!'

Rahikainen stopped responding. The tank in front turned off the road and headed toward them. The second accelerated fire to its maximum capacity to keep the first tank under cover. Cries of infantrymen started up again, and again they caught glimpses of men darting ever nearer. The defensive forces' fire slowed, just when it should have accelerated. It was clear that all it would take was a little shove for panic to take over. The ensign who had mined the road was lying in the ditch beside it. He rose to a hunched position and started running toward the tank with a mine in his hand. He made it a few steps forward before he spun around and fell a few yards from Hietanen.

### III

Hietanen clearly saw the bullets strike the Ensign, as his shirt rippled with the impact. For two seconds, Hietanen hesitated. The occurrence of this death right before his eyes made it all the more difficult to make a decision. Hietanen didn't really think. He just had some vague awareness that if he didn't do something, the tank would crush him, and if he tried to make a break for it, he would die running. The latter option would at least postpone the terrifying moment, and Hietanen was tempted to take it. For two seconds, he hung suspended in the scales. And then they tipped.

The tank was about two dozen yards off. A few steps out in front of him lay a fallen tree, whose upturned roots the Ensign had clearly also been trying to reach. They might offer him some kind of protection from the enemy's view. Hietanen quickly crawled over to the dead ensign and snatched the mine out of his hand. Moss flew up at his feet and angry squeals whizzed past his ears.

Hietanen's breathing felt strangely constrained, as if he had just plunged into an ice-cold swimming hole. His lips were stiff with tension, fixed in a sort of horn-shape. It was as if his entire consciousness had been frozen. It refused to consider the significance of these angry blasts, as if shielding itself from the terror such considerations would induce. Hietanen darted quickly behind the upturned roots.

Just then he heard Rokka's voice yelling, 'Now shoot like hell!'

Hietanen was panicked and trembling with anxiety. The urgency ringing in Rokka's cry struck his over-excited consciousness as a warning of some new, unknown danger. Then he realized that the call was intended for the others.

It occurred to him he did not know if the mine was functional or not. He didn't know anything about it except that it was supposed to explode under pressure. It was a little late for sapper training, however. The time was now or never.

A vision of the tank tracks rolling beneath their fenders flashed through his mind. Right there . . . right there . . . And then he threw. The weight of the mine made aiming next to impossible, and a kind of prayer-like wish flickered through Hietanen's consciousness as he hurled it. Then he hurriedly gathered up some moss and tossed it at the mine, to serve as some sort of camouflage. It seemed to catch a few bits of debris too. Then he glimpsed a sight that sent a shiver down his spine. It would have to fall under the right track. That much was already clear. Only then did the precariousness of his own position suddenly dawn on him. Would the tree base be enough to protect him from the force of the blast? He sank down behind it, opened his mouth and pressed his hands hard against his ears.

Two seconds later, it was as if the pressure of the whole world suddenly descended upon him. He didn't experience the explosion as a sound, but rather as a numbing, thudding blast – and then his consciousness went dim.

When it returned, he saw that the vehicle was still, tilted slightly to one side. It was still obscured by dust and smoke. He saw that the men closest to him had their mouths open – but he couldn't understand why, as he couldn't hear the hysterical shrieks of joy bursting from the line. His head was still sort of numb, so he wasn't sure what to do next. He just lay there, looking back and forth at the tank, then at the men, who were yelling at him, 'Yes, Hietanen! Woo-hoo! Bravo, Hietanen!' The praise was all wasted, however; Hietanen couldn't hear a thing.

Then he saw a leg appear beneath the vehicle, then another, and gradually a man's mid-section came into view. Suddenly it jerked and fell motionless. Hietanen looked back and saw Rahikainen's exhilarated face, though he couldn't hear him yelling, 'Pull off the line! I'll take care of the rest!'

Only then did Hietanen start to come to his senses. He leapt quickly back to his previous position and crouched to a squat behind the rock.

'Stay under cover! I'll finish him off.' Rahikainen shot a few rounds into the tank's hatches.

From the way he addressed Hietanen you'd have thought he was at least half responsible for the tank's destruction. The squabble of just moments ago had left him in an uncomfortable position. It made Hietanen's feat feel like a crushing comeback to his words, which was why he was now trying to restore his self-respect by adopting a caring, protective attitude toward his brother-in-arms.

Hietanen himself lay behind the rock, his body trembling through and through, as if from a severe chill. The more his senses returned to him, the more he was overcome by horror. It was as if he were now being forced to endure all the terror he'd blocked out during his dash. All his fear was concentrated into a single image that he couldn't get out of his mind. He saw the tank tracks beneath the fender about to run him over. The image was so vivid and powerful that for a moment he thought it was real and very nearly made a break for it.

He stayed put, however, his reason exerting at least some power over his imagination. He dug out a cigarette and managed to stuff it into the holder with trembling hands. It wobbled in his mouth and he grabbed onto it so forcefully that the thing snapped in two. With the fourth match, he finally managed to get the end of the cigarette lit, and the tobacco oil rose to the surface of the rapidly burning paper as Hietanen drew on it with hollowed cheeks.

Little by little the shaking subsided. He was already beginning to hear the men's shouting and shooting. For a little while he kept repeating, 'Good God. Good God', not even understanding himself what he meant by repeating it over and over. Then he remembered how he had thrown fistfuls of moss over the mine to camouflage it, and the childishness of the act made a smile creep over his face. And then it was accompanied by a strange joy rising up within him. Only now did he begin to understand what his action meant, and he exploded with laughter at the joy of victory. That was supposed to be camouflage?!

He laughed, and his laughter simultaneously released the previous moment's horror and the euphoric delirium of having survived it: of having accomplished this daring feat that elevated him to savior of the battalion.

Meanwhile, the combat situation had altered considerably. The second tank had retreated and the enemy infantry had also stopped their advance. Soon they stopped answering fire as well. Cautiously, the men began to raise their heads, noticing that the enemy had ceased shooting. They had retreated further back.

Koskela hurried over to Hietanen. 'How are you doing? My God! They oughtta give you leave for that. I couldn't watch when all that moss went flying up, I had to shut my eyes. And right at your feet!'

Hietanen couldn't really make out what Koskela was saying, though he was able to hear his voice now. So he just said, 'I have no idea. I haven't got the slightest idea. I just hurled it. It was just the grace of God that that ensign managed to get it all ready to blow. But I was scared all right! Holy bejesus was I scared! I didn't think I'd ever get that cigarette lit. It's just mind-boggling that a person can have a scare like that. But hey, we better go check it out.'

'That does it. I finished 'em off!' Rahikainen announced, coming to join them. He may have succeeded in deceiving himself, but he certainly didn't fool Koskela, who paid him no attention whatsoever. The three of them cautiously approached the vehicle.

It was silent, and when they had waited a moment, Hietanen banged on the side of it with the butt of his gun. He had shaken off his shock now, and gave himself up to a state of euphoria. In a voice that declared it belonged to the vehicle's destroyer, he bellowed, 'If anybody's still in there, now's the time to come out! Otherwise I'm gonna give this roof a blast that'll send you all the way to America! From now on, this tank is mine and I decide who drives it. *Idzii surdaa! Ruskee soldaat!* Come on out! Well, damn. I'm popping the hatches.'

Hietanen climbed up onto the roof and pried open the heavy hatch door. When he got it open, he looked inside and then called out to the others, 'These guys all got blood comin' out their ears. All's quiet.'

'Say, the one I finished off's a lieutenant!' Rahikainen shouted from underneath the tank, where he was cutting off the dead man's badges. 'That makes me as good as captain of the Russian army from now on. Now that I took down this lieutenant here.'

Hietanen had already forgotten their recent spat. He looked over the tank and exclaimed in sincere amazement, 'Jesus Christ, guys! Am I something or am I something! I'm pre-tty damn impressed! Say now, what does all this make me? Hero of Finland! If only this damn buzzing in my head would stop. Nothin' swollen up there I hope.'

'Oh it's swollen all right, but don't worry, it won't hurt'cha,' Rahi-kainen smiled. It was like an olive branch, the way he said it – and it made Hietanen laugh, as indeed everything made him laugh just then.

Then men and officers started gathering around the tank, burst-ing with congratulations. Even Lammio nodded approvingly and said, 'That's the way. That decisiveness was exemplary.'

The only remarkable thing about his congratulations was that nothing about them really felt congratulatory. The aloofness and expressionlessness of his thin voice always felt a little offputting, regardless of what he happened to be saying. Even Sarastie turned up. He took Hietanen by the hand, squeezed it and said pointedly, 'Having been aware of the previous state of affairs, I might under-stand better than anyone here just what you have accomplished. So first, many thanks. You'll be receiving a Liberty Cross at the next ceremony, and I'll get the paperwork moving pronto for your pro-motion to sergeant.'

Hietanen was a little perplexed. He still couldn't quite make out all the Major's words, but he got the general drift. Even if he was sincerely amazed at himself, he still found it rather embarrassing to be congratulated by everybody else. So, he just smiled and looked uneasily at the officers.

Sarastie resumed his battalion commander stance and down-shifted to the most general variety of small talk. Tapping the tank with his stick, he said, 'Ought to be a very successful model, this new one. But it looks like even their most skilled engineers are no match for Finnish courage and conviction.'

A moment ago, the Major had been praising Hietanen, but with these words he was already moving on to congratulating himself. The Major, like so many military commanders, considered the feats of his troops feats of his own. Failures, however, were the fault of cowards and adverse circumstances. To be sure, the Major had actu-ally been in a state of anxiety that exceeded even that of his men. They had at least been ignorant of how critical their position really was. Amongst other things, the battalion commanders as well as the advanced company commanders had received strict orders not to move back their command posts under any circumstances – meaning that, were it to come down to it, they were to go down at their posts.

Now, however, the situation was improving. The failed attack had shaken the enemy's confidence, and on top of that, the division had just sent word of its advance, so the artillery would be able to back them up as soon as they'd taken over the firing positions.

But Sarastie had just lived through a critical couple of minutes. Several of the automatic weapons had started to run low on ammunition. Every last reservist had been put into combat, and the men positioned on the far side of the swamp had been left with virtually no cover at all.

Following such an experience, there was reason to indulge in a moment's good spirits. Sarastie straightened himself up, feeling his energy return and his capabilities strengthen as he stretched out to his full, towering height. Power and potency seemed to surge through him with the blood pumping through his veins.

The importance of this operation guaranteed that it would be followed with great interest all the way up to General Headquarters. The Marshal himself might even be listening to the news at this very moment: 'An enemy attempt to break through from the west has been put down after heavy fighting by Battalion Sarastie. Other battalions have also repelled the enemy's slightly weaker attacks attempting to bring relief from the north and the east.'

The Major turned to his men. A joke came to mind, which Sarastie had actually come up with the day before, but decided to save for the appropriate occasion – which, it seemed to him, was now. 'Well, boys. Caught your breath now, have you? We got them right in the jaw this time. Let's go and give it to them in the seat of their pants next. They're after that nickel up in Petsamo . . . Well, you're all generous fellows, aren't you? Let's go give them all the nickel they want.'

The good cheer spawned by the successful thwarting of the enemy attack made the men laugh all the more heartily at the Major's joke, and Salo, who was standing nearby, exclaimed just loud enough for the Major to hear – or rather, just so that the Major would hear, 'Let's give it to 'em, let's give it to 'em! Ain't got no penny-pinchers here!'


# IV


Lahtinen and Määttä didn't have time to marvel over the tank. They were too busy scavenging ammunition from dead enemy soldiers, having nearly run out of their own in putting down the attack. Lahtinen was flipping a dead Russian onto his back so as to get at his pockets when he heard the Major shouting from across the road.

'Oh, stop crowing,' he grumbled. 'We're still here all right, but just barely. They're a tough bunch, that's for sure. Heading for us bolt upright, even after I sent four belts at 'em.'

Määttä was accustomed to Lahtinen's grousing and didn't ever take it too seriously. He just responded rather indifferently, 'Seems pretty convenient to have 'em running upright if you're tryin' to shoot 'em down. Anyway, it's a good thing we all got the same caliber weapons. They even thought of that.'

'Humph ... no. Nobody thought that far. The Whites stole weapons from the Russians back in the Civil War, that's why they're the same.'

'Weren't you the one who said it was the Germans who armed the Whites?'

'Yeah, they armed 'em with the guns they stole from the Russians out here on the Eastern Front leading up to '17. But hey, gimme that guy, the one still hangin' onto his rifle there. Come on, buddy, let go, lemme see if you got any rounds left in that magazine a yours. God damn it. You'd think I'd be able to manage against a dead guy. Humph. Nothin'. Just one little sucker in there. But hey, let's go over there behind that mound. That's where their machine gun was.'

When they arrived, they saw that the enemy had left their machine gun behind. Four bodies lay behind it. They found five full belts and half of a sixth in the feeder. Lahtinen collected the belts, chatting away happily, 'I'd say that belt was definitely worth it – one I shot over here, I mean. Paid us back nearly six times over! But wait, what am I talking about? These cloth belts have two hundred and fifty rounds in them and ours only have two hundred. We better give the other guys some. We can't even carry all of these.'

'That's plenty. But look how old that guy is, the one sprawled out over there. Could they really be running low on men already?'

'Don't be ridiculous,' Lahtinen grunted, though only out of habit, the bountifulness of their loot having stripped him of any real desire to get into a quarrel. His lips pursed in a contented smirk. He tossed the ammunition boxes over his shoulder and said as he headed off, 'We better switch to steel belts. These cloth ones are just damn rags. Anyway, listen, they're not gonna run out of men over there. When it comes to manpower and materials, that country's pretty well stocked. Now, the only thing is that over there, I mean, they've been looking out a little bit about what the people have to eat, rather than investing everything they have into sending packs of scoundrels out shooting in the forest. Meanwhile we've just been throwing the people's money to the winds! Guys spend their Sundays running around in the forest with rifles on their backs, and then come evening, they go around and give each other promotions. Over there, they've put some pressure on the fat cats so that all the people's bacon doesn't just disappear beneath the butcher's apron! But what's the use. Look, if they run out of men, they'll send over a fleet of fifteen million women soldiers. They train everybody over there, and that includes the little old ladies.'

'No way. Damn! Where's this at?' Rokka had caught the end of Lahtinen's tirade and tossed in his question with a sly smile.

''Cross the way. Hey, if you need any ammo cartridges, take some of these.'

'Would you look at that? I scrounged some, but I could take a few more. Those damn fellas's all huntin' for bread and badges, never mind 'bout gittin' any ammunition. But what were you sayin' just now? Some lil' ol' Russian ladies's gonna come fight us?'

'You don't know. It could happen.' Lahtinen was already grumpy and irritable, suspecting what was coming. Nor were his instincts incorrect.

'Well, if it comes to that, then you might say we're . . .'

'Well, at least we'd know where to aim! Got lots of practice,' Rahikainen chimed in.

'Might lead to some pretty intense hand-to-hand combat, hee-heehee. Then even Rahikainen might win his Mannerheim Cross, heeheehee.'

Lahtinen turned away with lips pursed, looking up into the tree-tops as if to proclaim that he would not deign to continue conversing with such people.

Then Koskela and Hietanen arrived and informed them that they were advancing immediately. Koskela had ordered Hietanen to report to the field hospital to rest, at least until his hearing returned to normal. But such a passive role was beyond Hietanen's powers in the wake of his great feat. Elation had made him too restless to lie still in one place. His joy was so earnest that no one really minded it. Even if Hietanen was still marveling at his own distinguished performance, there was a sufficient degree of comedy mixed up in the whole thing to make the men put up with just about anything. And Hietanen's jubilation wasn't just the product of his heroic feat. In reality it was the joy of having made it out alive. Now he was laughing again, talking about the shock he'd experienced behind the rock. 'Then, when I threw all the camouflage on the mine!'

'Move out!'

The joking and chattering ceased. Their carefree spirit vanished as suddenly as it had appeared. The men trudged on in silence, their faces tense and restless.

They ran up against the enemy again about half a mile later. The artillery had already caught up and so could prepare their attack, pushing the opposition back another hundred yards or so, but then the enemy stopped beside the clearing of a small village. They gave it one more push before darkness fell, but to no avail. Reluctance, darkness and exhaustion put an end to the offensive, and Sarastie decided it would be best to wait for the new day, even if it meant the wounded would have to hang on another night for proper care.

The battalion assumed its positions beside the village fields. There were some potato patches lying out in no-man's-land, and under cover of darkness, Rokka and Rahikainen snuck out to do some harvesting. Their digging was audible from the enemy positions, however, so Rahikainen abandoned the mission halfway through, as soon as the bullets started raining down around them. Rokka, however, took cover in a ditch and got straight back to it as soon as the enemy had calmed down. He brought back enough potatoes to feed his whole platoon and Kariluoto's besides.

They dug a hole in the ground behind their positions, started a fire and pretty soon potato soup was underway. They blanketed the fire in twigs and perched along its edge in the drizzly darkness. Only now did their nervous anxiety give way to hunger and exhaustion. The soup of the poorly washed potatoes oozed from the corners of their mouths as they ate greedily. Their three days' dry rations had run out that morning, so they ate the potato soup plain – but even so it tasted wonderful. Once they had eaten, the men not on guard duty stumbled toward the roots of the spruces to sleep and, despite the cold rain, slept like the dead. They were not demanding. Vanhala even fell asleep in a puddle of water – having fallen into it, he gave up the search for a better spot.

But somewhere deep in their nervous systems, fear was still keeping watch. If shots struck at a rapid tempo, the startled sleepers would jerk up to a sitting position, listening for an anxious moment, and then, when the bangs fell silent, slip back to the ground, sound asleep by the time their bodies were horizontal.

## V

The aid station tent was full. The dying men who had lost consciousness had been taken outside, as had the more lightly wounded. A low, plaintive moaning hummed through the spruce grove. The medics squatted – dazed – trying to make themselves immune to the surrounding misery. The worn-out doctor's nerves were frayed. It was painful watching men die when he knew many of them could have been saved by a quick operation. But out here there was no way he could operate. All he could do was bind wounds and give morphine injections.

One of the wounded men was dying. He'd been injured the night before, when the battalion had advanced up onto the main road. He'd taken a bullet in the lower part of his stomach, and he'd been in severe pain until early this evening, when his state of intermittent consciousness had begun to grant him some relief. The doctor stooped down beside him and the man opened his eyes. They gleamed feverishly and gazed up at the roof of the tent, on which the doctor's formless shadow spread, projected from the bright Petromax lantern behind him.

'So, how are you doing?' the doctor whispered, seeing that the man's consciousness had returned. The man didn't answer, but just kept staring at the shadow looming on the ceiling. Then his gaze turned toward the doctor. His lips moved, but no sound came. The doctor diverted his own gaze. He couldn't look into those fearful, feverish eyes that seemed to burn straight through him. Then the man's gaze turned back to the shadow. He started to mumble something and tried unsuccessfully to raise his head. He seemed to be in a state of overwhelming anxiety. The doctor pressed his ear to the man's face and made out the words, 'De-eath . . . Up on the ceiling . . . Lord . . . Jesus . . .'

The doctor pressed his hand down on the man's forehead, as he was still struggling to lift up his head, without success. 'Close your eyes. There's nothing up there. Are you in pain?'

The man did not calm down and the doctor was becoming impatient. He was a bundle of nerves as he crawled out of the tent and said to the chaplain huddled under a nearby spruce, 'Eerola hasn't got much time left. Why don't you go in there and try to do something for him? He's restless again and I just can't keep giving him endless amounts of morphine. He's vomiting even without it. Oh for God's sake, could they please get that main road open!'

The doctor's nerves and exasperation gave his voice an angry tone as he addressed the chaplain. He was hesitant to send him into the tent to talk with the man, as it would be agonizing for the others to have to hear the whole thing. Listening to somebody prepare for the end wasn't going to do any of them any good, lying there as they were, with fear in their hearts, awaiting their own deaths at any moment. This was why he generally tried to get the dying men out of the tent, as the two deaths inside had induced panic in the others. It was just that it seemed rather a gruesome task to carry them out into the rain, even if they were all bundled up and well past under-standing anything about the world around them. Practically speaking, it was still better to bring them out. The doctor cursed the Third Battalion's aid station, to whom he had lent his second tent, in deference to the fact that they had even more wounded men over there. One of their companies had ended up at the dead center of a terrible mortar barrage.

'We half-killed ourselves carrying that tent out here and now we can't even use it. Was it really necessary to halt the advance here?'

'The Commander said the men were so exhausted that there was no way they'd be able to launch a successful attack before morning. By the way, did Eerola ask for me?'

'No. But he's afraid of death and I think he was praying. Just try to calm him down.'

The chaplain removed his black rubber raincoat and hung it on a tree branch. Then he cleared his throat and focused. He had a habit of saying a little prayer to himself before performing his duties. The act had already become so habitual that it was entirely devoid of any genuine spirit of piety. The operation was more like that of a reaper who sharpens his scythe on the whetstone a couple of times at the end of each row, just out of habit.

Then the chaplain crawled into the tent. He had to squint for a long time before he could see anything in the glare of the Petromax. The stove radiated warmth into the air, which reeked of disinfect-ant. A medic was huddled half-asleep beside the stove. Wounded men wrapped in blankets lay lined up along the side of the tent. Somebody gave a low moan.

The chaplain crawled over to Eerola. The wounded man looked at him with restless eyes dimmed by fever and nearing death. The chaplain saw that his face was covered in beads of sweat. In this kind of situation, it was an unfailing sign.

'Brother, are you in pain?'

The man said something, but his voice got lost in his throat.

The face the chaplain looked upon was filthy and exhausted, already gleaming with a yellow sheen. There was something dark glimmering in the region around the man's eyes, almost like a visible manifestation of his suffering. You could see a line on his neck where his suntan ended but his skin remained filthy, and his flannel shirt collar glistened with grime, peeking out from beneath his sweater. Eerola was twenty. He was thin and lanky, having been underfed his entire life. As a day laborer on a large farm and a member of a family of hired hands, he belonged to a social group below which there were only vagrants and inmates of the workhouse. Heavy labor and light sustenance had left their mark on his physical constitution, but even so, a tough resilience within him fought death long and tenaciously. This young man had had a goal in life, which he had pursued, but which was now doomed to remain unattained for all eternity. He would have liked a new suit and a new bicycle – that belonged to him from the start and were meant exclusively for his use. But he had been obliged to hand his meager salary over to his family, so he had had to do without. And it had made him bitter, for in the world of his tiny town, these two items were the rightful belongings of any grown man. But it was in plain trousers and a suede jacket that he had left for the army.

The chaplain watched as the life that had cherished these dreams slipped away, little by little. He put his ear to the boy's mouth just as the doctor had done and made out a hoarse, wheezing whisper. 'Jesus . . . Jesus . . . take me . . . deliver me from here . . .'

'Brother, be calm. He will help you. Jesus will not forsake any of us. He will deliver us all to safety. Do not be afraid, brother. You are

His. He has redeemed you as He has redeemed all of us. You have borne your burden faithfully and Jesus will not forget that . . .'

The man's restless breathing evened out and began to grow faint. The chaplain whispered quietly into the dying man's ear, 'Jesus has forgiven your sins. He will grant you everlasting rest and peace.'

A brief, gentle shudder shook the dying man, two soft sighs escaped him, and the chaplain pressed his mouth closed and whispered, 'Amen'.

Over on the other side of the tent, somebody pulled a blanket over his head and muffled sobs began to emerge from underneath it. The chaplain was just about to head over to him when the wounded man who'd been lying unconscious beside Eerola suddenly started to speak. He had been stirring restlessly the whole time, obviously disturbed by the chaplain's whispering. The man, who was high on morphine, grunted almost incoherently, 'Jesus . . . Jesus . . .'

The chaplain bent down beside him, thinking he was praying. Actually, the man had lost contact with reality entirely. He was a tall, broad-faced youth. His wide, brutal-looking mouth revealed tobacco-stained teeth.

'Jesus, Jesus,' the man repeated over and over, the word from the chaplain's speech clearly having fixed itself in his mind.

Quietly, the chaplain said to him, 'Brother, shall we pray?'

'Jesus, Jesus,' the man repeated, only to himself. Then he suddenly burst out into a harsh, piercing howl.

'Shh, shhhh, calm now,' the chaplain whispered, but the man went on howling, foaming at the mouth as his eyes rolled back in his head. From underneath the blanket that had been muffling sobs just moments ago, there now came a shriek of 'Stop it, stop it!' as the man burst into a hysterical fit of tears.

'Ah-ha, oh dear! Oh, what a world! Please, dear people, please!'

The doctor crawled quickly into the tent and hurried over to the crying man, trying to calm him. The chaplain was completely at a loss for what to do and decided it was best to leave the tent. As he emerged outside, he heard a medic saying in a pained voice verging on tears, 'How much more can they suffer? Can't they at least be left to die in peace?'

The chaplain took his raincoat from the branch and crouched down to a squat. He prayed, half crying, that God would let the main road open and save the wounded men. The sobs died down within the tent, the doctor having managed to calm the man. The medics carried out Eerola's body and set it in the grove of trees behind the tent, the last in a long row.

Rain drizzled from the sky. The Petromax hummed quietly in the tent and now and again a tired, hopeless wail would emerge from its tarped awnings.

Guards stood in the darkness surrounding the aid station, keeping watch over this miserable grove, where the cost of the flanking operation was being paid out in pain.

## VI

During the night, the enemy retreated through the forest behind the point where the road had been cut off. They had abandoned their heavy artillery. Amongst other things, the second KV, or 'Klim', as they called them, engaged in the earlier attack had been driven into a swamp. The men were still skirmishing with the last of the enemy soldiers along the roadside when the ambulances arrived to evacuate the wounded. Many of them had been awaiting rescue minute by minute, hour by hour, for twenty-four hours. Slow, torturous waiting, unrelenting pain and the fear that the regiment wouldn't be able to defend that crucial stretch of conquered road had been steadily wearing them down. And, in the grip of this fear, they had watched the medics carry those who hadn't made it out to the line of corpses.

The vehicles' arrival prompted a surge of hysterical joy in the minds of the wounded. Even the weakest of them endeavored to demonstrate this with whatever strength he had. The prospect of delivery washed the recent hours of torture from their minds.

Moans and wails receded into the silence of the dark spruce grove, to be forgotten there for ever. The dead could no longer bear witness to their pain, and anyway, no one particularly wanted to inquire. Their suffering was theirs alone. They had given up everything else. They had been coerced out of everything, down to the last shred; but their suffering they were permitted to keep for themselves. It was of no use to anybody.

At daybreak, Sarastie's battalion reconnoitered the surrounding area. Kariluoto's platoon and the men from Koskela's who'd been attached to it were ordered to search the village on whose flank the previous evening's attack had been halted. The ambulances had already driven through it, of course, but the village hadn't yet been scoured.

One resident had been left behind. A man as old as the hills – a *starikka*, as the Karelians called them – who was nothing but a burden to anybody at this point, and had been allowed to remain behind for precisely that reason. He lived in a small cabin on the edge of town, and was gazing out of the window when gray-clad men began to flash between the buildings. There came one – crouching, lying in wait with his gun under his arm. He walked into the neighboring building and then reappeared in the courtyard. Others followed further behind and when their leader gestured to them with his arm, they threw their guns over their shoulders and calmly joined him. The starikka watched as each of them yanked off a stake from the courtyard fence. He was beginning to be frightened. What were they going to do with those stakes?

Then he gave a sigh of relief. The men threw their packs and guns to the ground and raced off to the potato patch.

When the men had dug up the potatoes, they washed them in a ditch with a speed only hunger can induce. Rokka scrounged a table from one of the buildings, along with a couple of chairs and a long bench, which he then proceeded to chop into firewood. They started up three or four campfires and soon potato-filled mess kits were boiling above them.

Major Sarastie strode down the main street of the village. He gave the Eastern Karelian buildings the once-over as he walked. He considered it his duty to have some appreciation for the beauty of their gable ornaments, even if – to be perfectly frank – he didn't understand the first thing about them. But paying attention to them was somehow part of the whole tribal spirit of the war, and Sarastie was a true herd animal, his occupation aside. So, once he realized that all the reports about Eastern Karelia described the local building style and gable ornamentation, Sarastie had to make sure he noted them as well.

His actual, and very matter-of-fact, opinion of these houses, however, was that they were not suitable for human habitation. Then he glimpsed something that genuinely intrigued him. A spring chicken just about perfectly ripe for slaughter was padding around the corner of some building. Sarastie was just about to call for his orderly when he caught sight of a block of wood somersaulting toward the chicken and whacking it in the neck. The chicken squawked and staggered a few steps, stunned. A private appeared from behind the building, nabbed the chicken by the legs, and – knick-knack! – snapped its neck.

'Hey, Private!'

The man started, looked at the Major and sprang to attention, the chicken still in his hand.

'What's your name?'

'Private Rahikainen, Major, sir.'

'And is Private Rahikainen aware that violating residents' property in these villages is strictly forbidden?'

'Major, sir, with all due respect. There aren't any residents. I conducted a full investigation.'

'I believe you are aware that in that case all property defaults to the state. I understand that has been made clear. They've certainly discussed the issue enough.'

Rahikainen stood with the chicken still dangling from his hand, dawdling his way through a response while trying to concoct some sort of cover-up. 'Major, sir. Indeed, I was aware of that. I haven't violated any property. This fellow here was damaged already. Hobbling on his feet. Probably got injured or something during all the fighting. He was definitely done for. I just thought that it'd be a waste to leave him. When he was about to die anyway.'

Sarastie thought this explanation was about as superb as anyone could have come up with in such a situation. He glanced rather wistfully at the chicken, and then began to chuckle at Rahikainen's phony, puppy-dog face. 'All right, take him this time. But let it be the last. Bull's eye like that deserves some kind of prize.'

Rahikainen played his role right through to the end. 'Yes sir, Major, sir! Better cut him open quick. So the meat doesn't spoil, huh?' And with that, Rahikainen was off. The others demanded that the chicken be cooked in the potato soup, and Rahikainen concurred. There was no soup pot to be found, but they made do with a bucket.

The only thing missing was salt, and Rahikainen decided to go and see if any had been left behind in the houses. After a few unsuccessful searches, he stepped into the cabin. The starikka was sitting on a bench at the back of the room, frightened and staring uneasily at Rahikainen. The sight of another person gave Rahikainen himself a start, but he calmed down upon observing how old the man was.

'Well! What kinda antique Finn are you?'

The starikka didn't reply, but stared mutely back at Rahikainen.

'Hey guys, come see! We got a prehistoric Finn in here. Beard, fur cap and all.'

The starikka blinked his eyes, watching the men as they stepped into the cabin.

'Well, hello there, grampaw!' Rokka exclaimed, taking a seat beside him. The old man leaned over toward him and answered softly, his voice wavering, 'Helo, helo.'

'Left ya behind, did they?'

'Ah, levd me here.'

'They leave you any salt, pops?' Rahikainen asked. 'We need some for our soup.'

'Ah, nodzing.' The old man was becoming anxious. He recrossed his legs the other way, glancing around uneasily.

'Didn't they leave you anything to eat?' Salo asked, moving in closer.

'Took everydzing. Levd me alone here.'

'Here's some bread for starters . . . I ain't got no more, but the supply crew ain't far behind us. They'll be sure to look after you. You're gonna have a chance to eat your fill for once. Who knows the last time you had anything to eat.'

The old man took Salo's bread with a trembling hand and looked at him hesitatingly for a moment, as though he might even give it back, but then tucked it into the chest of his quilted coat.

'Lissen, grampaw, you know if there's any other folks left in this town?'

'No. All dza people gone.'

'Too bad for them,' Salo said. 'We're just gettin' things set up around here. They weren't too rough with you now, were they?'

'Ah, rough, very rough.'

Rokka was scanning the room without listening to the old man. The rest of them, on the other hand, were prying the guy for every possible scrap of information about life in Eastern Karelia. He said almost nothing of his own initiative, but he answered their questions, concentrating primarily on figuring out what it was they wanted to hear. Salo was chief examiner.

'You had any parsons around these parts?'

'Ah, bevore, dzere vaz parzon in Pryazha.'

'They killed him, didn't they?'

'Killed, killed . . .'

'You got kids?'

'Ah, had two boyz. One killed, and odzer one beaten and taken . . .'

'Why'd they kill him?'

'Ah, did not go kolkhoz.'

'Did you have a house?'

'Had a houze. All taken avay.' The old man had caught on to his questioner's delight at hearing of people being killed or mistreated, and so started steering all his responses into this same general vein.

'Killed, killed. All killed.'

'You'll get that house back all right. And the churches won't be used as stables from now on, either. Gonna be a new start around here.'

'No more. No uzeing churchez like ztablez. Ah, dzat iz good. Dzat iz good.'

'But where are we gonna find salt?' Rahikainen demanded, vexed over the issue.

Rokka looked at the old man out of the corner of his eye for a moment. Then he clapped him on the back with a laugh and said, 'You sure know how to play 'em, grampaw. You're one crafty fella, lyin' 'bout this, that and the other. Well, lissen, serves 'em right for pryin' 'bout every damn thing . . .'

'I thought the old geezer was taking us for pre-tty wild ride . . .'

Salo looked almost hurt as he said, 'Lies? Maybe that's what you think. But that's what life has been like back here. And now he'll have a chance to see a better life, in his old age . . .'

'Personally I don't see what business we have with these kinds of folks. Seems pre-tty pointless liberating them or taking them prisoner, if you ask me.'

Rokka walked over to the stove. There was a stool sitting beside it with a basket on top, covered in a sack. Rokka pulled off the sack and the old man started and stood up.

'Lissen here, grampaw! Looks like you was cursin' those fellas over nothin'! They left you a whole basket a bread! See? Here, take a look. Guess they must'ta forgotten'na tell you.'

The old man was trembling, but Rokka burst out in a reassuring tone, 'Don't you worry. We won't take 'em from you. But if I find that salt I'm takin' me a pinch.'

They found some up on the shelf – coarse, brown salt.

'In'nat case, I'm takin' my pinch. Lissen, grampaw, we'll give you some a our soup in exchange. You can have some cigarettes too. Give 'im some, fellas.'

The men pressed some cigarettes into the old man's trembling hands. Rokka watched Salo, laughing, 'Lissen, let 'im keep that scrap a bread you gave 'im earlier, too. He gave you a whole song and dance for it!'

Salo tried to save face by joining in the others' sniggering. Forcing a laugh, he said, 'Old man sure does know how to pull a fellow's leg. He's studied up all right.'

They left the old man in peace and set off to cook their soup.

A column drove down the main road and Sihvonen exclaimed excitedly, 'Must be new troops! Maybe we get some time off the line.'

New troops had been a perennial source of hope for some time now. If ever the men so much as glimpsed an unfamiliar squad, they eagerly inquired after its regiment number. The others took no interest, having been disappointed far too many times already, but Sihvonen headed over to the roadside and asked, 'What unit?'

'Weapons company transport.'

'Which weapons company?'

'First. Don't you know your own company's drivers?'

'Huh . . . oh, right. I didn't mean that . . .'

'Well then, what did you mean?'

'Aw, go to hell!'

'You messin' with me?'

'Just go . . . go!'

Then Mielonen came from the command post. 'All rrrighty, boys, we're heading out on the offensive.'

No one said a single word. Dejected heads hung low. The soup was half-cooked. They tied the bucket to the end of a pole and carried it over their shoulders. Maybe there would be enough time to let it cook through on the next break.

# Chapter Eight

## I

'That's how far it is to Petroskoi.' A dirty, black-stained finger traced the road leading to the city on a map of Eastern Karelia purchased back at the canteen.

'Matrusa's around here. Then there's Polovina, then Vilka.'

'And Pos Rudan, heehee! And the Village of the Decisive Third Kolkhoz, heehee! And Red Plowmensville.' Vanhala was endlessly amused by the Eastern Karelian place names, which sounded strange to his ears. The new communist names were particularly hilarious, and made him laugh almost as much as the slogans in their own Information Bureau pamphlets.

'Once we make it to Petroskoi, I'm not moving a goddamn muscle for two weeks,' Rahikainen declared.

'War ain't gonna stop there,' Rokka said. 'You think that town's so important Russia's gonna collapse soon as we take it? You better not. There's a whole lotta globe back there behind Petroskoi.'

'Well, let there be whatever. I'm not going.'

'No, no. No way.'

'No.'

'No.'

'No.'

'No.'

'Well, no. Not further than that.'

*Pow, pow, pow, pow . . . oooo . . . oooooo . . .*

'Advaaance . . .'

*Pa, pa, pa, pa, pa, pa, pa, pa, pa, pa, pa, pa . . .*

'Medii-iiics . . .'

*Pa, pa, pa, pa, pa, pa, pa, pa, pa . . .*

Their clothes were full of holes, as were their shoes. The creases in their faces had deepened into furrows, and their sprouting, adolescent beards made their filthy skin look even darker. Somehow or other they had been hardened against everything now. Grumbling and griping were rare. Solemnly, silently, they listened as each new assignment was explained, their bodies still trembling with exhaustion from the last one. Somewhere out in front of them lay Petroskoi. That was their final destination. All questions would be resolved as soon as they reached it. And even if they weren't, they still weren't going beyond that point. They rallied the last of their energy on the basis of this general understanding. Petroskoi, Petroskoi, the golden city, toward which they strove, through pain and suffering, like pilgrims.

They considered it almost like the right of their regiment to remain in the city once it had been captured. All the regiments advancing toward it probably nurtured the same thought, for the same reasons: 'We've been in all of the worst fighting, and besides, our strength's run out.'

The opposition grew ever fiercer the nearer they drew to the city. The more exhausted they became, the more demanding the tasks that confronted them, and they were continually obliged to push the limits of their physical capacities. But it was becoming apparent that the bow had been stretched to the breaking point. Even the weakest counter-attacks could set them back now. Their frayed nerves couldn't withstand situations they would have dismissed as skirmishes before.

When they were about four miles from the city, the Third Company's Commander, Lieutenant Autio, fell, shot by eleven bullets. Which is to say, that is how many bullets managed to strike him upright, before he collapsed to the ground. It was one of the most beautiful deaths they had witnessed. The men had begun to falter in an attempt to repel a counter-attack. Some had started disappearing from the line when, in an effort to restore their courage, Autio rose to his feet and yelled, 'Remember who you are! Not one step backwards!'

His body literally rippled as a hail of light-machine-gun fire punched straight through it. Kariluoto took over command. Autio's death brought Kaarna's demise flooding back to him, and for a moment he was thrown back into his old, rather theatrical state of mind. The scene felt like a repetition of the first, and the likeness compelled Kariluoto to prove to himself that some difference in him set the two scenes apart. The alder branches rustled in his ears, but he rose and yelled, 'The Third Company is now under my command and is to remain in position!' Who would dare abandon his post after that?

One of the soldiers nearby did. He was just starting to crawl backwards when Kariluoto's shouting prompted the enemy to increase fire in their direction.

'Where are you going?'

The man didn't answer, but cast his eyes furtively to the ground, and Kariluoto's high-minded spirit evaporated. He started cursing at the man and humiliated him into returning to his post, but the incident left Kariluoto with a bitter taste in his mouth. No, there was absolutely no room out here for a man's solemn, spiritual side. This was a place of base, bare-faced brutality. Even Kariluoto had sometimes wondered what endowed him with the moral right to drive other men to their deaths. To deride and humiliate them, to strip them of all honor and manhood if they failed to obey his command.

But these were thoughts of a moment, thoughts he himself dismissed as the product of over-exhaustion. The nearness of Petroskoi filled him with excitement in anticipation of its conquest.

On the last evening of September, they reached the outskirts of the city.

They lay out in the dusky twilight before the fortifications at Suollusmäki, contemplating the enemy dens and positions reinforced with barbed-wire fencing.

'Snuffin' out a hell of a lot of lives over there.'

'Well, not ours, far as I know,' Koskela said. 'We won't be attacking over there. Some other units are coming in to attack and we're turning off to the north.'

'Fuck. Of course. Of course they're not letting us into the city.'

The conversation went no further. It was too bitter a discussion to continue. They watched solemnly as the sky lit up behind them and listened to the howling shells soaring overhead.

'How in the world are the people going to pay for all that damage?' Lahtinen asked.

'I don't know. But that looks like a pre-tty shitty place to be,' Hietanen said.

'Damn assholes, shooting everything to bits. There won't be anything left!' Rahikainen grumbled.

'Maybe we ain't headin' in there at all,' Rokka said.

'Awful lot of force in those shells,' said Määttä.

'Offensive Operation Underway! Heeheehee. The deafening voice of Finland's artillery makes itself heard! Heehee,' Vanhala giggled. He sat down on a tree stump and nibbled on a piece of bread he'd scrounged from a dead enemy soldier. He'd scraped off the bloody part.

## II

The first morning of October was clear and beautiful. The sky was a cloudless, transparent blue. If you looked upwards, so you couldn't see the autumn landscape, you might have thought it was the middle of summer.

The men advanced through the thicket, following the power lines. They weren't directed northward after all, but received orders to cut off the roads leading north from the city. A rocky, forested ridge in front of them still blocked the city from view, but everything around them signaled its nearness. Small footpaths crisscrossed through the thicket, and the whole landscape had an 'inhabited' feel to it, between the wood boards, paper scraps and other bits of garbage people tend to leave behind.

The first to glimpse over the ridge was a fellow named Viirilä, a beast of a man, with a large head and quite a mouth on him. This boorish creature was the eternal thorn in the officers' sides and he had regularly spent time in confinement during peacetime. But since they'd been at war, Viirilä had demonstrated a bravery verging on lunacy – often, as now, voluntarily walking out in front as a scout. Were it not for this intrepid fearlessness, the man would hardly have been forgiven for the obscene parody he made of the whole blessed war.

He stopped as he reached the top of the ridge. 'Hey, Finnskis! Petrozavodski gleams in the dawning light of the homeland.'

'Really?'

'Yeah, and there's smoke coming from it. Looting little Finnskis are already having a field day down there.'

They climbed hurriedly up the ridge. An airstrip opened up in front of them, and behind it rose the clustered buildings of Petroskoi. The wide, open surface of Lake Onega stretched off into the blue-gray horizon. Columns of smoke rose from the city and the odd shot still rang out here and there.

'There she is.'

'So that's the shantytown we've been killing ourselves over.'

The city's gray, ramshackle appearance came as something of a shock. There were a few white, stone buildings mixed in with the collection of shacks, but that was it. That was the whole city – what a disappointment! The landscape itself was beautiful, though. The smoke-tinged air shimmered blue above the glinting lake, and further off in the steel-blue haze you could just make out some landmasses jutting out into Lake Onega.

'Haa . . . alt!'

The company came to a halt and sat on the ground to admire the view. Undeniably, they were overcome with a sense of fulfillment. There she was: the city for which they had persevered through all those obstacles and misery. Now they had reached their destination, and here their war would end. For some reason, they believed such a thing was possible.

Rahikainen was impatient. 'What are we standin' round here for? The other units are gonna snatch up all the good stuff before we get there!'

Rokka leaned on his gun and said, 'I don't give a damn 'bout all'at. Oh, but if that town were Käksalmi!'

'Hear hear,' Susling replied wistfully, though it was more home-town pride than genuine yearning that drove him to say it.

Koskela didn't say anything. He sat on a rock with his face to the sun. Had he said something, it would have been, 'Sun feels awfully good.'

Hietanen was on his knees. He was silent for a long time at first, but then he launched into an extravagant address. 'Hello, Petroskoi! You object of our most fervent hopes! If only all the boys were here to see you. All the guys who kicked the bucket trying to make it out here. Here we are, even though they tried to hold us back at every turn. Boys, this is a historic moment. One day they're gonna write war songs about this. One day the kids'll be singing about the day we came crawling on our hands and knees to Petroskoi. Mm-hmm. It's a kind of thing that doesn't happen every day. There lies Finland's new-est city . . . I bet they've got saunas over there too. Say, I itch like hell. I get a good four or five lice every time I take a swat under my arm.'

'Are you complaining about your lice?' Rahikainen scoffed. 'I've had one on a leash round my belly button for a couple of weeks now. Name's Oscar. No lie, he's about a quarter-inch long, with a Liberty Cross on his back. But what are they having us hang around here for? I sure hope they aren't plannin' on sendin' us out to Suoju. I heard the reserve units refused to go any further. Which makes us the ones they're gonna shove out into the next mess.'

'I'm not going up to Suoju.' Määttä was sitting on a boulder with his arms wrapped around his knees, staring thoughtfully out over the city.

'Yeah, and if they send you?' Sihvonen asked.

'Won't send me alive.'

'Lissen, Koskela, you hear what these fools are sayin'? It's mutiny they're talkin' 'bout! Say, what the hell you got goin' on over there?'

Koskela was lying belly-down on a rock, using a twig to bait ants into attacking one another. Two ants hurled themselves into battle just as Rokka was speaking, so Koskela just said, 'Not now!' He was smiling – that curious, private smile of his, evident only in and around his eyes.

Kariluoto walked over. He had taken off his cap and the wind was ruffling his hair. He walked with his head held high, cutting a stiff, noble profile. He felt unwittingly like the blond, conquering knight of the West, standing atop his hill and gazing out over the conquered city. Even his face had taken on a look of cast steel, though Kariluoto wasn't aware of it. One of the greatest moments of his life had just taken place. A company commander of the Finnish infantry, he had watched as the blue crosses of the Finnish flag rose up onto the flagpoles of the tallest buildings of Petroskoi. Whatever the journey out had cost, for that moment it was forgotten. There he stood, son of the independent Finland, the young crusader, with a strange lump caught in his throat. He was moved.

Then he cleared his throat, pulled up his holster so his belt wouldn't sag, took a deep breath, and said, 'Well, men. There she is. The Jaeger Brigade and troops from the First Division have manned the city from the south and southwest. As it went, we were not called upon to carry out that mission. But let whoever should march in first, march – the fact remains that we were the ones who opened the road. And if history tells it otherwise, then history lies. There are still a few stragglers destroying what they can down there, but that will all be over soon. We are to remain here and make sure no one is permitted to escape. So, take a breather, but keep your eyes peeled.'

'Are we going to get some time off the line?'

'I don't know, but let's hope so. All right, men. Our company was the first to see the city. I mean, the first of the troops advancing from this direction.'

'Yeah, and Viirilä saw it first!'

'Me first, mpaahaahaahaa . . . mpaahahahaha! I saw it first!'

Kariluoto managed a weak smile. While he had to recognize that Viirilä was the bravest man in the company, he still felt a kind of aversion toward him. It felt blasphemous, somehow, to think of this large-headed ape at a moment like this. Even just the man's outward appearance was repulsive. The hunched back, bowed legs and that massive head. His clothes were always half falling off. And as for his pack, the man didn't even have one. He just let his filthy mess kit dangle from the belt loop of his jacket. His pockets bulged with various belongings, and there was a spoon poking out from the bottom of his trouser-leg. Sometimes Kariluoto seriously wondered if the man was insane. Grunting and laughing and muttering things that rarely contained anything that made sense – just as he was doing now. Blurting things out and then bursting into grunts of laughter, shaking his head. 'Mpaahaahaahaahaa! Private Viirilä . . . mpaahaahaahaahaa! Guard of the Homeland mpaahaahaahaahaa . . .'

Kariluoto walked off to the side in embarrassment. It was too difficult trying to find anything in this man that would be appropriate to the moment Kariluoto had just experienced.

Time passed. The shooting in the city had ceased, and they could discern movement within it.

'Snatched right out from under our noses. Won't be anything left over there,' Rahikainen lamented, gazing longingly out over the airstrip.

## III

At first it looked as though they weren't going to enter the city at all. But at dusk they received an urgent order to march in and take up positions as an occupying battalion. Apparently, somebody had found a massive keg of liquor – which may have been left there intentionally – and the previous occupying battalion was now riproaring drunk and looting the city.

They advanced down the 'May First Road', at some point coming across a large tractor stuck in the mud. Random, drunken shots rang out all along the streets, whistling past their ears and frequently forcing them to take cover. The descendants of the Hakkapeliittas, Finland's fabled war heroes, were celebrating their victory, three centuries later.

On turning one corner, they found themselves facing a party of four: a captain and three privates. Two of the privates were dragging the Captain by the armpits, his body having gone entirely limp, and the third was walking out in front playing a mandolin. The Captain's legs trailed along the ground and his head hung down over his chest, though he would occasionally raise it up to bellow out some garbled exclamation.

'Damn it, why don't you try to walk by yourself for a while,' one of the guys said to the Captain he was dragging. 'We drank just as much as you did, but you're like a wet dishrag.'

'Hey Hessu, play . . .' the Captain blurted out. 'Play *With swords we draw the dividing line . . . From Ladoga straight to the White Sea! . . . Not we to be shaken, though fate should present . . . dadada deeda dee dee da da!*'

'Here, you try walking a bit . . .'

'Walky walk walk. *Deedeedadadadadadeedeeda . . .*'

The Captain swung his head and bellowed, '*Not we to be shaken, though fate should present . . . Roads arduous, we will prevail . . . Not one tribe of Finland from us shall be rent . . . Our bonds are too great to assail!* . . . Well, looky there, what unit's that?'

The Captain noticed the approaching battalion and started bellowing, 'Welcome to Camp Finland! Howdy do . . . what units are you? Present yourselves! I am Captain Usko Antero Lautsalo . . . but you can call me the Wrath of God. Terror of the Russkis, Number One . . . seeing as the Wrath rolled right over them . . . Hessu, play so these guys can hear the great Captain Lautsalo's approach . . .'

Lammio ordered the Captain's entourage to get him out of sight, but received only brazen responses of, 'Go to hell! We're in the Captain's command and no lil' loo-tenint's gonna tell us what to do.'

It was clear that the men had decided to take advantage of their drunken fraternity with the Captain, thus rendering Lammio powerless, as he couldn't actually arrest a superior officer. It was a bitter pill to swallow. They were like the servants who usurp their master's power in his moment of weakness. 'Listen Usko . . . Hey, Usko . . .'

The Captain noticed Lammio. He tried to stand up on his own legs and put on an absurdly comical sternness. His head swerved indecisively from one shoulder to the other, and the energy he was expending to keep himself imposingly upright was fast petering out.

'Lieutenant . . . I ask you . . . I am Captain Usko Antero Lautsalo . . . and I am asking you, I, who earned the name the Wrath of God in the Winter War, I am asking you, what right do you have to order my men around . . .' Then the Captain shook his head, hiccuped, and forgot both Lammio and whatever it was he had been talking about, bellowing, *'Maaa-ay the na-aation of Finland forever be faith—*hick! . . . hick! . . . *faithful and valiant . . .'*

'I consider it within my rights to alert your men to the inappropriateness of their behavior,' Lammio said.

'Hick! . . . hick! . . . I do the commanding . . . hick! . . . and I command you to advance, my brave boys. We've still got half a bucket of booze . . . don't we?' The Captain stared at his men searchingly for a moment, awaiting their assurance, and when they offered it, he continued, 'Hessu, play . . . Everyone should hear the arrival of the great Usko Antero Lautsalo, Captain of the Army of the Republic of Finland . . . hick! . . . Advance. We've taken Petroskoi. Made the dreams of centuries come true . . . hick! . . . Play "Hessu" . . . Hee . . . hee . . . advance . . . *Lit with flaaaaames of desire, we are burning with rage. He who thiiinks he can last, let him stand in our way . . . Once a Northern man has set out to wage . . . War, be afraid!* Hick! . . .'

No sooner had the drinking party disappeared around the corner than the bellowing vocals started up again, accompanied by strains of the mandolin . . .

Then they came upon two privates.

'The oldest guys in the group . . . but I mean, they've had us spearheading . . . out in Vieljärvi, fuck . . . He chickened out, the Sarge, I mean, but I said gimme that goddamn submachine gun . . . left eighteen of 'em lyin' there . . .'

Then they saw their first civilian resident. It was a woman, dragging her mattress God knows where, looking harried and frightened. She was an old woman, wearing all thirty of her handkerchiefs on her head, boots on her feet and a quilted overcoat tied with a woolen sash. The woman frantically quickened her step as some drunk who had been walking toward her from the opposite direction started walking beside her, slurring strangely, *'Maatuska . . . maatuska . . .*

Russki mama, babydoll. *Kuksitnaataa . . . Finski kuksitnaataa . . . Liepuska . . . finski* bread for you *. . . yepatnaataa* me need fuck you *. . . yeputtaa yeputtaa . . .*'

The frightened woman sped up, but the man persisted by her side, repeating his words over and over. He took the woman by her wrist and patted her bottom, '*Russki Maatuska . . .* Good Bessie *. . . yeputtaa . . .*'

The woman slipped inside some building, leaving the baffled forest warrior to stand in the street and recover from his disappointment. He was a large man and big-boned. A reddish beard covered his face. His shirt glistened with grime and half of its buttons were open, the other half being absent entirely. A large triangular swath of fabric was torn out of the knee of his cargo trousers. He'd rolled his trouser-legs up twice and his wool socks peeked out from underneath.

The man shoved his powerful fists into his pockets and started to stagger away, bellowing, 'Onward! Marshal Mannerheim cries . . . aim between the Russki's eyes . . .'

Kariluoto had already taken a few steps toward the man when the latter had taken hold the woman, but he abandoned the effort once he saw her escape into the building. He felt ashamed, and angry. These people . . . these people . . . where did these people come from?

But the sight of the woman had brought Sirkka to mind. This woman was already on the older side, and looked a little Santa Claus-esque with all those clothes wrapped around her, but the sight of her had made Kariluoto's thoughts drift to women nonetheless, and thus, quite naturally, to Sirkka. So exquisite was his relationship with the girl that he could think of nothing ugly in connection with it. In his mind's eye, he saw only that lovely, slender face, those slim shoulders and bosom, which he had occasionally brushed up against, by accident. His whole body shuddered as a sharp longing flooded through him. When, oh when would they grant leave?

What a marvelous thought. Home – a conqueror of Petroskoi. He knew he would be promoted soon. Lieutenant Kariluoto. A youth of twenty who had taken over command when the Company

Commander fell and succeeded in putting down the enemy attack. Yes, this was Petroskoi. Maybe they already knew, back home.

Kariluoto looked back. The company was marching double-file behind him. 'Finns March into Petroskoi.' How many times had he heard his father and his friends talking about Eastern Karelia, even when he was a child? Of these kindred people, sighing beneath the yoke of foreign rule, whose liberation was the duty of the Finnish nation – a duty that should never leave their thoughts. They ought to think about it at mealtimes, at work, ponder it while preparing for bed; and during the night, visions of it ought to fill their dreams. And now it was here.

They were liberating Karelia.

A rowdy group of men carrying boxes and bundles on their backs came around the street corner. Kariluoto was so absorbed in his thoughts, however, that he didn't pay any attention to them. His battalion hadn't yet taken over the guarding of the city, anyway, so it wasn't their responsibility to arrest drunks just yet.

Shots and yells rang out. Bonfires were still ablaze over in Ukkossalmi, lighting up the autumn sky with bloody curls of light.

Petroskoi descended into the darkness of her first night as a Finnish city.

'*Laadaadaa dee daadaallalalaallaa . . . daa deedeedaadeedeedaadada . . .* and I'm saying to the doctor . . . *you* take a piss in those bottles, mister . . .'

The keg had been destroyed, but the men had managed to get the liquor into buckets, which they were now lugging toward their lodgings.

## IV

Life was good as an occupation unit. A fellow could explore the city at will and amass all kinds of fascinating experiences – such as rounding up all the city's madmen after some drunken soldier released them all from the mental hospital, for example. If they were liberating the city, he protested, they were supposed to free everybody behind bars! That was his story, and what could you do? The explanation was perfectly logical. Walking the streets, they were amazed to encounter young Russian men wearing civilian overcoats over their army uniforms: fellows who had abandoned their units and taken it upon themselves to resume life as civilians. The Finns couldn't really hold it against them – seeing as they would happily have done the same.

The men had been explicitly ordered to protect the houses against theft, but what difference did it make who owned each old vinyl record, Russian string instrument, button and knick-knack these thieves rounded up? There wasn't anything decent to be found in the whole town. They had to protect the residents, but once the keg of liquor had been destroyed and almost all the other units had left the city, life was so quiet that even that wasn't much of a burden. They tried to make friends with the local residents, who took a little while to get over their initial shyness, but then began interacting with them quite freely.

One or two of the men had already found himself a girl – Rahikainen first, obviously. His urban existence was like a chapter unto itself. It was as if everything in that conquered city had been made expressly for him – scraps, hungry residents, women, labyrinths, massive army depots. He played the businessman to a T. Not so much because it would get him anything in particular as because it was just his mode of operation. He didn't know what to do with himself unless he had some scheme or other in the works. And here, where greater opportunities presented themselves to the enterprising entrepreneur, well – he pounced. His principal operation consisted of procuring food for the hungry inhabitants, generally against payment in the form of young women's services. He scrounged up some icons for some art-connoisseur military official, even if he did think the man was nutty to give him money for those mildewy pictures. The older and less entrepreneurial privates could safely turn to him with their needs regarding women, as he already knew all the ones willing to sell themselves for bread. He sold the mother of his own seventeen-year-old ladyfriend to some guy from the veterinarian unit in exchange for two packs of cigarettes.

They enjoyed life. They had no duties to perform, save the occasional round on guard duty. And the fact that they were cleaning out a Russian barracks for their housing indicated that this state of bliss was likely to continue.

The city was no longer Petrozavodsk, nor even Petroskoi – it was now Fort Onega, Finland. Lenin's statue had been replaced by a Finnish field cannon, and their ownership was established throughout the town in every possible way.

Rokka, Hietanen and Vanhala were walking the streets shoulder to shoulder, routinely failing to salute the officers they happened across. All sorts of occupying units had turned up in the city, and admittedly their general comportment was such that our friends would have happily been thrown in the brig before demonstrating their respect toward such individuals. They had passed by several officers without incident when a certain captain approached them from the opposite direction, having spotted them from quite a way off. When the trio pretended not to notice him, he stopped and said, 'What's this? Why don't you salute?'

The Captain was wearing a peaked cap, shiny boots and spurs. He'd pulled the brim of his cap down slightly over his eyes, so its edge cut a 'menacing military line' across the upper half of his face. His self-important air seemed to center around his pursed lips, which emanated a kind of pinched, forced militarism.

The man's formality and gruff, military air exacerbated the men's already hostile attitude. At first they said nothing, so the Captain repeated, with increasing irritation, 'Answer me! For what reason do you fail to salute your superior?'

Rokka started to smile. It was that same subtle, shifty smile that signaled he was feeling mischievous. And indeed, it made the Captain fly into a rage, particularly when Rokka replied, 'We didn't notice ya.'

'What are you grinning at? Notice! In that case, it's a matter of even greater concern! An NCO who can't see a superior officer in the same street! How are you going to see the enemy out on the terrain?'

Rokka's face fell. He tilted his head to the side and, holding up his finger in a performance of utmost seriousness, began, 'Now you lissen here, Cap'n. We got this situation here that rides on colors. Now me, I don't see shades a gray so well. But brown, well, brown's no problem, so I git on just fine with the enemy. But our own officers's all dressed in gray, so you see, I don't always notice 'em. That'ssa root of it all. Now shiny things I do see, so I spotted those spurs a yours right off – don't you worry 'bout that. I sure done noticed how spankin' sparklin' you are, Cap'n, yesssiree.'

'What's your unit? What is your unit? Name! Tell me your name!' The Captain was suffocating with such fury that he couldn't properly formulate the command he was trying to issue, and instead just kept repeating, 'Unit! Unit!'

'Kuopio Kicksled Company! Heeheehee!' Vanhala wasn't typically one to be so bold, but Rokka's example had inspired him to slacken the reins a bit and anyway the opportunity was just too tempting to resist.

'I'm placing all three of you under arrest. To the main guard station. March!'

'We're gonna make a run for it, fellas. Vanhala . . . gimme the records.'

Vanhala was carrying a gramophone and a packet of records, so Rokka snatched the latter to lighten his load. Hietanen and Vanhala realized that Rokka wasn't joking, and that they were about to make a break for it. A few yards up ahead, a tumble-down alleyway turned off the street, as if made to order. They disappeared down it, leaving the Captain in the street screaming, 'Stop them! Stop them! Haaaa . . . alt!'

The trio dashed down the block, crossed the next street, turned a couple of corners, and figured they were safe. Breathless and panting, Rokka declared, 'Shame to run out on a fella like that, but I sure ain't takin' an arrest for sumpin' as stupid as'sat. Would'a grown into such a stink, we'd a been two weeks tryin'na git out of it.'

They stole backward glances now and again as they continued on, but there was no sign of anybody on their tail.

The Captain himself hadn't attempted to chase them, and the privates walking in the streets made themselves scarce on hearing his shout. There was no question that they sided with the trio and were not about to turn them in, even if they feigned trying for the sake of appearances.

Vanhala giggled with delight. It was the first time he'd pulled one over on an officer. 'Diversion operation successful! Heeheehee!'

'But what are we gonna do about this fellow?' Hietanen gestured toward the Lieutenant Colonel heading toward them, sitting astride his thoroughbred horse and looking around him, evidently enjoying the splendor of his own magnificence.

'This round, we pass,' Rokka said, slipping into the jargon of the card-player as he ducked through an archway. Hietanen and Vanhala followed and together the three of them watched as the Lieutenant Colonel rode by.

Continuing on their way, they found themselves walking behind two army officials and an army chaplain who were chatting away animatedly as they walked in front of them. '. . . but at first glance it would appear that the Vepsians have been best at retaining their national character . . .'

'The most reasonable thing to do would be to let the Orthodox faith die. Since Bolshevism has worn it down so much already. All efforts at resuscitating religious life should be carried out along Lutheran lines. From now on, all children's baptisms should be left to the evangelical faith. Of course, it's not a question of religious persecution, just managing things in a natural way . . .'

'You have to distinguish between different kinds of Russians. The whole resettlement issue will probably be resolved very quickly once the Germans take control of all of European Russia.'

The army chaplain and the military officials turned down another street. There was some sort of Army Bureau in the building on the corner, and a private was standing in the courtyard holding a horse harnessed to a church buggy. A lieutenant and a beautiful Lotta emerged from the building, and the Lieutenant bowed to the Lotta in a rather exaggerated display of cordiality, saying, 'If your graciousness would deign to step in? I would like to request the honor of showing you Fort Onega, Finland, from the height of a church buggy.'

The Lotta laughed as she stepped into the buggy and said, 'You're hopeless . . . Oh, wouldn't I?' The driver clicked his heels to attention and handed the reins to the Lieutenant, then they set off on their drive, the buggy jerking about on its springs.

'Well, I'll be darned . . .' Rokka said, chuckling. He sniffed love in the air, and the whole thing gave him a hearty laugh.

Then they stopped and stared at a sight that quickened the metabolic functions of their whole bodies. A Finnish cleaning unit of young women was coming down the street toward them. They were a group of student volunteers who had come to clean the city. They moved as a group, and even attempted to march in step with one another, though without much success. They managed to get it just close enough so that you could tell what they were trying to do. The girls wore brown overalls, wooden shoes and garrison caps that didn't quite cover the 'wildly unruly' locks of hair peeking out around the edges. Their clear, girlish voices sang, '*Russkis won't stink up Finland for long . . .*'

The trio watched them wistfully, in so far as men of their nature can accommodate feelings of wistfulness. Even Rokka gazed keenly after the girls, though he was the father of three.

'Let's go see Veerukka, fellas. We got our ladies too,' Rokka said, and the others were happy to follow.

There was one place they went to meet girls. It was entirely innocent, though, as the girls there did not tolerate advances of any sort. There were three of them: one Russian and two Karelians. The men would come and play Vanhala's gramophone for the girls, who would in turn perform Russian dances for them, which they were more than happy to watch.

'But hey, wouldja let me go get some bread first? I've still got a few pieces. I wanna take 'em to Tanya and Alexei.'

There were two orphans living in the same building as the girls, whom Hietanen had taken under his wing like adopted children. The children would rush out to meet him whenever they saw him coming, and Hietanen was in the habit of bringing them whatever food he could get his hands on. Which was why he now wanted to go and get something to bring, so he wouldn't have to disappoint them. Rokka and Vanhala understood the whole thing very well and readily agreed.

When they got back to their lodgings, Hietanen realized that he actually had very little bread left, so he decided to go ask Mäkilä for the next day's rations in advance. A spat between Rahikainen and Mäkilä was underway in the storeroom when he got there, as Mäkilä had accused Rahikainen of snitching sugar from his supply.

'Aw, please, Pops. I couldn't care less about your storeroom. I got bigger bags to dip into round here if I want.'

'Chuh . . . well, that's no secret.'

'Hey, listen,' Hietanen broke in. 'Gimme my rations for tomorrow, wouldja? I need 'em.'

'It is not distribution time right now. And besides, there's too much bread floating around this city.'

'Look, I'm just asking for my own rations.'

Mäkilä forked them over, mumbling about bread and women so pointedly that Rahikainen thought it a splendid opportunity to take matters into his own hands. ''Fit's makin' ya jealous, Pops, I can help you out. I've got just the girl. Only speaks Russian, but you don't need much language for that. And knockers like you've never seen.'

Mäkilä didn't respond. He just cleared his throat and retreated into his storage cupboard looking mortally offended. But Rahikainen hurried after Hietanen, asking 'What kind ya got?'

Hietanen smiled mysteriously and whispered, 'By God, there's not another girl like her! Used to be some kind of big cheese in these parts. Part of the Young Communists' League, or something like that.'

'Naw . . . I got one just like that too. But it's true, what I was telling Mäkilä. If you're ever in need, or you know somebody who is,

I'm happy to take care of it. Not askin' much in return, either. She's a little roly-poly maybe, but whew! those knockers. Like two little piggies with their backsides in the air.'

'Holy . . . well, look, I'm good. See ya!' Hietanen shot off and Rahikainen started dreaming up other schemes.

As Rokka, Vanhala and Hietanen were approaching the girls' building, Tanya and Alexei ran out to meet them, shouting, 'Heroo!! Heroo!!'

That was their convoluted rendition of Hietanen's first name, 'Urho', and it never failed to crack him up. Alexei was eight and Tanya was six. Their father had been killed right at the start of the war, making them war orphans. They never asked for anything, they just watched Hietanen closely, waiting for him to reach into his bread bag. Hietanen would purposely dawdle awhile, keeping the children dangling in suspense. Not until they reached the courtyard did he pull out the bread and give it to them. They both thanked him in Finnish, though neither of them actually understood a word of the language. They clasped the bread to their chests, as their mother had instructed them to bring home anything anybody gave them. Hietanen glanced at them and yelled, 'Alexei! Down with the Russkis!'

'Down viz da Russkii!' Alexei shouted, laughing, without a clue what he was saying.

There was a third child in the courtyard as well. He was a boy of maybe six or so, wearing a grown man's shirt and trousers, the legs of which had been rolled up so they wouldn't drag on the ground. On his head he had one of those pointed, so-called 'Budenovka' caps of the Red Army. The boy watched the men closely and silently retreated further away the closer they came.

'Alexei and Tanya!' Hietanen called to the children, who were on their way up the stairs. They stopped and Hietanen gestured them to come back. 'Give him some of the bread. I'll be sure to bring more next time.'

The children didn't really understand what he was saying, but they gathered he was talking about the boy and said, 'Grisha'.

'C'mere, Chris-ka!' Hietanen called, but the boy just looked at him, hesitating. Only when Hietanen pulled out the bread did the boy cautiously start toward him. As soon as Hietanen placed the piece of bread in his hand, the boy spun around and bolted off as if he were running for dear life. Hietanen gave a hearty laugh. 'Wouldja look at that little one go!'

Then they headed toward the girls' quarters. Hietanen had happened upon them right away that first morning they were in the city. He had stepped in to check the building, his gun poised under his arm, and had suddenly gone red with embarrassment on realizing that he was staring into a pair of beautiful eyes belonging to a girl staring down the barrel of his gun.

The girl was Vera, an Eastern Karelian schoolteacher. After the city had fallen, she'd taken in two of her friends to live with her. Right from the start Hietanen felt some sort of bashful subservience in Vera's company. He didn't dare visit her alone, but always brought Rokka and Vanhala along for moral support. And no wonder. Vera was the kind of girl who would have made just about any man a bit uncertain of himself. First of all, she was exceptionally beautiful, and on top of that she had a calm, proud way about her. Her sharp features were expressive, but strong and stately at the same time. She looked upon the occupiers kindly, but from a decidedly elevated vantage point – perhaps because she was a committed communist, but above all because she was aware of her spiritual superiority over the three of them. But she frequently chatted animatedly with them, and she loved to dance. Little by little, Hietanen had become her favorite, as well as that of her housemates. They knew Hietanen brought bread for the children in the building, and they demonstrated their appreciation for this in their own spontaneous way.

The girls were making tea. Vanhala had a few dirty sugar cubes that had been rolling around in his pockets for quite some time, which he now fished out and offered to the girls. The humble offering was accepted – seeing as when the Russians pulled out, the girls had been left with next to nothing. It hadn't occurred to them to stock up on anything in advance, so they were out of just about everything within a day or two.

Vera was practically silent. She sat staring into a corner of the room, and Hietanen gazed at her profile, whose even regularity was so beautiful it downright frightened him. He had never seen girls like her before, save a passing glance as some fancy car sped by his milk route back home.

'What'ssa matter, Veerukka?' asked Rokka, who was not fond of reflective types. 'C'mon, why don't you start dancin'? That'll send your worries whirlin' away.'

'Be quiet! She misses her fiancé,' Hietanen said, blushing.

'Verotshka doesn't have a fiancé,' Nina, the other Karelian girl, said.

Vera smiled, but her face fell quickly and she said, 'Why did you come? Why couldn't you just leave us alone?'

'Now lissen, Vera, don't you start in on'nat,' said Rokka. 'You're the ones started the damn thing. Took m'farm! You think we've wrecked things here, you oughdda go see what kinda state Kannas is in! We wouldn't be here if you all'd just left us alone.'

'Ah, listen . . . who came . . . Hitler came . . . But he will be made to pay.' Vera spoke boldly, particularly once she realized that it didn't set off these men's tempers. She never fawned over them, nor did she soften any of her positions, or demonstrate the least deference toward them.

Hietanen was somehow ill at ease. It seemed rather awkward to oppose Vera, even if he knew that she was a communist, and thus the victim of propaganda. He tried to steer a middle road, granting that Hitler was an aggressor, but pointing out that in the Finnish situation, things had been different.

'Then why did you point your riffle at me?' Vera asked, smiling.

Vera's 'riffle' made them all laugh, because although she spoke near perfect Finnish, being a schoolteacher, she didn't quite know how to pronounce all the Finnish terms properly.

'How was I supposed to know who I was going to find?' Hietanen asked, continuing in all seriousness, 'I recognize that war is nothin' but trouble for both sides, no matter who started it. Brings a whole lot of misery on all kinds of people who never did anybody any harm. Like all the kids, for example.'

'And you bring 'em bread. Lissen here, Veerukka, you say we're all a bunch a troublemakers, but Hietanen here took out his own rations for tomorrow so he could bring 'em to Tanya and Alexei.'

Hietanen flushed red with pleasure at Rokka's praise in Vera's presence, but his insides turned upside down when Vera then rose and, without a word, kissed him on the cheek.

He tried to laugh, but couldn't quite manage it, and failing, directed his energies angrily toward Vanhala, who giggled as he gasped, 'Our boys are sharing their own rations with the children of the kindred nations, who have been suffering from undernourishment under Bolshevik rule . . .'

Hietanen hadn't managed to say anything before Vera flared up on his behalf. Vanhala practically froze in terror when those beautiful eyes flashed angrily at him, accompanied by a rapid fire of words uttered in a voice nearly trembling with rage. 'You don't give anything to children. You obviously eat everything yourself, or you wouldn't be such a great *sangia priha*.'

'A great *sankia priha*? What'ssat?' Rokka asked, laughing, and Vera made a rounded movement with her hands to indicate Vanhala's plumpness. With this, Hietanen finally regained his footing and burst out laughing loudest of all. Vanhala's own laugh was heartiest, however, as he repeated, giggling, as if practicing the pronunciation of his new name, 'Great *sankia priha* . . . heehee . . . Sankia Priha the Great!'

Hietanen boisterously started demanding music, and Vanhala began fiddling around with his gramophone, getting it ready to play.

'What'll we play? Should I put on Stalin's speech?' Vanhala had several large records of Stalin's speeches. He played them frequently, repeating some of the more clearly distinguishable Russian words over and over to himself.

'Hell, no. Play "Yokkantee"!' Rokka cried, campaigning for his favorite.

'Nah, let's have "Army Battalyon"!' said Hietanen, a fan of marches.

Vanhala did not reveal whose wish would be granted. Then, strains of 'Yokkantee' filled the air. It was a Russian-style rhythm that girls often danced to, and it was indeed with this hope in mind that Vanhala selected it just now. No sooner did the first notes reach his ears than Rokka's whole body came alive, moving in time with the music. 'Lissen, Vera,' he said, 'you dance alone. Those legs a yours move so goddamn fast.'

Vera hesitated at first, but then began. Through the slower, opening measures, it was as if she were focusing, concentrating her forces into the fast, feral movements that eventually accelerated into such a dizzying crescendo that the three of them could no longer follow what was going on at all.

For Rokka, this fiery finish was the most interesting of all, and he waited for it, exclaiming, 'Not like that, not like that. Like last time! Quick like that!'

When Vera's dance began to accelerate, Rokka clapped his hands and every part of him came to life, moving in time with the music.

'That's it, that's it! You see, fellas, see how this girl can dance? That's it, Veerukka! Holy Mother a God, that girl is fast.'

Vera danced. Perform she did not – rather, everything about her seemed to declare that she danced for herself alone. The music filled her entire body, which responded to its tiniest nuances, and it thrilled her, propelling her in some kind of ecstatic trance. When the dance ended, a restrained smile emerged on her face, as if proceeding from some internal satisfaction that the dance had given her.

The three crusaders sat dazed in astonishment. They didn't understand the beauty and precision of Vera's dance, which would have afforded her easy passage from this sitting room to the most demanding of public arenas. They were just amazed at how fast she was.

As they were leaving, Hietanen lingered by the door as Vera came to shut it. He reached out, playfully unclasping the Youth League pin from its resting place on her blouse, sitting upon her impressive breast. His little finger experienced the trembling pleasure of pressing slightly against it, and then, practically petrified, he said, trying to make his voice sound playful, 'Think I might take this, to remember you by?'

'Take it!'

Hietanen was immediately embarrassed at the awkwardness of his flirtation and turned to follow the others. Vera looked after him for a long time, her eyes full of compassion, but there was something in her gaze that made Hietanen sense that this could not continue. He could not quite attain Vera, and he understood that, vaguely and indistinctly. And besides, what could ever have come of it anyway?

He was feeling rather wistful and mixed up when he caught up with the others, though uppermost in his confused emotions was the tiny, minute joy of having touched Vera with his little finger. And it was this feeling that prompted him to blurt out, 'I have to say, the women here are something else . . .'

'And they kiss you on the cheek. You should've stayed! The tribes of Finland unite!'

Hietanen was so swept up in his own emotions that he didn't quite grasp Sankia Priha's joke. But it nonetheless prompted him to limit his praise of Vera to her dancing, in order to demonstrate to everybody that there was no silly sentimentality in his admiration of the girl.

'Man! It's crazy how a person can turn like that! Only time I ever danced, trying to turn those girls was like, I don't know – moving one of those heavyweight plows they make over in Fiskars.'

'Lissen here, Sankia Priha the Great!' Rokka said, laughing. 'We ain't takin' Hietanen there any more. He might git all heartsick on us and then he'd be no use at all.'

'Heehee! The children of Kaleva reunite . . . Heehee! No longer lost strands blowing in the wind . . . Heeheehee!'

Only now did Hietanen realize that they were mocking his most sacred emotions, and he flew into a rage, vehemently attempting to defend his masculinity by making it clear that his soul certainly didn't have anything like goodness or beauty in it. 'Now don't you go thinking I'm the one who's gonna start getting all gushy first here. I don't go in for that kind of thing at all . . . No way . . . I'm just a happy-go-lucky kind of guy. I don't give a shit, damn it!'

Then he fell silent, figuring that he had convinced the others he was guilty of nothing so shameful as taking pity on hungry children or falling for a girl in any way that exceeded commonplace flirting.

Near to their lodgings, they came upon a group of small boys asking for bread and cigarettes. They tossed over a few smokes, figuring the children would take them back to their fathers. The boys expressed their thanks by counting off down the line all the Finnish curse words they knew. They had obviously figured out how to earn cigarettes from the soldiers, and supposed that the same trick would work as payment too. One little fellow emerged from the scuffle without any cigarettes, and so chased after them quite a way, attempting to win them over by yelling at the top of his lungs, 'Sheeeet! Sheeet!'

Vanhala found this hilarious and tossed the kid a cigarette. As they neared their lodgings, they heard strains of an evening prayer service underway. Strains of the company's hymns echoed through the dark city: '... *miiiighty fo-o-ortress is our God ... A buuulwark never faa-a-ailing ...*'

They turned cautiously down a back road so as to avoid being seen.

That evening Hietanen sat gazing out of the window, singing off-key, '... *even in the fiercest fighting ...*'

## V

The next day there was a parade. They didn't have to do anything for it but maintain order in the city. A few men from their battalion had been selected to take part in the parade, but nobody from Koskela's platoon. They did receive medals and promotions, though. Koskela was promoted to the rank of lieutenant, Hietanen received the sergeant's stripe the Major had promised him, and Määttä was promoted to corporal. Just about every man was awarded a medal of some sort, and admittedly, the Second Class medals were starting to be rather like prizes for participation.

That evening they moved into the barracks. After a hell of a lot of work, they had finally managed to make it suitable for habitation. They were not pleased about the move, as they sensed that the old buildings had permitted a freer lifestyle in every way. Nor were their instincts incorrect. As soon as they were in the barracks, Sinkkonen, who had also been promoted in the recent sweep, to master sergeant, ordered the company to fall in by rank into four lines. It was as if the old army brat was suddenly possessed by the devil from the moment he set foot in a barracks. After having been put in his place upon his first presentation to the company, he had kept quiet, but now it was clear that he had decided to settle the score.

He strutted self-importantly in front of the company, clearing his throat, stretching out his neck, and ordering the men to count off.

'One . . . two . . . three . . . four . . .' The men counted off lethargically, as if expressing their opinion of the exercise by making their voices even more apathetic than usual. When the count-off was over, nobody called out any absences, though Sinkkonen could obviously see that neither the third nor fourth row was complete.

'How many absences? Are you men sleeping or what? Why didn't you call out the absences?'

'Who's had time to count 'em all?' a voice yelled from the back.

Sinkkonen ordered whoever was yelling to keep his mouth shut, but then somebody else shouted, 'We lost seven guys from our platoon. Twelve were wounded, but eight of 'em came back.'

'What, what . . . what kind of talk is this?' Sinkkonen was struggling against the pressure of the crowd. His self-assurance had abandoned him, and to mask its loss he began lashing out at the company. 'Clearly, there are certain men here who imagine the army is no longer able to maintain discipline. That is a serious mistake. Men in the back, report the number of absences from count-off.'

'All right, all right, two,' somebody said, and the Master Sergeant considered victory his. A moment ago he had been feeling very pleased to stand before the company, as he had been planning to give a speech about various issues relating to their move into the barracks. Speaking before ranks like these was one of his greatest pleasures – and now it had been spoiled. Nevertheless, he began. 'Now that the company is being housed here in the barracks, I would like to call your attention to a few matters regarding routine chores and responsibilities. Impeccable cleanliness and order are to be strictly maintained. Every article of the barracks duty regulations is to be observed. In light of the circumstances, we will permit one exception, which is that you are not required to salute NCOs upon their entry. Only the Company Master Sergeant need be saluted as usual. And then, esteemed NCOs . . .' (A few muffled sniggers emanated from the ranks, and even the NCOs laughed, with the exception of one or two men.) 'Quiet in the ranks! The NCOs will lodge separately in designated NCO quarters. You are to ensure that your quarters are kept thoroughly in order.'

Just then Rokka's booming voice interrupted Sinkkonen's speech. 'Well, shit, no. That don't work for me at all. Suslin'n I take our tea together and everything else together too. Either I bunk with him or he comes over in'na NCO section with me.'

Sinkkonen had not forgotten Rokka's spoon-wagging nor his lecture. His composure abandoned him and he nearly screamed, 'Silence! Keep your mouth shut over there. You will go where I order you. Is that clear?'

Rokka smiled. But there was a menacing note behind the customary, playful calmness of his voice as he replied, 'Now lissen, don't you start talkin' big with me. You know what happens when you start tryin'nat. You really think you can just slap those reins and make me jump for you like a new recruit?'

Without a word, Sinkkonen set off for the Company Command Post and returned with Lammio in tow. Lammio waited for the silence to intensify, and then said with frosty authority, 'Corporal Rokka.'

'What'ssa trouble, friend?' His voice rang out with such wholesome innocence that the whole company had to laugh. Lammio glared at the men and said pointedly to Rokka, 'You will stay in the NCO barracks just like the others. Is that clear?'

'We'll see 'bout that this evenin'. Now lissen, I don't needa git into too much of a tizzy 'bout this here, but you wouldn't happen'na know when we're gonna git some leave now, would you, Louie? Here I am a family man and I been out here months already. Would you back me up if I put in a request?'

Lammio was once again uncertain whether Rokka was being direct with him or making fun of him. In any case, he was offended by the man's disrespectful tone and said, 'Corporal Rokka. As far as I am aware we have made no agreement to dispense with the customary formalities of address between an NCO and his commanding officer.'

'Nope, we ain't, but there ain't no time like the present. Antero's m'name. You can use it any time you like. I'll just call you Louie 'stead a Lieutenant, since you're a bit younger'n me, n'all.'

A low snickering rustled through the company. For the first time in his career, Lammio was at a loss. Threats of the court martial flashed through his head, but as pathetic as his instincts were, even he could tell that this time there was nothing more he could do. Rokka's arrogance was so unshakeable that Lammio had taken it to be the product of pure simple-mindedness. But when he realized that Rokka understood precisely what he was doing, Lammio also gathered that the man wasn't going to back down, even when faced with the strongest of military punishments: the death penalty. The issue was further complicated by the fact that the man in question was one of their best soldiers – and where would that leave them? Lammio still thought Rokka was trying to get away with bravado on account of his bravery, failing to grasp that these were two sides of the same coin.

Now Lammio was just looking for the best way out. He ordered the men to attention and rattled off, 'I sentence Corporal Rokka to four days' labor without relief as punishment for disrespecting a superior officer. The punishment is to be carried out in the form of four extra days of guard duty. At ease.'

Lammio rushed off, for fear that Rokka would do something to exacerbate the situation further.

Sinkkonen ordered the company to disperse and endeavored,

unsuccessfully, to slip out of Rokka's sight. Rokka grabbed hold of his shoulder strap and held it so tightly that the Master Sergeant was forced to halt. Rokka laughed, but it was precisely his laugh that Sinkkonen feared, for behind it lurked the menace of utter indifference. Sinkkonen sensed that, once the customary fear of disciplinary measures ceased to protect him, nothing, in fact, did.

'Hear that, Master Sarge? I'm punished. Four days without relief. I'll be damned if we didn't do months and months without relief to git us out here in'na first place. You wanna tell me what I was bein' punished for in'na Winner War when they kept me out in Taipale for three months without relief? You tell me that, Master Sarge!'

Sinkkonen stiffly muttered something about the necessity of discipline and Rokka shoved him away in contempt, laughing as he said, 'Oh, we got discipline like you never dreamed of, Master Sarge. But hey, lissen here, you go your way and I go mine. We don't git on so well the two of us, see?'

Sinkkonen hurried away, relieved to have got off so lightly. Rokka didn't move into the NCO lodgings or perform any extra guard duty, and no one attempted to make him. The issue hadn't actually been so important to him as all that, but they had certainly managed to make it important, so obviously he couldn't back down. And so the Finnish soldier emerged victorious from one more struggle for independence.

The incident provoked restlessness within the company. There was a great deal of discussion about it that night, and then, to top it off, a rumor began circulating that they were going to be sent to the front. The men were feeling irritable, as the return to formal barracks living and boot camp-style discipline felt like an insult, particularly in light of their achievements that summer.

Lahtinen thought his moment had come, and started spouting off again about how everything would turn out in the end. 'I mean, Timoshenko's giving it to the SS over there in Rostov-on-Don, that's all I'm sayin'. And you know how it goes: when the falls freeze, the ducks are fucked.'

'I dunno,' said Salo, who had also acquired a medal in the recent handout and so was in a mood to salute even the Master Sergeant. 'As soon as summer comes back round, they'll start drivin' in those wedges with the tanks again.'

At three o'clock in the morning, the company was called to alert. The men awoke to see the officers moving about in full uniform, and immediately suspected what was afoot.

'The company is preparing for departure. Vehicles arrive in one hour.'

Then came the cursing, followed by murmurs and whispers. 'We're not leaving.'

Lammio heard their murmuring, but pretended not take the least note of it. He ordered the men to hurry up. Some of them lethargically started gathering up their clothes, but most of them looked like they had no intention of going anywhere.

'Hurry up, hurry up. We've only got one hour.'

'We're not leaving.'

Now even Lammio could no longer pretend not to hear. 'Who said that?'

'We're not leaving.'

Murmurs rose here and there.

'Is that so? I disagree. Anyone who is not ready for departure in one hour will present his case before the court martial.'

The men gathered in their quarters, urging one another not to leave. They appealed to the fact that they had been promised a long period of rest once the city had been taken. Actually, they hadn't officially been promised anything. They had just harbored this hope themselves, and hope had given rise to rumor. The fact was, life in the city was good – too good, and it came as a sharp blow, suddenly, to have to leave it.

As usual, the majority of the group remained undecided, waiting to see which way the scales would tip. Lammio turned to the NCOs and ordered them to prepare for departure. He managed to get them moving, but the men did not follow. Time passed and Lammio was beginning to grow irritated. 'I am saying this for the last time. Prepare to head out! Anyone who fails to follow orders will do well to remember that the maximum sentence for such an offense is the death penalty.'

'Fuck it . . . our fire don't hurt any worse than the Russkis'. Bring it on!'

'Bring it on! Send the whole goddamn circus up in flames.'

'Anyway, we're not leaving without a change of company commander.'

'Koskela for company commander! Then we'll go.'

Lammio didn't find this insulting in the least. It was genuinely inconceivable to him that he himself should be the object of the men's distrust. 'This is not some kind of Red Guard that elects its company commanders by shouting out votes. Is that clear? I am ordering you for the last time. After that I will advance to other measures.'

Koskela had remained silent the whole time, standing off to the side. Now he went over to his bed. Calmly, as if nothing had happened, he said, 'Better get moving, I guess. The convoy'll probably be late just like every other time, but anyway. Don't take too much extra junk with you. The instruments are pretty nice to have around . . . I guess we can manage to take 'em along somehow or other.'

Slowly the men of the Third Platoon began to pack up their belongings. No one made a sound. The quiet lieutenant standing in the middle of the room was like some sort of solid, stilling force, draining them of all desire to protest. The most remarkable thing of all was that, in spite of everything, the men sensed that Koskela was on their side. The weight of his presence – of him, personally – compelled them to action, but it aroused no bitterness in them. It just felt evident and natural that they should leave, once Koskela had commanded it.

The men from the other platoons skulked by, hissing quietly so Koskela couldn't hear, 'You mean you're leaving? Don't back down now, damn it!'

'What else are we supposed to do?'

The men in the Third Platoon were angry, as it felt rather awful to be the source of the splintering – still, it did not occur to any of them to go against Koskela. And with that, the whole company began preparing for departure. Backing down was easy for the rest of them. 'What does it matter? If the Third Platoon's going . . .'

Koskela was silent. His face was expressionless as he paced back and forth, but he was following the tenor of the company the whole time. He knew that the others would follow the Third Platoon; he was only a little afraid that Lammio would open his mouth again and turn the tide on the whole matter. But, luckily, even he remained silent.

This time, the convoy was prompt. They loaded up quickly, and the battalion set out. The first snow had fallen overnight and the vehicles roared through the city in its weak, glittering light, turning onto the south-bound road.

'Where are they taking us?' somebody asked Koskela.

'The Svir. Sounds like they've crossed the river.'

'Hey, Rokka! Cheer up! Looks like we're all doin' duty without relief – for who knows how many days!' Hietanen wasn't thinking of Vera. Their departure had banished any such thoughts from his mind. Only her Youth League pin remained, tucked in his wallet.

Rokka seemed the least bothered by the departure. 'Sankia Priha the Great! Play us sumpin' on'nat record-player a yours. It'll work sittin' in your lap, won't it?'

Vanhala's new name had been established. He set the gramophone in his lap and it started to play, skipping and jiggling. Rokka clapped his hands together, swayed his shoulders and sang, '*Yokkantee and Yokkantee and yommaiyyaa . . .*'

The silent, dusky forest flashed by along the roadside.

# Chapter Nine

## I

'Come out,' the Military Police Lieutenant commanded in a stiff, unnatural voice as he opened the sauna door. The guard standing beside it asked in a nervous rush, 'Can I go now? You don't need me anymore, do you?'

'On your way.'

The guard practically sprinted away, as if afraid they might still call him back. The Lieutenant stepped back from the door, allowing the two privates to exit the sauna. They stopped just in front of the threshold and waited in silence. They saw the dim, winter morning just on the point of daybreak, and, above all, they saw the group of Military Police officers, the Lieutenant and the military judge standing off to the side. The army chaplain had left, as the men had refused to receive him.

One of the men was tall and carried himself very upright. He brushed his disheveled blond hair off his forehead. His face was strong and masculine, with a flinty toughness that was evident even in the dim light. He looked at the Lieutenant, but the latter averted his eyes, as if unable to endure that burning, penetrating gaze, which only the knowledge of imminent death can bring to a man's eyes. The other fellow was smaller and seemed to emanate a sort of numb nervousness. He trembled silently the whole time, as if he were freezing. The blond fellow was twenty-five at most, his shorter companion already well into his thirties. Both were bare-headed and beltless, wearing their combat jackets.

The military judge read out the same sentence they'd heard the night before at the drumhead court martial. It felt strange to hear it announced so officially that they had abandoned their guard post and refused to return to it. Sure, they remembered it all right. And then they'd been brought before the court and sentenced to death. And that was it. The past eleven hours in the dark sauna had sufficed to make it clear to them what it all meant. They were finished. In truth, they were dead already, both of them. All that remained was the official confirmation. They had played out the whole execution in their minds so many times that the actual event no longer terrified them.

The older man was trying to distract himself so as to avoid thinking about the whole thing. The younger one, however, was seething with hatred for his executioners. The Military Police were the enemy, depriving him of his life. And he maintained his anger instinctively, as if he understood that it would keep his head upright and make death easier to face.

When the military judge had finished, the younger man hissed, 'Gimme a cigarette, you motherfucking piece of shit.'

The military judge and the Lieutenant scrambled to pull out their cigarettes, racing to offer him one. The man's swearing only seemed to increase their eagerness to serve him. The harried Lieutenant fumbled around for a light and some MP officers in the line rattled their matchboxes at him. Every one of them was eager to cater to even the smallest whim of the condemned.

The Lieutenant hesitated. Should he let the men finish their cigarettes, or get things moving right away? Dragging out the ordeal felt torturous. Better to get the thing over with as quickly as possible. He had ordered several people to be shot, of course, but they had all been either communists or enemy spies, so there was no question about shooting them. This was the first time he was executing their own soldiers.

The younger of the condemned men made his decision for him. 'All right, butchers. Get to it. I'm getting chilly.'

The MP officers were startled by the shrill little laugh that slipped from the man's mouth as he spoke. The other man just trembled like an aspen leaf, not saying anything, and obviously not seeing or hearing anything either.

'Blindfolds,' the Lieutenant said to his men. They hesitated.

'You, go get them.'

'I'm not going.'

'Oh for fuck's sake, don't start squabbling. I'm not dying with a rag over my eyes. I think I've stared down more gun barrels from the front than you have from behind, even if you are executioners.'

'And you? Would you like one?' the Lieutenant asked the other man.

He just shook his head. Then the younger man stepped quickly over to the sauna wall and assumed his position. His companion followed suit. The MP officers fell into line, their guns grounded.

The order rang out. Rifles rose. The older man turned his head to the side and a quiet whimper escaped his lips. But the younger man stared straight down the gun barrel with such conviction that somehow he seemed more the condemner than the condemned. Just yesterday he had been an ordinary young man, who, in a moment of thoughtless defiance, had disobeyed a lieutenant whose arrogance he hated, just like everybody else in his company. This morning, having spent eleven hours in the dark sauna with death for company, he was a grown man of great experience.

The rifles sounded in one, unified bang. The men beside the sauna wall sank into the snow. The MP officers hurried toward the bodies and gathered them up with gentle deference.

And one more incident receded into the past.

## II

'Attention!'

The battalion, assembled in the snowy forest clearing, stiffened to attention. Major Sarastie took out a sheet of paper and began to read. The men listened, a bit perplexed. They already knew what had happened. What was the point of reading it out? Two men had been executed because they had abandoned their guard post and refused to return to it. As soon as they'd heard that the sentence had been carried out, the men had gone after the MP officers who'd done the executing. They didn't catch them, though – luckily, seeing as they were probably the least guilty of the parties responsible for the crime.

When the Major had finished reading his memo, he added, 'So! This sentence was carried out as a reminder to the insubordinates out there that you do not joke with the army. I hope, and I trust, that in this battalion, such a reminder is not necessary. However, should the need arise, the Code of Military Justice will be brought to bear to the fullest extent of the law.'

Only now did the men understand why the notice was being read to them. They were being threatened. An attack on the Svir River had provoked a surprisingly strong resurgence of enemy activity, and the opponent they presumed to have been struck down now appeared quite capable of counter-attack. Sarastie's battalion had been tasked with carrying out the counter-strike. It was merely as a precautionary measure, in other words – to foster the necessary spirit and morale amongst his men – that the Commander had decided to read his memo just before departure.

## III

Beneath the clear winter sky, the crackling, crashing and booming was constant. The battalion pushed on toward the enemy's service road to force it out of a village they'd retaken over a month ago. The two armies had been tied up in a bloody scuffle over the village for a long time, but the enemy wasn't giving up its prey. And now, they meant to take it. Sarastie's battalion had received strict orders to cut off the service road and keep it closed.

The barrage was concentrated further back to their left, on the bald peak of Kalju Hill. After three bloody, failed offensives, the remnants of a Jaeger Border Patrol battalion had finally managed to gain a firm foothold on the hill. Its slopes were littered with bodies, as the enemy had had no means of withdrawing and the fighting had grown exceptionally fierce. The Jaegers had managed to keep their spirits up through all three failed attempts, and when the fourth brought them to the hill, the Siberians fell in their foxholes without a single man surrendering. Now the enemy artillery was firing back with a vengeance, and the Jaegers were crouched out there amidst the bodies, apathetic and terrified, in the middle of the mayhem.

This hill, which had been sleeping peacefully since time immemorial, had suddenly become an item of utmost importance. A thin, blue-veined hand had pointed it out on a map: 'Taking that hill is an absolute prerequisite to retaking the village. It controls the surrounding swampland for a one-mile radius, and in any case we won't be able to cut in very far without it because it would be too hard to get supplies out to the men in front, and they could easily end up isolated.'

This 'prerequisite' having been fulfilled, Sarastie's battalion had started its advance.

Lahtinen, Määttä and Salo were pulling a supply sled through the deep snowdrifts. Sihvonen was following behind with the brake cable, trying to help them along by pushing with a ski pole. They had been attached to a covering rifle platoon, but were lagging behind on account of the sled. It was so heavily loaded down that it sank through the snowdrifts and dragged against the ground. At first the men had tried to advance on skis, but the weight of the load kept making them slide backwards, so they'd loaded their skis onto the sled and proceeded on foot. Streams of sweat poured down their bodies, despite the freezing temperatures. Panting and cursing, they followed the ski tracks of the platoon out in front of them. Heads buzzing with exhaustion, they could make out the clatter of combat, but the crashing was so faint and confused that they had no way of knowing where their own soldiers were versus those of the enemy.

Salo proceeded out in front, frequently on all fours, as the weight of the sled kept threatening to force him over onto his back. Määttä pulled silently, but powerfully, keeping an eye out for lumps and hollows in the snow so as to keep the sled moving as efficiently as possible. Lahtinen pulled with the whole weight of his towering body, and whenever the sled got caught on a rock or a tree stump, he would lurch against it, yanking his rope in a furious surge of determination and swearing grimly, 'God . . . damn . . . it.'

They took little breaks in between, sitting on the sled and catching their breath. Lahtinen panted, 'God damn it! Come on, bullet, come and kill me! Of all the shit jobs! And meanwhile the fat cat sits back in his rocker, counting up his profits from black market grain. Hell, if somebody just turned up here, somebody who wasn't all mixed up in this shit already, I mean, you know what he'd say? A guy who doesn't necessarily know the ways of the world or anything, but just knows the sensible, necessary stuff, I mean? He'd be downright flabbergasted. Grown men dragging a goddamn toboggan back and forth through the forest!'

Lahtinen paused for a moment to control his temper, which he then proceeded to vent in the form of a dialogue between himself and this rational creature of his imagining. 'He'd take a look at these shovels and crowbars and ask, "Are you going to build a road or dig the foundations for a house?" And what am I supposed to say? What could I say but, Ye-ahh . . . not exactly . . . we need these to bury ourselves in the ground so we don't get killed. Then the little pain in the ass would wonder, "What's that extraordinary contraption you have there? What do you do with that?" . . . Huh-huh. What do you do with it? You'll see . . . Mmhm. I gotta fight out here even if I don't know what the hell I've got to fight for. My life, I guess, but I'm pretty sure I could do a better job of hanging on to that somewhere else. I haven't got any homeland and I left religion back in confirmation classes. I got something resembling a place to live, but it's the company that owns it. Fight to protect your parents, the chaplain says! Well, hell, I've only got a mom, and if some Russki thinks he can do something with that old bag then by all means, he can have her . . . Well, hell! Let's get to it. God damn these tree stumps! Tugging at you like little beggar boys . . . Would it kill 'em to chop 'em a little lower?'

The journey continued. Lahtinen's anger was channeled into the hauling effort. Though he did yell at Salo, who had let his rope go noticeably slack, 'You pull, too, God damn it! You haven't even broken a sweat!'

Salo's rope tightened and over their huffing and puffing came the very sensible response, 'I ain't tryin' to break a sweat. Just tryin' to get this sled to move.'

They started to hear intense firing out in front of them on the left, and suspected that the battalion had reached the enemy service road. They were just about ready to drop with exhaustion when they finally caught up with the platoon, which had already fanned out into formation. Lahtinen decided by himself that the machine gun should be positioned right in the middle of the platoon, in a cluster of trees jutting out of the forest. He recognized immediately that it was the best spot. On the whole, he was a good machine-gun leader, as he knew how to organize things so the weapon would be useful.

The area they needed to cover was extensive, and the Ensign leading the rifle platoon was apprehensive about the mission. His platoon was supposed to cover the flank of the advancing formation, so it absolutely had to hold its position – and it was very likely that the enemy would do everything it could to keep its service road open. The Ensign trudged through the snow to the machine gun and said, 'That's right. This is the best spot.'

His position of responsibility had made him feel a bit isolated, so he continued chatting, sociably, 'We may be able to get through without any resistance, but if they come at us, you start shooting full blast.'

Lahtinen was still pissed off about his recent exertion and snarled irritably, 'Of course we shoot! You think we're gonna sit here sucking our thumbs while they mow us down?'

The Ensign, baffled at Lahtinen's outburst, continued on his way.

## IV

The cold grew worse. The horizon receded into a bleak, cold red as the winter sun sank down behind it. The snowdrifts between the trees began to take on a blue sheen. Darkness fell over the dense forest, making its dead silence feel even deeper.

Lahtinen was on his knees behind the machine gun, keeping

constant watch over the immediate terrain. The others were a bit further back, gathering around a pitiful excuse for a campfire. Sometimes the freezing temperature caused crackles up in the branches, and occasionally you could hear the low clink of metal as the guards moved the bolts on their guns to keep them operable. They could hear firing off to their left. A light machine gun sent a couple of rounds echoing through the icy forest several times over. The artillery fire had died down. All they heard was an occasional string of booms from the artillery battery and the whistling of shells overhead.

Lahtinen's boots were frozen – as was his snowsuit, which rustled whenever he bent over. A louse bit his neck, but he didn't bother to scratch it, as he couldn't bring himself to pull his hand out of the warmth of his mitten.

The snow crust crackled in the forest. Lahtinen went rigid and listened closely. Then the sound came back. Somebody was trudging cautiously through the snowdrifts with carefully weighted steps.

Lahtinen's heart started to thump. He sank down slowly onto his stomach and slipped his hands up into the grips. The sound continued, growing louder. Soon it was accompanied by the rustling of several legs, followed by the clanging of metal.

'Hey,' Lahtinen whispered to the infantry guy lying a little way off. 'Enemy's moving. Straight ahead.'

The man raised his head and whispered in a suffocated breath, choking with anxiety, 'Yeah, I hear.'

Then he passed the word, 'Alert. Neighbors ahead.'

Safeties clicked. The alert rippled down the line.

Lahtinen stared through the trees at the clearing and suddenly started. There was a man in a white snowsuit standing with a gun under his arm, scanning his surroundings. It was as if he had appeared like a ghost, and Lahtinen had no idea when he had arrived. Then another one appeared behind the juniper bushes, and the first beckoned to him with his hand. Lahtinen released the safety on the gun and set the thumb of his frozen mitten on the trigger. The man's upper body rose above the sight.

Lahtinen breathed anxiously. Straining with tension, he waited for more enemy soldiers to come into view. He was only afraid that the infantry guys would start in too early with their rifles, as the men within eyeshot were clearly scouts, which meant that there were even more enemy soldiers not far behind. At the same time, he was in the grips of the perpetual fear of the machine-gunner: would the weapon work? The freezing temperatures had made some of its moving parts go stiff.

A bang sounded beside him, and Lahtinen nearly exploded with curses, but then he pressed the trigger. A great wave of relief rolled through him as the gun obediently began hammering out rounds. The man in front dropped into a heap like a collapsible pocket-knife. The fellow behind him tottered for a moment, as if deciding which way to fall, before dropping down on his side.

'Positions!' Lahtinen cried out hoarsely to the group of men behind him. There was no sense in whispering anymore. A few shots rang out from the forest, but the enemy was nowhere to be seen. Then the firing ceased and all they could hear was crunching snow.

Määttä, Salo and Sihvonen tossed some snow on their feeble campfire and hurried to the machine gun. Behind them, the guys from the infantry platoon did the same.

'What's over there?' Sihvonen asked, when they had reached Lahtinen. The latter was scanning the ground out in front of him and didn't respond. The machine gun gave off a sizzling noise. The hot grease hissed against the metal, which even in the midst of all the excitement reminded Lahtinen of an old omen his mother had always talked about when their stove made that sizzling noise. Supposedly it was a sign of death.

Maybe Lahtinen's fear manifested itself in his recollection of this sinister omen. Nevertheless, he refused to wallow in the fear the memory brought on and turned to Sihvonen with a blank stare, replying with his usual crotchetiness, 'Well, whatta ya think? Now who could possibly be over there? Who might be shooting from that direction, now, you tell me.'

Sihvonen shut up, hurt at Lahtinen's cutting reply. They scanned the terrain carefully, but didn't catch so much as a glimpse of the enemy. Only the crackling of the snow led them to the conclusion that the enemy must be regrouping for an attack.

The Ensign showed up on their right just as his deputy platoon leader turned up on the left. The Ensign endeavored to keep his voice calm and businesslike, but was unable to conceal his anxiety as he said, 'There's even more rustling over on the right. I think we're up against some stiff opposition. This isn't a question of a few scouts.'

The deputy didn't even try to mask his uneasiness, but declared grimly, 'Nope, definitely not a question of scouts. The forest's rustling way past our furthest positions, and someone's giving orders over there in front of the fourth squad.'

'Can't you stretch out the line?'

'How the hell am I supposed to stretch out the line when the men can barely shout to one another as it is?'

The Ensign lost his temper and snapped, 'You've got to spread it out! Put a light machine gun at the head. And tell the leader of the fourth squad to keep a special eye out on his flank . . .'

'I've already put a light machine gun out there. But it's not going to be much help. Its shooting range is fifty yards.'

The Ensign didn't say anything. He'd been dreading a situation like this the whole time they'd been at war. Death on one side, and Major Sarastie's withering glance on the other, accompanied by the emphatically declarative question, 'And so you had to turn tail. Well, what the hell have they got over there?'

Then some sympathetic friend would feel awkwardly obliged to console him, 'That kind of thing can happen to anyone.'

The Ensign lived in perpetual fear of finding himself in a situation in which everything would rest on his shoulders alone. Would he be man enough to hold his ground as an example to his men, to maintain discipline if they began to falter?

He would have to be. Such an encounter with the Major could not come to pass. They'd hold the positions, and if there was no other alternative, then let the end come. The Ensign took a deep and decisive breath of air, filling his lungs far below his heart and saying in a voice full of strength and assurance, 'Here we stand and here we stay. There's no alternative. The battalion is in combat and we are responsible for protecting its flank.'

Lahtinen hissed back at them, 'Shut up back there! Listen! There's a hell of a lot of chattering going on across the way.'

The Ensign fell silent and they listened. Low voices came from out in front of them, mixed with the crunching of snow. Lahtinen glared at the Ensign and said accusingly, 'I mean, it's none of my business, but it seems like we might want to start doing something here. That's not just one company back there, guys. If there's anything that's clear around here, it's that we're in for it. You'd better send a runner to request help. And he'd better tell 'em straight out that a troop of guys who are already half-dead isn't gonna cut it.'

'I already sent word,' the Ensign replied, 'but I didn't request the reinforcements, because there aren't any.'

'I see. Well, that's a different story.' Lahtinen resumed scanning the foreground with a scowl on his face.

The Ensign and his sergeant turned back to one another. After a brief consultation, they decided to send another runner to update the battalion on the situation. 'Tell them we can't be responsible for holding the line if we don't get help.'

The man set off, happy and relieved, and the others gazed enviously after him. There goes one guy who's getting out of this alive.

The gravity of the situation prompted the Ensign to take on a collegial tone as he said to the Sergeant, 'Well, do what you can over there. They can't fly away in these deep drifts, either.'

The Sergeant turned to leave, tossing his rifle over his shoulder and calling back with a sort of bitter, hopeless defiance, 'Snowdrifts aren't gonna stop 'em. Well, so long, then. See you on the other side.'

## V

It was nearing five o'clock. The snowdrifts gleamed ever bluer as the forest settled into dusk, and the last, cold strains of the clear, winter daylight faded away. The glimmering snow helped the light linger a little, but in the groves and thickets, dusk had already gained the upper hand.

Commands rang out from the enemy side. Lahtinen scowled at his companions. Anxious and frightened as he was, he was overcome with a sort of hopeless, malicious glee, as if he were reveling in the fact that, now, things were as bad as they could possibly be. As the others stared silently into the forest, Lahtinen thought he would remind them just how bad a fix they were really in, and said, 'We're toast. Just so you know.'

No one responded. Only Määttä slowly stretched out an ammo belt, and Lahtinen took the silence to mean that the men still didn't realize or recognize how hopeless the situation was. So, he dutifully resumed his missionary efforts. 'So now we fight in the name of our faith and family. Humph. Gotta earn those wood crosses they're gonna stick up on top of our graves.'

No answer. Salo released the safety on his gun. Lahtinen was losing his patience. What the hell was going on? Why didn't these guys realize how hopeless their position was?

'If we have to hightail it out of here, the machine guns better not get left behind. Just so you know.'

'I'll take the gun-stand,' Määttä said quickly, with deliberate nonchalance. He may have sensed that, in his fear, Lahtinen was lashing out, paying them back for all the laughs they'd had at his expense. But the hopeless, malicious glee fell from Lahtinen's voice and he grew frank and businesslike as he issued the men with their instructions. 'Määttä and I shoot the machine gun. You guys cut down everything you can with those rifles. And remember now, every round's gotta strike. Aim for the belly, that's the way to take a guy out of the game. Aim for one that's closest and take 'em down in turn. And don't shoot blind. What I mean is, every time you shoot, shoot to kill.'

'Uraaaa . . . aaa . . . aaraa . . . uraa . . . raaa . . .'

The men drew in their breath. Every nerve was on edge as their bodies prepared to give their all in carrying out their minds' orders. The cold had evaporated, banished by their over-excited bodies and anxious breath. It was the most stirring moment of battle, a silence charged with excitement that suddenly erupts into a clattering crash. It was as if the first shot startled tens and hundreds of fingers into pulling their triggers, so that for one moment, all the weapons cracked in unison before their fire petered out into its various forms.

Lahtinen shot with his jaws clenched firmly together. His first prey was an officer clad in white furs. Then he turned his attention to a machine-gun squad trying to reach a position under cover of some pines.

One man made it in time. The enemy's call to charge echoed over a terrifyingly wide range. From their own positions, they heard only the clamor of ceaseless firing, though once they made out a hoarse, anxious cry on the left: 'Light machine guns over here! Get the light machine guns over here . . .'

The advance halted in front of the machine gun. The enemy was trapped in its fire, and Lahtinen was rapidly shooting to both sides. He glanced at Määttä and said, thinking to fend off any accusations, 'I can't see them, I'm just boosting morale, see.'

Määttä didn't say anything. He was just making sure one belt after another made it into the feeder. The machine gun was already beginning to glow with heat.

Things to their left had fallen suspiciously silent, and suddenly Sihvonen gasped, 'They're making a run for it. We'd better go, too!'

Lahtinen also saw the running men and screamed to Sihvonen, 'You're not taking off before the rest of us!'

At that moment the Ensign came running up on the right, yelling, 'Get in position! Go back! Who the fuck gave you permission to retreat?'

Further off one of the guys running yelled, 'They're circling round from the left!'

The Ensign called for his deputy commander, 'Penttinen! Sergeant Penttinen!'

'Penttinen's dead. Head's shot through like a sieve.'

'And Lehtovirta and Kylänpää.'

'They're cutting through on the left!'

'The light machine gun's still back there along with both guys. I saw them get Aarnio from three yards away.'

Panicked men poured in from the left, yelling about one disaster after another. Hoarse, the Ensign screamed, 'Turn around! Get back in position!'

A few of the men returned to their positions, but just then they were hit with a hail of enemy fire and one of them fell, crying out softly. It rattled the others so much they lost all will to hold back the enemy. Even the guys on the right, who'd been spared these traumas, were beginning to join the flight. Lahtinen started detaching the machine gun from its mount, as he could see that there was nothing to be done but try to save the gun. Salo and Sihvonen had already fled.

The Ensign also realized that the situation was hopeless. He was about to set off toward the left to see if there was any chance of holding the enemy back, but just then he spotted a hand rising from the snow and heard a wounded man scream, 'Guys! Don't leave me! Please, guys, please . . .'

The Ensign dashed over. He called for help from Sihvonen, who was just running by, but Sihvonen just pressed on with eyes like saucers. Salo stayed back to help, however, and together they started to pull the wounded man behind them.

When Lahtinen saw what was going on, he put the machine gun back on the gun mount and said to Määttä, 'Clear out the sled and put that guy in it . . . Hurry. You go help. I'll hold 'em back while you guys take care of him . . .'

Määttä went. With one heave he dumped the contents of the sled, then pulled it over to the wounded man. They raised him into the sled and started pulling it to the forest for cover. Some of the Ensign's men came back to help, so Määttä and the Ensign stayed to wait for Lahtinen.

Lahtinen was firing indiscriminately across as wide a range as the spin on the gun mount allowed. He glanced over his shoulder and, seeing the sled slip into the forest to safety, rose to his knees to grab hold of the gun.

Määttä and the Ensign shot randomly toward the enemy, trying to give Lahtinen some kind of cover. The enemy had spotted him, and their bullets were sending up bursts of snow all around him.

'Leave the machine gun and run!' the Ensign cried, figuring it would be impossible for one man to get the machine gun out all by himself. Maybe Lahtinen didn't hear, or maybe he just couldn't imagine abandoning the weapon, but in any case Määttä and the Ensign watched as the hulking youth swung the entire machine gun assembly over his shoulder and began crawling toward them. When Lahtinen fell, they thought at first that he had stumbled, but when he didn't get up, Määttä yelled, 'Lahtinen!'

No answer came. The snow-suited man lay prone and motionless. The front leg of the gun-stand stuck straight up behind his neck. Määttä and the Ensign waited for a moment for some sign of life, then began to trudge away in silence. Abandoned skis littered the terrain behind their positions, but there wasn't time to gather them up.

The machine gun sizzled as it sank into the melting snow, its casing hot from firing. Water pearled and joined and slowly began to trickle down the exposed blueberry leaves. A few, sparse drops of blood had stained it red. They dropped from just behind Lahtinen's ear, where the bullet had lodged.

# VI

'You all whacked or what? Where you comin' from?' Rokka clapped the gasping man on the back.

'Over there . . . over there . . .'

'Don't you mumble now . . . What's goin' on over there?'

'All the guys . . . done . . . killed the whole platoon.'

'Now, don't say that! Here you are, still alive! And there's s'more fellas comin' over there. What happen'da the machine gun? Where's Lahtinen?'

'Still back there. Nobody made it out alive.'

'I don't think we're gonna get anything out of him,' Hietanen said, leaning on his ski poles. The only assistance the battalion had sent was Rokka's rifle, and Hietanen had tagged along. The two of them suspected they were too late to be of use as soon as they ran into the first retreating soldier, who was still in a state of shock.

Rokka let up on the man, and as more breathless runners turned up, he and Hietanen got a clearer sense of what was going on from the guys who had their wits about them. Määttä and the Ensign brought up the rear. No sooner had the Ensign rejoined his men than he flew into a rage. 'You motherfucking pansies! That's the last time you're going to pull that stunt. Sure, just run like a flock of goddamn chickens without so much as a glance behind! And forget about bringing the wounded guys! If even one of you abandons his post again, you'd all better know what you're in for.'

'Where's Lahtinen and the machine gun?' Hietanen asked Määttä.

'Lyin' back there side by side,' Määttä replied flatly, as if he couldn't care less.

'There was nothing to be done,' the Ensign said, as if making excuses on Määttä's behalf. 'This man did everything he could. He and I brought the wounded man back. It wasn't this man's fault. He's the only guy worth his salt in the whole outfit . . .'

'Look, I don't care whose fault it was. All I asked about was Lahtinen and the machine gun,' Hietanen said, a bit sharply, as he didn't like the sound of the Ensign's accusations.

'Me, too,' Rokka said. 'Lissen, they're gonna be over here soon, too . . . Better git the fellas set up.'

The Ensign realized there were more critical things to attend to than berating his men and quickly started organizing the defense. He was still hoping to stop the enemy advance, so, letting up on his tone of a moment before, he bellowed, 'We'll knock the fight out of them yet, boys! Get into positions. Try to dig some foxholes in the snow. And if you can reach into the ground, even better.'

Spurred on by a new wave of hope, the Ensign pulled himself together and moved decisively. He asked Hietanen to take charge of the men coming in on the far right wing, as his own platoon had lost its deputy commander as well as both of the squad leaders who'd been on the left. Hietanen got the troops into formation and Rokka searched for a good spot for the machine gun. They had too many men for one gun, now that Lahtinen's team was on hand as well, so they decided that just Määttä and Vanhala would stay with the gun, and the others would join the firing line. Rokka himself went over to the Ensign and said, 'Lissen, Ensign! Where do you need a real top-notch fella? 'Cause you're lookin' at him.'

Rokka's self-assured declaration made the Ensign grin, despite the gravity of the situation. He was aware of Rokka's reputation, however, and knew he was as good as his word.

'The ends of the line are the worst. Take a few men with you and cover the far left. Head out just past the end of the line and keep your eyes peeled . . .'

'You betcha. Hey! You, with the submachine gun! Come with me! And gimme that gun.'

'You might want to take someone else with you,' the Ensign whispered. 'Lampinen was on the left back there just now, so he's a little traumatized. And anyway his nerves aren't exactly made of steel.'

'Don't need quality. Just somebody a keep the drums loaded. C'mere! Now lissen, I'm a comedian, see – you come with me and we'll have ourselves barrels of fun. Grab some ammo there, much as you can walk with.'

They set off.

Rokka trudged through the snow, his quiet companion lugging ammunition behind him. The moon began to shed some light on the dark forest. Snow glittered in the gaps between the trees, but menacing, mysterious shadows emerged from the thickets. The shadows stretched long, as the moon had only just begun to rise.

Rokka and his companion passed the last man on the line and continued on a little further. Rokka chattered away, whispering to his silent companion, 'Hot diggity! These are some dandy felt boots I got me back there on'nat service road. Lil' tough gittin' 'em off a that fella's feet, though. Already good and frozen on him, they were.'

The man didn't respond, he just glanced around, petrified. Suddenly Rokka stopped and raised his hand. A lump rose in Lampinen's throat when he saw what had prompted Rokka's halt. Before them lay a small, frozen swamp, and dozens of snow-suited men were tramping across it double-file – toward them. Rokka beckoned Lampinen to his side, and carefully they pressed themselves into the snow.

'There's nothing we can do,' Lampinen said, his voice trembling.

'Now how you gonna know 'til you try? Aw, shucks, what a trick! They heard us makin'na racket and figgered out where we was so they could send troops round and surround us. Can I smell it or what? And here I am this whole time feelin' things ain't quite what they seem.'

The enemy was advancing slowly and recklessly. They didn't have any scouts, despite the fact that, at the moment, they were crossing an exposed swamp. Perhaps they were just so confident in their mission that they figured that kind of thing wasn't necessary. Rokka and Lampinen sank themselves deeper into the snowdrifts, Rokka whispering instructions the whole time. 'These drums here's full. Soon as I plow through 'em, you refill 'em, hear? Just make sure you always put the full ones in the full pile, so they don't git mixed up. And you just keep calm. Just like Rokka here. We ain't got no troubles. They're the ones gonna be in for it pretty soon. Hey, you know howd'da sing? You might hum a lil' sumpin', soft-like. Keeps the spirits up. Lil' strategy for the mind, see? Just think a any crazy ol' thing, 'sall good in a spot like this.'

Rokka knew his whispering wouldn't reach enemy ears, since the rustling of the men's snowsuits would drown out any smaller noises. Double-file, they trudged laboriously through the snow as Rokka steadied the sight.

'See that officer out in front? Soon as his shadow hits that lil' spruce there, he's meetin' his maker. That's what I say. 'Nen after him, I start in on'na rest of 'em. Look at them all lined up! Waddlin' along one after the other like sittin' ducks. Poor bastards! Don't know what's about'ta hit 'em. Pretty soon you're gonna see how the Lord takes His own. Now, You lissen up up there, ol' man! If any a those fellas's sinned, You take mercy on him, hear? Be quick now! They're gonna start headin' up to You soon.'

The shadow of the officer walking in front was nearing the

spruce tree. The man never knew what happened to him. All he saw was the dark rim of the forest, the snow glittering in the moonlight, and his own shadow, whose head was just reaching the tip of a young spruce tree. His eyes may have glimpsed the muzzle flash, but he never had time to grasp its meaning.

A few cries and random shots rang out, but Rokka's submachine gun cut through everything, hammering away like a sewing machine. Rokka was cool and calculating as he killed – an ability made possible by his particular kind of constitution. His eyes were sharp and his mind moved swiftly, unfettered by fear, as his hands carried out its commands with sure and extraordinary accuracy.

A few of the men darted off, trying to make a break for it. Others tried to crawl along the snowdrifts. A few shot randomly, but the dry hammering of the submachine gun was difficult to locate.

Having mowed down the front of the line, Rokka started in from the tail end. First he shot down the men nearest to the forest's protective edge. The man nearest to safety was always next up, and Rokka hammered steadily toward the center of the group as the situation advanced. Men dropped like flies in the snowy clearing. One hopeless fugitive ran wading through the snow to the edge of the forest, and a glimmer of hope may even have flickered through his mind as he crossed into the shadow of its cover. But then the hail of bullets struck, and again, one more motionless lump sank onto the snow. Others tried to dig themselves down into the drifts and return fire, but no sooner did anybody shoot than the snow around him would fly into the air and his weapon would fall silent.

Lampinen lay beside Rokka, dripping with sweat from head to toe. Hands trembling, he tore open the cardboard boxes and filled Rokka's empty drum magazines. He was nearly mad with fear. He was reassured somewhat by Rokka's face, which wasn't even anxious, just stealthy and alert; but the whole situation still struck him as highly unstable and far from equal. They might be surrounded at any moment. And on top of his fear he was overwhelmed with horror at this staggering slaughter. Whenever he glanced over at the swamp, he would glimpse some guy trying to crawl away on his last legs, until Rokka's merciful bullet would put him out of his misery. Heart-rending wails and cries for help pierced through the din. Never in his life had Lampinen witnessed so great a massacre, and although he had no particular humanitarian anxiety about such things, the ruthless slaughter somehow struck him as monstrous.

Lampinen heard an angry, buzzing blast, and the submachine gun fell silent. A frightened cry escaped him as he looked at Rokka. He saw that his fur cap had slid off. His head hung limp over the butt of the gun and a red rivulet of blood was trickling from his hairline down to his cheek.

Lampinen dropped the magazine and started crawling away. Now that he was alone, self-control abandoned him completely and, choking with horror, he imagined that the enemy was at his back at this very moment, about to shoot a stream of bullets straight through him. He was just about to get up and start running when he felt a hand seize his ankle, and with a strangled gasp and protruding eyes, he turned back to look.

Rokka squeezed his leg and smiled. But to Lampinen, even the smile was sickening. Rokka's face was distorted by pain and stained with blood, and his grimace gleaming in the moonlight looked more like that of a cackling devil than anything human.

'Where you headed?'

'Nnnn . . . n . . . no . . . nowhere.'

'C'mon back where you were, then. I thought you'd run off somewheres. Don't you go runnin' off, damn it. I'd run outta drums . . .'

The submachine gun started up again. None of the men remaining was running anymore – those that were left were just trying to crawl through the snow to safety. A few of them even made it, but the number of survivors represented just a tiny fraction of those who had advanced into the middle of the clearing.

'That'ssa one done it, lil' sucker behin'nat spruce. You shot a furrow down my scalp, and for that you're gonna git half your head blown off. Like that . . . an'nat . . . an'nat. Just lookit how that fella went down in'na snow! You see how that drift just swallowed him up? Damn! Don't you mess with Antti Rokka.'

Movement on the swamp slowed. There was some fire coming from the rim of the forest, but no signs of attack anywhere else. The moonlight, clear as ever, bathed the bodies strewn about the swamp. A low moan would rise now and again, followed by a sharp, quick string of shots from Rokka's submachine gun. His head bare, his face lit with a faint smile, the cool killer guarded his prey, eyeing it down to the very last sign of life.

A rustling of skis sounded somewhere to the rear. The lieutenant from the Jaeger Platoon slid up behind them. 'What's going on?'

'Ain't nothin' goin' on no more. Lissen, you go git the line and stretch 'em over there alongside a swamp! Neighbors might give it another go. Guess you fellas came to give us a hand anyway, huh?'

'Yeah, yeah, that's why we're here.' The Lieutenant sent his companion back to the line while he himself remained marveling over the bodies.

'It was just you, shooting?'

'Well, sure, you might say that. Neighbors over there tried'a chime in every once in a while, but nothin' much came a that. Did gimme a nick in'na head, though, the bastards. Clear knocked me out for a second there.'

'And I was all ready to run,' Lampinen confessed meekly, as if to establish that he had no intention of denying his fear. Rokka gave a good-spirited chuckle and said, 'Sure were! Gave me a good laugh when I came to and saw your foot right there next to me, 'bout'ta push off for the rear. 'Nen it flashed through my head that you thought I was a goner. I reckoned you'd git a hell of a start from a dead man pullin' your leg! But lissen, you bandage up my head now, all right? Ain't bleedin'. Cold's stopped the blood, but you better wrap it up anyway.'

Lampinen started binding the wound. He wasn't at all embarrassed about how scared he'd been, and said in a voice full of humble admiration, 'I don't know much about these things, but man, you're one hell of a shot.'

Rokka raised his mitten and started lecturing in his schoolteacherly voice, 'Now, you see here. Here's how it is. You turn tail, and you can hightail it all'a way to the Gulf'a Bothnia. They'll chase after ya, no doubt about that. But if you stay put and don't give an inch – well, whadda they gonna do about it? Wouldn't be quite right to all fall in'na same pit together. That'ssa whole key to defensive strategy right there. There's nothin' more to it than that and there never will be. But gaddamn it, don't swaddle me like a babe! Pretty soon I ain't gonna be able to see or hear nothin'! Say, Lieutenant, gimme a smoke. I left mine back in'na transport.'

'Here, take the whole pack. I've still got another.'

'Naw. Now, aren't you a big-hearted bastard? I like you lots, Louie. You go see if those fellas all got felt boots on. 'F they do, then tomorrow I'm outfittin'na whole platoon with 'em!'

There were no felt boots on the bodies. They checked the next day, once the enemy had ceded back the reconquered village. The wedge that had been pushing toward the service road had forced them to return to their original line. Fifty-two bodies were found lying in the swamp. By Lampinen's count, Rokka had emptied seventeen drum magazines. The weapon showed it too. The barrel was stretched beyond repair.

After the fighting, Major Sarastie assembled his battalion again and thanked them for a job well done. He said that their role in the counter-attack had been decisive. The battalion had fought well, and even the Regiment Commander had sent his congratulations. He had ordered that the battalion be recognized for its dauntless fighting spirit.

The men didn't really understand how this time was any different from any other time, but anyway, apparently they had fought well, because somebody said so.

And to revitalize that fighting spirit within them, they had even shot two privates in front of a sauna wall in the next town over. It would have been rather incredible, after all, if such a thing had had no effect whatsoever.

# Chapter Ten

## I

Mäkilä was pacing back and forth beside the field kitchen. He spotted some potato peel on the ground, picked it up and tossed it into a crate. Though the sight of the potato peel had aroused his general distaste for the 'undying barbarism' of his present company, he was actually in an exceptionally good mood. The machine-gunners had emerged victorious from a scuffle with the Third Company over grazing land for their horses, and so had triumphantly taken control of the forest meadow in question. Mäkilä was to be thanked for this coup, as for so many other matters concerning the company's maintenance. Sinkkonen, the Master Sergeant, had proven utterly incapable of managing things adequately. Appeals to the rule book or the customary proceedings were of no help out here. The circumstances required initiative and punch – and Sinkkonen had neither. Which was why the machine-gunners frequently found themselves suffering the consequences of his ineptitude compared to the other master sergeants, who knew better what they were about and how to hold their own. It was only Mäkilä's staunch, hefty pressure, combined with the men's own enterprise, that evened things out, despite the fact that Mäkilä's inferior rank put him in something of an awkward position with the other master sergeants. 'But we have to try something. Touching a hand to your cap's not going to get anybody too far round here.'

The early summer evening was already on the wane. The glints of sunset flickering between the trees had already vanished from the pond's surface, and dark shadows were stretching long from its western rim. Mäkilä would have gone to bed, but he didn't dare. Rahikainen was leaning against the field kitchen, chatting with the guard. Angling to steal something. Mäkilä didn't even have to wonder anymore whether Rahikainen was up to something – which was why he was still up, hanging around, for fear the guy on guard would slip up and get himself swindled.

Finally Rahikainen left, lazily making his way down the path. When Mäkilä saw him disappear around the bend, he crawled into his tent and went to bed. Rahikainen walked a little further down the path, then stopped and gave a low whistle. The answer came right away. Rahikainen followed it and after tiptoeing a little way, found Rokka perched on a rock.

'It's next to the field kitchen, on the pond side. Won't be easy, but I'll manage.'

'Who's on guard?'

'Sipilä.'

'All right, 'attl work. I'll git to it soon as I git over there. You just make sure you're ready when'na time comes.'

'Careful that asshole doesn't shoot you.'

'Oh, I'll be fine.'

They parted ways. Rokka pressed into the forest and Rahikainen started tiptoeing back toward the path. He crawled under cover of the bushes until he was a few yards from the field kitchen, then stopped to wait. The guard was smoking, looking at the pond glimmering between the trees. The supply guys' tent was just a little way away, but over there everything was quiet.

A thud sounded in the forest, and the guard turned quickly, slipping his rifle off his shoulder and under his arm. A branch rustled in the trees, and the man released the safety on his gun. Then he took a few steps toward the noise and paused, listening, and Rahikainen slithered over to the field kitchen and grasped the soup vat sitting overturned beside it, then started pulling it quietly into the bushes.

Another thud came from the forest. Masking his fear in an artificially raspy voice, the guard called out, 'Password!'

No password came, but the supply guys emerged from the tent in their underwear.

'What's over there?'

'I don't know. Something made a noise.'

'Must be birds rustling around.'

Rahikainen had already pulled the soup vat into the bushes and left the men to wonder over the cause of the mysterious noises. He returned to their previous meeting point to wait for Rokka, who arrived promptly.

'How'd it go?'

'Take a look!'

'Aw, shit, that's swell! All we gotta do now is screw the top on and we're all set.'

Rokka tossed the vat over his shoulder and off they went. Their tent was pitched in a little clearing in the forest, and some of the guys were lying around it. The two men stopped before they'd left the cover of the trees. Rahikainen gave a low whistle.

'C'mon out! Coast's clear.'

Rokka and Rahikainen's arrival aroused lively interest. Everybody gathered around the tent, except the guy on guard. Shouts of joy burst forth as the men spotted the vat. They crowded around it, touched it and inspected its interior. Vanhala stuck his head inside and let out a yodel. 'Ba-aaha-aahha-aa!!'

He must have enjoyed the sound of the echo, judging from the massive grin spread across his face when he removed his head.

The first section was 'standing down', in other words, laying a road. The company had organized their time off the line by section, and each rest period lasted one week, during which time the guys on their break would stay back somewhere by the supply crew and lay a log road extending toward the front line. It was the first day of Koskela's section's turn, and they had decided a long while back that when their next break came, they would make home brew. The lack of a vessel was their only concern, and since they knew there was no use in asking Mäkilä for such a thing, they had decided to steal it. Koskela had agreed to the plan, seeing as he could hardly use his position to pressure Mäkilä, under the circumstances. And anyway, even Koskela's authority would hardly have induced Mäkilä to surrender his pot for such nefarious purposes.

Määttä and Vanhala went to fill the pot with water. Then they added a bowl of boiling water to it. Rokka took the helm, while Koskela tossed in brief, occasional words of advice. First, Rokka poured in the sugar they had collectively saved, followed by the precious yeast obtained through many tricky twists and turns. Finally, in went the pieces of bread each man had saved from his rations.

Then they screwed the lid shut and shoved the vat into a corner of the tent, covering it in coats and backpacks. The joy of anticipation gleamed in all of their eyes. Vanhala put his ear to the side of the vat. 'Hissing already. The oppressed are rising to power in there.'

'But we can't just leave it sitting in here alone,' Hietanen pointed out. 'Somebody's gotta stand guard. Mäkilä might suspect we took it and come and inspect the tent.'

Koskela looked like he was thinking. 'Nobody's really allowed to just hang around here. But doesn't anybody have some kind of injury? Maybe somebody could go to the aid station and ask for sick leave.'

'I got a sore throat!' Rahikainen broke in, but Koskela replied, 'No. It's gotta be somebody legit, somebody they're not going to question. Salo, you got any kind of injury you could go complain about? Wouldn't occur to anybody to suspect you of trying to get off.'

'I do have a sore on my foot. But it's almost dry already.' Salo was very flattered, taking Koskela's selection as a straightforward compliment and missing its insulting insinuation entirely.

Salo removed his boot when Koskela ordered him to show him the wound. 'Scratch it a little. And in the morning before we set off, rub it so it gets all red. Then go ask for first aid, really earnestly.'

'Tell 'em like this,' Rokka instructed, 'tell 'em it ain't that it hurts so much, it's just that it rubs when you put on'nat boot, see. And tell 'em that it's been that way for a long time, but it don't git any better so long as you have to keep movin' it all'a time.'

The next morning Salo went to the aid station and obtained his sick leave, though only for three days. But now that this precious wound had attracted the attention of the whole section, it got so much worse that after three days Salo really did limp to the aid station and easily obtained three more days' leave. So he was able to guard the vat, whose absence had caused a great hubbub amongst the supply crew. Even Mäkilä wouldn't have thought to suspect that it was Koskela's men who had taken it, mostly because it would never have dawned on him what they would do with such a vessel. Otherwise he would certainly have linked the coincidence of the vat's disappearance with Rahikainen's movements near the kitchen around the same time and drawn the obvious conclusions.

The life of the entire section began to revolve around the vat of home brew. When the men returned from laying the road, they hurried directly to the vat. They listened to it and tapped gently on its sides, and when they forgot about it for a moment, somebody would ask, 'What's hissing over there under the packs?'

'Bubba's in there.'

For some reason the jug of home brew had acquired the name 'Bubba'.

'Seems like things've been quiet an awfully long time. Be a damn shame if we got called up before he was done. We'd have to drink him as is.'

'That won't happen here. They need all the boys they got down in Crimea and Kharkov.'

'What have the Fritzis got brewing down there, anyway?'

'Let 'em brew whatever they want. All we're worried about here is what's brewin' in Bubba.'

'In my town, we had this one old guy, this Heikki Vastamäki, who cursed like a sailor. And one time the minister stopped in to ask for something to drink, and this Heikki, he pulls the blanket off his keg and says, "Beer brews like a bastard and grain floats like shit, but why the hell is a pastor here askin' for it?"'

'And once, in our town—'

'But I was saying—'

'Or then this one time—'

The low rumble of fire echoed from the line, ersatz coffee bubbled over the campfire and, in the corner of the tent, the home brew was hissing away.

## II

June 4th, 1942, was a glorious summer day. The Marshal was celebrating his seventy-fifth birthday, and the event consumed the whole of public life. For those in the army, the day was remarkable because it brought with it one bottle of liquor for every five men: 'cut cognac' it was called.

'But just one thing. When we start getting sloshed, we can't make a racket. So if anybody in the group starts looking for a fight, we all take him down together, OK? What do we do to him?'

'Butter his balls in rifle grease.'

'OK.'

'OK.'

'Sh'we get things rolling with Mannerheim's liquor?'

'Cut cognac, heeheehee! What do you think you cut cognac with?'

Hietanen measured out the drinks into field cups, and when everybody had some, they took a group swig. Hietanen raised his cup and said, 'So, hey, cheers! To our good luck! Better dedicate the first one to Lady Luck for sparing us so long.'

Cups turned bottoms-up and the bliss of the celebratory drinks settled over the men.

'C'mon, that's nothing, let's have Bubba!'

'What are they gonna say tomorrow when they find out where the soup vat's been?'

'Bah! Don't worry about tomorrow!'

Hietanen shared the home brew around and they gulped it down, coughing and choking. No one would have dared criticize it, seeing as it had already afforded them the joy of anticipation, which made its waters sacred. It was beyond reproach. They downed another round and grew drunk with glee, more from the pleasure of knowing that they would soon be drunk than from the actual alcohol, which hadn't had enough time to take effect.

Conversation grew livelier. A sort of radiant joy seemed to rise in each of the men. They were quick to laugh at even the most pitiful jokes, and a powerful atmosphere of camaraderie and fraternity soon reigned within the tent.

'Aw, shit, it warms a belly to the depths!' Rokka smiled. 'Hey! Koskela! Why ain't you over at the command post? They got the big shots' liquor over there.'

'Nothin' as big as this jug here.'

'You sure don't do much drinkin' with them other officers.'

'Why should I? Right here's where I come from.'

Faces here and there were already flushed pink, and Salo was off to such a rip-roaring start that he was already singing Koskela's praises. 'No, guys. Say what you will, but there's not many sections got a top dog like we got.'

Koskela didn't pay him any attention, and none of the others was quite drunk enough to start launching into public confessions just yet. They stuck to praising the home brew.

'Stiff stuff. Starting to feel it, boys!'

They drained one cup after another, and soon the conversation turned to the various phases of the war and the friends who had fallen. 'It's been rough, boys. Guys dropping like flies . . . you remember the time we flanked the road for that shitty encirclement and the stretchers were dripping with blood? That guy was tough all right . . . I mean, if you wanna tell it straight, Lehto was tough as nails . . . guy killed himself for nothing . . . Yeah . . . sure was . . . sure was . . . Lahtinen was as good as they come . . . got 'im in the back of the ear . . . Aren't many guys would of even started lugging that machine gun back.'

'Lissen, Koskela,' Rokka said, 'you oughdda make 'em git another stripe for Määttä, now that he's replaced Lahtinen as squad leader and all. Not that those ribbons are worth anythin', but since that's how it's done and all. He's a good fella.'

Koskela hadn't said anything yet. Little by little he had started looking around at the others, always fixing his steady gaze upon whoever happened to be speaking. Now, weighing his words, he said, 'I know the guy.'

Salo turned to Koskela, hands flailing. 'But look, Koski! Maybe I ain't the best, but I still done purty good, ain't I?'

Koskela looked at each of them again, staring at them for a long time. Then, weighing his words as carefully as before, he said, 'Tough crew.'

'Yeah, I say so too. And no other crew better come stompin' all over us.' Hietanen might have been the drunkest of them all, bobbing his head as he spoke, hair falling in his eyes.

'Hey, guys, put my share in a bottle, huh? I'm gonna go check out the villages,' Rahikainen said.

'On the other side of the Svir? How you figure you'll do that?' Hietanen asked.

'They got convoys driving over all the time. But there's a big encampment even closer to here where they got some ladies laying a road. The guys on leave said so. Whatta ya say, boss?'

Splotches burned red on Koskela's cheeks. He stared silently at Rahikainen for a long time and finally said, 'Guys come and guys go, and that's their business. I'm not going to give you permission, but if you want to go AWOL, that's your responsibility, not mine. Tomorrow morning we head for the line right after we eat, and if you're not there then, you'll get hit with ten times normal guard duty. The things we have to do, we do – otherwise, we might as well be Lulu's chickens on the loose. Remember that, and you can go.'

'Okey-doke! If I'm alive, I'll be there. You betcha. Now gimme some a that home brew, huh?'

They eyeballed Rahikainen's share and poured it into two bottles, which he wrapped in his blanket and stuck in his bag before taking off.

'What the hell you takin'na blanket for?'

'A man's gotta put something down! Who's gonna lie on the bare ground?'

When Rahikainen had gone, Rokka said, 'Yup, I bet he makes it.

That fella there's gonna make it through this whole war without a scratch. Too slippery for even a bullet'ta catch, that one.'

'Yeah, but Jesus, come on. Now I don't wanna be mean or anything, but I have to say, it's pre-tty rare that Rahikainen puts himself in the line of fire.'

'Sure is!' Salo chimed in, pointedly. But Sihvonen, not exactly belonging to the fleet of the fearless himself, was not eager to discuss heroism and sniffed, 'I don't know about that. Every man here's been scared.'

'Scared . . . scared. Everybody gets scared, some guys just know how to hide it better . . . There ain't no such thing as a guy who ain't afraid of death.'

They all raised their voices in agreement, save Rokka, who smiled and said with a wink, 'Now, don't talk nonsense, fellas. How could I be scared a sumpin' I ain't never seen? But hey, fellas, let's play sumpin'! Lissen, Sankia Priha the Great, put on "Yokkantee!"'

Vanhala dug out his record-player. Its spring was broken, but Vanhala turned the record with his finger, which worked well enough. The rhythm was a little off, but in their current state of bliss, nobody noticed. They played 'Yokkantee' and 'Army Battalyon', records they had named according to the words they could make out the most clearly. One or two of them even took a crack at singing along, belting out garbled, vaguely Russian-sounding noises over and over again.

Eventually Vanhala got tired of turning the records and their attention drifted off in search of the next source of amusement. At one point, somebody finally remembered it was Mannerheim's birthday, but they didn't drink to him just then because they were saving the home brew, and by the time they poured the next round, Mannerheim was long since forgotten. But Vanhala had promised to sing in his honor, and since the others were eager to hear something, he began,

> Shackles of the nation tremble with frustration
> Finland's cup of misery has reached its very brim

Casting off the chains of tyrants, Finland rallies up the finest
Forces in the noble nation, braced for battles grim . . .

'Goollord, boy! That'ssa rebels' song you're singin'!' Rokka
exclaimed, but Koskela motioned Vanhala to continue. He'd found
the rhythm in his fingers and was tapping in time with Vanhala's
song, even humming along here and there. Koskela had known the
song as a boy, since back before the Finnish tenant farmers had won
the right to own their land, the Koskelas had been quite red indeed.
Two of Koskela's uncles had been shot at the hands of the parson's
son, a Jaeger trained in Germany, at the base of the hill by the village hospital. Thanks to his sturdy constitution, Koskela's father
himself had made it out of prison camp alive, but only barely. The
Koskelas had rented their farm from the parsonage, and it was to
the parson's severe disappointment that he had one day glimpsed
this phantom of a red scoundrel staggering home to claim the farm
now lawfully his. Afterwards, the elder Koskela had gradually softened, and when his two younger sons fell in the Winter War, and his
eldest was promoted to the rank of officer – making him nothing
less than a legend in their little district – the two uncles' graves by
the hospital hill came to be noticeably better kept. The elder Koskela
wasn't particularly surprised by his son's promotion, seeing as he
himself had commanded a company in the Red Guard, and if by
some stroke of luck he had managed to escape execution himself, it
certainly wasn't because he hadn't been a hell of a rebel. Of course
his son would have inherited his military gifts: his bravery and
strength, his calm, steady intelligence.

Even in the parson's estimation, an improvement of some
sort had taken place over the course of a generation. So, if now,
in his drunken revelry, the Koskela boy was humming the Red
Guards' March, the parson was none the wiser, and even if he
were, he would certainly have forgiven him. The rebels' anthem
sounded curious indeed in the mouth of an officer, but Koskela
just kept asking for more and the slap-happy Vanhala kept it
coming:

Fat administration, beyond saturation
Lawless, lynching minions, executions without trial.
No one knows as chaos rages – will our nation's hist'ry pages
Tell of revolution or of reconcile? . . .

There Vanhala's song ended, as he was unable to continue, having dissolved into chortles of laughter. The lynching minions and raging chaos cracked him up especially, and he kept repeating the words over and over between fits of giggles. It was as if he could just taste the hopeless naïveté of the lyrics and wanted to suck out every last drop of their sweetness.

And so the celebrations continued until at last the home brew ran out, and they moved outside. They played Vanhala's gramophone now and again, belting out their own bastardized renditions between songs. Koskela himself didn't sing, but urged the others on all the more insistently for all that. He listened closely, as if there might be something remarkable in there, amidst the din. He had never really been interested in songs and such, and indeed, his expertise in such matters was rather weak. He didn't even know the names of the songs, which was why he kept having to say things like, 'Guys, do the one with Lotta Lundgren and the stable nags!'

A miserable melange of belches and bellowing rang out:

Beneath the shaaady pines
There lies a waaaaar canteen
Where Lotta Lundgren, she
Boils up the weak caffeiiiiiine . . .

Echoes rang through the densely wooded grove, mingling with explosions of artillery fire in the background as the cannons boomed in the Marshal's honor.

'Hey lissen, Sankia Priha the Great! Play "Yokkantee!" I'll dance. I'll dance like Veerukka in Petroskoi . . . You fellas remember?'

Hietanen dug Vera's pin out of his wallet and started swinging his head back and forth as he hollered, 'I I I I remember!!!!!!!! Hahaa . . . Do I remember!!! The pin of the Soviet Socialist

Republics . . . Take a look, boys . . . I remember all kinds of things . . . Hahaa!'

Vanhala played and Rokka danced, attempting a rather peculiar rendition of Vera's spinning, but demonstrating marvelous virtuosity in doing so. Hietanen spread his arms out and shouted, 'Hahaa! Listen, everybody! Big shot here's giving a speech! I am the defender of our homeland. We didn't want anything at all 'cept to build our houses and saunas in peace. And build up this country . . . Hahaa . . . Hink hank hoonaa . . . *Niemi's big bull climbed the Santaranta hill, his big ol' balls a-dangling* . . . Blessed are the airheads, for they will never drown . . .'

Rokka spun faster and faster. '*Yokkantee an' Yokkantee* . . . Aw shucks, that's swell! Suslin's on leave . . . gonna bring me back a package from the missus . . . *Yokkantee an' Yokkantee* . . . Looka here, Hietanen, watch me dance . . .'

Hietanen was completely gone. He staggered about with his arms stretched wide, shouting, 'Look, boys! I'm an airplane!'

He swerved around back and forth, vrum-vrumming his lips. 'Look out, boys, Messerschmitt coming in!'

At that point Vanhala's gramophone went silent and its operator, bubbling with delight, joined in the airborne antics. 'I-16 swooping down on the left, engine's howling at max rotational speed, pow pow pow! Vicious air combat . . . Warriors of the skies in the thick of battle, pow pow pow pow pow . . . The last knights of war, pow pow pow pow!'

They veered around each other, arms extended, vrumming and pow-pow-ing, and in between Vanhala would shout, 'Heroes of the great blue skies . . . with their engines roaring, eyes sharp, hands firm, and hearts steeled, our fearless aviators take on enemy predators . . . pow pow pow pow pow pow pow . . .'

Hietanen tripped on an alder stump and crashed down. And there he remained, unable to get up. Vanhala swooped round in an elegant whoosh, engine roaring, and yelled, 'Pull the parachute! The plane's going down! Heeheehee . . .'

'Plane's going down! Whoa, I'm dizzy . . . Everything's spinning like my head's turning round,' Hietanen slurred, pawing at the grass as he tried to grasp it in his hands. Vanhala yelled into his ear, 'You're in tailspin! Jump! There's no way you can turn it around . . .'

But Hietanen's plane was falling with ferocious speed, spinning and whirling through its descent. No longer in a position to leap, its pilot fell with his plane into a fog and then, complete darkness. Vanhala left him there, disappointed that their battle had been cut short.

Somewhere off to the side, Määttä, Salo and Sihvonen were sitting around on a rather large boulder. Salo was lecturing the others gravely, his hair flopping in his eyes, 'In our county the will-o'-the-wisp is real bright . . .'

Sihvonen turned his head away and swatted his hand as if fending off mosquitoes, 'Oh please, come off it . . .'

'Well, I think it's true. Old people's seen it. Even seen crossed swords over the spot.'

'Oh, stop it . . . Lapland witch tales. Maybe way up north they have some of those wonders.'

'But who here's from way up north, then?' Määttä asked. 'I mean, where I'm from's so far up, we brew our coffee over the northern lights.'

Määttä had been totally silent the whole time, and even the home brew didn't appear to have had much effect on him. Now he stared at the rock and proposed, 'Now that there's a rock. What do you say we lift it?'

'I don't think so . . . that one's not comin' up.'

Määttä circled the rock, contemplated it in silence, then grabbed hold of the corners that offered the best grip. The rock was almost as big as the man himself, but lo and behold, up it came, a few inches or so. Määttä straightened himself up, clapped the dirt off his hands, and said, 'Didn't I say it'd come up?'

Sihvonen estimated that his odds were just about nil, but Salo took hold of the rock and gave it a yank. The rock didn't budge, but Salo suddenly grabbed his back with both hands. 'I pulled something in my back. Shit! If the damn thing hadn't turned like that, I think I'd a gotten it up.'

'You just lifted it the wrong way if you put your back out,' Määttä said, gazing at the rock with an air of calm superiority. But Salo was still holding his back, his face contorted with pain. Maybe he actually had sprained his back. Hadn't his foot started to hurt too, after he mentioned it?

Rokka had stopped dancing. Vanhala was playing Stalin's speeches to himself and Koskela had started off toward the command post.

'Koskela! Where you goin'?' Rokka called after him.

'Jerusalem!' Koskela was groping his way uncertainly along the path, beltless and hatless, the front of his combat jacket undone.

'You goin'na the command post?'

'I am going to the Führer's Headquarters.'

They inquired no further, gleaning from Koskela's evasive replies that he wasn't about to tolerate other people's meddling in his affairs.

He set off decidedly, though not without a swerve off the path here and there. Stiff and unflinching, his blue eyes stared into the grove of alders. Between hiccups. Then he stopped and belted out, '*O, crash! Lake Oooonega's waaaters . . .*'

## III

A group of the battalion's officers had gathered in the machine-gunners' headquarters to celebrate. It was more comfortable there, since it was located furthest away from the front line. It certainly wasn't the renown of Lammio's hospitality that had prompted their selection. Kariluoto was there, as well, having been promoted to lieutenant in Petroskoi. He'd left his company in the care of a platoon leader and set off to join the party. He'd been downing drinks with great gusto and was already spouting off about the task of being an officer. 'The only way to influence a Finn is by example. And then you have to spark his ambition. A private feels his subordination in relation to his superior, and that feeling has to be directed so as to persuade him to carry out acts that will make him feel he's rising up to the level of his superior. But above all, no weakness . . . lock it up inside of you, whatever it is. On the outside – like a rock.'

Lammio was sitting at the table in his best uniform, decorations splayed across his chest. Pale-faced, he was nodding off in a drunken stupor. Some young ensign was lying on his back on Lammio's bed, saying, 'Oh my drunken brothers. *Helsinki is in my heart, and in my sight . . . oh that happy city of delight . . .'*

Kariluoto remembered Sirkka. 'Hush . . . shhh, Jokke. Don't get me all revved up . . . I remember . . . I remember . . . That time I danced that tango of yours. *Taa daa didadaa dida dida dida dii daaa dididaa . . .'*

Kariluoto looked rather amusing sitting on the bed demonstrating his tango moves. 'Sirkka's tango. *Taa daa dii di . . . ta dida daa daa diidi . . .'*

A slim ensign with spectacles was sitting on Mielonen's bed, the latter having been driven outside by the party. Interrupting Kariluoto's wistful tango, he suddenly burst out singing, *'Die Fahne hoch . . .'*

The 'Horst Wessel Song' made Lammio come to. He rose, swerving as he attempted to straighten himself up, then shouted behind the door, 'Bursche!'

The orderly stepped inside and stiffened to attention.

'Fill the glasses.'

'Yes, sir, Lieutenant!' The orderly poured the drinks and disappeared. Lammio raised his glass and said, 'And now, a drink to the officers. Gentlemen, our task is clear. We are the backbone of the army. On our shoulders Finland will rise, or fall. Gentlemen, unswerving we follow, wherever Mannerheim's sword may lead.'

*'Zum Kampfe stehn wir alle schon bereit,'* sang Spectacles, and the glasses clinked.

'Backbone,' Mielonen muttered behind the door. 'In that case, we got a weak link in your spot, my friend.'

Even the calm and eager-to-please Mielonen was beginning to feel that he had had enough. It wasn't until the advance had stalled, setting them in the deadlock of a positional war, that it had really become clear what it meant to be Lammio's battle-runner. The crowning glory was the Lieutenant's mongrel mutt, which he was obliged to refer to not as 'it' but as 'him'. Mielonen had actually conspired with the orderlies to tie 'him' to a twenty-pound rock and launch both into the pond, but the next day Lammio had put in a phone call to one of his buddies higher up in the division and requested a new pup. They decided not to repeat the stunt, since they knew that while one incident might escape notice, systematic dog drownings were likely to arouse Lammio's suspicions.

Mielonen rose as he saw Koskela approaching and walked down the steps to open the door. He was rather stunned when Koskela, contrary to all Mielonen's prior experience with the man, growled in a voice looking for a fight, 'Who the hell are you, the goddamn doorman?'

'I'm Corporal Mielonen, Lieutenant, sir,' Mielonen said, rather bewildered. The contrast of Koskela's outburst with the tact and discretion he had always demonstrated before made it all the more upsetting. Then Mielonen noticed Koskela's hazy, dilated eyes, realized what was going on, and stepped away from the door as Koskela said, 'Well, if that's who you are then don't go falling over yourself to open doors like you were a doorman.'

'Yes, sir. I mean no, sir, Lieutenant, sir.' Mielonen was so confused that he kept calling Koskela 'sir', despite the fact that they had been on casual terms for quite some time now.

Koskela stepped inside. Hair rumpled, buttons undone and slightly unsteady, he lurched to the center of the room and said, '*Zrastooi.*'

The others didn't appear to take much notice of Koskela's arrival, nor his curious Russian greeting, but Kariluoto lit up at the sight of him, calling out, 'Well hello, old man! Where have you been? Why didn't you come along with the group? Hey, orderlies! Let's have a glass for my boy Koski here. Here, take a swig from mine – there's some first aid for you.'

Koskela drained Kariluoto's glass and took a seat on the bench. He stared at each man in turn, one after the other, without saying a word. The orderly came round to fill the glasses, then disappeared.

Ensign Spectacles started in again on his interrupted solo, *'Die Strasse frei den braunen Bataillonen . . .'*

Koskela started staring at the singing officer. At first, the man just kept on singing, but soon the strange fixity of Koskela's gaze began to make him uncomfortable. Assurance fell from his voice and even the melody turned tail as he struggled to remain self-possessed in the face of this unflinching stare. Finally, he was forced to stop singing entirely.

Suddenly Koskela said, *'Siberia bolshoi taiga.'*

'What's that?' the Ensign asked uncertainly, his voice strained.

Koskela didn't answer him, instead saying in the same husky voice, *'Dobra hoo-ya.'*

Now the Ensign was entirely unnerved and flew into a rage because of it. 'Who is speaking Russki here?'

'Koskela the Finn. Eats iron and shits chains.'

Kariluoto realized that Koskela was looking for a fight, and offered him a drink to distract him, but Koskela shoved his hand aside and started to count out insistently, *'Odin dva tri pyat . . . Odin dva tri pyat . . .'*

'Have you got something against me?' Spectacles asked, growing ever more furious. But Koskela just continued on in his curious tongue, *'Union sovyet sosialist . . . tis . . . list . . . k republeek . . . Holodna karasho maatreeoshka dee-yay-vushka krashnee-soldier komsomolski homoravitsha bulayeva Svir . . . Dada dai dada! Dada dai dada . . .'*

It finally dawned on Spectacles that it was the foreign language of his song that had prompted Koskela's carrying on. 'I can speak Finnish too,' he said. 'And you might do well to stick to it yourself.'

'Guh . . . gun . . . gunners . . . *Dada dai dada! Dada dai . . . dada.* Martti Kitunen, Hunter of Bears . . . *dum-dee-dum dee-dum-do Jack Frost blows the windows . . .'* Koskela sang. The tempo mounted and Koskela hissed the words through clenched teeth, *'Father Christmas in his snow frock, tousled hair, snow-cape and gray sock—'*

On this last syllable he suddenly rose and punched the Ensign, who had also risen and was standing beside the bed. The officer was knocked unconscious and collapsed onto the floor, his spectacles sailing off into the corner.

The others rushed to contain Koskela. Even Lammio tried to grab hold of him, but was sent flying into a wall like a cast-off glove. Just then Koskela took hold of the heavy bench and swung it up into the air, saying, 'Stay back, damn it. Or I'll shift to second gear.'

'Koski, calm down,' Kariluoto urged, but Koskela no longer recognized him. The ensign lying on Lammio's bed seized Koskela's arm from behind and got him to drop the bench. Then the others were able to get a hold of him. Spectacles came to and started spitting the blood out of his mouth. Lammio called for Mielonen, who came inside with the orderlies on his heels.

'Tie this man up . . . Tie him up!'

They managed to get Koskela face-down. Five, maybe six men were lying on top of him, but he still wriggled around like a bear beneath the pile of them. At last they got three belts around him, and Koskela was helpless. Nevertheless, he clenched his teeth and growled, 'I'm not giving up, damn it! Damn it, I'm not giving up.'

Then they carried him off to his tent with a sizeable brigade in tow. Kariluoto walked beside him, chatting to try to calm him down, until finally Koskela asked, 'Who're you?'

'Why, I'm Kariluoto! Don't you recognize me? It's me, your old friend.'

Koskela lit up. 'Well, hello there! So long, boys . . . Where we going?'

'To lie down. You're tired.'

'Tired . . . Old Lady Koskela's boy never gets tired . . . *Then Antti of the Isotalo's came by . . . singing all the way from Härmä da-dye . . .*'

The casualty rate in the tent was rather high as well. Only Rokka and Vanhala were still up. Määttä had actually taken the initiative to go to bed, but the others had just dropped out on the field, as it were.

Vanhala was playing Stalin's speeches and Rokka was telling tales of yore. 'Looka here . . . I keep this lil' almanac with me all a time, see. And then one time I go back home with the missus to her parents' place and here I am flippin' through this almanac here so her ol' man asks, "Anythin' in'nat book a yours 'bout the fishin' for t'marra?" 'Nen I read, "Fish's swimmin' this time a year an'na pickins's good". And shucks! Next mornin'na ol' man comes back with a whole heap of 'em, and he says Tommo went out and bought all kinds a books, too, but no good ever came a any a those. Shoulda seen how the ol' man was worked up! But then'na next day he asks me again and I read him the same bit, but he doesn't catch a damn fish all day. So then he gits all sore 'bout the whole thing and won't open his mouth for three days. And then there's the missus, who got sore 'bout it, too, cause I put one over on her ol' man.'

Vanhala's head was nodding off as he turned the record, but he laughed nonetheless and said, 'The missus got sore . . . the missus always get sore.'

'My missus never stays sore long. You know, Sankia Priha the Great, you know what you do with a missus when she gits all riled up at you?'

'Give 'er a good whack 'cross the backside, heeheehee.'

'Stop that. I spinn'er round in a polka and I'll be darned if that don't set things right. But hey! What the hell is'sat? What'ssat they're draggin'? Those fellas gone and killed Koskela?'

They went to meet the traveling party and Rokka growled from a good way off, 'What the hell'd you folks do you gotta drag a fella back like that? What'ssa matter, boy? Somebody take a crack at you?'

'Well, hullo, sharp-shot. Who took a crack?'

They lowered Koskela to the ground and Kariluoto whispered to Rokka, 'Try to get him to go to bed. He got carried away and we had to tie him up.'

Rokka loosened Koskela's bindings and led him over to his tent. Koskela put up no resistance. He had no idea what was going on around him, and just babbled as he stumbled along, leaning on Rokka's arm. 'Hullo, you old Taipale vet. Let's sing Lundgren . . . *da da da off with the stable naaags . . .*'

Koskela dropped off to sleep as soon as he hit the tent. Rokka tossed a coat over him and came back outside.

Lammio was trying to play sober, and failing miserably, though the ruckus had dispelled his drunken haze quite a bit. He looked around at the men lying about here and there, a few of whom had vomited up the rice porridge consumed in honor of the occasion. 'Lovely . . . Very attractive . . . Well, that clears that up. The whole platoon's in the same state. What have you been drinking here?'

'Home brew. Bubba had such stuff in'nim that me and Vanhala here's the only ones left standin'! We'd offer our guests some, 'ceptin'nat we're all out, see . . .'

'You are responsible for the section until Koskela and Hietanen have sobered up. And what do you suppose would happen if we were called to alert now?'

'Well, shucks, me and Vanhala here'd go set up a machine gun and empty some belts over there, and there, and there, and there. We'd send such a hail a bullets in each direction as would settle that alarm right then and there, don't you worry. Lissen, you better not have any more to drink now, hear? Otherwise I'm gonna end up bein' company commander. Not that I couldn't do it, a course, it just wouldn't be quite right, see.'

At that, Lammio could say nothing, so the officers made their exit. The whole festive mood had been spoiled, and Lammio even started enumerating Koskela's less favorable qualities for the others' benefit. 'It is not always the case that personal courage makes a man suitable for the rank of officer. When they asked me about possible candidates for officer training, I thought of Rokka and Hietanen, but I decided against it. And this kind of thing proves that I was right to do so. As good a man as Koskela may be, he lacks the sense of tradition and the true spirit of a real officer. He doesn't fit into civilized circles – which is why he buddies up with his men and then vents his resentment in a drunken outburst. There is no other possible explanation. I wouldn't have believed it of a man so calm and restrained.'

Kariluoto hiccuped. His spirits had suddenly plummeted. Everything Lammio was saying made him feel so sick that he somewhat uncomfortably started speaking up in Koskela's defense. 'Sure, but he was totally drunk. Home brew can make anyone like that, for no reason at all.'

He remembered the shots whistling from the bunker, and how Koskela had crawled toward it, loaded down with satchel charges on both sides. And he knew that it was he, and not Koskela, who had received all the credit for that breakthrough. But it wasn't his fault. He'd done everything he could to make sure everyone knew what Koskela had done. Kariluoto could feel himself growing sober, and in his numbed state he was suddenly ashamed of the whole drunken evening and everything he might have said over the course of it. Goodness, how far away all of this was from the center of things, from that point upon which the reality of all these events turned! Kariluoto didn't return to Lammio's quarters, but turned off toward his own command post without a further word of explanation.

Rokka and Vanhala dragged their compatriots into the tent for the night. They brewed a pot of ersatz coffee and drank it between themselves.

Mosquitoes swarmed in the beams of sunlight streaming from the evening sky, and from high in the treetops of a nearby spruce came the hollow call of a cuckoo.

## IV

They awoke the next morning to the rustle of Rahikainen's return. Rumpled heads began to rise along the edges of the tent, eyes red and squinting, tongues wriggling about in their dry, sticky mouths. Hietanen looked around, spotted the empty vat and said, 'Well! Never taken part in a war operation like that one before!'

'You ended in a tailspin, heeheehee!'

'I can't remember a damn thing. But hey, let's put on some coffee. I need something anyway. My mouth tastes like a cat took a crap in it.'

Koskela got up too. He wrinkled his forehead in concentration, but evidently the effort yielded no insight into the festivities of the previous evening, as he subsequently asked, 'So, uh, how did everything go yesterday?'

Rokka laughed. 'Went pretty good for everybody else! It's just you they had'da take prisoner over there at the headquarters.'

'Did I go over there too?'

'Sure did. Fellas carried you back. Bound hand and foot.'

'What for?'

'You started a fight over there.'

'Mm. Mhm . . . I see . . .' Koskela ran his fingers through his hair, gave a grunt and fumbled idly with his backpack. Then his face resumed its customary, expressionless mien, and he asked, 'Well, did they say anything about it? Did anybody get hurt?'

'Naw, nothin'na worry 'bout over there. I hear the Second Company's ensign was spittin' blood, but it probably done that fella good.'

'OK. Well, if that's the worst that happened, it doesn't matter much. Better take that vat back to Mäkilä. And start getting all this equipment into piles. We're leaving right after we eat.'

Vanhala looked on inquisitively as Rahikainen lay down to sleep, and when it looked as though he might doze off without any confession at all, Vanhala finally asked, 'So, you roll out your blanket?'

Rahikainen had been waiting for somebody to grant his return due attention, and now, smiling mysteriously, as if to make the whole thing more significant, he said, 'Boys, I'm sleeping from now until it's time to eat. Don't wake me up before then! Oh, and I gave the other bottle to the guy standing guard, he traded me some Swedish crackers.'

Rahikainen pulled his blanket up over his head and fell asleep. The others started boiling up the coffee, reminiscing with rather half-hearted smiles about the previous day. Then, in the middle of everything, up rose the tent flap and in crawled Mäkilä.

'Well, hello! C'mon in!' Rokka called out. Mäkilä didn't reply. His eyes went directly to the soup vat and stayed there as he cleared his throat.

'You lookin' for sumpin'?' Rokka asked, looking at Mäkilä out of the corner of his eye.

'Chuh. Who stole it?'

'Nobody stole it,' Hietanen said. 'The guys found it over there next to the path.'

'Chuh. Right next to the field kitchen. Chuh.' Mäkilä inspected the vat. He refused to look anybody in the eye, and just kept coughing to himself, looking cross.

'It's dented.'

'Well, I'll be darned. So it is. But lissen here, don't you worry. We'll fix 'er right up. Sankia Priha the Great, gimme that piece a wood there.'

Rokka took the piece of wood and started banging the pot back into shape, as Mäkilä watched out of the corner of his eye, as if he were thinking, 'Bang away! It's not going to make it any better. It's ruined.'

Koskela wondered for a long while whether he should say something. He felt it was his responsibility to offer some sort of explanation, but then, what was there to explain, really? Finally he asked, 'You, uh, didn't need it while it was missing, did you?'

Even Koskela was not going to be spared this time, regardless of his rank, position and whatever virtues he might possess. In Mäkilä's scales, none of these carried much weight beside the offenses of drunkenness and theft on the front. He muttered angrily over his shoulder, 'Chuh! Course not . . . Don't need anything to transport food in if all you fellows need is beer.'

Koskela couldn't help smiling as Mäkilä silently hoisted the vat onto his back and set off, dripping with disapproval. Hietanen chased after him, pleading, 'Hey, gimme a few of those salted herring from the kitchen, wouldja? I need salt something awful.'

Mäkilä marched out in front, fuming silently, his vat bobbing about on his back. Hietanen lumbered along behind him, pulling at his waistband with one hand and scratching his head with the other. He kept up his campaign, undaunted by Mäkilä's outraged silence. 'Come on, you can spare a couple of herring. I'll pay you back swell for 'em sometime, somehow or other. You oughtta at least help out an old friend.'

No answer. The vat just bobbed on, and Hietanen shifted into sentimental gear. 'C'mon, wasn't I the one who whispered you the answers about the moving parts of a machine gun back in NCO training? And I always let you off easy when it was my turn to be drill leader. You could at least pay me back for that with two or three herring. Or even five, really.'

There was some truth in Hietanen's pitch. He was talking around the issue discreetly, though, as whispering in class was hardly a remarkable event. In actuality, Hietanen's help had been of a more profound nature. Quiet and devout, Mäkilä had frequently fallen prey to the rowdier boys' shenanigans, and a sharp command from the brawny, broad-shouldered Hietanen had shut up his tormentors more than once. It was for this reason that Mäkilä conceded to open his mouth. 'That was a long time ago. And why should I go get you a salted herring for your hangover? I'm not a doctor. If you don't feel good, go to the field hospital!'

'C'mon, gimme a couple!'

'Why don't you go drink some more of your beer? That'll get rid of your hangover.'

'Well, there isn't any left!'

'Go steal another pot from somewhere and make it!'

'You gonna be sore about that stupid pot till the cows come home?'

At that Mäkilä finally blew his top. 'Stupid pot? What does one little pot matter? If I didn't fight tooth and nail to hold onto stuff around here, you lot would take everything! I have to feed and clothe one hundred and fifty men with my bare hands. I've got one guy sitting all starched and spiffy in the office dugout, ordering people around, but as soon as anybody comes round sniffing for something, it's heels together and aye aye, sir! Yes, sir! Yes, sir! Without so much as a thought of holding his ground! I'd take a foxhole out there on the front lines over this job any day! If I just sat around here sucking my thumb, everything would disappear in one fell swoop. First you get drunk, then you make a racket, then you start fighting, and now you come chasing after me for salted herring! But just let things heat up again, and then everybody's got Our Father on the tip of his tongue.'

Hietanen was both irritated and extremely amused by this yoked creature in front of him with a vat bobbing about on his back. He knew which teat to tug to get the milk he wanted, though, so in a voice of pure seriousness and sympathy, he declared, 'Well, look, you took the words right outta my mouth. I don't lead that kind of sinful life at all. You sure got a tough gig, don't I know it. Never a moment's peace for you. You gotta watch this stuff like a hawk day and night. Look, I wouldn't a taken the vat, but the other guys took it. What was I supposed to do, tell you? That would have put me on the outs with my own gang. Sure, I guess you can understand that. But come on now, gimme a couple of herring!'

Mäkilä didn't reply, but Hietanen's hopes rose, as he suspected this silence boded well for him. Mäkilä dilly-dallied in the kitchen, fiddling around over here, and then over there, while Hietanen sat on a rock, waiting impatiently. He wasn't sure if he should keep pushing or not, as it could be that Mäkilä was stalling deliberately and that a renewed request would make him change his mind. Finally, Mäkilä went to the little dugout-like hole where he stored the rations. He returned a moment later with one miserable, measly herring dangling from his hand.

It was rare that Mäkilä gave handouts, so to him this occasion felt downright momentous. There was even a sort of chummy warmth in his voice as he said, 'Make sure nobody sees you eat it. Otherwise I'll have the whole lot of them after me. And don't come asking for anything else for a little while.'

'Cheers.' Hietanen was annoyed at first. But then, he had to laugh at this pathetic little herring that looked as though it had died of starvation. He could imagine how very great the gift was in Mäkilä's estimation though, so he tried to keep a straight face as he said, 'Well, gee, this'll last me a good half a year! Thanks so much, really, thanks a ton.'

Mäkilä stalled, fiddling awkwardly for a moment. He blushed with embarrassment, and after clearing his throat for a good while, said, 'It's not right for you to drink like that. We're about to set out again. At four o'clock this morning they hit a dugout dead on over at the third emplacement. Couple of boys gone and three taken to the field hospital in pretty weak condition. Chuh . . . send-offs can be pretty quick. What condition will our souls be in when the time comes?'

Hietanen was not fond of having people fret over his soul. He personally had never been too concerned about what kind of shape it was in. Somehow or other it seemed to him that since the government had sent him out here, it would probably look after him if he died and make sure its fallen soldier's sins weren't taken too strictly into account. The government had ministers to straighten things out with God, after all. Hietanen's discretion and debt of gratitude prevented him from letting Mäkilä see any of his irritation, however. So he said solemnly, 'Yee-eah . . . Don't have to tell me. Folks definitely get to thinking about that stuff when things get rough. When the lead's really coming down. But people are funny, soon as it's over, they just start singing all kinds of things and swearing like sailors. But hey, look, I gotta run. And thanks again, thanks a ton!'

Hietanen tossed the herring into his mouth as he left. He didn't have the heart to chew it, so he just gulped down the sad little runt Mäkilä had enlisted to save his soul.

## V

The section departed as soon as they'd eaten. Lammio remained out of sight, managing things with Koskela via Mielonen, who acted as go-between. As far as Koskela was concerned, the whole spat was forgotten. He tossed his pack onto his back with his usual nonchalance and said, 'Well, onwards, huh?'

Vanhala put on a Savo dialect – which cracked him up and which he did not refrain from using frequently – and commanded himself, 'Rrrrrrifles over your shoulder and forward, march!'

He heaved his gun over his shoulder in accordance with his own command and started off, grinning to himself. The others' glumness at having to depart prevented them from enjoying his antics, though.

Their spirits had reached a new low. Out in front of them there was a dugout and a trench. Other than that, life was pretty unremarkable. Things had been very quiet leading up to the spring. In April they had put down a significant enemy attack, though admittedly it had looked like a pretty close call at one point. The enemy had cut in deep from the side, but finally they managed to push them back and hold on to their critical bridgehead on the south side of the Svir.

The arrival of summer did brighten their spirits somewhat. Even Koskela looked into the dense forests running beside the log road and thought, 'Wouldn't the cows have a field day here?'

Sturdy grass had emerged from the damp soil. It was warm. It made you want to just sit on the grass and let the sun shine on you.

The men marched behind Koskela in silence. Only their heads bobbed slightly whenever a boom sounded out in front of them.

'Headed for Mount Million,' somebody said. 'Bet those fellows're making a run for their foxholes.'

Rokka glanced around. Nothing but solemn faces and steady shoulders swinging in unison. 'What's troublin' you fellas? I was thinkin' I might clear the air with a lil' singin'. I've tried just 'bout everythin', see, but makin' up a song's sumpin' I ain't never tried my hand at yet. Whadda ya say, fellas?'

Rokka's shoulders began to sway as he improvised, '*Mmbada go we gadda go we gadda go . . .*'

Vanhala scuttled over to Rokka as if he were a magnet. '*If you have a heart within you, gay or weary, come join into Singing Finland's Song*, heehee!'

Hietanen perked up as well. 'Hey, guys! I know. Let's make a kinda rat-trap that'll catch 'em alive. We can write some whoppers on scraps of paper and stick 'em round the rats' necks and set 'em loose. Then when the guys from the next dugout meet up with 'em, they can listen to what the little monsters have to say by reading the tags.'

'Hang on, boys, I got it!' Rahikainen said. 'There's that guy from Salmi in the Second Company knows Russian. If we have him write in Russian, then we can send the letters 'cross the way.'

'Let's make 'em good and dirty, heeheehee.'

'Yeah, yeah. They'll be able to see us just round this bend. Let's turn off into the forest.'

# Chapter Eleven

## I

Their bunker was situated beside a small, alder-covered hill. On the other side of the hill, there curved a trench leading to a machine-gun nest at either end. On the left, the trench continued on into a shallow communication trench connecting to the neighboring stronghold. On the right, the land dropped off into a soggy ditch, beyond which you could make out more positions. A bit further off the terrain rose, and there sat Mount Million and Mini-Million, the 'advanced posts from hell', the latter of which was worse. They were perched on a treeless hill, which came under enemy fire from three directions, because the line turned sharply to the right just behind the hill. The spot generated plenty of bad news, even during quiet periods. Each unit had to man it for two weeks at a time, so the hill was like an almanac by which the whole sector kept time: 'So and so many weeks 'til it's our turn.'

In front of the position lay a swamp, and beyond the swamp, the 'Devil's Mound', complete with mud-log enemy gun-nests. The Finns had taken the hill twice, but holding it proved to require constant, heavy fighting, so they had ceded it back both times. Only the low ridge extending from the bottom of the hill had been held, and indeed that was where both of their advanced positions were now situated. It didn't make much difference anyway, whether the line wandered this way or that at any given point, as the thing looked like it had been drawn by a nitwit to begin with. And, of course, it had been – drawn by the feuding egos of two states, both of whom had decided, 'From here we will not retreat'.

They had squabbled over these hillsides in the autumn of 1941, tired of it, and then abandoned the mess just as it was on both sides.

The positions were littered with the remains of Siberian soldiers. No one had bothered to bury them over the winter, and by the springtime nobody could bring himself to. By this time they had dried out and turned white. Nothing but hollow sockets peered from beneath their helmets.

Koskela's platoon had reinforced their bunker with beams scrounged from a neighboring town's *tshasovna*, one of those Karelian Orthodox chapels, so they didn't have any of the bedbugs that plagued the bunkers reinforced with timber scrounged from people's houses. It was Koskela who had seen to this, further enhancing his reputation amongst his men. 'Son of a bitch thinks of everything.'

A masonry oven made of round stones sat between the door and the window. Bunk beds lined the walls. Koskela's solitary bed lay below the window. The men had insisted it go there, though Koskela would have been just as content to sleep in a regular bunk. And once again, the trivial proceedings revealed a curious fact. While the men in other platoons begrudgingly addressed their officers as 'sir', turning the show of respect into a mockery, Koskela's men sought to make everything a little bit better for him than it was for themselves.

The steady monotony of the positional war brought out Koskela's quiet, solitary side even more than before. He would lie on his bed staring at the ceiling, and might remain there for hours at a time without saying a word. He had taken it upon himself to do rounds on fire-watch, half out of a sense of duty, half out of a hankering for the solitude of the night shift. He enjoyed pitter-pattering around by himself in the quiet night. His favorite task was trapping rats. He would lie motionless for a long time, holding the wire trap open beside a rat-hole, and as soon as some meddling rat would cautiously step inside, he'd pull the snare shut. Then his solitary face would light up with a wide grin as he dangled the squeaking rat before his eyes, whispering, 'Well, whatta ya know! Hullo, gramps!'

Then he would let the rat out of the trap and say, 'Ga home! But make sure I don't ever catch you round here again.'

Once in a while, just as the summer night was giving way to

morning, he would sit outside, looking as if he were day-dreaming. This wasn't precisely the case, however. His attentive eyes would be following the early morning birds, and if one of the guards happened to pass by, Koskela might say, 'Folks talk about those carefree birds up in the sky, but I've never seen a man work that hard for his bread.'

The men wrote letters, took turns standing guard, and made rings. Rokka and Rahikainen set up a business: Rokka did the making and Rahikainen did the selling. It was worth it for Rokka, even if he knew Rahikainen cheated a bit in the accounting. He didn't say anything, because the amount of money wasn't really worth it, and because he knew that, for Rahikainen, the whole appeal of doing business lay precisely in these little ruses.

Rokka had a vast supply of ring-making materials. Once, while they were watching some air combat, a Russian fighter plane had been shot down. It had fallen a little way away from their bunker, prompting Rokka to stick some pliers in his pocket, toss a hacksaw and a submachine gun over his shoulder, and take off after it.

Lucky for him, the fighter plane had fallen in no-man's-land, and the Russians had managed to get a security squad to the site to guard the wreck. Otherwise things would have been all cleaned up before Rokka could have got there. As it was, teams of scavengers were walking away disappointed when Rokka arrived. He was certainly not planning to return empty-handed, however. He managed to talk the braver of his men into joining him, and the rest tagged along behind. The Russian patrol squad vanished when Rokka shot their leader and let loose one of his terrible howls, which frightened even his own comrades so much that the less hearty among them took to their heels.

The wreck was surrounded by a terrific hubbub. One guy was lusting after the measuring gauges, somebody else wanted the parachute silk, and a third guy was after the pilot's mangled, blood-stained leather jacket. Most of them wanted the light metal alloy to make rings with, though.

Their time was cut short, as the Russians sent out a sturdier squad, compelling the 'freebooters' to make a hasty exit. By rights of leadership, Rokka was permitted to take his pick of the loot. With the triple-blade, fighter-plane propeller over his shoulder, he returned to the bunker crowing far and wide, 'Don't think those wartime shortages are gonna pose much threat to my raw material supply! But goollord, how we ran! What with those Russkis on our tail, we had'da press our tongues to the bit like a team a sled hounds. I wouldn'na managed to git this fella out if he hadn'na already come loose on his way down.'

As a result of the excursion, all of the men from the neighboring battalion who had gone with Rokka ended up assigned to the next patrol. The 'patrol volunteers', as the command put it.

Hietanen and Määttä were the most avid card-players in the group. Hietanen routinely lost his entire daily allowance, and when it ran out, he would explode into a long, post-game fury. 'Jesus! Why am I so goddamn stupid? What was I thinking pulling that last card? I'm sticking to fifteen from now on.'

Then he did an extra round of guard duty for fifty marks, and when he'd managed to lose those, he scratched his head and said, 'No. Goddamn it, I'm pulling nineteen. Might shoot it all to hell but I'm sick of being stingy.'

And so the others always knew where they could find Hietanen at any given time, and that evening Hietanen wrote in his stiff hand-writing, his tongue sticking out the corner of his mouth and following his flourishes, '. . . send meat, bread and butter. And send a little cash, too, so I can pay for my cigarettes. Sincerely, Urho.'

He never played with the money he got from home. 'But it's not worth trying to save this petty cash. It's not like I'm out here for the money.'

## II

Rokka rubbed a darning needle along the ring's surface, polishing it up with a few final touches. He raised the ring up to the window, checking it in the light, and then said to Koskela, lying on the bed, 'Lammio's clear forgotten'na come git that propeller a mine. He says it belongs to the government. Gaddamn it, if I go fetch the booty fair and square, it belongs to me. You think he knows what kind a whippin' he'd git if he came 'n' took that piece a metal from me?'

'He won't take anything,' Koskela said, rather awkwardly. He found all of the squabbling between the men and the officers bothersome.

'I don't believe it. Lissen, you don't hear how that fella bangs on and on about discipline. The sharper fellas can't stand goin'na war themselves, so they send fellas like him out to do it. And they start returnin' everythin'na discipline. 'Fyask me this whole business's gone to hell. Nothin'ssa way it oughdda be any more. The men don't know what's comin' and they start seein' everythin' like it was a joke. Pretty soon they ain't even gonna care who wins any more. And those clowns think they're makin' things better by keepin' ever-body in lock step. I can't even figger out if they believe it themselves or not. It's hard'da imagine grown men actin' that unreasonable . . . Keep the men in lock step! Gaddamn it! They spend all their time buildin' fancy chimneys for their command post and makin' a contest outta whose's the best. Ain't nothin' gonna come outta that. I've started'da wonder 'bout some a that stuff those fellas do.'

Rokka polished the ring quietly for a little while and then said suddenly to Koskela, 'You think we're gonna lose this war?'

Koskela stared at the ceiling for a long time and finally said, 'They're pressing on pretty well down south.'

'Ain't that that worries me. They're actin'na way a bumblebee does when he's caught in a spiderweb. More he tears in, more tangled up he gits. Last year I thought they was gonna make it all right, but come fall I already guessed there wasn't a chance in hell a that. Don't take a whole lotta wits to figger out what's goin' on. If they'd a struck then maybe, but any chance we might'ta had was gone by the time winter come.'

'Yeah, you might be right.' You could tell from the tone of

Koskela's voice that he'd given the matter some thought and didn't think Rokka's conclusion at all implausible.

Rokka, for his part, cast the matter aside and said, returning to his former carefree self, 'Well, anyhow, this ain't the time to worry 'bout none a that here. Would you believe I sent six thousand marks to the missus, all from these here rings?'

'Why not?'

'Hey, all you heroes out there! Mess tins's boilin'.'

They had built a grate to set atop the stove to make coffee. There were a few mess tins full of boiling water on it now, and the men wandered inside to stir in packets of coffee substitute.

'Million's still takin' it hard from those six-inchers,' Rahikainen announced, sitting on his bed, which was pasted with a series of pictures cut out of *Signal* magazine: 'Sabine before her bath', 'Sabine bathing' and 'Sabine after her bath'.

'Must not get much sun down there,' Hietanen said.

'We ain't gonna git much round here, neither, if you all don't quit stirrin' up a ruckus out there on guard duty. Sankia Priha the Great, you better quit hollerin' at them the whole time, hear?'

'Heeheeheehee!'

Koskela got up and went to the window, having spotted a few strange men heading down the path to their bunker. 'So here are the delayed reinforcements.'

The door opened and four men stepped inside. Koskela's men stared in wonder at the private who entered first.

He was a man of towering height, in his thirties, with big, earnest eyes staring out of his long, horse-like face. The real cause of their astonishment, however, was the bow and arrow dangling from the man's shoulder. He snapped stiffly to attention and, without moving a muscle, addressed Koskela in earnest, gravely respectful tones.

'Is this the bunker belonging to Lieutenant Koskela?'

'It is.'

'Lieutenant, sir! Might I have a word?'

'Don't see why not,' Koskela replied, amused.

'Are you yourself Lieutenant Koskela, sir?'

'Yes.'

'Lieutenant, sir! Private Honkajoki A, A 1: the first A designates my first name, Aarne; the second A and the one, my fitness grade. Reinforcement reporting for duty in the Lieutenant's platoon. Prior service in the Fiftieth Infantry Regiment, Second Company, machine-gunner treated for injury in the military hospital and re-assigned here by the Personnel Replenishment Center. Hereby reporting for active military duty, firmly prepared to sacrifice my own blood, as well as that which I have received via the military hospital's blood transfusion service, in the fight for our homeland and the freedom of our people.'

The man remained standing stiffly at attention until Koskela issued the permission to be seated he had been waiting for.

'Well, welcome. There's some beds over there. Two guys stay here and two guys go join the other section. You can decide amongst yourselves who goes where.'

Vanhala hesitated a moment, then hissed to Koskela, 'Keep archer-man here.'

Vanhala was afraid of losing out if horse-face didn't stay, having sensed immediately that an arsenal of pranks lay behind the man's peculiar front. It wasn't like Koskela to dictate anything he didn't have to, though, so he let the men decide their assignments amongst themselves. The three others were new recruits fresh out of boot camp, eager to join the other section so as to get out of the bunker with the officer whose presence intimidated them. So, it naturally worked out that Honkajoki stayed, finally designating one of the new recruits to remain with him – a boy who shyly whispered that his name was 'Hauhia'.

The men selected beds for themselves and began settling into the bunker. Honkajoki placed his bow carefully in the gun rack, and Rokka asked him, 'Ain't got much faith in those weapons next to yours, huh?'

Honkajoki replied politely, his full attention fixed upon Rokka, 'In light of the rapid development of weaponry and technical equip-ment that is currently in use in this great war, I find that from the point of view of the nation's defense, the adoption of new weapons is essential.'

Everyone's attention fixed upon this curious crusader, and Koskela asked him, 'Whereabouts you from?'

'Lieutenant, sir! My mother brought me into this world in Lauttakylä, but I was still a babe-in-arms when my parents relocated to Hämeenlinna, where I grew into a young man. I then grew into manhood all across Finland, as I led a very mobile life, which I might mention in passing is a reflection of my peripatetic nature. Which is to say, I have a solid dose of the explorer and the researcher in me. In truth, I am a scholar.'

'What kinda work you done?' Hietanen asked in turn. Honkajoki turned politely toward him and answered in the same stylized tones with which he had addressed Koskela, 'Sergeant, sir! I have earned my livelihood in forestry. More precisely, in pine-cone collection. That is merely how I've earned my living, however. As I mentioned, I am a scholar. My interest lies in creating new inventions, and my most immediate objective is the creation of a perpetual-motion machine.'

'Don't you know nobody can come up with that kinda thing?' Hietanen said half-seriously, as he was always something of a hard-liner when it came to anything related to the spiritual or supernatural.

'Indeed, I am thoroughly acquainted with all the difficulties associated with this invention, but I do not permit them to discourage me . . . Aha, perhaps I'll take a brief respite. Incidentally, how are the guard duties organized here, if I might be permitted to inquire?'

'Both machine guns are guarded at night, just one during the day,' Koskela said. 'You can each do a shift with one of the other guys so you have a chance to figure out the lie of the land and see how everything works around here. Might be good for Hauhia to do two shifts that way, maybe even three. Rokka, take this fellow along next time it's your turn and show him the ropes. And Hauhia, try to remember everything he tells you – somehow things look a lot more harmless than they actually are around here. What's your age class?'

'1922, Lieutenant, sir!' Hauhia snapped to attention as he responded, and Koskela said, 'OK. That'll be just fine. And you can drop the "sir". We don't stand on ceremony around here. We're all pretty informal, so just make yourselves at ease. This only applies to me, of course. With the other officers it's a different story.'

'Understood, Lieutenant, sir!' Hauhia stiffened to something like attention even though he was seated, the fear of superior officers having already developed into a reflex.

## III

Honkajoki lay down and went to sleep. The others ceased to marvel at his peculiar conduct, figuring that the man belonged to that class of guys who come out of the woodwork in a long war, ready to engage in any senseless shenanigans that will help them and others pass the time. The man had already assumed this role so thoroughly that he no longer even knew how else to behave.

Hauhia, on the other hand, didn't sleep. He would have been happy to set off immediately on guard duty with Vanhala, but Rokka said, 'Come with me. Sankia Priha baits the neighbors too much. 'Fyou head out there cold with him, some sharp shot'll nab you real quick.'

'Have you lost many men?' Hauhia ventured timidly. Rokka looked at him for a moment as if weighing his words, and meanwhile Rahikainen cut in, 'Rare day we don't have somebody bite the dust.'

'Don't lissen'na him. He's full of it. Just tryin'na scare you. We don't even man Mount Million for another two months yet. But don't you go out alone, hear! You keep that in mind.'

'I have been in an air raid,' Hauhia said, but added hastily, 'Though of course that's nothing compared to a real war.'

'Ain't no war more real than that,' Rokka said smiling, and Hauhia fell silent, thinking Rokka was smiling at his childishness. He looked around at the bunker and the men inside it. He would have asked many questions, had he dared. He was intimidated by Rokka and

Hietanen, not to mention Koskela. The fear of NCOs that the training center had drilled into him was still strong in his mind, and he watched and listened nervously as Susling said to Koskela, 'Toss me that paper.'

'Here, grab it.'

Rokka shoved his ring-making materials under the bed and said, 'Awwright, boy. C'mon! Papa's gonna show you how we fight a war.'

'Which weapons?'

'They got 'em out there, don't worry.'

They climbed out of the bunker into the connecting trench, and Rokka led Hauhia behind a small turn in the trench, where there was a pole.

'This here's the toilet.'

'Are those pamphlets?'

'Yup. Neighbors's even provided us with toilet paper.' Rokka showed him the pamphlets, in which Finnish soldiers were encouraged to kill their officers and switch over to the Red Army.

'You see what's written on'na other side? If a fella's got this note with him and he surrenders, they're obliged'da keep him alive. So keep that in mind. Take it with you when'na time comes.'

Then they continued on their way.

'Over there's the second team's machine gun. We only guard that one at night. These here're the gunners' nests. Their guard's over there. Hey! See anythin'?'

The guard glanced up from his novel to look in the trench mirror, then replied, 'Nope.'

Rokka explained to Hauhia, 'Now, don't you read on duty, even if that fella Ukkola is. So now, git this in your body head to tail: your head don't ever come up above the level'la the trench. Just about everybody we've lost round here's somebody who lifted his head up just a second too long. You needa look out, you use the periscope.'

'Sure, sure.'

'Sure sure. You don't realize they just saw you.' Rokka yanked Hauhia away from the slit in the trench the machine gun fired through. 'I ain't jokin' with you here. Every word counts. Whoever's over there may've just caught sight of you through his binoculars. It's a nice summer night and all, but don't you go driftin' off to dreamland for all that. Death's not the type to marvel over the scenery, see. Seems like it's about time for a cigarette break. You smoke?'

'Yes. But they didn't give us anything when we left but the cigarette ration.'

'I'll give you some. I can give you a whole pack when we git back to the bunker. Would you lissen'na that loudspeaker?'

'Men of Finland. Kill your fascist officers and come join us.' The loud, crackling voice emanated from the Devil's Mound.

'Fascists got knocked off a while ago. Now we're on to the communists!' Vanhala's voice rang out from the other side of the trench.

'Men of Finland. Come get bread!'

'Why don't you come get some butter to put on your bread? Heeheehee.'

'He pulls that stuff all'a time,' Rokka said half-angrily, though he was also amused by Vanhala's constant baiting. Ukkola smiled too, and said over his shoulder, 'He's even rigged up a new telegraph signal. Two shots spaced out, then three right in a row. Tap . . . tap . . . tap tap tap. And then they answer. Some crackpot over there just like him, naturally.'

'Hitler's black bandits have lost countless men and all kinds of technology. Working soldiers of Finland! You are spilling your blood while the Germans are raping your wives and sisters.'

'Uh-huh, and even the younger mothers are getting more than their fill. Heeheehee.'

*Papapapapapapapapa.*

The alders rustled and Hauhia threw himself to the floor of the trench.

'Did they hit anything?' he asked, panicked.

'*Russki vintovka, hutoi vintovka*, heeheehee.'

'There you heard it. Let's go git that nutcase outta here!'

Vanhala was watching the Devil's Mound through the periscope. The periscope was made out of two mirrors and a tube made of wooden boards. So many men had been killed by enemy snipers that now the men were forbidden from aiming without it. They had also been ordered to wear a helmet, but in keeping with tradition they had conducted an 'experiment' that left the helmet shot through with holes, so now it lay rusted on the side of the trench.

'Quit shoutin', gaddamn it!' Rokka said, when they finally reached Vanhala.

'The neighbors started it . . . heehee.'

'And they can put a stop to it, too. Now shove it, gaddamn it! What you doin' with that file?'

'I was just filing a notch across the head of this bullet. Makes a nice long whistle when it blows.' Vanhala set off, laughing as he went. He was particularly amused at the raped wives and sisters and, giggling, he dreamt up lines in his head, 'Evil German soldiers rape valiant, hearty Nordic women.'

Rokka surveyed the foreground in the mirror and ordered Hauhia to take aim. 'That's how you gotta check every time. There're fourteen bodies out there. Memorize where they are so you don't forget. If the enemy comes out sometime, you don't wanna mix up the dead and the livin'.'

'When did they die?'

'Last fall. We weren't in this sector then. There ain't nothin' but bones and maggots underneath those rags by now. See those bunkers over there on'na mound? They're aimin' from over there too. If you're lucky, you can spot a helmet sometimes. I'd like to git me one a those sniper rifles with telescopic sights and start takin'na real crack at 'em. At the beginnin' I used'da try for 'em, but then I started this ring business and I ain't had time for it. I'm tryin'na send a bit a money to help out the missus, see. She's tryin'na rebuild stuff down in Kannas. But don't you try takin' any shots at 'em for a lil' while yet. You gotta be pretty sharp to nab those fellas. And you gotta stick your own neck out, see.'

Rokka continued to lecture and instruct for the entirety of the two-hour shift. 'If they come out, then you pull on this cord here. It rings a bell back in'na bunker. And if anythin' happens, just don't panic. Aim sharp and keep steady. Knock off a couple a rounds straight away at the start, that'll quiet down the others and slow 'em down.'

'What is it like, shooting people?'

'Dunno. I only shot enemies.'

'Aren't enemies people?' Hauhia asked, smiling. Rokka's playful, careless reply struck him as funny.

'No, they ain't. Or anyway I dunno. The fellas up top say they ain't. Dunno what else they could be, but lissen, don't you go squabblin' with your conscience over all that. Or at least put it off 'til later. Fellas 'cross the way'll be happy to commit that sin if you don't wanna. I don't worry 'bout that kind a stuff. The higher-ups doin'na commandin' can worry 'bout that. They're the ones's responsible. Antti Rokka shoots and makes rings. And that's what you're gonna do too!'

'I'm not pitying them,' Hauhia said with contrived manliness, though no sooner had the words left his mouth than he was ashamed of them. For no other reason than that he feared Rokka might take him for a braggart. Hauhia had fallen under Rokka's spell immediately. He considered himself quite lucky to have been retained in the first section. To his mind, Rokka was the concrete realization of everything he had heard and read about soldiers on the front. Soon he would be just like that himself. Hauhia was under the illusion that war makes a man courageous. Reflecting for a minute, he asked, 'They say you get used to being afraid. Is that true?'

'Git used'da bein' afraid! Don't you dare. Fear's bad company, hear? You shake him off quick and make sure he stays off.'

The ground shook as a six-incher aimed straight at Million went off. Hauhia clung to the trench floor, face-down, until Rokka ordered him to get up. Embarrassed, he explained that he couldn't tell which blasts were harmless and which ones weren't. But to his astonishment he heard Rokka saying gravely and sympathetically, 'Lissen, there ain't no such thing as a harmless blast. They're all dangerous. You git down whenever you hear one. Ain't no shame in'nat.'

Two hours later, Rahikainen came to relieve them. The other machine gun was already being guarded now as well. Määttä had brought Honkajoki along and was showing him around and acquainting him with the foreground. Honkajoki had his bow over his shoulder and his arrows in a woven birch-bark quiver. Määttä wasn't sure there was any point in explaining things to this man, as he seemed somehow dubious. Maybe they had better not leave him alone on guard duty at all.

'I have indeed grown accustomed to the duties of the sentinel over the course of my military career. But has Corporal Määttä heard the story of the unfortunate guard?'

'One in particular? Day before yesterday some poor sucker got a shell on the head over at Million.'

'An unfortunate incident indeed. But I was referring to the guard on Finnish Public Radio. Has Corporal Määttä not heard his laments? I am overcome by a feeling of unspeakable despair every time I hear his wistful voice, *"I stand on guard alone, oooout here in the lonely night."* I do not understand how it is deemed permissible to keep one man continuously on guard. No one ever comes to relieve him. A truly startling state of affairs.'

'Yeah, it's uh, just that we don't have a radio.'

'Excellent. I will be spared many painful moments. But might the Corporal be aware of any good juniper groves in this vicinity? I believe I need a new reinforcement to ensure the pliancy of my personal weapon.'

'Some over on that hill.'

'Thank you. Perhaps I'll procure a spare as well. The battle for our nation's survival may well grow heated.'

Määttä watched the man out of the corner of his eye. He was reassured to see that, regardless of his odd babbling, Honkajoki did at least scan the terrain in the mirror with a sharp and vigilant eye.

## IV

Rokka took Hauhia along for one more shift that night, and the next afternoon the boy was permitted to do a shift on his own. In the morning he asked Koskela for permission to go and visit his friends from the training center over in the neighboring position.

'Go ahead. But take the communication trench and keep your head down.'

'Yes, sir, Lieutenant.'

Hauhia still couldn't quite manage casual conversation with Koskela. He set off in his excitement to tell his buddies about everything he'd seen and experienced. Koskela, for his part, just kept staring at the ceiling, wondering how anybody could be so excited about war.

Over at the neighboring position, Hauhia hardly let his buddies get a word in edgewise. It did not cross his mind that all of his stories might be old news to them by now. 'Our position's in a fucking dangerous spot. You can't raise your head at all! But the boss is solid. He just lies on his back on his bed, wiggling his big toe in between the others. They think guys like us are all babies, but they did gimme some smokes. If it'd been up to me I'd have gone on guard duty by myself right away, but they wouldn't let me. They said they were sure I'd be fine, but they're under orders not to let guys go out alone the first time. Our machine gun is fucking amazing. It even has an accelerator. At least seven hundred rounds a minute, if not more.'

'We've got the same kind.'

'Yeah, but I heard our machine gun has knocked off the most. We've got this corporal. Might even get a Mannerheim Cross soon. Guy from Kannas.'

'We've got some pretty tough guys over here too.'

'But there's this one guy at our post who's a real daredevil. Just yesterday he yelled over at the neighbors, even though it made them pepper the area so damn hard the whole forest was shaking.'

The new arrivals made their coffee substitute and drank it together. The owner of the mess kit admired the new soot that had accumulated on its side. Almost like the combat vets' tins.

They whispered amongst themselves in a corner of the bunker, conscious of the childishness of their conversation. Hauhia had more to brag about because he was on his own – and so without anyone to rein in his imagination.

'All right, bums.' (Hauhia was from the country, but he had made friends with the 'Helsinki crowd' while at the training center.) 'When are we gonna get leave? The older guys'll rotate out first, of course, but we're next in line.'

'Thank goodness machine-gunners don't have to go out on patrols.'

'You can volunteer. But it's not required.'

'Don't think I'll be volunteering.'

'I don't know. Might be nice to go see what's going on. That Rokka guy said something about taking me with him if he went out sometime. That's the corporal I was just talking about. But hey, I've gotta be back on guard duty at two. Come by our bunker round four, when I get off duty. Take the communication trench, but remember, don't raise your head. Lead poisoning is fucking dangerous. Bring some sugar with you, we can make some coffee. I'll let Koskela know, the boss I mean. And you don't have to be all official in front of him. That kind of stuff makes him laugh. I was really casual with him right away.'

'Oh we don't do any of that official stuff. This morning I was sitting in front of the bunker when the commander for this whole stronghold arrived. And I just pretended I didn't even notice him.'

'Don't forget to come. You'll even get to see some Russki-rot. There's fourteen of them. Almost reached our positions. Must have been in a pretty tight spot at some point.'

'There's dead guys here too. The neighbors even took this spot and held it for a couple of hours. The guys said they used hand grenades to get it back. Even the bunker was so covered in bodies that there wasn't even space to put your foot down.'

'Our position's never been taken. The guys load up all the barrels to stop them in their tracks before they get there. But we're headed up to Million pretty soon. Guys get killed up there all the time. Well, see you later.'

Hauhia hadn't even noticed that he was already sort of aping Rokka's gestures and tone of voice. Once he was back at his bunker, he kept glancing restlessly at the time. He was annoyed with himself for having told his friends about what friendly terms he was on with

Koskela. And now when they came . . . He tried to address Koskela casually a couple of times, so he'd be more used to it, but the words evaporated in his mouth every time. Finally, timidly, he began, 'Have you been the leader of this platoon for a long time, Lieutenant, si—?'

'Since peacetime,' Koskela said flatly.

'You must be a regular commissioned officer, then.'

'Overtime. Means I'm a reserve officer in a regular officer's job.'

'Were you in the army already in the Winter War, si—?'

'Yup.'

'As a platoon leader?'

'Yup, there too. I was a squad leader first, then a platoon leader. But I dropped back to company commander by the end.'

'What do you mean "dropped back", si—? Ahem . . . ahem,' Hauhia coughed awkwardly.

'Well, by that time the company didn't have more than sixteen men left in the ranks. My platoon had at least thirty to start out with.'

'Did you destr—, ahem, bust up any tanks?'

'A couple that had been buried underground in Lemetti. But Hietanen over there's the one that blew up a KV.'

'Oh yeah? You knock it out with a satchel charge?' (Hauhia was already as comfortable with Hietanen as he was with his friends.)

'Mine. Look, don't believe all that stuff guys tell you about fighting tanks. Most of the folks talking about that stuff never seen a tank in their lives. I was such a panicked wreck when I threw that mine, even I hardly know what happened. And I guess I was shaking a good ten minutes afterwards too – so much I couldn't even get a cigarette to stay in my mouth. Even now I sometimes have these dreams that I'm watching that tank track moving underneath its fender just about to drive right over me. Then I wake up in this horrible sweat . . . I just hope I never see another contraption like that as long as I live.'

Koskela looked up from the *Karelian News* and said, 'You can head out there by yourself now. But if you're not feeling too sure yet, you can just say so. You don't have to go alone. I can come along, or Hietanen here, if you want.'

'No . . . no, I can manage.'

'Don't doubt that at all. I'm just afraid you don't quite realize how dangerous it is out there in the quiet. Just don't raise your head! Only look out through the mirror. And don't take any unnecessary shots. Do not shoot, even if you see something – unless they're actually making a run at us. Keep an eye on the nearby surround-ings, too, they're pretty crafty in snatching prisoners. Once they came up on a guy from behind and seized him in broad daylight. But if something happens, don't panic. Just shoot immediately, don't hesitate and stay calm. Striking first is half the game. And don't rely on the fact that the infantry guy on guard is keeping watch. He's probably thinking the same thing about you. Maybe I'll go with you.'

'I'll be fine!' Hauhia burst out, and then he left a few minutes early, as opposed to the old guys who always tried to shave a few minutes off their turns in the changeover.

'Remember what I told you, now!' Rokka called after him.

'Can't do more than that,' Koskela said. 'Guy's been given all the advice there is.'

Hauhia went to relieve Vanhala from his post. He bounded eagerly over to his station and gave a Rokka-like shout, knowingly using Vanhala's nickname: 'All right, Sankia Priha, off with you!'

'I hereby hand over responsibility for the front. There's some infantry guy's rifle in the shelter, but don't use it unless you have to. Bastards'll make you into a hero real quick. You just stay here real quiet and grow into one of Finland's terrifying deep-forest warriors.'

Hauhia turned the mirror. He looked at the outlines of the gun-nests set against the smoky afternoon sky. All was calm, drowsy and still. Even the faint, far-off rumble of cannon fire over toward Bulaeva didn't seem to disrupt the sleepy atmosphere of the front. An unbroken silence reigned. Even the dark bodies lying out in front of their positions seemed to have hardened into place ages ago, melting into the general stillness.

When he'd had his fill of looking around, Hauhia dug out some paper from his shirt pocket and started writing on top of a cigarette crate. He felt slightly guilty doing so, but tried to mitigate his guilt by glancing up at the mirror every time he'd written two or three words.

Each time he checked the bodies and counted them, afraid there would be too many. Some living guy might have crawled in amongst them and might be lying in wait, ready to pounce. Hauhia had heard of things like that happening.

Suddenly a shell went off on Mount Million, and Hauhia dropped for cover, then remembered the previous evening and straightened himself up right away. A dozen or so shells went off in the space of half a minute.

Hauhia stopped writing and started looking at the machine gun. It, too, was mute and still. But to Hauhia, the dead object seemed mute precisely because in his mind, it was capable of speech. It was like a story locked in steel. Hauhia imagined this story in his head, mostly false and unfounded, like the stories the Information Bureau fed to people who couldn't tell the difference. He hadn't seen the faces unnaturally distorted with anxiety behind it, nor heard the hoarse, panicked screams and commands, the nervous swearing and cursing, nor Kaukonen's moan as he died with his face pressed into these handles. He knew nothing of the dark, rainy autumn night when it had lain beside the muddy path, the night that Lehto and Riitaoja had died.

'Good-looking gun. I wonder if there's water in the jacket? Be nice to rattle off a few rounds.' Hauhia looked through the periscope and gave an exclamation of surprise. A helmet was moving in one of the nests. Now it was still. Hauhia seized the rifle from the shelter, repeating to himself in justification, 'I won't shoot it, but just in case.'

He looked out again. The helmet was still there. For a while the urge to hunt and the fear of disobedience battled it out in his mind. Then he stepped into one of the machine-gunners' nests and carefully raised his head. 'Immediately . . . before he has a chance . . . I'll stick these twigs in front . . . they won't be able to see from way over there . . .'

He set a juniper branch in the nest's open slit, stuck in the gun and, hands trembling with excitement, tried to focus the helmet in the sight. He retained consciousness just long enough to feel the sharp blow strike his head and see stars fade into view before he thudded to the trench floor and blacked out.

## V

Vanhala's gramophone was now equipped with a new spring and some Finnish records its owner had brought back with him from his leave. Their favorite, 'Life in the Trenches', was spinning round at the moment and Rahikainen was lying on his bunk singing along.

> When the bend in the road led to war
> no one knew what our lives held in store
> which of us would return from the trenches
> which of us, disappear evermore.
> Life out here in the trenches, you see
> was the lot cast us by destiny
> And it may be destiny's ending
> that the bullets one day sing for me.

Rahikainen had a good voice, and he could even hit the high notes with no greater strain than a slightly furrowed brow. Vanhala was cracking up at the song's wistful, naïve lyrics, and at the sight of wily Rahikainen crooning with such heartfelt devotion.

> Come my fair-haired beloved to me
> bind my wounds, keep your love company
> surely you wouldn't leave me to wither
> you who know what my suff'ring must be.
> In this land where I cry out in pain
> to the tune of the bullets' refrain . . .

Rahikainen suddenly interrupted his song. Revealing that it occupied his thoughts only marginally, and that he was in fact preoccupied with more important questions, he said, 'No, I gotta start exportin' over to the neighbors' sectors. This market's gettin' too saturated. How many you got finished over there?'

'This fella here makes eight. Whadda I engrave on here? "1942"? "Svir, 1942"? Lissen, Rahikainen, we can cook up a new model. Then they'll keep sellin' here in our sector. Fellas'll buy more if it's sumpin' new.'

'How about the Coat of Arms with the Lion of Finland?'

'Picture from the five-mark coin? Price's gotta go up five marks then.'

'They'll go for it. Long as you do a nice job.'

Rokka was just hurrying to get down to work, when the cow bell hanging from the ceiling began to ring. The wire coming from the guard post was moving.

Koskela rose. 'What's that boy up to?'

'Alarm.'

Chaos set in. They yanked their boots onto their feet, grabbed their weapons from the rack and, thus equipped, ran for the trench. Honkajoki seized his bow and arrow, but he did at least take along a real gun as well. Vanhala remembered Rahikainen's song and giggled as he climbed the stairs, 'To the bullets' refrain! Heehee. As chaos rages, heehee!'

The bunker was empty. In their hurry, no one had thought to stop the gramophone, so 'Life in the Trenches', having played to the end, was now scraping out, '*eeeyaow, eeeyaow, eeeyaow*'.

As soon as the men were outside, they quickly gathered that there was no attack underway, since the infantry platoon hadn't been called to alert. So it was just something concerning their guard. As they advanced toward the guard post, they suspected that the inexperienced Hauhia had panicked, and so sounded the alarm. Things became more complicated, however, when they saw that the guard post was empty.

'Something's up over there,' Koskela said, dreading what it might be.

The face of the guard approaching them in the trench told all. The man looked earnest and rather pale, though his voice was brusque as he said, 'Better send up a new guard and cross the old one off the ration list.'

'Sniper?'

'Yeah. That gun was over there on the parapet. I guess he meant to shoot it, but the bullet never left the barrel. A helmet popped up across the way, but it was so absurdly high it must have just been bait. Then there came a bang and I suspected he'd raised his head up to peek so I came over. Then I sounded your guys' alarm.'

'Goddamn it! What did the lil' monkey do that for? And after I just spent four hours tellin' him about that exact thing! If he'd a lived, I'd be givin' that boy a swift kick in'na rear.'

'Shouldn't have been out here alone yet.'

'Yeah, though nobody can say that he didn't know,' Koskela said. 'None of us got half as much advice as he did.'

'No, we didn't.'

And so they ceded responsibility to fate.

Hauhia lay crumpled on the trench floor. In the middle of his brow, perfectly centered between his eyes, there was a small, blue hole. The point of entry had not a single drop of blood along its edges, but the back of the boy's head had been partially blown off. It wasn't an unfamiliar sight in itself, but even so, somehow or other the boy's accidental death felt more horrible than the others that had occurred amongst them. Most of the men were only a couple of years older than Hauhia, but even so, he somehow seemed like a child to them, and that made his fate even more upsetting.

Rahikainen took over for the rest of the guard shift and the others carried the body to the bunker. They set it in the front entryway and wrapped it in tent tarps. Koskela notified Lammio and Kariluoto of the incident and requested a heavy barrage on the Devil's Mound. Artillery fire had not previously been allowed without permission from the Commander, save to counter an enemy attack, and in order to obtain permission Koskela told Sarastie that he had seen a lot of movement up on the hill. Sarastie wondered why the Artillery

Commander hadn't notified him of the commotion, but he trusted Koskela so unconditionally that he granted permission. The men, too, were amazed at how naturally lying came to Koskela.

'Let the damned pigs squeal a little while,' Koskela said as he lay down on his bunk. 'The kitchen cart can take the boy back.'

They waited awhile, and soon the bunker windows began to rattle with the pressure of the first blasts a couple of miles off.

'It's the big gun over in Itävaara.'

'Could be Korvenkylä.'

'Nope. When'na fellas fire from Korvenkylä they hit to the right a that pine there. Lissen'na the rumble.'

Even quiet Susling said bitterly, 'Just git 'em good this time.'

For once they really did hate the enemy. Practically a crime, beating that kid to the punch. In any case, whatever the reason, Hauhia's death was a much more powerful agent in stirring their fighting spirit than the Military Police's execution of those two men by the sauna wall.

The barrage was still underway when Hauhia's friends arrived at the bunker. They had seen the body wrapped in tent tarps in the entryway, but in their state of anxiety at the explosions, they hadn't looked at it very closely. There were four of them, two infantry guys and the two replacements. Frightened, they scuttled quickly into the bunker, sugar cubes and rye crispbreads in their pockets. The first fellow stood at attention and said, 'Lieutenant, sir! We're here to see Private Hauhia. We were all in the same group.'

Rokka polished a ring. The others lay silent. Nobody wanted to be the one to tell the boys what had happened, so the task fell to Koskela.

'The unfortunate fact of the matter is that we've lost Hauhia. Sniper got him. Body's back there in the entryway.'

The boys tried to retreat behind one another's backs, embarrassed to be seen by this officer. The ones furthest back hesitatingly made movements to leave. Then Koskela added, 'Look, we have to take lessons from one another. Your own experience sometimes comes too late. Now, believe me when I tell you guys that games and reality are never far apart out here. They're all mixed up together.'

'Yes sir, Lieutenant.'

'Can we see him?'

'If you want. But make sure you wrap him back up properly.'

The boys didn't linger in the entryway long. They felt the same way the others had felt looking at Vuorela one year before. Glassy eyes, twisted gums, contorted, yellowed skin.

That evening Vanhala thought he'd put on the gramophone, but Koskela said, clearing his throat, 'Maybe not today, OK? We'll put it on again tomorrow.'

He had taken Hauhia's half-written letter, thinking it might be better that it not end up in the hands of his family.

*Out here, somewhere 10/8/'42*

*Dear Family,*

*I am now on the front line. There's a lot of explosions out here. I arrived with some friends last night and now I'm standing guard. I forgot to ask the Lieut' for the postal code for this sector, but I'll fill it in at the end. There are bodies lying all over the place. They weren't shot down that long ago, but they are already full of worms. Put lots of salt in the meat when you send it. Packages take a long time to get here. A barrage just started over at the neighboring position. We're supposed to go up there soon, but don't you worry, I'll be fine . . .*

# Chapter Twelve

## I

Vultures circle eyeing bloodied heroes dying –
Of this endless slaughter will we never be relieved?
Blood-thirsty souls slurping gore, raven swarms lurking –
Not until the Finnish people's freedom is achieved.

'Blood-thirsty souls slurping gore! Heehee . . .' Vanhala was chanting his satirical verses again, though his own blood had been running rather thin for a while there. He had volunteered to go out on a patrol, or rather he had traded one of the infantry guys four shifts of guard duty in exchange for a patrol. He had returned pale-faced with a bullet in his side. Now he was back from the military hospital, but in his extended absence the others had come to realize just how important the little giggler was to them. When someone gazing out of the bunker window spotted Vanhala returning from sick leave, they all rushed out to meet him, shouting raucous welcome greetings, and Sankia Priha's face, grown rounder with his leave, stretched wide into a hearty grin.

Honkajoki was hard at work on his perpetual-motion machine, which was always just on the point of reaching completion. Rokka had given up his ring scheme in favor of a lamp-stand manufacturing operation, and Rahikainen had stayed on as sales manager. Rokka wasn't a shabby salesman himself, but this arrangement allowed him more time to work. Määttä was awarded another stripe, but other than that, the life of the platoon continued on uneventfully. Even their autumn 'turn on the Millions' came and went without any casualties.

With the start of a new year, they began to receive impassioned bits of news, courtesy of the Devil's Mound. The fighting at Stalingrad was nearing its end, and things were not looking good – and the urging and entreaties of previous propaganda broadcasts had been replaced by a threatening, frightening confidence in certain victory. It was during this time that Honkajoki's bow became legendary. It was their new secret weapon, in which all hopes were invested, and Honkajoki paraded from bunker to bunker lecturing about it.

'Bottle up one of "Onega's Waves" now so you'll have something to remember her by when you retreat!' the loudspeaker would declare, to Vanhala's untold amusement. Once he'd been listening to the radio at the neighboring position when, right in the middle of the soldiers' evening prayer service, interference crackled into the background, shrieking, 'Blast those bridges, boys!'

The startling contrast had set Vanhala giggling for weeks.

Little by little the idea of defeat settled in. The army made no effort to fend it off, save a few senseless, small-scale charades. A few lively diversions and wood-chopping tasks were devised to keep their spirits up. The men in the trenches knew perfectly well what was coming, but they soldiered on with determined nonchalance.

Kariluoto went off to the Army Academy and returned a captain upon completion of his course. He was immune to the general lowering of spirits, his recent engagement having distracted him from any concerns about the future of the homeland. Inhabitants of the Third Company bunker became thoroughly acquainted with the virtues of a certain girl by the name of Sirkka. Like all lovers, Kariluoto naturally assumed that everyone took great interest in his happiness, and anyone who could bring himself to lend him an ear would never stop hearing about the girl. A certain telephone operator had become engaged around the same time, and so instantly became Kariluoto's bosom buddy – in so far as a captain and a private can be bosom buddies, that is.

Lammio had already been made a captain as well. He hadn't changed in the least – at least, not for the better; and as the situation deteriorated, he figured that the only way to combat it was to enforce tighter discipline. Koskela wasn't promoted, for the evident reason that there were no positions above his open in the battalion, and Sarastie was reluctant to lose him to another, even if the Regiment Commander had suggested such a possibility. So, Koskela was paid in decorations, and to ease his own feelings of responsibility, Sarastie repeatedly promised him that the next company commander post to open up was his.

Koskela himself wasn't particularly concerned about the matter. He had firmly resolved to leave the army as soon as the war was over, so he had no particular use for promotions. He lay on his bunk and took part in the quiet life of his platoon just as he always had.

The winter passed and a new summer came. Germany's defeat became ever more apparent, and Salo alone was able to hang on to his faith. Even the events in Italy didn't rattle him. Whispers about his steadfast devotion circulated amongst the others, and after each notice of a defeat somewhere, somebody would bait him, 'Seems like now might be a good time to pull out those secret weapons, don't you think?'

But Salo would just gaze over their heads into the beyond and say, 'They'll come. They'll come . . . They're just waitin' for the enemy to get closer before unleashing 'em. I heard they got some eight-inchers over there behind the lines. There'll be plenty of iron all right, once they decide to let 'er rip.'

'Well, I'll be darned. In that case we ain't got nothin'na worry about!' Rokka said – and still Salo managed to remain uncertain whether he was being mocked.

A quiet bitterness had appeared in Rokka, making itself felt now and again. He knew that the ring money he'd sent down to Kannas for the new house had all been for nothing. He wouldn't live in that house. The firmer this conviction grew in his mind, the more resentful he became of the officers' ongoing rivalry in kitting out their bunkers. 'Now they're makin' log lounge chairs. Guess those fellas think we're gonna be sittin' back by the fireside 'til kingdom come.'

One afternoon in the summer of 1943, he was sitting on guard duty, carving decorations into a curly-birch table lamp-stand when a colonel suddenly took him by surprise. The 'surprise', in truth, was purely the product of the Colonel's imagination, as of course Rokka had noticed him a way off and just hadn't bothered to hide the piece of wood. The Colonel was some sort of inspector charged with taking stock of who knows what. He was on a typical inspection round, deemed necessary for whatever reason, collecting observations to compile into some kind of high management report, which would be distributed amongst the divisions, and possibly even read by somebody somewhere before being shoved into a file.

The Colonel was not particularly different from any other Finnish colonel, and dreamt up nothing more than the trusty classic, 'Well, well, what have we here? What do you think you're doing?'

'Standin' guard. And you know, a guard's a kinda fella you shouldn't just up and yell at . . . on account a he's got great responsibilities to attend to.' The Colonel's tone of voice had made Rokka bristle instantly. He sat carving his lamp-stand in defiance, though not without glancing up into the periscope sharply and frequently.

'What are you doing?'

'Carvin' a lamp-stand. Ain't you got eyes? But it's got its shape pretty good now. Gonna be a beauty that's hard to beat.'

'Don't you know you're on guard duty?'

'Sure do. Why else'd I be out here? You can see for yourself I'm on guard duty, sittin' here lookin' in'na periscope! That's what bein' on guard duty is.'

'What is your name?'

'Rokka, Antero. No middle name.'

'You'll hear about this.'

The Colonel left. Rokka continued to sit calmly, carving and keeping watch. He didn't say anything of the incident to the others in the bunker, and he was already beginning to think that maybe the Colonel's threat had been empty when he didn't hear anything more about it for two days. But at the end of the second day, Koskela received a phone call from Lammio with orders to send Rokka and his squad to clean up the area around the command post and decorate the path with some rounded stones along the sides. Koskela didn't quite follow the whole command, as it sounded too absurd, even coming from Lammio. But he replied carefully into the phone, 'Yup. I'll convey the order.'

This 'convey' was Koskela's way of establishing that he did not stand behind the command. And in a voice that announced as much, he repeated the order to Rokka. The latter was silent for a moment, then said perfectly calmly, 'If anybody want'ssa go, you all feel free. I ain't goin'.'

'Why, without our leader?' Rahikainen exclaimed, aghast. 'But how're a bunch of bumblin' privates supposed to manage all by ourselves?'

'Decorate with stones, he said . . . ? Heeheehee!' Vanhala snickered, giving no indication of leaving. Susling's vote obviously fell with Rokka, as he followed his friend unconditionally.

Koskela notified Lammio of the group's refusal, adding stiffly that he would not personally get involved any more than his position required – in other words, issuing the command and notifying them upstream of the men's refusal to comply. Lammio then ordered Rokka to the command post, to which Rokka replied, 'Sure, why not? I can pay 'im a call.'

He set off, humming, stooping to pick berries along the side of the path as he went. He managed to dawdle a good couple of hours on his way to the command post, causing Lammio's irritation to attain new and unprecedented heights by the time he arrived. He stepped easily into the bunker and, unbidden, took a seat, plonking his cap onto the table. He was carrying five sturdy straws of hay skewered with berries, which he plucked off one by one and popped into his mouth as he spoke. Before Lammio had a chance to utter a word, he burst out, 'So! What'ssa trouble?'

Lammio turned his words over in his mind for a while before he spoke. 'Listen, Rokka. You seem determined to incite conflict with your flagrant disregard for the disciplinary code.'

'What'ssat? You just talk straight with me. I'm a farm boy from Kannas, see, and I don't understand all those fancy words a yours.'

'You act as if military discipline did not concern you at all.'

'It don't concern me at all.'

'Well, it's going to concern you now.'

'It sure ain't gonna concern me enough to grab a besom and start sweepin' up after you all.'

'Besom! Might you be so kind as to answer me in Finnish?'

'Don't you know what a besom is? 'Swat we call a broom over in'na East. Which word you think is right? And say, when you luck out, does that mean you got lucky or you're shit outta luck? Gaddamn it! How is it that we got men from the East an'na West squabblin' over these things a whole war long and we ain't got nothin' figgered out?'

'I am not a specialist in regional dialects, I am the Commander of this company, and I intend to make it clear to you that there is such a thing as military discipline.'

'Gaddamn it. And I'm supposed'da cut the grass an' line up lil' pebbles on'na edge a your path. What the hell were you thinkin' when you cooked that up?'

'You talked back to a colonel on his inspection rounds and the complaint came to me, urging me to punish you. Punishment did not seem to me appropriate to the offense, so I selected this task instead, as a means of determining whether or not you meant to comply. Should you fail to comply, then and only then will I press the matter further. I ordered your squad to come along as well because they comport themselves exactly as you do. Your example has borne fruit, congratulations. Your predecessor Corporal Lehto was just the same, and following in the footsteps of the two of you, the whole platoon has become a bastion of insolence and bravado.'

'You really think I'm gonna obey that order?'

'I would urge you to, I really would. You are entirely alone – there's nothing you can do. Your insolence triumphs just so long as the army is willing to tolerate it, and its tolerance stops here.'

'You think I'm afraid'da you?'

'Not in the least. I grant bravery its due respect, being a brave man myself. But you have been demanding too high a price for it for a long time now. I've yielded to it more than I should have, more than regulations properly allow. I've been waiting for you to come to your senses. Given your capabilities, you could be a soldier of the highest class – were you suitable otherwise. If you behaved like a proper soldier, or rather like an officer of superior rank, I could hand you a Mannerheim Cross as if it were a cigarette. It's been awarded to lesser men than you. I am fully aware of the fact that, amongst other things, you saved this battalion from an extremely dangerous situation last winter, sparing us who knows what destruction. I am willing to grant that in terms of fighting, you are the best man I've seen, and I've seen some real daredevils, but you cannot continue on with this misguided idea that that fact excuses you from everything else.'

Rokka plucked a berry from his skewer and said, half-seriously, 'Mannerheim Cross! Those come with a pot a dough.'

'I already told you it's a no-go. It would be like making a poster boy out of insubordination. Your insolence is more dangerous to this army than Honkajoki's mockery of it, which, incidentally, I am also putting a stop to. You have an opportunity to redeem yourself by bringing your squad to carry out the task I've assigned.'

'Nothin' doin'.'

'That means the court martial.'

'Means a whole lot more'n 'nat. Now you lissen'na me, I been thinkin' all this over too.' Rokka's easy joviality had vanished. Slowly his entire body began to shake, and though his face struggled to maintain some sort of smile, his voice was trembling with fury. 'Now lissen here, friend. Don't you play games with me. You think you're gonna break me, but believe you me, you won't – no more'n any a the others that's tried. Lissen, you know my wife down in Kannas is pregnant and out there cuttin'na rye all by herself? And you, you bumblin' bird-brain, you wanna play games with me, make me line up pebbles along your path? Gaddamn it! You really think you can push my patience just as far as you please, don't you? Here I spent a year makin' rings whose profits're sunk in'na walls of a new house I ain't never gonna see. And now I'm makin' lamps so

I can scrape together enough to build me another one. And you all're settin' up your Headquarters, usin'na gaddamn blow torch to weld decorations on'na your furniture so you can take pictures for the newspapers! "See how these fellas fixed up the Headquarters for their esteemed officers!" Sure they done it, when they been damn well ordered to! Well, I ain't doin' none a that. You got that? Can't you see what's lyin' in wait for all of us? You think the neighbors gonna come say, "Sure, you just sit back and stay there long as you please"? Won't be long now before we're all in for it. Half of us ain't gonna make it outta here alive and you clowns are raggin' on us about discipline. You're gonna be shootin' your own men soon if this game goes on long enough. But I am tellin' you now, don't you go pullin' me in'na that mess. I do what needs done in a war, but I don't go in for games. You do whatever you please. You send me 'a the court martial if that's what you want! You just better remember that fellas like me don't die like dogs. You all shot those two fellas back there by the sauna wall, but you ain't gonna shoot me that way. It's gonna cost you a few of your own buddies first. You just keep that in mind. I'm outta here.'

Rokka snatched his cap, grabbed the strawful of berries that had tumbled to the ground, and left. Lammio said nothing – not that he would have had a chance to get a word in, anyway. He was a bit embarrassed, somehow or other. The sincerity of Rokka's rage had managed to jar his consciousness at least a bit. He felt helpless for a moment. Squabbling any further felt fairly pointless after such a speech. But then he began to wonder if Rokka hadn't been putting on an act, threatening him that way. And then he remembered how he had even thought to grab his stick of berries as he left, and Lammio became more and more convinced that he had been duped. The man was a daredevil, to be sure, but now he was just trying to wriggle off the hook by putting on a show. If he had been in earnest, he wouldn't have remembered his berries in the midst of such an outburst.

Lammio got in touch with Sarastie and stated his case. Sarastie hesitated at first, but when Lammio pressed him, embellishing the story as necessary, the Major finally concurred that Rokka should be brought before the battalion for an official inquiry the following day. Sarastie was aware of Rokka's reputation – both the good side and the bad. He hesitated for a long time. Lammio's reasoning was valid. The man was famous for his bravado – the incident with the Colonel was hardly an isolated event – and his insubordination had made him a legend within the ranks, inspiring the men's admiration. He set a dangerous example. But was opposing that example any less dangerous? The man was also the best soldier in the battalion when it came to personal combat capability. That, too, had become legendary. And then to send the guy out to hoe some swamp for a couple of weeks? Maybe knock him down in rank as well? What kind of reaction was that going to provoke amongst the men?

Sarastie regretted that Lammio had ever been brought into the matter. It was really a little over the top, trying to force the man into submission by slamming him into such a demeaning assignment.

But Sarastie also felt that his own authority had been compromised – so, he concurred. Inspectors couldn't be going around reporting such things about his battalion.

## II

This incident took place during their 'turn on the Millions'. This time their lot fell to the stronghold on the right, 'Mini-Million' – the worst one. In terms of the terrain, the two posts were actually the same position, but the men distinguished them from one another because they were manned by separate infantry units. They were situated on the same rise. 'Mini-Million' was on a downward-facing slope on the right side of the ridge, which tapered off into the narrow bay of a neighboring lake. They manned the area up to the head of the lake, and after that they maintained contact with the guys at the next position with the help of a messenger patrol squad. The enemy positions were about a hundred to a hundred and fifty yards off. The terrain rose behind them, and the Millions were under direct fire from that slope, while being simultaneously under fire from the right, as well as from the back, where the lake's inlet curved around them. It was precisely this crossfire that made the positions so dangerous. The fortifications had been poorly constructed, due to their proximity to the enemy. Amongst other things, there was no barbed-wire fencing at all, and the shallow trenches, lacking any structural reinforcement, were continually collapsing under the constant shelling. On occasion it could be quiet even here, but for the most part things tended to be lively on one side or the other, more so than at any of the other positions.

After his visit to the command post, Rokka was quiet and irritable all afternoon. He offered no explanation of the incident other than saying, 'What's to know? Fella asked the only stuff those clowns can think to ask . . .'

It happened that he had the graveyard shift that night, from midnight to two a.m. He relieved Vanhala and made sure the hand grenades and submachine gun were all in place. He could hear the infantry guard coughing off to the left. The machine-gun nest was on the far right, thirty yards from the lake, and the messenger patrol guys kept in contact from there.

The August night was almost dark because of the heavy cloud cover. A gentle wind rustled the grass in the foreground, and Rokka kept sharp watch, listening attentively. After he'd been on duty half an hour, he took the flare gun from the niche cut into the trench wall and shot off a flare. He hadn't heard anything special, but it amused him to shoot the flares. The bluish light would flicker for a moment in the air, giving Rokka a chance to inspect each rise in the terrain. Nothing but grenade craters, a few bodies and the gun-nests looming further off. Rokka ducked his head, knowing that his flares would bring about two outcomes. First, the enemy would shoot off a few rounds, and after that the guy on guard duty in the neighboring position would get restless and shoot off his own flare. The perfect regularity of the sequence made Rokka smile. He was of a mind to answer the submachine-gun fire, but he restrained himself, as it would prompt more fire in return, as he also knew from experience. It would make the enemy hit the positions with some direct cannon fire, in other words.

A rustling sounded from the communication trench and Rokka took the submachine gun under his arm and turned toward the noise. He suspected the messenger patrol from the neighboring position must be approaching. The men suddenly popped up right in front of him, before he had even been able to distinguish them from the darkness. Rokka kept his submachine gun at the ready the whole time.

'Who'ssere?'

'Just us. Home team . . . Oh! Sankia Priha's off duty already.'

The men had come to know Vanhala by his nickname. They knew Rokka as well, and lingered for a moment to chat. Rokka was rather taciturn at the moment, however, so the men returned quickly to their position.

After the men left, Rokka thought for a moment about his old plan to blow up the enemy gun-nests. He had looked out many times, even laying out the route of how he would crawl over. He wouldn't have started considering the gamble if it hadn't been for the idea he'd hatched that the stunt might earn him a leave. But this time the whole scheme seemed like a waste.

'They'll slap me in'na can for sure. That'll be it for my leave. Bastards do that and I'm finished. I ain't doin'na damn thing after that. And when I ain't even done nothin'! Gaddamn it they ask stupid questions, and in that awful tone of voice, like I was some kinda criminal . . .'

Rokka was fretting over the affair, as he knew perfectly well how much trouble it might cause him. But he was also resolutely decided that he was not going to back down. 'Even if they up and shoot me, damn it. Anyway, I ain't wastin' any more time thinkin' about this nonsense. There we are!'

Rokka reinforced his mind's movements by dropping his shoulders, as if to slough off the burdensome, bothersome weight of the whole issue. He slipped naturally into just the right means of eluding these useless worries and wonderings.

He hunkered back down to his previous vigilance on guard duty. Actually, Rokka always lived in the 'here and now'. All that existed for him was the night, the rustling grass, the voices carrying over from the enemy side, and the odd shot that would ring out now and again. Lammio and military discipline were distant, unrelated trifles that had nothing to do with his guard duties.

A blast exploded with a flash of light. For one second, a red flame illuminated the curve of the trench. Not until after the explosion did he hear the boom of the launch.

Rokka quickly ducked down into the shelter in the trench wall. Another shell exploded about a dozen yards off. Shrapnel sailed through the air and dropped onto the parapet. The barrage continued intermittently for about five minutes. Rokka scrambled out of his shelter and shot a flare, but then hurried immediately to the neighboring gun-nest. The terrain in the foreground was empty, but the cannon fire was picking up speed. Then a short pause ensued, followed by a few shells.

When the firing had stopped, Rokka held his breath and listened for a long time, but no unusual noises followed. Soon he was restored to his previous calm and stood quietly at his post. Then he heard the tiniest of rustles coming from behind the communication trench. A clod of dirt fell onto the floor of the trench.

Rokka held his submachine gun under his arm ready to shoot and took a few steps from the gunner's nest toward the communication trench. He suspected the patrol squad was back again, but the uncertainty of the clamoring gave him pause. Normally the men didn't bother much about trying to be quiet.

Rokka was no more than a yard from the bend in the trench when the rustling sounded again directly behind it.

'Who'ssere? Password!'

A towering figure appeared before Rokka, and a great deal happened in the space of the next few seconds. Rokka was about to shoot right away, but the thought of the patrol squad that had just been there cost him a precious tenth of a second. The impression still fresh in his mind, he hesitated for an instant rather than following his initial instinct, and in that same instant the barrel of his gun was pushed to the side. In a flash Rokka grasped what was happening and, in the blink of an eye, began moving without hesitation. They were going to take him prisoner. Rokka quickly loosened his grip on his submachine gun, giving up the struggle over it and instead pulling the same trick that had just been pulled on him. He shoved the hand holding the pistol aside. The pistol went off as Rokka howled, 'Help! Sound the alarm! Enemy in'na trench!'

The man was already upon him as he yelled. Rokka's plight was desperate in the extreme. The man wrestling him was at least as tall and powerful as he was, and his first move had revealed him to be both quick and determined. And Rokka glimpsed another one behind him. Luckily, the trench was so narrow that the men behind couldn't get around right away and so had to stay behind the man fighting with him. Rokka knew that as long as he remained in this position, he couldn't be struck or shot, as the man acted as a shield protecting him. The pistol went off again, but again missed, as the man's wrist was stuck fast between Rokka's arm and his side. The pistol was within Rokka's reach, but if he let go of the man's hand, he was done for. The enemy squad must also have realized by now that the operation had misfired, so they would no longer have any interest in keeping Rokka alive and would just try to get themselves out as quickly as possible.

'Guard! Help!'

A submachine gun started shooting into the air about twenty yards off, and Rokka could see over the shoulder of his opponent that it had attracted the attention of the man behind him. But there were even more men beyond him. Both wrestlers grunted, teeth clenched, and the Russian hoarsely tried to say something to his friends, but Rokka's forehead happened to be pushed up against his mouth at just that moment. Rokka was trying to whack his head into the man's face, but he couldn't manage to get any force into the blow.

It was clear to Rokka that he was going to have to try something soon. The situation couldn't continue this way for long. The man standing behind had already raised his submachine gun into the air to strike Rokka, despite his friend's head.

Rokka let go of the man and seized just his right hand, the one holding the pistol. It shot a third round as Rokka wrenched it away. The man threw a punch at him from the left, but struck only his shoulder. Rokka couldn't shoot, as the pistol was backwards in his hand, but in the fierce rage of self-preservation, he funneled all of his might into a blow directed at the man's head. The back of the pistol cracked against his face, and in the same moment Rokka grabbed him and shoved him on top of the man behind him. When that man then shot his submachine gun, the muzzle flash of the barrel nearly singed Rokka's eyebrows. The recoil was enough to knock the man over, however, giving Rokka enough time to turn his own pistol around in his hand and, in the same blink of an eye, finish off the third man in line. Rokka yelled instructions to the neighboring guard, ordering him to shoot down the communication trench. 'I'm in'na nooka the nest! Don't worry 'bout me, just shoot!'

But the guard couldn't understand what he was trying to say. Nor would he have been able to shoot, as there were still a couple of bends in the trench between him and the men. He still hadn't managed to get any closer, as the struggle had lasted only a few seconds.

The second Russian was scrambling to his feet, but no sooner had his head reached Rokka's knee than the latter's boot struck, sending him sinking back to the trench floor. Rokka was filled with the wild rage of desperation. He acted with all of his might, but directed each movement carefully, for his rage was not the blind rage of panic. He did not hesitate for the briefest moment; rather, he was immediately aware of everything. In pushing the man from his lap onto the man behind, he knew that he would then be in danger from the ones behind him, because they would be free to shoot. That was why he had not shot the fallen man, but the third. The trench leading to the guard's nest was empty now, but Rokka fully suspected that more men awaited him just beyond the turn in the trench. He couldn't escape, as that would require climbing up onto the parapet, and that would certainly be the end of him. He couldn't just stand there and wait either, though, because as soon as the men behind the bend deduced that their buddies were dead, they would surely send a hand grenade sailing over the corner of the trench. It was a matter of seconds once again, so Rokka didn't grab his own pistol, which was a few steps behind him, but seized the weapon of the man he'd kicked onto the trench floor instead. He made sure the job was done by giving the man another kick in passing as he jumped over him.

A soldier loomed behind the bend in the communication trench, and for just a fraction of a second he was unsure whether the man coming toward him was a fleeing countryman or an enemy. He hesitated for the same reason Rokka just had. But his luck was worse, and he died, letting out a panicked scream and falling to the ground. Rokka heard a trampling noise behind him, from which he deduced that the rest of the pack had come to the obvious conclusion about their failed mission. Because if it didn't succeed right away, all was lost. A close-combat situation in the trench would only mean bad news for them.

The neighboring guard also dashed into view round the bend in the trench and was just about to shoot when Rokka howled, 'Don't shoot, gaddamn it!'

'Where are they?'

'Gone . . . Lissen, you take care a those two fellas, one of 'em's at death's door for sure. But the other one I just kicked with m'boot. Don't kill 'im. I'm takin' 'im prisoner.'

Rokka chased after the fleeing men, fearing the messenger patrol squad might run into them in the trench. But the men made it out in time. Nothing but reeds rustled along the lake's edge as they disappeared, and Rokka saw them off with a few farewell rounds. Just then, one of the men from the messenger patrol yelled from the edge of the lake, 'Password!'

'Aw, damn it. What was it? It's Antti Rokka here . . . Hang on, I got it! Karelian . . .'

'Bear.'

The patrol guys asked what was going on, and Rokka ordered

them to stay and guard the water's edge for a little while. 'Lil' bastards came from over there. Gaddamn it! Fellas ain't dumb, that's for sure. Ain't their fault if I'm not headin' back with 'em.'

By the time Rokka returned to the guard's nest, the whole position was manned, the infantry guard having sounded the alarm. Rokka was already entirely calm by then. He was perfectly aware of all the nuances of this incident, and affected a lighthearted joviality even greater than he actually felt. To Koskela's query he answered offhandedly, 'Well, we had ourselves a wrestlin' match, see. Finland v Soviet Union. I scored us a clear win. Might'ta broken a couple a rules, but then, fellas did gang up on me.'

'Clear win . . . heehee! Looks like that win was hard-won. Just died, heehee. Face all bashed in . . . heehee!'

Rokka looked panicked. 'Naw, damn it! 'Sother one still alive? All he got was a boot in'na head.'

Rokka calmed down once he heard that the man was still living. He was sitting in the trench spitting blood, Rokka's boot having knocked out one of his teeth.

'We're takin' care a this fella here from now on! I need 'im. Lissen, Koskela, don't you say nothin' about this here wrangle. And you, Lieutenant, don't you report nothin' either. We'll give 'em a lil' surprise tomorrow. They promised leave to any fella gits a prisoner. I'm deliverin' mine personally to the command post tomorrow.'

Koskela, who was aware of Rokka's scheduled interrogation, could guess why Rokka needed the man. The lieutenant from the infantry platoon also promised not to send a report before Rokka himself had delivered the prisoner. He didn't know anything about the disciplinary issue, but when Koskela asked, he conceded, even if it wasn't exactly allowed.

They took the prisoner into the bunker and threw the other bodies up over the banks of the trench. They inspected their Russian prisoner more closely in the bunker. The man's lips were badly swollen, so you couldn't tell much from his face, save that he was a churlish, fearless man somewhere in his thirties. He looked them fiercely in the eye, clearly prepared to face down anything, even death, if need be. The man wasn't wearing his shoulder insignia, but his general tenor gave them reason to wonder whether he might be an officer. Rokka fetched him some water and the man washed the dirt from his face. 'Lissen, you take this rag and soak it in'na cold water. Then stick it on your mouth. Look . . . Right there, I think.'

Rokka tended to the man, who accepted his assistance, even if he didn't seem exactly grateful for it. He inspected Rokka closely, however. His interest may have been piqued by the insane fury with which Rokka had defended himself. Maybe he was regretting that his team had ended up attacking a man too tough for them. Koskela's men also suspected that this prisoner was more valuable than the ordinary sort, as they generally didn't select just anyone to take prisoner.

They sent for the fellow over in the neighboring position who spoke Russian – the same guy from Salmi who had written the messages on the rat-collars – and started listening to the prisoner. He refused to say anything at first. Then, finally, he offered up Private Baranov as his name, but the interpreter also suspected he was lying about his rank, and said so. The man fell silent again, but eventually identified himself as Captain Baranov. He had probably reached the conclusion that there was no point in keeping his rank a secret, and that it might actually be better to let it be known, which was indeed the case. The men immediately began to treat him with greater deference, and if the disclosure meant that they were going to require him, as a captain, to disclose more information than they would have asked of a private, well then, so much greater was his opportunity to lie.

Finally, he also admitted to being the leader of the kidnapping mission. But as soon as the interpreter started asking questions about things over on the Russian side, the man fell silent, saying only that he had been sent on this mission and knew nothing whatsoever of his own side's state of affairs. Of his own squad he offered more information. The man whom Rokka had killed with the back of the pistol had been an NCO specially trained for the task. He was the one who was supposed to capture the prisoner. The failure, the

Captain explained, resulted from the fact that Rokka had heard them coming and so had managed to turn around.

'Lissen, that ain't why it failed. You tell 'im straight out it was 'cause Antti Rokka here happen'na be standin' guard. But you tell 'im they did one hell of a job plannin' that trick. You tell 'im I know their whole plan. They been spendin' lots a nights watchin' how our patrol squad comes 'n' goes, plottin' their whole operation off a that. First they set the cannons goin' so the guards would take cover. And meanwhile the fellas crawl along through the reeds ... He's still wet from it too. Then they thought, the guard'll think it'ssa patrol squad comin'. That's what I thought, anyway. I'd thought about takin' that same route myself, cuttin' through the reeds over to their side. That's why I thought it might be them. You remember, Koskela, how I said we oughdda put more guard posts along the shore? You're a right sensible fella, that's for sure. I'm gonna make you a cuppa tea. Then in'na mornin' when there ain't nobody sleepin' no more, I'm gonna play you "Yokkantee". Then you and me's gonna head over to the command post together. Fellas'll git'ta do their official inquiry on us both!'

Rokka was happy as a clam. He hummed along as he boiled his water for tea, and, drinking it with his prisoner, chatted on about the merits of the world, none of which his companion understood in the least. Then Rokka ordered his prisoner into the bunk to sleep. The man went to the bunk, but he didn't sleep. Rokka, on the other hand, dropped off as before – instantly, without so much as rolling over onto his side. The guy on fire-watch kept an eye on the prisoner, and all the weapons were removed from his reach. They were perfectly aware that he was not the type of man to let even the slightest opportunity pass him by.

III

Rokka awoke the next morning in splendid spirits, though his prisoner's mood was even more dour. He drank the tea Rokka gave him, but the playing of 'Yokkantee' he endured only because he had ears through which he had to. Rokka, on the other hand, threw in a couple of spins as he danced along, at which even Baranov's scowling eyes betrayed the tiniest trace of a smile.

'Lissen now, you cheer up, hear! We'll head off to prison together. We won't have no worries there. We'll make lamp-stands. I'll teach you how. You might'ta tried'da knock me down with the butt a your submachine gun, but you got a boot in'na face for it too.'

Rokka had been ordered to appear at the command post at nine o'clock, and a few minutes before nine he turned up with his prisoner in tow. Lammio was there, as well as some ensign who had been given the task of taking the minutes. Rokka's case was so important that Sarastie himself had chosen to attend the interrogation.

Sarastie's bunker was rather modest, as he didn't share the frontline architectural aspirations of the other officers. Rokka stepped inside, bringing Baranov with him, and in place of the standard military greeting, declared with a natural chipperness, 'Mornin'! Here I am! Koskela mentioned somethin' about me bein' called over here.'

The officers' moods underwent a small revolution. They had just been engaged in a stone-faced, 'scientific' discussion about the importance of discipline at the current time, as morale was sinking very low. And into this general atmosphere now popped the much-discussed problem child, with his 'Mornin'!' greetings and – on top of that – a prisoner, about whom they had received no information whatsoever.

'Whaa— Who is this?'

'This fella here? Why, he's the Baranov boy!'

Sarastie was quick enough to realize that Rokka was up to something, but suspected it would be revealed to him soon enough. The Major couldn't help laughing as he gazed at Rokka. The latter stole a glance at the officers as if weighing the impact of his entrance. Otherwise he was entirely nonchalant, as if there was nothing exceptional in the least about the situation.

'The Baranov boy,' Sarastie repeated. 'May I ask why you brought him here?'

'I took 'im prisoner last night, then I thought that if we were doin' this here inquiry, we might git his over with at the same time. I heard you might be threatenin' me with some kinda prison sentence, so I thought maybe the two of us here could go together. Two birds with one stone like.'

The prisoner was so important that the officers paid no attention to Rokka's jibe and just asked how the prisoner had been taken.

'Fellas came to take me off to Russia! But I told 'em that it wasn't gonna work that way, on accoun'ta I gotta go to this court martial, see. Three of 'em died in the scuffle, but I held onto this fella here. Good lookin' guy like he is. I done spoiled 'im a little with that kick in the jaw, but he'll git over that all right. Baranov here's a big fish. He's a cap'n.'

Sarastie was increasingly interested. 'How do you know that?'

'Sotti questioned him over in'na bunker already. He's from Salmi, see, so he knows Russian. Oh, he's a cap'n all right. He was chief a the commando.'

Rokka explained the incident in greater detail, and Sarastie phoned Koskela. Putting down the receiver, he looked at Rokka for a moment, considering him carefully, and then asked with a smile, 'What kind of man are you, anyway?'

'Who, me? Don't you know me? I'm Antti Rokka. Farmer from Kannas. These days, poster boy for Tikkakoski Tommy Guns.'

The ensign assigned to take the minutes endeavored to keep a straight face, as he didn't dare laugh before a major, but seeing that Sarastie himself had lost it, the Ensign burst into laughter as well. Only the two captains, Lammio and Baranov, remained straight-faced. Rokka himself was quite earnest, though slyly, vigilantly keeping tabs on the situation. He had evidently decided to relish the ordeal as much as possible, hopefully getting out of the threat of the court martial without being humiliated, and maybe even doing some humiliating himself.

'How did you manage this? Really.'

'I shot, hit, head-butted and kicked, that's how. They were some tough fellas, lemme tell you. I almost didn't make it to this here inquiry for the court martial.'

Sarastie turned to the Ensign. 'Take the prisoner out and send for the interpreter. That man is valuable. We've been after him a long time.'

The Ensign and Baranov left. Rokka called after them, 'I don't think you're gonna git much outta that fella. He's tough as nails. I sure seen that all right. Good thing I heard those fellas comin'! Who knows what might'ta happened with this here court martial if I hadn't? That's the way it is with these things in wartime, see, just dunno what's gonna come at you one hour later. Everythin's always gittin' mixed up with the regulations and such. Downright irritatin', ain't it? But whadda you gonna do?' Rokka lifted his hands and shrugged his shoulders, as if to lament the whole state of affairs.

Sarastie thought for a moment. He was having some difficulty reaching a decision on the issue, as it aroused too many conflicting impulses within him. He couldn't help marveling at this man and being amused by his sly, calculating glances. The Major had already gleaned what Rokka was up to. He could actually see the situation with greater clarity than Rokka himself. The Major knew that Rokka had backed him into a corner. In Sarastie's mind, the case had broader implications than it did in Rokka's reckoning. Rokka experienced it as an isolated event, but the Major saw the conflict of opposing principles within it. And Sarastie was hardly without his own personal motivations, either. He felt personally insulted, even if he would have insisted that this feeling was exclusively derived from his conviction that discipline had to be maintained no matter what.

'Tell me seriously, what makes military discipline so onerous to you that you feel obliged to oppose it at every turn?'

'I don't know a damn thing about military discipline. Never had any need for sumpin' like that. And I ain't opposin' anythin' but this here order sayin' I'm supposed'da go put rocks along somebody's walkway. I already told Lammio here all I gotta say about it. This fella here's the cause of all this!' (Rokka pointed his finger at Lammio.) 'He's been pickin' on me ever since I turned up! It's always sumpin'. But he ain't never said anythin' to me that wasn't downright trivial. It ain't never anythin' important. It's always just some stupid whim a his. I'll tell you all one more time. I was happy to come fight this war. I wanted'da go back to Kannas. And it just so happens that I'm the kinda fella ain't none of you ever gonna equal. And I'm tellin' you, you put any other fella out there last night and he'd a been a goner. What more do you want from me, gaddamn it? It's not that I'm tired a curtsyin' to you all, it's just that it ain't no use out here, so I don't do it. Lissen, I ain't out here because a you. I got a wife and kids and you want me to jump like a dog whenever you say hup? What for? It ain't gonna change nothin'! Look, I done figgered out we're gonna lose this war. And the closer it gits, the stupider the shit you clowns come up with. You send me to the court martial, but believe me, you sure ain't gonna see me kowtowin' to them bosses. We're half a million fellas out here. And you think that's why we're here? So that there's always somebody standin' in front a you with his heels together blabberin' "Yessir, Yessir . . ."?'

Rokka fell silent and began staring out of the window, as if to underline the fact that anything said from here on out made no difference whatsoever. Sarastie sought to invest his voice with severity as he said gravely, 'No, that is not why. But this act you refer to as "kowtowing" is an external sign of discipline, and its absence signals an absence of discipline. And an absence of discipline means that those half a million men out here are powerless to carry out the task they have been brought here to perform, namely, the defense of Finland. And you might keep in mind that they are not all like you. There are countless other pig-headed Joe Blows out there who possess only your faults. And that claim of yours, that the war has been lost, is not true. No war is won without setbacks. Because of their lack of expertise, men in the ranks have a tendency to come to conclusions on matters whose significance they do not understand. Nothing decisive has happened yet.'

Rokka heaved his shoulders and laughed with cutting bitterness. 'Don't understand! When you throw hundreds of thousands of men into a encirclement to die, there ain't much to understand, that kinda sign speaks for itself. You think we'd a done that if there was anythin' else we could'da done? It's done. I known that a long time now. But about arrangin' those pebbles.'

Lammio had been silent the whole time, but now he asked the Major for permission to speak. The request was entirely unnecessary, but Lammio wanted to emphasize his own willingness to comply with convention. 'Tell me, Rokka, where do you propose to find a company commander who would tolerate as much as I have tolerated from you? Be reasonable.'

'He he. Reasonable. As if your game had some kind a reason! Lissen, you ain't planned things out too carefully when you started this here brouhaha. You just gone and followed your whims without any real basis at all. Don't you start throwin' that stuff at me! You, flatterin' yourself about how brave you are and all those ideals you think you're defendin' . . . Git that ensign a yours! Let 'im take this all down for the record. Gaddamn it, I have had enough! My patience's got its breakin' point too.'

Lammio looked to Sarastie, awaiting his decision. The Major rose and said deliberately, straightening himself up, 'The battalion can operate very well without you. No man is indispensable in a war, no matter who he is. I am granting you a pardon. More precisely, I am granting you a pardon indefinitely. Not because I think we have any obligation to pardon you, but for other reasons. And my proposal is this. You will not breathe one word of this to anyone, nor will you swagger around puffed up over how we've decided to settle it. And from now on, you will follow the rules just like everyone else. Now, if you go singing this in the streets, then it becomes a question of authority, and if that happens, I will set the mill to grind. I hope you understand the opportunity before you – not only for your sake, but also for my own and that of the army. I do not personally have any need to break you, but should the occasion arise in which it becomes necessary, that, too, can be arranged.'

Sarastie drew a deep breath and threw back his shoulders. Mobilizing the towering stature of his body, he felt assured of his own might, affirmed by the very fact that he could afford to grant such a pardon. He flexed his muscles beneath his jacket and expelled any feeling of defeat from his heaving chest, and so was free to grant forgiveness from on high.

Lammio did not need to engage in any body–soul affirming exercises. The issue was no longer his responsibility, and besides, it seemed to him that Rokka had been humiliated, even if he would have supported a movement by the Major to set the mill in motion immediately.

Rokka, for his part, was pleased with the whole arrangement, though he wasn't about to sign off without conditions. 'I already said I do what needs done in'na war. But lissen, you tell Lammio here to leave me alone. If he don't quit those games a his, there won't be no end to our squabblin', that's for damn sure.'

'You are granted no special exemptions from the disciplinary code. As I said, your behavior will determine how your case is handled henceforth. Dismissed!'

Rokka left. No sooner had he made it out of the door than he was back to bargain. 'Hey! I just remembered. We're promised a leave in exchange for a prisoner. So I'm due fourteen extra days. 'Specially seein' as I got me a cap'n.'

The Major shook his head in wonder at the man's audacity. Rokka acted as if everything that had just happened hadn't occurred at all. 'Well, you'll get it. No denying it belongs to you. Stick the request first in the pile. To be honest, I only regret that you've made it impossible for us to grant you a Mannerheim Cross.'

'Well, that's sumpin' too, but it ain't no humdinger after all, fifty thousand marks. I nearly made that much offa rings and lamp-stands.'

Rokka finally left for good. He hummed and whistled as he set out, happily swinging his head from side to side. After he'd gone a little way he noticed a rabbit by the side of the road, just bounding out of sight. In the blink of an eye, Rokka was after it, crashing through the thicket as he chased the creature out into the middle of it. The rabbit couldn't run at full speed yet, being only about half-grown, so Rokka was able to keep right on its heels. 'Don't run away! I wanna take you to live with us in'na bunker! I ain't gonna hurt you . . .'

Not understanding Rokka's promises, the rabbit just sped up, and after running about a quarter of a mile, Rokka decided it was no use. Huffing and puffing, he returned to the path, shaking his head at the rabbit's escape. 'Well, I guess we woulda hadda scrounge up grass for the little fella. And seein' as I'm headed off on leave . . .'

His breath had evened out by the time he reached the bunker. 'Damn near caught us a rabbit on my way back! We could a had a pet.'

'What did they say?'

''Bout what?'

'The prisoner and everything.'

'Oh, they didn't say nothin'. I'm takin' off on leave. I got me a leave!'

Only to Koskela did Rokka report what had happened at the command post. Lammio was quite restrained from then on, and said nothing further about the incident – nor about a Mannerheim Cross, for that matter.


# IV


Italy fell definitively over the course of the autumn. The most recalcitrant men in the battalion were rounded up and ordered to carry out drills designed to re-establish discipline. Honkajoki was amongst them, as Lammio had started following the man's intrigues ever more closely and decided that he posed a menace to morale. Some captain was assigned to oversee the close-formation drills, but he could see from day one that he'd been given a hopeless task. What, for example, was he supposed to do with this tall hulk of a man who stood in the ranks with a bow over his shoulder and responded affirmatively, in the most courteous of terms, to everything he said, then systematically performed every single movement incorrectly? And what could he do with that thug named Viirilä, whom he had difficulty even looking at? And crowning it all was the knowledge that Viirilä, like a surprising number of these delinquents, represented the cream of the crop within the battalion.

The general rule was that men were released from the exercise when they knew how to execute the drills properly. Or rather, when they decided to execute them properly, as there was no question they all knew how. But the Captain ended up having to relax this rule rather generously, as otherwise the drills would have drilled right on into eternity. The last men remaining were Honkajoki and Viirilä. They sat beside one another with equal measures of indifference. Honkajoki had traded his bow for a gun at the Captain's demand, but that was indeed the only concession the Captain managed to get out of him.

Some sergeant was giving orders and the Captain was supervising. 'About face, fall out!'

The men turned and ran backwards in accordance with the command. Honkajoki headed headlong into a sizeable spruce, and then, chest pressed up against it, continued running in place until finally he pretended to notice the tree, backed up slightly, and steered himself around it. Viirilä bolted out at a fierce clip, trampling a juniper grove on the way.

'Halt! Fall in!' the Sergeant called out. Honkajoki stopped and ran back to attention in front of the Sergeant. But Viirilä pretended not to hear, and just kept barreling on.

'Stop! The command was to fall in!' the Sergeant yelled.

Viirilä stopped, swung his head like a horse chewing on a bit, and let loose a long whinny. Then he shot off, running, stopped again, and started pawing at the ground, snorting through his lips like a skittish horse. Then he kicked and neighed, 'I-I-I-eeew.' He then resumed his startling speed once more, ran up to the Sergeant, and stopped beside Honkajoki.

'What is this? Cut the horseplay!' the Captain said in affectedly stern tones, which nonetheless betrayed his hopeless exhaustion.

Viirilä didn't respond, he just pawed at the ground, glancing at Honkajoki.

'Stop it!'

'I-I-I-eeeew!' the horse kicked and whinnied.

'Continue with the drill,' the Captain said to the Sergeant, seeking some exit from the hopeless situation.

Viirilä gave up his horse impersonation and executed the drills so astonishingly well for a while that the Captain had already resolved to excuse him from the drill when Viirilä, turning the wrong way, started inventing his own gun routines, which were so ludicrous that the Sergeant lost it entirely and the Captain had to turn away to conceal his laughter.

After devoting a week to the two of them, the Captain admitted defeat and quietly put an end to the discipline refresher courses.

The drills did not improve Honkajoki's ways. Whenever he wasn't working on his perpetual-motion-machine, which is to say fitting together some whittled pieces of wood, he roamed about as a self-appointed 'enlightenment officer'. For two years now he had managed to keep his perpetual-motion-machine project going, and whenever he thought it had receded to the point of being forgotten, and thus that it might attract attention again, he trotted it out.

Vanhala tagged along for many of Honkajoki's charades, but he was promoted to corporal even so, on account of his soldierly accomplishments. These had been honed even further one day when Vanhala, standing guard, had singlehandedly fended off an invading enemy patrol before the others had even managed to get into position. The stripe provided Vanhala with quiet delight for a long time, as it was such an easy target for poking fun.

At the beginning of that winter, Hietanen was wounded in the thigh by a shard from some shell, but the wound was so slight that he was only away at the hospital a month or so. He was the same spirited Urho-boy as before, but a gravity and manly maturity had begun to appear in him, little by little. In part, this was due to the deteriorating situation, but it was also on account of the very natural fact that they had all advanced in age somewhat over the course of the years. Hietanen served as platoon leader whenever Koskela was away on leave, or off filling in for some company commander who was away on leave. He and Määttä were just as devoted to their card games as ever, and the same ruckus would fill the bunker until Hietanen had lost all his pay.

Of all of them, Susling was probably most affected by the unfortunate end the war was clearly approaching. For him, as for Rokka, it meant a concrete loss, but while these developments made Rokka ever tenser, in Susling they seemed to bring on a paralysing depression. Even Rokka wasn't able to keep his friend's spirits up, though he never stopped trying. In this matter alone, Susling was unable to place his unbounded faith in Rokka's thoughts and moods as he usually did.

Around Christmas time, the German battleship *Scharnhorst* sank in the Arctic Sea.

'Buttons are poppin' off one by one, boys.'

'Must have been stitched on with matches from the start, hee-hee . . .'

Honkajoki popped into one of the neighboring bunkers with his bow.

'May peace be with you.'

'How's it goin', archer-man?'

'Thank you for inquiring. A frost warning has been announced.'

'No Eastern frost nor Northern freeze shall stay us in our course!'

'Let us hope, indeed, let us hope. But one is obliged to recognize that at the present moment, felt boots and quilted coats would be of capital assistance.'

A private was sitting on one of the bunks, his eyes burning with the 'holy' gaze of the believer. And, despite the risk posed by the Lieutenant lying on another bunk, he said, 'Sure, make fun if you want, but we need warm clothes around here.'

The Private was actually something of a lone wolf, much as Lahtinen had been, and it was significant, somehow or other, that he now dared to make such comments.

Honkajoki seized upon the issue. 'My brother-in-arms' comment was clearly intended in an exclusively literal sense. In that regard, I am quite agreed. But in so far as you may have been extrapolating from these items of clothing to consider their significance within the broader framework of world events, then in the name of freedom of information I must forbid myself from pursuing the inquiry any further.'

'How's the perpetual-motion machine coming along?'

'It has reached a very critical phase. I am waiting for one point of obscurity to clear up. Everything else has been worked out, but one small issue remains unresolved. That is, I have not been able to eliminate the difficulties presented by friction and the gravitational pull of the celestial bodies. In the void, which presents none of the difficulties of gravitational forces, I would be able to set it in eternal motion, but under the given conditions I must pursue another solution.'

The men didn't understand a word of Honkajoki's speech, but its comically distinguished intonations made them laugh. The Lieutenant, on the other hand, was put off by Honkajoki's prattle and turned irritably away.

After droning on for half an hour, Honkajoki prepared to leave, but before he did so, he removed his cap and clasped his hands, saying, 'Because it has already grown late, perhaps I shall stay here and dedicate an evening prayer to this humble abode. Shield us from the enemy's ploys, and above all its snipers and direct-fire cannons. The daily rations could also stand to be a bit more generous, should You still have any untapped stores You might call upon to fulfill Your children's needs. Grant us at least tolerable weather, that our shifts on guard in the name of Your cause may be slightly more entertaining. Moonlight would be most welcome, indeed, as it alleviates our anxiety and aids us in the conservation of our limited flare supply. Protect all the patrols, guards, seafarers and drivers, but do not trouble Yourself unduly over the men in artillery. Protect the Chief Commanders and the Chiefs of Staff, and the less consequential bosses as well, provided You have the time. Protect the Commander of the Army Corps, the Division Commander, the Regiment Commander,

Battalion Commander, and, most especially, the machine-gunners' Company Commander. Finally, individually and as one, protect these Distinguished Leaders of Finland, that they not bang their heads into the pines of Karelia a second time. Amen.'

Had Honkajoki caught a glimpse of the Lieutenant's face as he left the bunker, he would have known immediately what had prompted the summons he received the following day, ordering him to Lammio's bunker.

Now, Honkajoki was no Rokka, and the difference was evident in the unmasked fury and disgust on Lammio's face as the solemn man stepped before him to attention, his bow over his shoulder, announcing, 'Captain, sir. Private Honkajoki reporting for duty.'

'I can see that. Just what kind of enlightenment officer do you think you are?'

'Captain, sir. In these challenging times no support to morale is to be sniffed at.'

'You're cultivating defeatism. Are you working for the enemy?'

'Captain, sir. My honor as a soldier prevents me from answering such an inquiry . . .'

'Your honor! I'll give you the honor of a court martial summons if these disparaging speeches about the army and its management don't stop. Do you have any idea what this nation's security rests upon?'

'Captain, sir. It resides upon the noble shoulders of Carl Gustaf Emil Mannerheim, Marshal of Finland.'

'Precisely. His and those of his army. And you are a parasite within that army. The flea that thrives only in filth.' (The image wasn't Lammio's invention, but rather that of the Battalion Commander.)

'Captain, sir. In my understanding, the flea is not the cause of filth, but merely a symptom. Or perhaps I have misunderstood the Captain's suggestion.'

'Don't get smart with me. Are you a communist?'

'I am an inventor. My original occupation was, indeed, in pine cone collection, but I hold the pursuit of knowledge to be my principal vocation in life.'

'Are you insane?'

'Captain, sir. Such questions can never be resolved by the very person of whom such a condition is suspected. It falls to those around him to determine his case.'

'Very well. I have determined that your mockery will cease. I am giving you a serious warning. The army has plenty of means for disposing of unwanted entities. This subversive activity will end. We cannot afford to admit the enemy within our ranks, even clad in the gray uniform of the Finnish army, which incidentally is far too respectable to be worn by the likes of you.'

'Captain, sir. For a very long time indeed I sought with the keenest of interest to divest myself of it, but the disappointment of this desire over my long experience certainly justifies my suspicion that the esteemed Captain's suggestion cannot be in earnest. Which is, indeed, regrettable. I shall let it pass, however, and request your permission to put forth my own understanding of the present circumstances.'

'Wouldn't that be something.'

'In so far as the enemy's advance is concerned, I would consider the situation merely temporary. Communism will collapse under the weight of its own impossibility – underground forces are already at work to that end. The final conditions of peace will be dictated by Finland. Our position as a superpower affords us that prerogative. I have never considered communism to be a significant factor in any way. To begin with, the grain transfer system within the kolkhozes has been robbing farmers for twenty years. They've even been stripped of seed grain. And in the second place, a more important point. As soon as the people return to the land claimed by the Red Army, revolution will ensue. The government will lose all control, because the Germans will have removed all the barbed wire.'

'Get out!'

'Yes, sir, Captain. But I would caution you against a certain other actor. In my opinion, the greatest threat we now face is that of the Yellow Peril.'

'Out! Out!'

'As you wish, Captain, sir.'

# V

The skeletons sheathed in their chiffon of decay emerged from the snow for a third time. Water trickled through the trenches, and guards gazed through strained eyes at periscope mirrors. The calm only deepened, though the snipers still struck their targets now and then, and enemy patrols increased.

A feeling of great resolution hovered in the spring air, however. The men endeavored one more time to rally their hopes of salvation. 'Rommel's striking back against the invasion!' And then: 'The tank wedge is pressing east again.'

'If they could just drive them back to the sea, we might have a different game on our hands.'

'It's not gonna happen, guys,' Hietanen said. He was perhaps the most pessimistic of all of them, surprising as that was to the others. Another change had appeared in Hietanen as well. The boisterous fellow would sometimes stare blankly off into space. Such moments were rare, certainly, and Hietanen's lively, wayward spirit was quick to return, but he saw something in those moments. Maybe it was just that, in any case, the future was going to bring heavy fighting and more men were going to die. Him too, probably.

Koskela had been more prepared than the others from the outset, so nothing much changed in him. The same was true of Rahikainen. His business ventures had ended, though, as nobody was buying lamp-stands anymore.

'We could make coffins,' Rahikainen suggested slightly bitterly to Rokka, but the latter brushed him off, 'Naw, we ain't doin'nat. They can bury you just fine without.'

'The gravedigger always gets the last laugh. Heeheehee!'

Once when Kariluoto was making his rounds on the Millions, a shard from a shell blast got him in the shoulders and put him in the hospital. Koskela served as the Third Company's interim commander and Hietanen filled in as platoon leader.

By the end of May, the battalion had set up a smashing canteen for themselves, whose grand opening they celebrated with a round of entertainment and saccharine-juice. They were planning a movie theater for the regiment's sector, which was to be a state-of-the-art example of its kind. Another round of wood-chopping tasks were doled out as well, and Hietanen was forced to wage a real psychological war with his men before he was able to get anyone chopping.

They hadn't even all started when the command came that they were to cease.

# Chapter Thirteen

## I

'You mean you're gonna leave Sabine there for Private Russianov to rape?'

'Let 'er stay. She's pretty well treated.'

They were packing up, somber-faced and silent. Honkajoki took his pieces of wood, considered them for a moment, and stuck them into his pack. 'This could set them on the proper path. It could be that they are already as near to a solution as I myself.'

'Yeah, yeah. That's right. Back we go. Now that we've practically rotted into the ground here.' Sihvonen was angrily yanking at his pack in an effort to get it shut, as if it were the miserable angles of his belongings that were to blame.

Hietanen stood silently in the middle of the bunker, looking around at the others' preparations. His own belongings were already packed and ready to go. Three years earlier, he had stayed up waiting for their departure from the burnt clearing barracks, bouncing around boisterously. Now he stood quietly, without saying a word. Koskela was still filling in as Third Company Commander, so Hietanen was in charge of the whole platoon.

Rokka packed up Susling's gear, as the last guard shift had fallen to his friend. Hietanen ordered Rokka to oversee the first section's departure, as he himself headed off to the neighboring position to see about the other section. Hietanen had already ordered the machine-gun transport to the side of the road close to the front line.

The phone had been taken away, so they awaited the messenger's arrival with the command to pull out. When it came, they fetched the machine guns from the nests and left. From the bend in the road, they saw the silhouette of the Devil's Mound carved against the sky for the last time. A small screen of guys from the infantry company stayed behind to cover as they disengaged.

The transport vehicles waited by the roadside, and when Hietanen had arrived with the second section, they loaded up the machine guns and marched to the company's designated gathering point. Once the other platoons had arrived and the usual fuss over proceedings had run its course, they began to withdraw.

The road of defeat began quietly. They ceded the Svir bridgehead without any fighting. They passed the abandoned bunkers, products of two-and-a-half years of nibbling away at the earth. The artillery positions were empty. The bitter, silent march led them behind the river that had become so famous. Once over the bridge, Vanhala ran down to the river's edge, filled a bottle half-full of water and swung it in the air, chuckling, 'Some of "Onega's Waves!"' He hadn't forgotten the propaganda from Devil's Mound.

'Won't be hearing too much of that song no more.'

'Guess this stream won't be Finland's border.'

'Who the hell cares? At least this goddamn shitshow is done with.'

'Oh, it ain't over yet.'

'Down in Kannas, the guys are running with their tails between their legs.'

'Wonder what they're going to make us swallow now.'

'We're gonna pay for every last tree we chopped down over here, boys.'

'Mm-hm. And so are our children's children.'

'Well, I know one thing for sure,' Rokka said. 'We're gonna be hungry now that we're on'na move again. Rations are enough in a positional war since you don't gotta move, but from now on, fellas, we all better start scroungin' crumbs again.'

'We're a little low on wheat, but chaff we have in spades.'

'Stop bragging.'

Twilight fell. The path rustled with their footsteps. And off marched the Finnish private – his tilted cap crumpled with the tell-tale folds of its owner, his shirt unbuttoned at the top, his trouser-legs rolled, and his face set in a tense, bitter grimace. One man from the ranks drew in a deep breath, slowed his step into a slack, workaday rhythm, and started to sing. Along with the profane words ringing out into the summer night, there came the cry of his soul, voicing the bitterness of three years' useless fighting, as if, in this cry, he might scream defiance at all his enemies.

And here my song begins, a story for the ages . . .

## II

A low rumble filled the hazy, smoke-filled air. Incessant air raids and artillery fire kept the surface of the earth in a state of perpetual shaking. The constant drone of fighter squadrons whirred overhead from every direction. It was as if the whole world were burgeoning with some menacing force that kept bursting forth in howls and explosions.

For the retreat, Sarastie's battalion was put in a combined combat division commanded by Lieutenant Colonel Karjula. At first they retreated quickly along the poor forest roads, but then the front line caught up with them and the fighting began to intensify.

Bit by bit they ceded back the Eastern Karelian roads they had conquered in such bitter fighting three years before. They were tired and resentful once again – and hungry, just as they had been. The physical exertion took its toll on their food supply, but the poor organization of provisions meant that even the former portions now came irregularly and were often small. Of course, sometimes there was an over-abundance of food, as large quantities of the army's supplies would occasionally have to be destroyed. Then, even a hungry soldier might manage to sneak into a storage depot and steal all the food he could carry. Rahikainen put his skills to work on behalf of Hietanen's platoon once more, often keeping them from going hungry and sometimes even improving the state of their clothing. Once he even wormed his way into some barracks that was under heavy artillery fire, boldly risking his life for the ten pairs of new boots he triumphantly emerged with. Had so dangerous a task confronted him in a combat situation, Rahikainen would never have carried it out voluntarily. The only downside to the whole affair was that no one had been able to carry anything with him that was worthy of exchange for such goods, so Rahikainen was obliged to give everything away for free. Every last one of them was short on cash, so even purchasing was out of the question.

The platoon made it through the beginning of its journey without any casualties. The one exception was Honkajoki's bow, which he had been faithfully dragging along with him. It was left behind at some position when they had been obliged to make a rather swift exit. Honkajoki had been about to grab his weapon as he left, but just then one of the assailants, who had already managed to duck into the bushes beside him, shot a hole through Honkajoki's shirt. So the bow stayed, and Honkajoki bemoaned its loss, gasping out between breaths as their sprint finally ended, 'It would give me great gratification to employ an expletive at this moment, despite the gravity of our current situation. At the very least, I must say: damn that Bushki for depriving me of my personal weapon!'

Honkajoki wasn't bitter. For him, the defeat seemed to be as insignificant and irrelevant as every other worldly circumstance. At one point he went missing for three days. Four men from the First Company disappeared around the same time, and it was decided that they must have left for the 'pine cone platoon' – in other words, deserted. But then Honkajoki turned up again. He had simply been carrying out some reconnaissance work a little way behind the camp, he explained. In truth, he had been with the group of deserters, but at some point he had become separated from his companions and decided it might be best to return to the fold.

Otherwise, the platoon's fighting spirit was probably in slightly better shape than that of the other units. Koskela was away, but he had left an indelible mark on the platoon, and Hietanen and Rokka were not the kind of men you desert lightly. Hietanen never urged anyone on. He would just toss his submachine gun over his shoulder and start walking, and the others would follow suit. He had changed, as if in the blink of an eye. Maybe the change was just more striking in him because he had been so conspicuously rambunctious before. As his solemnity grew, so his bravery seemed to increase. A defiance had appeared within him whose roots were laid bare whenever anybody voiced any political *Schadenfreude* over the defeat and Hietanen barked out briefly but threateningly, 'Shut up!'

He wasn't the type of leader to safeguard the morale of his platoon. No, he was the type who realized, from the moment the defeat came, that his former wayward patriotism had been integral to his whole attitude toward life, and that the blow of defeat was a blow to the very foundations of his being. The man in him had allowed the carefree boy to revel in the times of success, but with the arrival of defeat, he stepped forward and took its burden upon his own shoulders.

Generally speaking, Rokka remained his former self. He might have fought even better than before, but he demonstrated no wasted heroism. When he saw that a situation was hopeless, he, too, would stop trying, as he knew perfectly well that even if he held his position, the guy next to him wouldn't. Once he even said that a pointless death was higher treason than desertion. The rumors that deserters were being shot struck him more sharply than any of them. It was lucky that he didn't run into any high-ranking officers during that time, as the rage the rumors had fostered within him might well have landed him in an inescapable stew.

Salo remained steadfast. He believed in their ultimate victory in spite of everything, and the less basis there was for his belief, the more stubbornly he stuck to it.

A few days after Midsummer, they were in the midst of retreating. Low-flying Sturmoviks were harassing the column from the air, and somebody yelled, 'Run for it, boys!'

'But our own fighter planes'll show up purty soon, don't you think?' Salo said, his comment pushing one embittered man to the point of rage, as it was precisely the absence of their own fighter planes they were perpetually cursing.

'Show up, you goddamn fool! They were out there flyin' round when nobody needed 'em, but where are they now? Those boys up there don't seem to have any problem keepin' on our tail.'

In his rancour, the man was just looking for any means of praising the enemy, but Salo retorted, 'They'll keep on our tail as long as we keep lettin' 'em! If we just keep on runnin' away, whatta you think's gonna happen?'

'Shut – shut – shut the hell up! If this road's good enough for the rest of us, it's damn well good enough for you.'

The truth was, in terms of his capabilities as a soldier, Salo did belong to that vast majority of ordinary men. He fulfilled his duties, for the most part, but you couldn't exactly call him a hero. The other men felt his recent words had overstepped his normal frame of operation, however, as the established understanding amongst the group did not afford him the right to accuse others of cowardice. Salo fell silent, but when the ground-attack planes returned, instead of taking cover, he took aim at a nearing plane, steadying his rifle on the side of a tree. He didn't look at any of the others, nor did he hear Hietanen's furious command to take cover, he just aimed with movements so calm that the intention behind their contrived performance was unmistakable.

He shot one round and was loading a new cartridge into the barrel when the Sturmovik opened fire. Salo fell, and as soon as the commotion died down, the men hurried toward him. He was pale, but calm. His left leg had been hit, so its bones were badly crushed, and there was no doubt that Salo would walk with a prosthetic leg to the end of his days, if he made it through alive.

Uncomplaining, he endured the horrific pain as the medics removed his boot and bandaged the crushed leg. Beads of sweat pearled on his forehead and his body stiffened frequently from the pain, but he withstood it all without a sound. No doubt he had always wished to be a braver man than he was. Perhaps this incident afforded him some kind of compensation for the feeling of inferiority that had been gnawing away at him the whole war – which his insistent belief in victory had only brought to a head. For the smug superiority with which the others mocked his belief had been facilitated, in a way, by his mediocre abilities as a fighter. The shock brought on by the injury raised him up into a mental state that made it possible for him – this time – to step outside of his usual self. His voice was cuttingly calm as he said, 'We ain't gonna start cryin' over a little leg now, are we? If we were runnin' away, well now, look, I'm rid of the thing that was makin' it all worse.'

The men of the platoon bade Salo farewell as the medics lifted him into the ambulance. As they waved him off, and each of them uttered something or other appropriate to the occasion, a note in their voices announced that with his unnecessary sacrifice, Salo had bought their respect. They never saw him again, but those who remembered him recalled him as a brave and courageous man. The last impression covered over all that had come before, and even the faith in victory that had provided them with so much amusement ceased to be stupidity and was transformed into an indomitable will.

The retreat continued. Soon they no longer remembered that there had been this man by the name of Salo in their platoon. The ever-intensifying fighting kept their minds fixed on fear, hunger and the vain hope of rest.

## III

The machine-gunners' command post was situated beside a winding forest road. There were sounds of firing over by the front line, and heavy shelling was underway between the front line and the command post. Lammio and Sinkkonen were receiving replacements, whose orders the company secretary was filing away. The secretary had been made a corporal as well, and seeing as there were eight young recruits amongst the replacements, he affected a lofty, superior tone of voice as he inquired after their details – never mind the exploding six-inchers making the ground shake even at the command post. It was indicative that the man was clearly aping Lammio's gestures and intonations in his managerial role.

In addition to the boys, there were also three men over forty who had been called up out of the reserves. All the replacements had dug foxholes to protect themselves from shrapnel, and they crouched down into them every time a shell crashed to the ground.

Lammio stood tapping a stick against his boot as he spoke with the Master Sergeant. 'It would be best to assign the old men as drivers and have the younger men who are driving now join the infantry. Send four of the new recruits to Hietanen, that platoon's down several men. Also, I received word that Kariluoto has rejoined the battalion and resumed leadership of his company, so Koskela can return to his own platoon. Only temporarily, of course, since he is to be transferred to company commander of some other unit. They'll probably move him to the Third Battalion, since they've been suffering heavy losses amongst the officers. I know Sarastie doesn't want to give him up, because he's afraid we will soon have need of him in his battalion, but under the current circumstances accommodating his opinion is hardly going to be an option. Well, it will all be sorted in due course, and Hietanen is certainly up to the task. These men just need to be fed before we send them out to the line.'

'Yes sir, Captain.' Sinkkonen turned to the older men. 'We're going to pull the younger men from the supply vehicles and assign them to the infantry platoons, then put you fellows in as drivers. Do you know how to drive a horse? What was your name again?'

Sinkkonen gestured toward the large man with a dark complexion who was sitting beside his foxhole looking glum and chewing nervously on a blade of grass. The man flinched angrily, diverted his gaze from the Master Sergeant and grunted, 'Hname . . . hmph . . . my name . . . Fuck you!'

Lammio stepped closer to the man. 'I do hope you know your own name.'

The straw wriggled its way from one corner of the man's mouth to the other. 'Papers's over there . . . hmph.'

'Answer me properly. How is the secretary supposed to know which file is yours?'

'It's the last one, of course. That one that's left.'

'State your name. What kind of game is this?'

'You oughtta know. Knew it well enough to come drag me outta my home. Hmph . . . that's right. So fuck off!'

Lammio was about to raise his voice when he remembered the stern warning he had received about not provoking the men any more than necessary, and so restrained himself. But Lammio didn't know how to behave except with the overbearing arrogance now deemed inappropriate to the situation – so his voice was helpless and uncertain as he said, 'Well, you must have a name at least.'

'Fine, it's Korpela,' the man growled, as if angrily throwing his name in Lammio's face, but only in passing. 'Private. Hmph.'

Korpela chewed nervously on his straw, then snatched it from his mouth and viciously tossed it aside. He didn't say anything to anyone, he just stared off into his own world, and when the Master Sergeant took the men to the field kitchen to eat, he threw his pack angrily over his shoulder and followed after the others, muttering something to himself that none of them could make head nor tail of.

After he and Mäkilä had selected which of the drivers would be reassigned to the infantry platoons, the Master Sergeant left Mäkilä to take things from there. Mäkilä was facing tough times. Any attempt at systematic organization was doomed. The book-keeping was a shambles. There was almost never any information about the strength of the food supply, as they frequently ended up having to feed divisions that had become lost or separated. Equipment vanished, as the drivers would quietly take it upon themselves to lighten their loads, and even the horses were dropping like flies under the strain of the incessant air raids on the supply vehicles. All of this only made Mäkilä more tight-fisted, however. The more equipment he saw destroyed, the more jealously he guarded what remained – as opposed to the rest of the men, in whom the situation had inspired something of an 'easy-come-easy-go' mentality.

Mäkilä distributed the men's food and was just assigning them horses when Korpela burst out angrily, 'Where are the fuckin' nags, anyway? Ones we're supposed to drive, I mean. So the fat cats of Finland can make their money in peace.'

Mäkilä wasn't about to get into something as pointless as fat cats' finances, so he just showed Korpela to his horse and said with a cough, 'Well, you take good care of this horse, then. Try to feed him whenever you can.'

Korpela just about exploded. 'Fuck you! I don't need you tellin' me what to do. I been drivin' horses my whole fuckin' life! Stop givin' me your goddamn instructions! You just look after yourself! Yeah, you heard me.'

Mäkilä had flushed red and started coughing. He didn't say anything more to Korpela, but his speech was more tense than usual as he addressed the others. Korpela looked at the harness, tossing and slapping the reins about angrily as he resumed his incomprehensible muttering. Mäkilä watched his shenanigans sharply out of the corner of his eye, but said nothing. Only when Korpela walked away from the carts did Mäkilä go set the harness in order. Then he asked the drivers, 'Whose turn for the soup run?'

Shells came crashing down all along the edge of the road, so it was no one's turn.

'Uusitalo! Your turn!'

The man in question swirled around angrily and started cursing. 'Course it is. Maybe you should try it yourself once so you see what it's like. Anybody can give other people orders.'

Without a word, Mäkilä fetched a horse from beneath a nearby spruce, harnessed it, and lifted the soup vat into the cart. He was just leaving when Uusitalo came over and said, 'Get the hell away from there and gimme the reins!'

Mäkilä blinked his eyes and looked past Uusitalo, giving the reins a tug as he said, 'Chuh . . . so . . . I'm going. This time.'

Uusitalo could see that there was no point in continuing the discussion, and Mäkilä set off. He walked beside the cart, figuring the horse had enough to carry with just the vat. They had to go over a mile, because the air raids obliged them to keep the supplies further back, as far from the front line as possible. After they'd gone a little way, a messenger cycling toward them got off his bike to warn Mäkilä. 'Be careful. They've bracketed the main road down there.

Bad news comin' down on both sides, little way past the mortar positions.'

Mäkilä didn't reply, but plodded calmly on, staring directly ahead. He passed the mortar positions and neared the point in the road where the shelling was concentrated, which was in a low, muddy spot at the bottom of a sloping hill. Once he made it over the hill, he paused to wait for a break in the firing. The shells came at short intervals, always in pairs. The boom from the launch was followed by a crackling whistle, which always paused just a second before the explosion. The horse snorted and quivered and Mäkilä held it from the bit. When a pause between launch booms stretched out longer than usual, Mäkilä figured that the artillery had quieted down and climbed into the cart. But just as he passed the halfway point, the booms on the hill started up again. For the first time in his life, Mäkilä struck the horse, who had started galloping frantically down the hill. The shells splashed mud up into the air a few dozen yards off, but the softness of the earth cut down on the schrapnel considerably. The horse reared up on its hind legs, snorted and started pushing the cart backwards. Mäkilä climbed down and began leading the horse on foot.

The next pair of shells exploded a bit further off. The horse flared its nostrils and took a few stiff steps before rearing up onto its hind legs again. Mäkilä patted the horse and tried to calm him, saying, 'Don't be scared! Here we go, nice and easy. This isn't up to people. It's all in greater hands.'

Mäkilä was speaking to the horse, though the words were actually intended for his own soul. Otherwise he was perfectly calm. His eyes gazed straight ahead, bulging only when the shells exploded, and he gave a throat-clearing cough now and again. The launch booms sounded once more, but this time the whistle was ominously short and quiet. Mäkilä saw the splash of grass-stained water strike his hand, and grasped the quiet whoosh and thump he heard before a red flame billowed up before him from a crater that had appeared in the road. He was blasted in two.

The horse fell sideways onto the pole of the cart hitch. There was a hole in the side of the soup vat, so when the weight of the horse and the downhill slope turned the cart onto its side, soup streamed onto the ground, as the hole in the vat was on the downward-facing side.

The horse managed to raise its head, struggled to get up onto its front legs, and let out a wild, agonized whinny. Then it sank back to the ground, tossing its head weakly a couple of times.

The next set of shells sent mud splashing over both of the deceased.

## IV

The machine-gunners were sitting beside their foxholes, awaiting their food. They were all silent and irritable. A few days earlier they had taken up positions along this brook, holding a bit of line connected to Lord knows how many others. The enemy had gone a long time without testing the line's endurance, so in that sense this situation was exceptional. Normally, their opponents shut down their attempted barricades immediately, forcing them to resume their retreat. They stared at the ground, their unshaven faces filthy, exhausted and creased with lines of bitterness. Sometimes a bullet would nick a tree and they would hear the rumble of a combat vehicle behind the stream. Further off they could hear the booming of an air raid, a sound that was rarely absent.

They were extremely hungry. Just two days earlier, Rahikainen had brought them a massive load of food scrounged from some bombed-out supply vehicle, but their moment of bliss had been short-lived. They couldn't turn away the men who came from neighboring units, hands outstretched, pleading, 'Give us just a little, huh? We haven't had anything to eat for two days.' Feelings of charity and generosity toward their brothers-in-arms were running even lower amongst these dead-tired men than their will to preserve the established order of Finnish society or the people fearing its demise, but they were so well acquainted with hunger that they shared every last morsel that they had.

It was an anti-tank detachment that came across Mäkilä while on their way to bring a new cannon to a devastated section of the line. The numbers stamped on the side of the soup vat enabled them to identify its owner and they brought him and the vat out to the platoon. So great was the disappointment brought on by their unsatiated hunger that the news of Mäkilä's death remained secondary to the fact of the shortage of soup. Rahikainen even went so far as to say curtly, 'That man was stingy all his life and managed to be stingy even in dyin'.'

They received one ladle of soup apiece and crumbled what little bread they had into it, then ate sparingly, as if they might somehow stretch the food that way.

It was Rahikainen who gave a laudatory eulogy for Mäkilä, however. 'That fellow there's the one offloaded the officers' junk into the forest. Did away with those icon-pictures the leader of the First Platoon was hangin' onto. The shit that nutcase collected! Not worth a damn cent . . .'

'We seen stuff better than that fly by the wayside. There's sacks a wheat flour they had in those supply trucks they drove in'na the lake. Didn't I tell you all they thought we'd be out here 'til kingdom come? They were still drivin' supplies out to the line when they shoulda been drivin' 'em away.' Rokka was sharing his cutlery with Susling, as the latter had lost his pack in some scuffle with the enemy.

'I done told you not to take it off your back,' Rokka added.

The men generally threw their packs on their backs immediately upon hearing an alarm, demonstrating their estimation of their odds of success, as well as the general state of their fighting spirit. Hence Vanhala's new name for their gear: 'Panic packs! Heeheehee.'

The others ate in silence. Rokka was the first to spot a group of men coming toward them along the road, and yelled, 'Damn it, lookit that! Kariluoto's headin' over. Well, I guess he's gonna see for himself now how it is . . . Got some men with 'im. Hang on, what the hell am I sayin'? Those are just pups's all those are.'

Kariluoto had returned, bringing the battalion's replacements with him. He took the men to the command post, where they met Koskela.

Kariluoto was overjoyed to see him after such a long time and burst out, 'Well hello, old man! Old Koski, still holding down the fort. Weeds'll outlive everything. God doesn't want them and the devil knows he'll get them in the end. I've brought some boys with me. Four men for the chatterbox team, too . . . your old platoon, I mean.'

Kariluoto was a happy man. He'd gotten married over his leave. He had returned to the front deaf and blind to the trains of wounded men streaming past. Newspapers full of the retreat and defeat had passed him right by. He'd grown thinner while he was away, and developed black bags under his eyes, and his lips were literally chafed from kissing. His lady Sirkka had bashfully remarked that he was going to wear herself out if he kept up that way.

With the perfect self-absorption of the lover, he had managed to block out the events that were crushing his entire world. Finland could not possibly capitulate, because that would make him, Captain Kariluoto, unhappy, and how could anyone do that, particularly now, when the wave of his life was at its very crest? Surely everyone was aware that he had just married a woman whose magnificence would astonish the entire world. Kariluoto's sharp-eyed mother had hinted that her son might have acquired a wife with a tendency toward carelessness, but that was precisely what made Sirkka so attractive to Kariluoto. She had such a charming way of forgetting things – and when Kariluoto found a one-mark coin in her stocking, which had been put there in place of a lost garter button, he melted at her adorable ridiculousness.

'New weapons,' his beloved papa had repeated anxiously, having realized that the tides of world history were not going to spare the idyllic corner of Northern Europe in which he had lived so happily. A secure government functionary's job during the week and exercises with the National Guard every Sunday – followed by all sorts of eager, utterly preposterous dreams about the future, backed by nothing but the untamed zeal and blue-eyed naïveté of a country that had won its independence just one generation before.

If a moment arose in which the son was obliged to take a stance on the developments, as well, he consoled himself with the fact of Rommel, or, in the worst case, with the Western Allies' friendship toward Finland.

Koskela stood waiting as Kariluoto bounded eagerly toward him, his hand outstretched. He had the glow of leave about him, emanating from his clean clothes, freshly cut hair and gleaming boots, upon which dust seemed out of place.

Koskela clasped his outstretched hand and said, 'Well, well. Hello, there. And congratulations.'

Kariluoto was suddenly unsure of himself. His boisterousness vanished – and only now did he realize the reality he was being faced with. He could see that Koskela's cheekbones stood out, that his eyelids were red and swollen, and that his forced smile was strangely contorted.

'Thanks,' he said quietly, then asked with some hesitation, 'How are things?'

'We're here. Moved since you been away.'

'Yeah. Tough times. Why don't we get these men split up and then go find a place to talk? I've got a thing or two in my bag. I can take over the company after.'

'Yeah, sure. The Second Platoon is on the other side of the road, the First and the Fourth are on this side, and the Third is off in reserve. Our battalion demanded it for its own reserve, but gave in when they heard that its headcount was down to sixteen. The Jaeger Platoon is carrying out patrols on the flanks and there aren't any other reservists left. Everything feels so helplessly weak.'

'Sarastie seemed quite hopeful about the line along the brook. He thinks it'll hold.'

'Maybe. But both flanks are exposed. Well, they've been that way before, too. When there's no one left, there's no one left, no matter how unreasonable that seems. If only there were just one strong reserve unit to take the flanks!'

They divvied up the replacements and found a quiet place to talk, out of earshot of the messengers and phone operators. Kariluoto opened up his pack and started making sandwiches.

'I can offer you a drink, too, if you want.'

'No, no.'

'I just meant one.'

'Not worth it for the taste. But hey, how are things back in the land of the living?'

'Honestly, there's not much to report. But how are things here?'

Koskela grunted quietly and then fell silent for a long time before saying, a faint surge rising in his voice, 'It's all over. As over as it can be.'

Kariluoto gave a start. Uttered in this strong, bitter voice, the words felt so irrevocable that Kariluoto felt the end was at hand this very moment. 'I see. Who'd have thought – Germany. And we won't last on our own.'

Koskela didn't say anything for a little while. It seemed to Kariluoto that he was deliberately holding something back. He saw a muscle twitch in the corner of Koskela's eye and realized what kind of strain this seemingly calm man must have been under. Finally Koskela said in a strangely angered voice, 'This isn't a war. This is just horror after horror.'

'Yeah, the deserters,' Kariluoto said, seizing on the first thing that came to his mind of what this 'horror' might be. 'Have there been many?'

'Oh, they don't really have anything to do with it. The ones who actually desert, I mean. There aren't many of them, and mostly they're guys whose nerves are so fried they're no use anyway. But nobody wants to fight. The whole thing's like sand slipping through our fingers – like water, even. Nothing stays where it's supposed to.'

Koskela fell silent and his face resumed its former, motionless mien. Kariluoto didn't say anything either, sensing more from Koskela's speech than he really wanted to know. He knew him well enough to understand that he must be tottering on the breaking point of exhaustion, as there was no other way that Koskela would have been capable of such an outburst.

A long, embarrassed silence prevailed as they chewed on their sandwiches. Finally, Kariluoto said, 'How are things going for us?'

'The battalion, you mean?'

'All of us. All of Finland . . .'

'The way things go for losers. Getting the shit kicked out of us.'

Kariluoto's jaw trembled. He felt a dampness under his eyelids and his angry voice wavered as he said, 'No. By God, no! I can't stand it . . . I don't want to see it. Anything but that.'

'There's no hope. Not a trace.'

'So we fight hopelessly.' A savage note had crept into Kariluoto's voice.

'That's what we've been doing this whole time,' Koskela said, exhausted to the point of apathy. Kariluoto saw that he was embarrassed by the whole tenor of their conversation and wanted it to be over. They shifted into a more practical mode and Koskela explained their situation to Kariluoto. He would go back to leading his former platoon indefinitely, even if he knew it was only a matter of time before they transferred him elsewhere. The shortage of officers was becoming apparent, and they wouldn't be able to keep lieutenants like him as platoon leaders for long. The battalion actually had a couple of company commander vacancies that were being filled by men younger than him, but they had been filled while he was serving as Third Company commander, and besides, they were regular officers. Koskela had no professional ambitions mixed up in the matter, but he would have liked to stay with his own platoon. There was no way that would happen, however, unless he became commander of their own company.

When they'd finished eating, they set off to check on the positions. Koskela explained a bit about the stages of the retreat, and little by little Kariluoto began to understand just how complete the collapse had been.

V

The new recruits assigned to Hietanen's platoon were digging fox-holes for themselves. They were four in total, and Hietanen had left them all in the first section, as it was down by more men than the second. Actually, all the squads had been operating short-handed since the war began. It hadn't really been a problem during the positional war, as it had just meant that they had to stand guard more frequently, but as soon as the retreat began, they struggled to carry all of the equipment. Hietanen was instructing the boys digging foxholes. Three of them appeared to be taking the situation seriously. They said little and followed Hietanen's instructions with a harried submissiveness attesting to their general uncertainty. The fourth boy, however – a vigorous, blond youth – seemed instantly at home. Once he'd dug his hole, he sat down on the edge of it and said with a swagger, 'So, where these Russkis at, huh? I wanna start takin' 'em down.'

Rokka's head popped out of a pit. 'Goollord! You all hear this fella? Lissen boy, don't yell so loud, they'll hear you, and they'll all start runnin' for the hills once they realize you're here.'

'How old are you?' Hietanen asked.

'Eighteen, Sergeant, sir,' one of the boys replied.

'Well, I'll be damned. We were pre-tty young when we started but we weren't children.'

'Mother Finland wrenches babes from her breast and sends them out to protect her,' Rahikainen said.

Something resembling a smile rose to Hietanen's exhausted face. 'That's the first time I've been called "Sergeant, sir"! You all hear that? Just so you know who you're talking to.'

'New recruits with the fear of the trainin' center drilled into them,' Rahikainen said disparagingly. 'Now they're sendin' us young'uns and grandpas.'

'*Far and wide, our heroes rise up, coming forth to join the line-up . . .* heehee . . .' Vanhala, sitting in his hole, hands clasped around his ankles, started chanting the Red Guard's March again.

> Bureaucrats are dying
> hells and prisons vying
> for the wretched souls

of this sad, misbegotten land.
Far and wide, our heroes rise up
coming forth to join the line-up
fighting on through all that life and death demand . . .

'Fighting on, fighting on,' Sihvonen sneered. 'Except that there's no life out here. Should've just made it "death" . . .'

Koskela and Kariluoto then arrived. Koskela was to stay with his platoon from now on, and Kariluoto stuck around a moment to say hello. 'Hey. How are you guys doing?'

'Oh, fine. Ceding land to pass the time.'

Kariluoto spotted a guy from his former platoon and ran off to greet him – it was Ukkola, boiling up some water over a nearby campfire. Ukkola sat with his cap backwards, the bill over the nape of his neck. Machine-gun cartridges dangled from his waistband. He had no pack, just a breadbag and a rolled-up winter coat bound together with some hemp string. He had fixed his canteen to the barrel of his submachine gun and was dangling it over the fire.

'Hey there . . . How you doing, Ukkola?'

'Hey. Well, can't say there's anything too great about the job.' The man glanced over his shoulder and even Kariluoto had to smile. The image of him was so perfectly stereotypical, right down to the response.

'No, doesn't look that way. So this is what we've come to.'

'In cards it's the luck of the draw, and farming's a goddamn lottery, but this here, this is one hell of a course they sent us out on.'

'Isn't there anything we can do?'

'Sure, we can stir up a little nuisance, but that won't stop them. If we manage to hold the line in one spot it gives way somewhere else. And those guys move fast. First, they load up the air with iron and then they pounce on you like a pack of wolves. Those fuckin' Sturmoviks are hell. Shooting off shells and bullets so fast it almost looks like there's guys sittin' up on the wings shooting off submachine guns.'

Ukkola's water started to boil. He took the grease box for his gas mask and carefully emptied his packets of substitute coffee into it.

'This here's everything I have left. The supply guys have given their notice. We go whole days without seeing a scrap of food. Even the Good Lord Himself couldn't save this ship from sinking.'

Ukkola stopped speaking as he focused his attention on the boiling coffee. Blowing on his cup, he continued, 'I mean, once it goes, there's no getting it up again any which way. So, well. Hey, congratulations by the way. Didn't you get married or something?'

'Indeed I did. Thanks very much. Here's a couple of rye crackers. I haven't got much left since I already shared some with the guys in the First Platoon.'

'Thanks. There's more coffee over there – if you're interested, I mean. Couple of guys from the unit decided to make themselves scarce back at Pyhäjärvi.'

'Thanks, I don't have time right now. Yeah, Rajamäki doesn't surprise me, but Kuusisto and above all Rauhala was something of a shock.'

'Kuusisto lost it completely, and Rauhala, well, he was always a little braver than the rest of us, so I guess that's why he dared run off a little further.'

'At least there aren't any more deserters, though, right?'

'No, no more deserters. But as soon as those fellows 'cross the way start at it again, there'll be another round.'

Kariluoto continued on his way. It went from bad to worse. His feeling of depression only deepened with each encounter. Ukkola had more of a will to fight than most of them, and he had given up hope entirely. Kariluoto got the same reception from his entire company. The men answered his greetings with whines and whimpers. His former platoon mates congratulated him at least, and showed some kind of happiness at his return, but all in all, the feeble line that he inspected was dismal indeed.

# Chapter Fourteen

## I

*Vo . . . ooo . . . oooooo . . .*

Ground-attack planes were flying over the front line toward the command posts and artillery positions. The sudden roar overhead rent the atmosphere of normality and sent the men scurrying instinctively to the shelter of their foxholes. The unusual moment of calm had lulled them into that self-deception hope can induce, in which a man can imagine that, for some unknown and mysterious reason, the fighting might cease for a while. A couple of days of the quiet life had soothed their minds, but their tension was still so close to the surface that they quickly descended into the panicky anxiety that had become characteristic of the retreating troops. When the planes had passed over, they began to rise up in their holes, but quickly ducked back down again when an unbroken stream of low booms started sounding from the enemy side.

They had a few seconds to hope the barrage might miss before the first explosions exposed the vanity of such hopes. The ground lurched and shook. Screeches and moans filled the air and the miserable men's hearts pounded nearly to pieces in the midst of the grinding upheaval. They tried to hold themselves against the earth as tightly as they could. They dug their nails into the sand at the bottom of their pits, and somebody was even digging himself deeper into the ground with his shovel, like a child, one scoop at a time.

'Stay down!' a choked voice screamed somewhere, before being drowned out by the crashing explosions. Trees snapped like twigs as fire and columns of smoke rose up to the height of the treetops. Shrapnel, tree branches and clods of earth rained down in one flash flood, and somewhere a hot, whizzing shard struck a panicked man, who began screaming between cries of pain, 'Medics! Medics! I'm hit!'

Hietanen was lying face-down in his pit. He clenched his eyes shut, his strained consciousness registering each nearby explosion as it landed: 'And again . . . and again . . . and again . . . and again.' It was some kind of method of protecting himself, a way of banishing all the horror that this crashing and trembling awakened in his mind. He began to make out a pitiful wail and cry for help a few yards from his hole, and after wrangling with his fear for a few moments, he lifted his head to look. A few yards away, one of the recruits who had just arrived was struggling to crawl forward, dragging himself and screaming for help with a crazed, desperate look of horror on his face.

Hietanen leapt up. He grabbed the man and started pulling him into his hole, his face blue with anger as he yelled, 'I told you to stay in your fucking hole! And you got up!'

He had just given the boy a stern warning about not leaving his hole, because he knew from his own experience how hard it was to stay down in a barrage. As soon as terror got the upper hand on self-control, it brought about exactly this kind of stupid mishap in the middle of a onslaught. The heavy-handedness of Hietanen's warning might even have been partially responsible for provoking the man's action.

Hietanen pulled him along almost brutally, the fear in his mind having transformed itself into a blind rage directed at the boy. The whirr of shrapnel filled his ears, dirt rained down on them, and waves of pressure kept whooshing their clothes right up against their skin. Hietanen was on his knees, pulling the man by his hand and his belt. The man screamed ceaselessly, though more from the shock than from the pain, as his wound was not dangerous.

A hot wave of air struck Hietanen in the face at the same moment as a shard snapped the cartilage of his nose and tore open both of his eyes. He slumped over the recruit, who froze into a petrified silence as he saw these sliced, bloody eyes bulging out of their sockets.

The man tried to roll Hietanen off him, but he was so paralyzed with fear that he couldn't muster up enough strength. He turned his head away so he wouldn't have to look at the terrible, bloody face, and when he was finally able to get his vocal cords to function, he let out a long, horrible cry.

It startled the others. Koskela and Vanhala were closest and crawled over to help. They lifted Hietanen off the man and dragged them both into the nearest foxhole. Just then the barrage started moving further back. Koskela yelled to the recruits, 'New guys! Bandage the wounded, and if an order comes to retreat, then carry them with you.'

The others hurried to their positions, as they could already hear the rumble of a tank somewhere behind the stream, accompanied by rapid firing. A charge call rang out just then as well, but it became clear fairly quickly that it was a bluff. The enemy didn't attack, and both the yelling and the shooting gradually died down. The men wondered what the taunt was supposed to mean, but weren't able to make much more of it than that the enemy wanted to scare them rather than launch a genuine attack. This type of thing had actually happened before, so they weren't terribly concerned about it. Koskela ordered Rokka to keep an eye on the platoon and headed back to see Hietanen. In the previous moment's rush he hadn't actually had time to see what had happened to him. He had the impression that only one of the eyes was lost.

Hietanen had a bandage wound around his head, and he was just regaining consciousness as Koskela reached him. Hietanen moved his hand, touched the bandage, and murmured, 'What's the damage?'

Koskela took his hand from his face and said, 'Don't worry. Be still now.'

'Koskela?'

'Yup. Don't move. Got you in the nose a bit.'

Koskela turned to the men and drew his fingernail in front of his eyes. The men nodded. Then he raised two fingers and they nodded once more. The blood on Hietanen's shirt sleeve drew their attention to a small wound on the back of his elbow as well. They had bandaged it, trying to make it seem as important as possible so that Hietanen would direct his attention there. 'It hurts,' he grunted. 'Say, why's my forehead wrapped?'

'They got you in the nose. It's not too bad . . .'

'I know. I haven't got eyes anymore.' Hietanen's consciousness was returning ever more fully, increasing his pain along with it. The blow had anaesthetized him against the wound, but as the shock wore off, Hietanen was realizing what had happened. He squeezed his hands into fists and then straightened out his fingers. He held in his cry for a long time, but then there came a long howl that forced the frightened new recruits to turn away.

Cautiously, Koskela lifted Hietanen's head. 'Can I get you some water? Stretchers'll be here soon. I'll come with you to the side of the road.'

'No, I don't want any. Where are the guys?'

'At their positions.'

'Are we still there? Same old spot?'

'Yup.'

Hietanen lifted himself onto his side, letting out another howl. Then he went limp and fell onto his back. His breathing was quick and uneven.

'Are there other guys here?'

'The new guys.'

'Gimme a pistol!'

'Don't worry. They'll get you to the aid station soon.'

'I'm not gonna make it. My head's burning. Somethin' awful. Somethin' awful. I'm not gonna make it much longer . . . give it here . . . I'm gonna die anyway.'

'I'm not going to give it to you, you can be sure of that. There's no point. You're not going to die. You're totally fine otherwise. It just cut them open. Your nose's broken, but nothing else.'

Hietanen began writhing again. Koskela ordered the new men to run over to the medics and urge them to hurry up. They had already carried a few of the wounded over to the roadside.

Seeing as the enemy appeared to have calmed down, Koskela

allowed the men to come and say goodbye to Hietanen. Nobody could think of anything to say, as they all fully understood the enormity of Hietanen's misfortune, and felt the inappropriateness of the niceties they usually mustered to boost one another's spirits. Silently, they each passed through, touching the hand gripping the side bar of the stretcher. Between howls, Hietanen tried to make jokes, as even he could sense the paralysing tension of the situation. 'No eyes. No crying, then!'

When nobody answered, Hietanen sensed their sympathy, and as if to fend it off, he started chattering on in his old way. 'Well, it doesn't make any difference to me. Jesus, I'm not worried! I'm just a happy-go-lucky kind of guy. Little thing like this doesn't matter to me.'

The medics lifted the stretcher and started to carry it away. The last noise they heard was a long, pained howl. They knew quite well what it would take to get such a noise out of Hietanen, and so could guess what severe pain his torn eyes must have caused.

Koskela accompanied the stretcher to the roadside. The others who had been wounded in the barrage were already assembled there – six in all. Kariluoto had asked the aid station to send out an ambulance, and as it happened the vehicle was already there, having been just over at the supply post, where it had been sent to pick up the service guys wounded in the earlier ground attack. The doctor decided that the front line's wounded should come in the same load, so the ambulance had come directly out.

A bus that had been converted into an ambulance teetered toward them, swerving down the terrible road. The wounded men watched in horror as the driver snaked his way around the rocks with seemingly reckless abandon. They were afraid the bus would break down and leave them without transportation, and every one of them had a burning desire to get out of there before the enemy attacked again. Their fears were unnecessary, however, as the driver knew what he was doing. Generally speaking, these ambulance drivers had, over the years, learned to navigate even this kind of terrain, which no normal person would have dared attempt with even a horse. They knew they were in a race against death, as a wounded man's survival frequently hinged on his making it to the operating table in time.

The most seriously injured were placed in front. The vehicle's shaking was worse in the rear and it made Hietanen's head burn with pain, but he stayed in the back nonetheless, letting some guy wounded in his mid-section pass in front of him. The pain radiated from his brow straight through to the back of his head, burning into his back and down his arms as well. The medic even whispered to Koskela that Hietanen might die if the shard had cut deep enough.

Koskela refused to believe it, figuring that if Hietanen was conscious, his wound couldn't be as dangerous as that. He grasped his friend's arm and said, 'Take it easy. Life doesn't depend on eyes. If we make it through, we'll meet up again for sure. I'll come by sometime.'

Hietanen was in so much pain that he couldn't really focus his attention on Koskela any more. Turning his head away, he muttered over the moans and the cries, 'Keep in touch . . . Send my greetings to the guys! You take care of yourself . . .'

The driver ordered Koskela out of the ambulance and he stepped down to the ground. He stood there silently for a long time, even after the bus had disappeared around the bend in the road. Then he lit a cigarette and started slowly back to the platoon. The desolation that enveloped him now was deeper than it had been before. He'd been away from his platoon for a long time, but he hadn't drifted away from the men for all that. With each man that went, the platoon lost something. To him, the old platoon maintained a certain spirit, connected with the early part of the war and their success and energy in it. Each man they lost took a piece of that spirit, leaving in its place nothing but hopelessness and the meaningless absurdity of fighting. And Hietanen had been the closest to him, of all the men. And of all of them, he seemed the very worst suited to blindness.

But Koskela knew what he had to do. He would keep his thoughts fixed on what he wanted and away from what he didn't. Once again he shook off the discomfiting feeling that this senseless killing and suffering induced in him – the same one that had sparked his rage back when Lehto had shot the prisoner and the others had carried on about it like a pack of vultures. This was not the place for a human being. Koskela turned his thoughts toward the machine guns' new positions.

## II

Major Sarastie was sitting on a moss-covered rise, getting through one cigarette after another. Black bags sagged beneath his eyes, and the hand grasping his cigarette flinched nervously. His shirt was wrinkled and filthy. The swamps and the forests had rubbed the color off his boots. The bootlegs gleamed greenish-white. 'Shitty horse leather,' Sarastie thought in passing, as his eyes passed over them.

The command post was unremarkable. There was a phone and a campfire for making coffee. Messengers and signalmen huddled off to the side. There was no aide-de-camp, as the former one was now leading a Jaeger Platoon that had lost its leader. No replacement had arrived yet, and God only knew if one ever would.

Grenades whistled overhead. Ground-attack planes rumbled further back, harassing the supply train. Their own mortar choked out three coughs from somewhere nearby. The munitions shortage was affecting them as well. There were some transportation difficulties. The Sturmoviks were making sure of that.

Sarastie was worried about the exposed flanks. Encirclements were as established a part of this Russian advance as they had been of their own three years ago. But what could they do about it? They would have needed a proper reserve unit to take the wings, but where were they supposed to find one? There was the Jaeger Platoon, but they were carrying out the patrols, and there was one platoon from the First Company, but it was stationed out by the front line, just in case it should break. He couldn't take any more men from the line along the brook itself, as it was weak to begin with. And where was that going to land them – having guys everywhere, but spread too thin to do anything anywhere? Daring maneuvers had, of late, become a matter of necessity. He had been promised a sapper company as a reserve unit as soon as it finished laying some road, but as far as he knew, those guys were still over there. The combined combat unit's commander demanded 'iron-fithted operationth only'. As far as Sarastie was concerned, the Lieutenant Colonel was an idiot. Little love was lost between them, and in his irritation, the Major considered the Lieutenant Colonel's inability to pronounce the letter S just one more instance of his idiocy. The quarrel between them was nothing more than a typical manager–subordinate squabble, in which one party demands more than the other thinks reasonable. Whenever Sarastie was unable to hold back the enemy with his worn-out battalion, the Commander saw only one possible cause: that they had not pushed vigorously enough. What difference did it make how vigorously he, Sarastie, steamrolled onward if his men had run out of steam? There was nothing a commander could do about that. He had done everything he could. He had tried to understand the men, he had stressed to the officers the importance of their attitudes toward them, and he had given Lammio a strongly worded talking-to. It was time to give up the lofty stance of an officer, grab a pistol and join the ranks. Sarastie had read a great deal of military history, and a quote from Napoleon now came into his mind: 'I have been Emperor too long. It is time to be General Bonaparte once more.' Sarastie had been a hard-liner when necessary, but exercising the right to shoot his own men was something he considered unreasonable – immoral, even.

Yes, indeed. If he could just rally the men's spirits, then the line would stiffen up too. Everything hinged on that. There might even be some possibility of organizing operations once he could take stock of things. At the moment, everything was just resting on chance. The line might hold just as well as it might break. The men's ability to hold it was a hazier variable than it had been previously. A staunch, shared will was missing. There were just little spurts that might be flattened at the slightest opposition.

The Jaeger Platoon had just returned from a patrol off to the right, in an area that backed up to a broad stretch of swampland. Sarastie didn't trust the swamp, however, as he himself had carried out encirclements through tougher terrain than that, and experience had already made it clear that the Russians were just as capable. The returning patrol reported that all was quiet, but how much could one trust those kinds of reports these days? That slight uncertainty in the reporter's voice was a tell-tale sign that the men hadn't gone out quite as far as they were supposed to.

The defeat had increased Sarastie's tendency toward the philosophical. He had striven to take everything 'scientifically', even being a bit proud about it.

The Major took a swat at the mosquito that had just been buzzing in his ear, trying to smack it against his neck; but it slipped easily out of danger into the gust of air beneath his hand. His stomach gave a spiteful growl and a bead of sweat pearled on his brow as a momentary faintness washed over him. Diarrhea was endemic.

A guard suddenly emerged from the forest, gasping, 'Major, sir! The enemy!'

'Where?'

'Over there! In formation. With submachine guns under their arms.'

Sarastie ordered the messengers and signalmen into positions and set off himself in the direction the guard had indicated. He understood everything the moment he saw the enemy line advancing through the forest with men carrying machine guns behind them. They must be up against an encirclement, as a normal patrol wouldn't transport machine guns.

Sarastie ran back and ordered the hesitating men into position.

A couple of shots announced the fighting.

'I'll notify the front line and ask for back-up,' he yelled. The messengers and signalmen had taken to their heels and Sarastie spotted an enemy soldier behind a spruce. He pulled out his pistol and emptied the magazine. His hand had just reached the telephone handle when the first Russian shot off a long string of bullets. Sarastie was dead.

## III

The ambulance swayed with its moaning cargo down the potholed road. The driver watched the road carefully and turned the steering wheel, trying to gauge which potholes were the worst. The medic checked some wounded man's pulse. He got up and whispered to the driver, 'He's not going to make it to the aid station.'

The driver didn't respond, as the road demanded his undivided attention, and in any case there was nothing he could do with such information, seeing as he was already driving as fast as he possibly could.

Hietanen was lying at the back of the bus. He devoted all of his strength to keeping his body still, as every jolt sent sharp pains burning through his head. The pain shut out any possibility of pondering his unfortunate fate, and anyway his future life lay well beyond the reach of his concerns. He hoped merely that the drive would end soon, or else that he would die – just so long as he could escape this excruciating pain. Frequently, when the pain and misery became unbearable, his long, despairing howl would rise amidst the moans of the others.

As they neared the rise that led to the command post, they began to hear shooting over the roar of the engine, but it no longer aroused their interest. There was a bend in the road at the bottom of the hill, and just as the vehicle turned round it, the windshield shattered. The driver slumped down against the steering wheel, then rolled on top of the medic, who had fallen beside the gear shift. The ambulance hit a ditch and came to a halt. Bullets clinked through the body of the bus and flames began to flutter up from beneath the hood.

When Hietanen recovered from the stupor brought on by the vehicle's sudden halt, he got up. Screaming and moaning surrounded him. He groped about with his hands against the back door and pushed it open. The movement brought a new round of bullets sailing into the side of the ambulance. Someone was crawling by his feet and yelling, 'The ambulance is on fire! It's on fire! Help me out of here!'

'Where's the driver and the medic?' Hietanen yelled.

'Dead. Help . . .'

Hietanen pulled the man out and fumbled his way back to the rear of the ambulance, yelling, 'Anybody who can't get out, just grab my hand here! I'll pull you. But anybody who can make it, try to get yourself out. Everybody behind the bus!'

Somebody grabbed hold of his outstretched hand, and though the effort brought a sharp pain to his head, he pulled the man along the floor of the vehicle. The man screamed and wailed as his wounded pelvis dragged along the floor. There were six wounded men, but the two positioned up in front had been killed in the same shower that took out the medic and the driver. As he was dragging the man out, Hietanen heard the last of the survivors screaming for help. 'Help me! The car's on fire! I don't have legs! I can't get out!'

The screaming turned to choking, as the ambulance was beginning to fill with smoke. Hietanen made his way out of the back door with the wounded man and yelled, 'I'm coming right back! I won't leave you!'

The man who had made it out first, who had also been in the back of the ambulance, was the same new recruit that Hietanen had been wounded trying to help. He was actually in better shape than Hietanen was, but he was in such a state of shock that he couldn't think of the others and just tried to crawl to cover behind the bus. A bullet aimed straight at his head cut short his escape, though.

When Hietanen got the other man to the door, he lowered himself from the vehicle and pulled him out. The man suddenly panicked and started screaming, 'Get down, get down! He can see you! Over there!'

That was as far as he got. The shower struck the open doors of the bus and the man fell limply between them. Hietanen sank slowly down onto his side. His body shook for a long time as a shower of machine-gun fire tore through it. Sergeant Urho Hietanen was a happy-go-lucky kind of guy.

The ambulance burned, crackling and sparking. For a long time a choked coughing and crying rose up over the din, calling out, 'Come and help me! Why did you leave me? Can't anybody hear me? I'm burning. My blanket's on fire!'

The coughing went on for some time, then changed into a wild bawling. First came a long, drawn-out scream, and then, the voice clarified into words. 'Where the fuck did you go? I'm burning! Get me a submachine gun. I'm gonna kill you. I'm gonna kill everybody!'

The fire hissed. The voice choked and receded into coughs, and then, finally, a pleading whimper. 'Stop . . . stop . . . this is the Red Cross . . . For the love of God . . . stop, no more . . . I'm on fire . . . no more . . . This is the Red Cross . . .'

Then the voice was drowned out by the crackle of the flames. The organs of bomb squadrons boomed through the clear blue of the summer afternoon. In the south, toward Ladoga, an artillery barrage was rumbling.

## IV

Kariluoto was sitting at his command post eating a garden tomato – the last of the food he'd brought from home. He had come from the exultation of love smack into the middle of this misery, and the shock had sent his spirits plunging to a painful low. He had had enough of hearing about all the phases of the retreat. They attested to a total collapse. Columns harassed by ground-attack planes, destroyed supplies, the mood of hopelessness, the deserters, the reluctance to fight at all.

It pained Kariluoto to listen to these reports. On top of everything else, the defeat brought shame. He had thought the army would pull out fighting with everything it had, but the stories he heard revealed the truth, recounted in soldiers' bitter, sarcastic slang.

They had fled before as well. Been scared, run away – but at least they had been ashamed and tried to make up for it. Now no one thought anything of it. The men themselves would laughingly tell about how they'd run away, making a joke out of it. To be sure, there was not a thing in the world they were not willing to make into a joke, but it still pained Kariluoto to hear it.

He didn't actually condemn fear, having recognized the fear in himself long ago. He had even looked back on that baptism of fire and seen it for what it was, stripped of any self-protective shield. If he weren't company commander, who knows? Maybe he would be running away too. It was his position that compelled him to pull himself together.

He remembered the ghost that had haunted him. The gray-haired captain who had advanced under fire, body angled, shoulder high. Many times that broken voice had echoed in his ears: 'Give it another go, Ensign. They'll take off all right.' It had always made him groan with shame and agony. But eventually the specter had forgiven him, as Kariluoto came to realize that he himself had issued the same exhortation dozens of times. Kaarna's frame of mind from that day was well known to him now.

He did envy the men to whom bravery just came naturally. But he had devised careful protection against that. He had resolved for himself that that kind of bravery was merely pragmatic – it had no moral or ethical merit. Once, when they had been talking about Viirilä's insane bravery, he had smiled almost contemptuously, saying, 'Well, sure, and the horses out here are the least frightened of all.'

No, fear he was prepared to understand. But indifference – this bitter, biting mockery of their misfortune – it brought tears of anger to Kariluoto's eyes.

At first it didn't occur to him to pay any particular attention to the sounds of shooting coming from somewhere further to the rear. Only after some time had passed did it suddenly strike him that someone was fighting over there. A patrol, maybe.

Kariluoto cranked the phone handle, but there was no answer from Battalion Command. He called over a battle-runner and ordered him to go and get the Third Platoon leader from the reserves. When the man arrived, Kariluoto ordered him and his platoon to go and secure the main road heading toward the battalion's command post, and no sooner had the man set out on his task than the shooting started up again. This time the shots were coming from a Russian machine gun, a weapon that was rare in their experience. The sound made Kariluoto think of the ambulance. It must be just around that vicinity now. Then an even more important fact occurred to him. If there was a machine gun involved, whatever unit had turned up on the road was bigger than just a patrol. He tried the phone again, but to no avail.

He rounded up more men and sent them to help the Third Platoon as he himself headed for the artillery's observation post.

'Phone line's down. Mortars, too. We're trying radio.'

'Ask them to get me the Commander.'

When they finally got a connection, the artillery battery's firing position reported that connections were down at Battalion Command. According to their information, men had come from that direction saying that Sarastie was dead and that the enemy had cut off the road. The Jaeger Platoon was in the midst of trying to set up some kind of barricade on their side of the cut-off point. Then they reported that they had received more information. The mortar positions had been seized by the enemy and Captain Lammio had ordered the supply train to pull out while he rounded up all the men available to help the Jaeger Platoon.

Kariluoto's breath quickened. His hour of trial had come. He was the eldest company commander in the battalion save Lammio, and Lammio was on the other side of the cut-off.

'Ask them to get me the Detachment Commander.' Kariluoto lit a cigarette and took a long drag on it in an effort to calm himself. He tried to hide the trembling of his hands as he took the radio transmitter from the Ensign.

Conversation was difficult, as they had to avoid giving clear information for fear that someone might be listening in. The Commander gave his order briefly: 'Cut to minimum edge. No delay. Erecting barricade wetht. Help negligible. Pothition retention imperative.'

'I can curve.'

'Objective not curve but pothition retention. I am confident it ith not very thtrong. Quick attack will clear up. Hit hard. You choothe method. Over.'

There wasn't much left for Kariluoto to decide, actually. The Second Company and all the machine guns would hold the line along the brook. The First and Third Companies he would round up to carry out the attack.

When Koskela and the company commanders arrived, Kariluoto explained the situation. He assigned Koskela to take command of his own company. Koskela was looking at the map.

'If we pull off the line gradually and curve round between those ponds, we can slip out like a dog through a gate. They can't have many men securing that area, so far from the road. And as for holding the brook line, there's no way. They're not going to sit back and let us open the road just like that. The line can hardly hold with the men it's got on it now, much less with just the Second Company and the machine guns. In any case we'd better make a plan to destroy those two anti-tank guns.'

'The command was clear.'

Koskela clapped the map shut. 'Yup. But it doesn't change anything about the situation.'

'The Commander knows the situation. Explaining it to him isn't going to help anything.'

'Of course not. That's not what I was suggesting.'

The companies split up and the Second Company spread out to try to cover the areas the others had vacated. Koskela took Rokka and Määttä's machine guns with him. He knew, of course, that the weapons would make little difference in this attack, but he wanted the men with him, Rokka particularly. Rokka even left Vanhala in charge of the machine gun and promised to join the firing line himself. The men moved swiftly and determinedly. No questions, no dilly-dallying. The gravity of the situation had restored their old edge. They had wondered over Hietanen's fate for a moment, realizing that the ambulance must have been in a danger zone, but time had cut short their musings. Tonight, their lives were on the line, more precariously than ever before. Many of the men assigned to stay on the brookline asked to join the attack detachment, and Kariluoto took a few of the best.

The groups were set. The Third Company on the left side of the road, the First on the right. His own former platoon Kariluoto held in reserve.

Koskela had explained the situation to the company, adding, 'Guess there's just one way out of this fix – the old-fashioned way.'

But before setting out, he turned to Kariluoto and said, 'Soon as we set in, the neighbors are going to do the same. It won't make any difference how quick we are. They've been ready this whole time. The barrage earlier was just a cover for this encirclement. It's been three hours since then and you can see how they've dug their heels in all over the terrain. They've already got two or three loads of logs over there that they've started building bunkers with. Slipping into the forest is the only way out.'

'You know the order.'

'Yeah, I do. And I also know that the Commander has no idea what he's asking. He should come and open the road from his direction. But he has no idea how to do it. Problem is, it's even harder for us. Two hours from now you'll see what the situation is. When we have the Second Company retreating at our backs and the First and Third lying in shreds under the spruces by the command post. Good luck to any man trying to get out of that.'

Kariluoto diverted his gaze. He knew that Koskela was right, but while he had courage enough in him to make personal sacrifices, going against a commander's order was something that was beyond him. His voice cracked as he said curtly, 'There's an easy way out. Only hurts once.'

Koskela stole a glance at Kariluoto. It was the first time he had heard him take such a personal tone with him. Up until now, Kariluoto had always deferred to his views. Koskela knew it went back to those very first days of the war, and sometimes he had even been a bit embarrassed by it.

Koskela said nothing. Then, as Kariluoto left, a thought flashed through his mind, as if it were an axiom: That man will die today.

And then he banished the thought. 'Who knows? Maybe it'll work. And if we're going through with it, then in any case we have to do it like we believe it might succeed. Otherwise there's no point at all.'

Rokka was shoving hand grenades into his belt. He was on his knees beside the crate when Koskela found him. 'You think many fellas gonna die tonight?'

'I dunno. Anyway, now we just do the best we can.'

'Oh, you don't need'da pump me up. I ain't the pep-talk type. But Lord I hope you know how to pray!'

'Can't remember.'

'Well, try, y'hear? Sankia Priha the Great, he just laughed when'na fellas started puttin' their packs on, but it don't strike me we got much to laugh at.'

'Guess a straight face might be best for all of us this time. By the way, you can decide yourself which way you want to go. It would actually make sense to get together one shock troop, but we don't have time, and I guess the stronger guys will figure out what to do regardless.'

'Oh, I'll be all the shock troop you need, right here.' Rokka set off, humming as he went. *'Take my darlin' by the arm . . .'*

Koskela knew Rokka's singing was just for show. He knew their effort hardly stood any chance of success, but there he went nonetheless, humming away – humming to say that he was ready for anything, hopeless as things might be. In other words, the song meant: Come what may – no time to worry about that now.

## V

'Move out!'

A faint creaking sounded in the forest. No one said a single word. The men knew the drill. Holding their breath, they made their way through a security layer of men positioned in front of them, expecting shots at any moment. Sometimes one of them would glance at the guy next to him as if to ask something, and his neighbor's face would answer, 'Not yet.'

It was seven o'clock. A breathless hush reigned over the silent forest. They could hear shooting further out in front of them, on the other side of the enemy's encirclement. Evening sunlight bathed the bark of the trees. Winding through the forest was a cow path teeming with ants dragging twigs and pine needles to their nest. Occasionally a stripped, sun-bleached spruce branch would snap as a scratched-up boot happened upon it. Nobody was observing the beauty and quiet solemnity of the woodland, however. There were plenty of grave, searching eyes voraciously scanning the forest, but they were looking only for signs of the enemy so that they could strike first. Their scout was out in front. He slipped from tree to tree, bush to bush, trying to remain invisible. Suddenly the men following saw him drop to the ground and at the same moment came a shrill *Pi . . . piew . . . pieew . . .*

*Prr . . . prr . . . prrrrrrrrrrrr . . .*

It was the scout's submachine gun.

'Enemy ahead! Enemy ahead! Positioned on the slope! Alert down the line!'

The platoons fell into formation and the artillery observer ordered his men to fire. The barrage came quickly, but rather feebly, as the artillery positions were being harassed by planes overhead. No sooner had their own artillery fallen silent than the enemy started answering fire from behind. They were so near, however, that the Russian artillery observer couldn't fire close enough for fear of hitting his own men, so the barrage landed about a hundred yards behind them. It was still underway when Koskela's voice cried out, 'Shut 'em up, boys!'

'Shut 'em up . . . Shut 'em up . . . Shut 'em up . . .' The words spurred the men on, and they repeated them down the line verbatim, as somehow or other the command struck just the right tone for the situation. The men had decided that tonight they weren't messing around. And no wonder – for the situation was precisely the kind to ignite a Finn's fighting spirit. A mighty roar rang through the forest. 'Whooo-aaah! Mothuuurfuckuuuur! Hoooo-raaah!'

Viirilä's roar was easily distinguishable from the others, as he had his own, personal battle cry. Once, Kariluoto had mentioned in passing that the Catholics' battle cry in the Thirty Years' War had been 'Holy Christ, our Savior'. Viirilä had adapted this into the national style, which was better suited to his particular spirit. After that, the others' shouts were frequently drowned out by his blaring, inhuman roar of 'Holy crap, it's Satan!'

The roar sparked a deafening racket. It was as if a funeral pyre of dry juniper had been set on fire. Only at many times the volume. Three men in a row fell beside one root, and the others were searching for cover. The sides of the trees crackled and snapped, sending bits of bark and wood flying into the air, and constant, angry whistles hailed down onto the tufts of grass carpeting the forest floor.

Koskela was all the way in the back, surveying the situation. He could tell right away from the sound of the firing that the enemy's forces were spread at least as wide as theirs, and perhaps even wider. There was nothing to do but yell 'Straight on!', but the fire raining down from the gently sloping rise was so intense that the operation looked impossible.

'Soften them up with some fire first, guys,' he yelled to the men nearby, who then began searching for targets. Koskela himself located the machine-gunner, whose head fell as Koskela's submachine gun opened fire. A new head quickly rose in its place and the weapon started up again. Koskela got the new gunner in the sight and the man fell, but remained visible. They pulled the body away, however, and a new helmet rose into view. When it fell, no fourth followed, but Koskela knew that the men on the hill also understood what fleeing would mean. They weren't going to give so much as a yard without leaving their dead upon it. That much was clear from the beginning.

The firing didn't last long, though. The men were on the verge of losing all initiative, the first wave of enthusiasm having vanished. Something had to be done. He would probably have to intervene personally. Before he'd had a chance to drum up a plan, he heard

Rokka yelling a couple of dozen yards off to his right. 'Hey lissen, you with the light machine gun! Shoot at that mess'a sticks over by that pine. An' shoot like the devil!'

'What for?'

'They gotta light machine-gunner over there, see. And I wanna git me behind that stump. They'll kill me if they're left'ta shoot in peace. So you shoot real hard!'

The light machine-gun opened fire and Rokka got up. There was a flash of gray as he made a dash for the root, and only once he'd ducked behind it did the hail of bullets start whistling after him.

Rokka needed no more than a blink of the eye to figure out what was concealed in the mass of alder bushes he'd ordered the man to keep under fire. There was a pit in there with three men inside. One guy with a submachine gun and a light-machine-gunner with a fellow helping him. The latter had his light machine-gun, one of those Soviet 'Emma's, hammering away on his trail, but he himself was safely under cover of the stump. Flames fluttered from its fire damper, and Rokka could clearly see the man's broad-boned jaw pressed up against the butt of the light machine gun. He took a hand grenade from his belt and felt a wave of smugness wash over him, prompted by his perfect confidence that his target was toast. When his eye caught sight of a smooth pine cone, he snatched it and threw. He regretted it instantly, of course, but he just hadn't been able to resist, so what of it? The unexpected pine cone sailed smack into the pile of sticks. One of the men noticed it, but by then Rokka's hand grenade was already airborne. A panicked scream came from the pit, and the heads disappeared. The pile of sticks exploded into the air and Rokka made a dash for the pit. One of the six hands moved and Rokka shot it down as he ran.

Dirt flew up around the rim of the pit and Rokka pressed himself low, yelling, 'C'mon, fellas! I'll fire! You all know what's out there in front of us? Finland! C'mon fellas! Now!'

He determined which direction the firing was coming from, and as soon as it paused, raised his head and shot. No more danger from that pit. He glanced backwards long enough to see the platoon leader, Ensign Taskinen, rise up to yell something and fall in the same blink of an eye. Then he saw the guy with the light machine gun lying dead in the spot he'd just passed. Further back was yet another fellow, his head rolling back and forth gruesomely as he fell to the ground. Rokka cleaned out another pit whose dwellers hadn't yet caught on to what was happening.

As soon as he had stopped shooting, Rokka whirled around, as someone had thudded into his hole. It was Viirilä. He was making room for himself amidst the bodies and tore open one of the Russians' packs. He found a long, untouched loaf of bread inside, which he promptly shoved down his shirt, against his bare chest. He didn't have an undershirt. 'Ain't worth sporting an undershirt round here, like this job was better than it is, phahahaha!' Lice had taken over Viirilä's undershirt, and he had burned it over a campfire. 'Phahahahah!'

Viirilä's arrival had not gone unnoticed, and both men ducked their heads as dirt flew up about the edges of the foxhole. Viirilä stomped his feet on the floor of the pit and hollered, 'Hey, you over there! Yeah, you! What the hell do you think you're doin'? Uh-huh . . . Cut it out! Either that or I'm gonna come over there and take that gun off your hands myself.'

'Lissen. We clear out a couple a foxholes so the fellas can git in 'em . . . Then we steamroll 'em, see? You take the right, I take the left. You got any hand grenades?'

'Yeah, I got a two or three potato mashers . . . You know the French for "black cat"?'

'No, dunno . . . Lissen, now ain't the time . . .' Rokka was irritated, as the spot they were in demanded a quick follow-up, but he knew from experience that talking to Viirilä was like talking to a lunatic. The man had his own way of doing things.

Viirilä suddenly raised his submachine gun and fired a short burst, finishing off some man who had just raised his helmeted head above the edge of his pit.

'It's a dark miaow. Phahahaha!'

A hand grenade sailed toward them. As soon as it went off, Rokka raised his gun, knowing that its throwers would also be watching to see where it landed, and took out yet another of the most dangerous enemy soldiers. Viirilä peeked out at the terrain and squatted down in the pit ready to sprint. Then he commanded himself, 'Private Viirilä. Man the foxhole of the enemy soldier you have just executed, then fire at the Soviet soldiers' machine-gun position that is located at the base of that pine. The pine is situated in the eastern portion of the Greater Finland. In order to paralyze enemy morale, you are to strike up a spirited battle cry.'

Rokka had also spotted this same machine-gun position. It sat in the protection of a boulder that prevented any of their fire from reaching it. The same rock meant that the machine gun couldn't shoot at them either, but it was perfectly capable of annihilating anything in the pit Viirilä was eyeing. Rokka decided to shoot at the rock to subdue the men as Viirilä made his dash, and as soon as Viirilä rose, he opened fire.

Viirilä bolted off. Seeing him in his normal state, nobody would ever have imagined that this hulking beast of a man had so much speed and power in him. His army boots – two sizes too large – thudded down two or three times as he leapt between the pits. With his last thump, he roared, 'Holy crap, it's Saaaataaaan!'

Rokka kept the rock sparking with continual fire. The machine gun was silent and thus condemning itself to certain destruction. Viirilä's monstrosity of a head rose from the pit and he emptied the drum of his submachine gun into the enemy position. One of the wounded machine-gunners tried to crawl to safety, but Viirilä had already reloaded his gun, blurting as he fired, 'Stay with your group! Private Viirilä's orders.'

Just then Rokka took off. He made it to a strong shooting position as well, and the two of them cut an opening in the line of defense along the slope. It was no more than thirty yards across, but it was enough. When Koskela saw that Rokka and Viirilä had opened up the possibility for a charge, he joined the men himself and then, ordered it. The moment was, above all, psychologically opportune. The men closest had seen the feats of their two comrades and, fired up by their success, they pushed forward.

Hand grenades burst on one side, then the other. Fierce hand-to-hand combat filled the foxholes. Four hours later, Koskela's company was atop the slope's ridge, but its force of sixty-eight men strong had shrunk by seventeen.

They made it to Major Sarastie's headquarters and found his body stripped down to its underwear. There, a fierce counter-attack took them by surprise and fending it off proved no easy task. Määttä and Vanhala had to shoot through the belt of every last assailant before the attack was put down.


# VI


Kariluoto was crouched beside the remains of the ambulance. The bodies reeked something terrible. The ones inside had been burnt to a crisp, but Hietanen and the new recruit who'd made it out of the vehicle hadn't burned, only their clothes had. Hietanen's leather belt still smelled like it was smoldering.

The First Company had also managed to advance somewhat. The enemy had pulled back their position as well, when Koskela's attack pushed it out of its positions south of the road. But it had dug in its heels again and skirmishing had given way to heavy fighting.

Casualties were high. There was no blaming the men for any lack of effort this evening. The head of the First Company, Lieutenant Pokki, had fallen almost immediately. He had made the error of yelling condescendingly at some men who had halted in their advance, 'Come on, boys, move out! Nothing over there but a couple of loose-stooled Russkis.'

'Well, fuck, in that case, why don't you just kick 'em dead so we can get back over to our own side?' the men had muttered.

The Lieutenant lost his temper and stepped out in front, where a bullet promptly lodged itself in his throat.

The situation demanded some sort of solution. The firing had diminished perceptibly and Kariluoto knew from experience that this meant the men had lost their initiative and were lying under cover, shooting randomly. Koskela's word of the counter-attack had just reached them, and Kariluoto listened fearfully for those savage cries ringing out through the ceaseless shooting.

Something had to be done. Should they leave? Round up the battalion and curve around, pulling out through the forest? But there was the Lieutenant Colonel's command – which was also supported by the Second Company commander's recent message that the enemy had calmed down along the brook line and seemed to be stopping there, contrary to expectations. But pressing onward looked difficult. There were three bodies lying over there, side by side. Some wounded man was screaming and moaning as the medics hurriedly dragged him to cover. Then Kariluoto saw a man being dragged from the line on his side, and heard the man's panicky, trembling voice repeat, 'It's over, boys . . . the Virolainen boy's war is over . . . Virolainen's heading off.'

For the first time, Kariluoto felt that the responsibility for the men's deaths was his. Then he swallowed his feeling of doubt and yelled, 'Fourth Platoon, join the First Company's advance and take the enemy position directly ahead.'

Stopping here would mean that all the casualties incurred up to now had been utterly in vain. And besides, Koskela needed relief. Now was the time to strike. There were two options. Succeed and clear up the situation, or else . . . not curve around through the forest, but die.

The Fourth Platoon got itself into formation. Kariluoto had it join the First Company's clearly diminished line, hoping that the additional force would get the operation moving again.

Something of Kariluoto's mood took hold within his platoon. The men had seen how this slope devoured lives, but it hadn't crushed their spirit. On the contrary – it made them feel they had no right to be spared any longer either. They knew that Kariluoto had kept them in reserve because shared experience had made them a bit closer to him than the others. They were the last shot. Everything depended on them.

Kariluoto stepped beside them into the line. A savage call to charge rang out, and a terrific clatter ensued, swallowing up all individual voices.

Napoleon and the Old Guard at Waterloo. The comparison wasn't nearly as feeble as it might have seemed. Three years earlier, this same platoon had broken through the bunker line, and Kariluoto could still spot a few of the same men in the line: Ukkola, Rekomaa, Lampioinen, Heikinaro and a few others.

The men of the First Company joined the attack. Kariluoto yelled and shot with his gun under his arm, though he hadn't yet caught sight of the enemy. Just lead rain lashing against the branches and the ground.

'Yes, Ukkola!' he cried, seeing the man leap forward, shooting and howling. But right on the heels of his shout, a cry of panic escaped Kariluoto. Ukkola dropped his submachine gun and staggered to his knees behind a hill of blueberry bushes.

'Ukkola!'

'In the chest . . . I'm weak . . . so much for this boy's sprint . . .'

Ukkola didn't die, however, though he had thought he would. The medics pulled him to safety. Kariluoto continued to advance. He was soon forced to take cover, as the enemy was beginning to notice him.

Then Rekomaa and Heikinaro fell, one after the other. The men searched for cover, and Kariluoto was afraid the advance would get stuck again. Yelling, he rose to his feet and dashed to the root of a pine tree, shooting at the enemy, but with little effect, as their opponents were well hidden.

Cries for the medics rang out once more. Some guy from the First Company rose to his feet and threw a hand grenade. Kariluoto saw clearly how the shower struck him, and heard the man grunt softly as he died. Word came from the right that the squad leader had been killed.

Kariluoto urged the men on, but garnered nothing but a couple of short sprints. What was wrong with them? Then Kariluoto realized that in the space of the last ten minutes, the line had diminished almost to the point of non-existence. The terrain was empty to either side of him. And two more wounded men were crawling to the rear.

The enemy had been shooting furiously the entire time. They shot even though no one was visible, and the bullets brought up moss in ceaseless swirls. Kariluoto's mind was numb. The attack had failed. The First Company platoons attacking on the right sent word that they couldn't advance any further. The losses were disproportionate.

Banging and rattling rang in Kariluoto's ears in one heady, chaotic jumble. His consciousness swirled with panic. I've killed the company. I drove them to their deaths . . . I knew myself that this wouldn't work. I can't manage anything more with these men . . . Now they're even shooting Rekomaa's corpse.

The Sergeant's body was lying in plain sight, and some enemy soldier was pummeling it with his light machine gun so that the body shook with his fire. The sight was too horrific to endure, and Kariluoto turned his eyes away. Just a moment ago the man had been yelling and shooting, and now he was lying there bloody, shaking like a limp pile of meat as the bullets pounded into his back.

Firing was weak on their own side. Good God! There was hardly anyone left shooting. Kariluoto was terrified. His impression of the situation was more desperate than it actually was, as death had hit his immediate surroundings hardest, the men there having attempted the charge at his impetus. His former platoon was now more or less finished. As was the First Company's second platoon, which had attacked with them. Though in truth, neither unit had had more than a dozen men to begin with. And there were a few men helping the wounded.

One consolation did come, at least. Koskela's runner arrived from the south side of the road, announcing that the counter-attack had been put down and that there was a strong channel open in front of Määttä's machine gun. Even so, Koskela had said that he couldn't continue right away and, moreover, that his impression was that the operation was a lost cause. Kariluoto was to wait until they could both try again simultaneously.

'Wait! For what?' Kariluoto had surrendered to complete despair. Koskela wouldn't be any help. The enemy was strong enough to take on both of them. It didn't even need to move men. If he didn't make it through now, he wasn't going to make it through later either.

He pulled back slightly and headed down the line to the right. That would be the place to try from, in the Third Platoon's sector. Its leader was wounded, and Kariluoto took command of the platoon.

'Let's try again, men.'

No one replied. But the men silently prepared to charge.

'Advance!'

The movement sparked the enemy to fire full blast, and Kariluoto saw once more how the death of two men can bring their comrades screeching to a halt.

'I will not stop . . . I will not stop . . .' Kariluoto wasn't stepping forward, he was crawling. His face was snow-white, and his voice was stiff and strangled as he yelled, 'One more time, men . . .'

When the bullet struck, his mind burst with a strange release. He had three seconds to realize that he was dying, but in those three seconds he feared death less than he had in the entire war. He was almost content, as he realized, his consciousness fading, 'That's it . . . Now it's over . . .'

Jorma Kariluoto had paid his dues into the common pot of human idiocy.

As had Virolainen, Rekomaa, Heikinaro, Pokki, Vähä-Martti, Hellström, Lepänoja, Airila, Saastamoinen, Häkkilä, Elo, Uimonen, Vartio, Suonpää, Mikkola, Yli-Hannu, Kuusenoja, Kalliomäki, Vainionpää, Ylönen and Teerimäki.

They were all mourned from afar, soldiers who remained on the field. The names of Kariluoto and Lieutenant Pokki, the First Company's commander, appeared on the walls of their former schools. Russian work teams buried them all, along with the battalion's other dead, beside the swamp, not far from Sarastie's command post.

# Chapter Fifteen

## I

Upon receiving word of Kariluoto's death, Koskela immediately got the head of the Second Company on the phone. He suggested the man take over command. The Lieutenant turned him down, however. The honor held no allure for him, and besides, he knew Koskela himself was the better man for the job.

'I'll do it if you consent to a retreat through the ponds,' Koskela said.

The Lieutenant hesitated. He would have to get in touch with the Division Commander by radio first.

Koskela was irritated. In truth, there was no way he was going to continue with the attack, but Lieutenant Colonel Karjula might order the Second Company commander to do so. Koskela had been thinking they could just break off, and not get back in touch until all possibility of continuing this useless massacre of men had passed. He knew Karjula well enough to fear that the man might suspect him of exaggerating in his assessment of the situation.

Nor was he mistaken. But he declared flatly that at least the part of the battalion under his command was not going to continue the attack. The Division Commander was infuriated. He had assembled a weak force to secure the west side, and if the battalion pulled out from where it was, the enemy would immediately shift more men over to the barricade, which would enable them to push it off the road.

They were still arguing when a great clamor began over by the line by the brook. The phone rang and the Second Company sent word that a fierce attack was underway. Koskela brusquely apprised the Commander of the situation, to which the latter replied furiously, 'In any cathe, you are to bring the equipment back with you.'

'Not the anti-tank guns, at any rate. But the battalion I'll bring.'
Koskela put down the radio phone and said to the artillery observer,
'We're going to keep that guy off for a little while.'

Then the phone started ringing and the messengers, running.
Commands were clear, single-minded and thoroughly considered.
Koskela pulled the First Company back somewhat. Then he withdrew the Third Company from the south side of the road entirely
and set it up in defensive positions along the north side, so that the
line ran partially along the road, turned to follow the brook line, then
curved back around toward the north on the far left wing. Thus he
got the men into a horseshoe formation, and ordered the wounded
to be brought into its center. He had already had the wounded from
his own company carried to the north side of the road earlier in the
evening, as well as assigned a command group to make stretchers
out of stakes and tent tarps. At one point he had thought that they
might get the road open, but he had proceeded with his preparations regardless.

One of Kariluoto's men asked, hesitating, 'What about the
bodies? We brought the Captain's body out too.'

'The living are enough.' Koskela didn't even glance at Kariluoto's
body, nor any of the other dead. There was no time for prayers. He
was concerned with nothing but saving the battalion, which he had
decided he was going to do, come hell or high water. His face expressionless, he issued commands with businesslike brevity, and without
thought or question, the men obeyed.

He was most concerned about the Second Company's position.
How were the men going to be able to pull out under that kind of
enemy pressure? Koskela knew that that kind of withdrawal was
one of the most difficult operations to pull off, because in that sort
of situation the squads could easily get mixed up – panic, even. And
he couldn't send any help, as he needed to have a position ready to
receive them, through which the Second Company might pull out
safely.

Luckily, the guys manning the south side of the road were able to
disengage and retreat to safety before the tanks rumbled over the

defensive forces alongside the road. The tanks destroyed one of the anti-tank guns, and its men along with it, but the other went flying spectacularly into the air, its own men having amassed everything they had by way of explosives and ignited them all underneath it just as they fled. A barrel explosion would have destroyed the gun more easily, but it wouldn't have been nearly as impressive – and even in their mortal danger, the men really enjoyed the fireworks.

They left behind four machine guns, as well as some of the wounded, but considering the circumstances, Koskela was satisfied.

He sent the Second Company northward to spearhead the coming march. The First and Third Companies would hold the ring of the horseshoe henceforth. Then he gathered the machine-gun, mortar and anti-tank teams, as well as the artillery observers, in its center.

'Get yourselves into carrying squads of four. If we're short of stretchers, make some up quick. The wounded we carry and the machine guns we dump in the pond. We'll just keep one as a souvenir.'

Koskela looked around and saw Määttä, leaning on his machine gun. 'Want to bring yours?'

'Don't make much difference. Whatever you want.'

It seemed natural that Määttä's gun should be the one they kept. He'd been looking after it since the first days of the war, first shooting it, then leading its team – and now there he was, leaning on it, mute as a statue. Not once had any of them seen him hand it over to somebody else to carry. At the beginning, this devotion to a weapon the others detested for its weight and unwieldiness had just been a statement of the small-bodied man's quiet ambition, but over time it had become elevated into an ideal – the only ideal Määttä really had in connection with the war. He would have been able to toss it into the pond, but it was almost unthinkable that it would stay behind with the enemy unless Määttä's body stayed with it. It had fallen to the enemy for a little while, when Lahtinen had fallen and it had stayed with him, but Määttä didn't think he could be held responsible for that. After the enemy withdrew the next day, they had found it a little way from Lahtinen's body, and from that point on Määttä had guarded it like a precious inheritance.

Even if Määttä had answered his question offhandedly, Koskela knew that he had given Määttä something no decoration ever could ever have. With his question, he had attested before all of them to Määttä's superior ability to carry the machine gun.

The others hesitated at first. It felt strange to throw weapons into the pond, weapons they'd been dragging around the whole war long, often with the very last shreds of their strength.

'Just toss?'

Koskela grabbed the closest man's machine gun. 'Just toss. Like this . . . I don't have time for jokes.'

The water heaved and there it went. Koskela's irritation was as strange as the dumping of the machine guns – but dump them they did, as the men cast their hesitation aside.

'So long, buddy boy!'

'Have a good trip, you jack-hammering bastard!'

'No more tearing up my shoulder!'

Even the war hadn't quite killed the rascals in them. Their faces beamed with mischievous delight.

Enemy tanks were already on the road, their infantry forcing the men on the horseshoe into combat. In the interest of safety, Koskela set their course due north, designating the small, nameless ponds he had pointed out to Kariluoto earlier as their first destination. The First Company's patrol had determined that the flanking enemy forces had positioned men all along the north side of the road, and Koskela wanted to avoid running into them at any cost. Burdened down with their loads and the weight of their defeat, the men would be helpless if confronted with any significant fighting. He needed to get the battalion back to the road in one piece, and that was going to require a long detour.

He knew that he needed to get it there as quickly as possible, but even if it meant facing the court martial, Koskela had decided that they had taken enough reckless gambles for one day. Not even in their famous 'shitty encirclement' had they lost as many men as they had in this hopeless effort. The last three hours had been the bloodiest in the battalion's history. Koskela recalled Hietanen's charred body. Even the bandage around over his eyes had burned.

Koskela grunted.

## II

Vanhala, Rahikainen, Honkajoki and Sihvonen carried Ukkola.

He was in severe pain. The bullet had gone in through the chest pocket of his shirt. At first it seemed that the wound was not dangerous, but soon after their departure, Ukkola had started coughing, and blood rose to his lips.

'So it has punctured the lung, damn it. No wonder it feels like there's a nail in there every time I breathe,' he gasped.

The others tried to console him, but Ukkola knew the value of such speeches all too well. He had knelt more than once beside some dying guy, telling him over and over again how easy his recovery would be. He hadn't even feared death all that much, but this incessant pain was hard to take.

In an effort to cheer him up, Honkajoki started talking about his own injury, describing the wonders of the military hospital. Ukkola was heaving and writhing on his stretcher, but Honkajoki carried on with all his former aplomb. 'All of the finest women serve as nurses' aides. They are indeed heroic, as you will see. They do not even consider it below themselves to wash the leathery ass of a private. Why, those boys have risked their lives over there! With that curly, blond hair and strapping, athletic physique, you'll be a sensation. Don't you worry. Try to hang on just a little longer. I know how it feels. They carried me in a sled during the thaw. Careful, gentlemen. Careful you don't jar him.'

'Break!'

Vanhala sat down on a mound of grass and wiped his cap across his brow. Low moans sounded out in front of them. The infantry guys covering their passage stood off to the side. The dusk of the summer evening was just descending into darkness. A fine mist hovered in the damp air. And Vanhala was smiling. Not with glee, nor with bitterness, but as if he were weighing the whole evening in his mind and smiling nonetheless. 'They've suffered some losses, but our army is as unbeatable as ever as it retreats behind a new line of defense.'

Ukkola's face twisted into a smile. He'd spent hundreds of hours on guard with Vanhala.

'Ohhhh . . . as . . . chuh . . . chuh . . . as long . . . chm . . . ohhhhh. As long as . . . chm . . . we're still breathing . . . they'll be saying . . . chm . . . we're un . . . unbeatable . . . chm . . .'

'Here, let me straighten you out . . .'

'It's no use . . . chm . . . so long as there's still one . . . chm . . . left to slaughter . . . chm . . . we're not beat . . . chm . . . ohhh ohhh . . . What's it gonna take . . . chm . . . for us to be beat?'

'Does anyone have a handkerchief? Or actually, hand me a bandage.' Honkajoki wiped the blood from Ukkola's lips.

Vanhala put his cap back on his head. He knew that Ukkola in severe pain still couldn't be anyone but the old Ukkola, so he said, giggling softly, 'Undaunted even in his defeat, laughing proudly in the face of death, he looks beyond the avalanche that has buried the hopes of his homeland. Heehee . . . You heard it. We can't lose.'

The words Vanhala had just uttered were ones the men had recently heard on the radio, and Ukkola was amused just by the fact that Vanhala remembered such things so precisely. When they got moving again, he said, huffing, 'Hold on tight, Priha . . . chm . . . chm. If these lungs hold out . . . chm . . . out . . . then . . . sometime . . . chm . . . we'll go Priha . . . Ohhhh . . . huh . . . huh . . . get drunk . . .'

After they started off, the wounded man three stretchers ahead of them died.

The body was left at the base of a tree and the guys who'd been carrying the man started alternating shifts with the others. The dead man had been wounded by a shell out on the brook line and was already on his last legs when they'd set out. The men carrying

Ukkola tried to pass by the spot in such a way that their friend wouldn't see that the body had been left – but failed.

'If . . . I don't . . . chm . . . make it . . . then you'd cover me . . . with something . . . chm . . . oh who cares . . .'

One of the wounded men had lost it. 'Just don't leave me! If they attack . . . You promise? Come on, speed up! Hurry up . . . If we run into them, don't leave me behind . . .'

The men carrying offered no promises. They lumbered on silently, grunting and panting, and whenever the wounded man rose in a panic, they pressed him back down on the stretcher.

Ukkola's pain was increasing. He was running a fever and Vanhala wrapped his coat around him like a blanket. Ukkola put his arm over his eyes, giving a moan now and again, frequently accompanied by a litany of curses. Once when the stretcher gave a violent lurch, he seemed jolted out of his pained torpor, and said, 'Same . . . steps . . . Chm . . . step . . . together . . . boys.'

'I don't think we can get much of a sense of rhythm. Terrain's hell.'

Ukkola couldn't keep up a smile any more. More and more blood rose to his lips and his breath grew weaker and weaker. His coughing fits soon became so agonizing that even the guys carrying him had a hard time watching. He was shivering from the fever, and soon anything they could find was wrapped around him.

Four years of continuous malnourishment had not managed to diminish the life force of the country boy. Ukkola had been one of those athletes who turns up at every summer event, and although his results had remained unremarkable, the training had given him a kind of strength and endurance against which death could make no impression. It hadn't managed to make him lose consciousness yet, though he himself wished that it would, as did the men carrying him.

They reached their first destination. Koskela got in touch with the Commander. The man was in a rage. Everything had gone just as he feared. As soon as the battalion pulled out from the road, the enemy had brought its tanks up to the barricade and decimated it.

They would have to continue pulling out, and now the detour would be longer still, as they needed to reach a destination that was even further off. The Colonel himself designated the point at which Koskela was to meet up with the main road, saying finally, 'That ith the command. Your berry-picking excurthion endth there. Ith that clear?'

Koskela couldn't have cared less. He was immune to Karjula's criticisms – for even if he didn't ever descend into self-congratulation, he was still aware that not many men would have been able to get the battalion out in as good a shape as he had. Or as quickly.

The journey continued. The men carrying the stretchers were on their last legs, for although the burdens were not so heavy when divided amongst four men, the uneven terrain multiplied the strain many times over. Their progress grew ever more difficult.

One of the men carrying the stretcher in front of Ukkola's fell, and the wounded man dropped to the ground with a shout of pain. The fellow carrying regained his balance, gasping for breath, spat and screamed in a voice ringing with rage, 'Finnish president Risto Ryti and the National Orchestra proudly present . . . a polka: "Up Shit Creek Without a Fucking Paddle".'

Then he grabbed hold of the handle rods again and the power of his anger spurred him on for a little while.

Even Ukkola's carriers weren't talking anymore. They weren't up to it. Silently, concentrating all of their energy on their task, they toiled onward as Ukkola coughed and gasped on the stretcher in ever-increasing pain.

At three o'clock in the morning, as dawn was already beginning to lighten the sky, Ukkola shot himself with Sihvonen's gun, which had been left leaning against the stretcher during a break.

His carriers were looking off to the side, watching the infantry guys, and didn't realize what was happening until the shot went off.

They would have been happy to bring Ukkola's body to the road, but they were forced to abandon the idea, as the exhausted carrying teams needed to keep rotating and Koskela was urging them to hurry. But when they remembered Ukkola's plea to be covered, they hastily dug a shallow bed with their field shovels and set the body in it, wrapped in a tarp. Then they shoveled some moss and dirt on top to cover it up.

Even Honkajoki was solemn. Maybe it was just exhaustion, but then, death had become a constant companion that night, and it left little room for chatter.

As they were shoveling, Rahikainen said, 'Now, that guy would have made it. But everybody rings things up as he sees fit.'

'I guess Ukkola here was the last guy left in the Fourth Platoon who started in the burnt clearing,' Vanhala said. 'Man, I still remember that one time when we were new recruits, when the Third Company came back from a march and somebody had stuck this massive rock in Ukkola's pack. He'd cheated in packing it up. Hee-hee. Kariluoto was the one who stuck it in.'

'That guy was a real asshole back then – Kariluoto,' Sihvonen said. 'Grew up into a man, though. Guess they'll dump him in that pond too.'

They left Ukkola's grave and hurried onwards. There was no benediction. Nothing but Sihvonen's bitter outburst as he left: 'So that's how a Finn bites the dust these days. This country's done for.'

## III

The supply train was retreating.

It was early morning, but bright as day, so the drivers were worried about air raids. The vehicles had been camouflaged with underbrush and the horses' harnesses were covered in alder branches, and one of the drivers had even stuck a sprig in his cap.

'Keep wider intervals,' Sinkkonen shouted, riding his bicycle along the side of the road as he tried to pass the vehicles. Lammio was with him as well, since Karjula had allocated him the task of managing the supply train's retreat.

The old guy who'd been called out of the reserves, Korpela, was leading his horse alongside the vehicles. He had checked the carts for officers' bags and their other belongings, but the previous driver had already tossed all that kind of stuff into the forest, so there weren't any objects left for Korpela to hurl in his fury.

Sinkkonen was telling him something about aerial observation. Korpela glared daggers at the Master Sergeant and snarled, 'Yeah, order me to keep an eye on the sky! Why don't you just get out of the way? Yeah, that's right, take care of your bicycle so you can ride off on it when the time comes. 'Cause that's what you're gonna do all right.'

The battalion's Lotta was standing on the roadside. Raili Kotilainen hadn't snagged herself one particular man over the course of the war, but that was partially made up for by the fact that she had snagged several. The aide who had taken her picture by the captured mortar back at the start of the war had been dead for some time. At that point Raili was still a flower in bloom, but the war had worn her down as it had the rest of them. She had withered and lowered her standards so much that she had even succumbed to some anti-tank guy in infantry. *Sic transit gloria mundi*, Sarastie had observed.

The Lotta's bicycle was broken. She was tired and worn out. The men showed her nothing but their unmasked contempt and hostility. They showered her with obscene, insinuating abuse. Spotting Korpela, she thought she might turn to him for help. An older man, she imagined, would have some kind of fatherly sympathy for her.

'I can't ride this and I'm just so tired. And the heel of my shoe came off. Do you think you could give me a lift on your cart?'

Good Lord! The front-line Lotta! The sight of the woman struck Korpela the way a red banner strikes a bull. 'We don't haul horse shit on Sundays, bitch. Damn straight that's how it is.'

Lammio overheard him. First, he ordered the Lotta into the next vehicle and then he yelled, 'Private Korpela!'

'What's the problem?'

'What did you just say?'

'I said what I said. Yeah, and I meant that we've got enough shit to haul around here without hauling the Finnish officers' whore too. That's right.'

'Listen here, Korpela! You've gone too far. Now shut your mouth! One more word out of you and you will regret it.'

'Quit mouthing off at me, you, with your goddam fancy pants. Yeah, you heard me.' Korpela's fury had flared up full blast. He screamed at the drivers in a voice choked with rage, trying to pack as much biting contempt into his voice as possible, but mostly drowning it out in the overwhelming flood of his anger. 'Me-en! Hey, driiivers! Who's that bastard on my ass? Used to be the arse flies only swarmed round horses. They startin' to swarm round people now too?'

'You're under arrest. Hey, you, over there. Two men, over here! Confiscate Private Korpela's belt and rifle.'

There were no volunteers. Nor were they necessary. Somebody further behind was yelling, 'Heavy-duty tillers overhead . . . air raid! Sturmoviks! Get under cover!'

They turned the horses quickly toward the cover of the forest and everyone disappeared somewhere or other. Only Korpela remained on the road. His cart wheel got stuck in a ditch and the horse wasn't able to pull it out. The animal strained against its harness, pulling with all of its might, but the wheel just sank deeper into the treacherously soft soil at the bottom of the ditch.

Small bombs fell from the ground-attack planes and exploded behind them.

*Vo . . . uuuuuu . . . trrrrrrrrrrrrrrrr . . .* The plane droned over and machine-gun fire raked the road. When it had passed, more followed in its wake.

'Come on, you assholes, come and lift!' Korpela howled, but there was no help in sight nor did any materialize. Many men abandoned their horses and ran off deeper into the forest.

'Run . . . run! Just run like hell then! Leave your poor horse here to be killed, oh, that's fine . . .'

The carousel continued. Planes circled round and shells exploded ceaselessly, accompanied by the chattering of machine guns. The angry explosions of quick-load rifles grew nearer, then suddenly the back beams of Korpela's cart cracked. Korpela ducked for cover, but returned to his feet immediately and started yanking again. Having first taken the Lotta to safety, Lammio was now approaching Korpela's cart. He walked upright, with apparent indifference to the planes, and when Korpela noticed him, he flew into an unbridled rage. That man, flaunting his bravery!

'You stay the fuck away from me! Don't you dare touch my cart. I don't need any help from the likes of you. Yeah, you're damn straight I mean it.'

Lammio just continued toward him and suddenly Korpela threw the reins to the ground and stepped in front of him, saying, 'You get me a transfer right now! I'm moving to another unit.'

'What marvelous unit would that be? What is this . . . where do you think you're going to go?'

'Fuck you! I'll go all the way to hell if it means I can get you out of my sight!'

'Korpela, I am warning you for the last time. The defeat has gone to the heads of men like you, but do not make the mistake of thinking that this army is going to let you spit in its face, even in its defeat.'

'Ha ha ha. Who's spitting in whose face here? You asshole, you're the one that's been spitting in other men's faces for years! Yeah! Damn straight! You let go of that holster of yours or I'll throw it into the forest and send you right in after . . .'

Korpela turned, as another ground-attack plane was nearing them again. Heading toward his cart he hissed, 'Now . . . now . . . only now do I know what the high-born Finn really is. Ay-ay-ay-ay-ay. What he's really made of. I didn't quite think that. Wouldn't have believed it. But now I know. Ay-ay-ay-ay-ay.'

He tore at the harness and screamed in fury, 'Fuck it! Goddamn cart can stay there. Torturing poor, senseless creatures as if they'd done something wrong. Run away! What are you doing here letting 'em torture you? Come on! Yeah, you heard me!'

A plane neared them from behind. Flames fluttered down beneath it and the branches rustled. Korpela led the horse into the forest and, shaking his fist up toward the sky, he howled, 'You shoot, too, asshole! Shoot away! You just shoot like hell, here's your chance. Get it out of your system! Well, fuck!'

The plane pulled up and something flashed behind it. The frightened horse bolted off, galloping into the forest. For a while, it dragged Korpela along, as his hand was tangled up in the reins. When it finally slipped out, Korpela lay on his back. Lammio made it to the spot in time to see his eyes move for the last time. A great stream of blood was flowing out from beneath Korpela's body.

## IV

The ground-attack planes had flown off by the time the head of the battalion column reached the main road. Koskela radioed in a request for ambulances to evacuate the wounded, which arrived once the planes had disappeared. They began loading the wounded immediately. One of the stretchers held a corpse, as the man had died so near to the road that the men had just kept on carrying him.

Lieutenant Colonel Uuno Eemeli Karjula arrived. He was a bull-necked man with a stocky build who always spoke at a near scream, pressing his fists against his hips. The inner corners of his eye sockets pulled a bit too close together, which gave his small eyes a piercing aspect. Creases lined his powerful face. One hard, cruel line extended downwards from the corner of his mouth. His hair was always closely cropped, so that the strange, sharp crest along the crown of his head was exposed whenever he removed his cap.

This man had set out for the Winter War as a captain and had been promoted to lieutenant colonel in recognition of his personal fearlessness and indomitable will. His tactical brilliance might have left something to be desired, but his absolute unwillingness to retreat was generally understood to make up for it. Higher up, Karjula had a reputation for being a strong man – and that he undeniably was – but whosoever should end up near him or subordinated to him would, almost without exception, begin either to fear this man or to hate him. Once, after a quarrel with Karjula, Sarastie had gone so far as to tell his aide, 'And then there are men who would be criminals if armies and prisons didn't employ them. It's just pure chance that determines which side of the bars they'll turn up on.'

Karjula was absolutely enraged at the fact of defeat. He knew of no remedy besides 'iron-fithted operationth'. Leaving aside the retreat generally, he was furious that the battalion's withdrawal meant that the position of the entire combined combat unit was now in peril. There weren't many more miles left to cede before they would have to forfeit the whole position. The fallen Sarastie was treated to a real earful – even if, having died, he couldn't hear any of it. Karjula certainly didn't share the chaplain's belief that the Major could still understand him, but that didn't prevent him from abusing the man.

'Damn it! Why didn't that man have any rethherveth? Thquatting right by the road like that with no cover at all.'

Karjula chose to ignore the fact that he himself had approved Sarastie's operations, and also that he had promised to send him a sapper company for reserve before detaining said company laying a road. Just now the company was scraping together all that was left of the other machine-gun squads to form a barricade, but the best they could muster would pose no more than a weak obstacle for the enemy.

Koskela gave Karjula a brief account of the situation, though the Lieutenant Colonel struggled even to hear him out. Despite the presence of the many men listening, he said, 'Due to your hathty athethment of the thituation, the enemy ith now dethimating our flank. And on top of that, withdrawing the battalion through the pondth wath entirely unnethethary. A cothtly two hourth. And the loth of our betht pothition.'

Koskela spoke solely out of a sense of duty. He took no interest in Karjula's speech, knowing very well that no amount of reasoning was going to assuage this man's anger, which the calm tone of Koskela's voice seemed only to exacerbate.

'It has to be taken into consideration that I couldn't let the battalion's flank be exposed to the enemy under the circumstances.

Dividing into groups was too risky as we had to protect the wounded. And besides, the men were depressed by the casualties.'

'I have taken that into conthideration. I know what the thituation ith and I do not need any explanationth. But you thhould know that the battalion lotht thith fight only when you admitted itth defeat. Now hurry up and get the battalion into formation. Man the edge of that thwampland. Put a thuffithiently thtrong retherve unit on the flankth, and build it out of active troopth. The new anti-tank gunth will be here thhortly. I am trying to get the anti-mithile weaponth in tho far ath I am able. You take care of the battalion until Lammio hath finithhed with the thupply train and can rethume command. After that you will take over ath Third Company commander. The machine gunth go to Lieutenant Ovathka.'

His voice deadpan, Koskela said, 'I ordered them to sink the machine guns in the pond so I would have enough men to carry the wounded. I just kept one.'

Karjula's jaw dropped and closed repeatedly for a little while. 'In the pond. Thunk. Ma . . . chi . . . ne . . . gun . . . th . . . thunk.'

Karjula wouldn't have been so fundamentally enraged, had he not been obliged to recognize that the measures Koskela had taken were indeed correct. But that was precisely what he did not want to do, as it would have meant acknowledging defeat.

'Good God, Lieutenant! Mutiny . . . Deliberately aiding the enemy. I ordered you to bring the weaponth. Machine-gunnerth are machine-gunnerth, not medicth. And you were the battalion'th commander, not itth nurthe . . .'

Karjula at least realized that he was saying things that should not be said. Even the men had risen to their feet. Those who knew Koskela were hoping he would sock him to the ground, but Koskela just stood there, looking over the madman, his face motionless.

Trying to cover up his blunder, Karjula said, 'You may redeem your reputathion by holding the line. Get thome thteel into your thpine.'

Karjula had become cognizant of the men's presence and proceeded to grow furious with them, though he himself was the one who had mouthed off at Koskela in their hearing. Now he raved like a lunatic. 'And you men! What are you, thheep or tholdierth of Finland? You athume a pothition tho that either you hold it or you go down trying. You are wearing the thame uniformth ath the men who defended Thumma and Taipale, damn it. Thothe men knew how to die. You don't know how to do anything but flee. Thhame on you, damn it! I wouldn't dare to call mythelf a Finn if I abandoned the way you did. Whoever thtill dareth to abandon hith potht will find that there ith a thection of the Code of Military Juthtithe devoted to him. The game endth here. There will be no merthy requethted nor granted. Ith that clear? Now, to your pothitionth!'

Honkajoki went wide-eyed and dropped his jaw in a look of feigned astonishment. Then, in an official, important-sounding voice, he asked Vanhala, 'Corporal Vanhala. Are you a sheep or a Finnish soldier?'

'I am the World's Greatest Forest Fighter! Heehee . . .'

'Indeed, yes, indeed.' Honkajoki sighed, as if in doleful resignation. 'One hope I do retain. That the war will end and I will serve as a stud in a great farmhouse.'

Viirilä was sitting off on his own, munching on the loaf of bread he'd scrounged from the enemy soldier's pack the previous evening. Seemingly unintentionally, he blurted out, rolling his head, 'A man came from Arimathea and poured water on his head.'

The others didn't understand what Viirilä meant. Probably just blabbering on senselessly again, as he tended to do, not really meaning anything by it.

'Phaahaahaa . . . Bring on the rough and tumble. Long live anarchy and bloody duds! Bring on a storm that'll send foot-rags flying to the tips of the North Star to dry . . . Phaahaahaahaahaa,' he burst into his familiar, raucous laugh. That was Viirilä – ready to kill and just as ready to pack up and go home. Or, rather, go anywhere in Finland, as he wasn't from any place in particular.

Koskela started organizing the men.

They asked for food. There wasn't any, but someone would look into it. Silent and bitter, they began digging foxholes. The unit covering them pulled back, retreating behind their line. The sappers mined the road and to some extent the roadsides as well, but the barricade wasn't nearly strong enough. There was plenty of exposed terrain between the swamp and the road.

Lammio took over command of the battalion and Koskela returned to the Third Company. He was quiet and pensive. He issued instructions in a low voice as if he were somehow tired and depressed. Määttä's machine gun was positioned beside the swamp, close to the road. Another platoon was operating as a normal infantry platoon under Rokka's command. Koskela stopped beside Määttä's position and sat down on the ground, leaning against a tree trunk.

He looked out over the swamp. The sun had already climbed above the treetops, and it warmed his face. He sat still for a long time, as if he'd been turned to stone. Every last tremor seemed to have disappeared from his face. His wide jaw and high cheekbones were pronounced beneath his weather-beaten skin. He was thinner. Even the dent in his jaw seemed to have deepened. His eyelids were rimmed with red. A pained crease quivered around his mouth. He had turned thirty-one years old the day before yesterday. He hadn't remembered until the next day. Nor had it meant anything to him.

The world had fallen silent for a moment. Even the far-off noises of battle. It wasn't at all typical, as lately the enemy had taken to intensifying its efforts with each passing day.

Koskela leaned his head back against the tree trunk and allowed his eyes to sink shut. He could feel the warmth of the sun on his face, whose skin had grown rough and sensitive from exhaustion and lack of sleep. His mouth burned from so many cigarettes, and his empty stomach made him feel weak. He could hear the clink of nearby shovels and the men's quiet voices. An image of Karjula rose up in Koskela's mind. He wasn't insulted by the scolding he'd received. He knew that Karjula couldn't take these kinds of disappointments without venting his irritation at someone, whoever that might be. Karjula had to pick a scapegoat so that he didn't wind up one himself, and he needed to find some sort of pretext for his choice. There was no weak point in Koskela's sense of honor. He forgot the whole thing. Then he forgot the whole prevailing state of affairs. He grasped only warmth and the faint exhaustion of his body. The present moment faded away and he slipped into the space between dreams and wakefulness. He heard voices emerging from Määttä's gun. He heard Hietanen's voice, and a sort of panic came over him. Something was awry, but he couldn't figure out what was wrong. Then Rokka said something. Hietanen laughed. Koskela grew more and more alarmed. What was there to laugh about now? Everything wasn't as it should be. His breath started heaving as he clenched his empty fists in anxiety. Hietanen's face came nearer to him and laughed. It was black wrapped in the charred bandage, which still had little whitish strips around the edges of the blood stains.

'Want a smoke?'

Koskela started and opened his eyes. Why was Hietanen standing there like that – black – with a pack of cigarettes in his hand? Määttä gazed in wonder as Koskela's eyes stretched wide for a couple of seconds, as if he hadn't quite understood the offer. Then Koskela took the cigarette and said, 'Oh . . . yeah . . . I mean, thanks. I guess I fell asleep.'

'So I see. It's just that that engine over there's started rumbling already. Don't seem like they're giving us any downtime.'

'No, no.'

Määttä sat down to smoke as well, and Koskela relaxed against the tree trunk again. His recent dream had upset him. Why had he seen Määttä as Hietanen? He felt wretched and all mixed up. Some kind of restlessness was gnawing away at him, but he couldn't find any reason for it.

'How much longer am I going to hang on out here?'

Where did that sudden thought come from? He didn't usually allow such thoughts to enter his mind. Then he remembered what he had been thinking the last time he saw Kariluoto alive: That man will die today.

Was his number up next? Why was all of this coming to mind? For God's sake, here I am telling fortunes. It's nothing but exhaustion.

That's where this whole numb depression's coming from. I had a dream. He must have been dead before the flames reached him. The man was full of holes, at least. But the ones who were in the ambulance – that must have been pretty horrible all right. Koskela had been in such a panic himself over the situation that night that he hadn't had time to think about anything. But seeing it was terrible. That's where that sight a second ago came from, too. Yeeeesh. Seeing a guy you know in that kind of state . . .

*Pi piew pieeeeeeeeeeeeeeeew* . . .

'OK. They're here. And we're going to be up against them pretty soon, too. Better keep our eyes peeled.'

# V

Koskela lay in a foxhole. The ground trembled and swayed. Sand blew down from the upper rim. A piece of shrapnel whirred closer. The noise intensified until the side of the ditch suddenly caved in.

'How the hell did they move those guns so fast?' Koskela cautiously raised his head, but quickly ducked it back down again, having spotted a column of smoke rising into the air close by. Dirt rained down into his pit.

When the barrage fell silent, Koskela heard a call to attack. The first shots were already whizzing by. On the left, Määttä was hammering away with the machine gun as if his life depended on it. Koskela overheard Honkajoki saying as he ran by their position that the Lieutenant Colonel was lying down, but nonetheless declaring gravely in a voice thick with fear, 'Damn it! Now'th the moment we could really use those anti-mithile weaponth.'

Undoubtedly. Three tanks were coming down the road, tearing up the surrounding roadside with their guns. Koskela ran past the shooting men, who, in their nervousness, were aiming at the tanks, which was of course pointless. A grenade from one of the tanks killed somebody, and a panicked cry rose nearby, screaming, 'They're gonna run us over! Guys! They're gonna run us over . . .'

'Stay in position! They're not going to run anyone over. It's mined over there.' Koskela yelled as loud as he could in order to make himself heard over the din. He knew that if the men didn't hear his order clearly, it might easily induce a general panic. There were several short-range defense guys lying in the ditch alongside the road. Koskela crawled over to them.

'Got any satchel charges?'

'Yeah. But these won't get anywhere close . . .'

'I'll try. Couple of you guys come with me!'

'It'd be better to try from the pit. Ditch here's too shallow.'

Of course it would be better. But Koskela was quite sure that by then it would be too late. The men would flee before the tanks came within range of the pit.

Satchel charges were almost entirely ineffectual by now, as the tanks were well secured, but there was no other option.

Koskela set out. Two men followed. The first tank stopped and then turned toward the side of the road. The drivers were already fairly sure that the Finns didn't have any anti-tank equipment. Otherwise they would have started shooting it well before now. The tank advanced boldly. Bullets crackled in the pine branches and direct fire blasted into the roadside.

Straight ahead was a curve in the ditch, where it swerved around a boulder. If he could just make it there.

Koskela made it. He squatted down on his knees and waited. The tank seemed as though it was starting to hesitate, but kept approaching nonetheless, shooting continuously. Koskela tried to calm himself as much as possible. He knew from experience that this kind of situation called for presence of mind above all else. You couldn't try from too far away, and you had to focus on the task and block out any distractions. You had to try to forget where this toss was happening. To do it without thinking about the danger or what it meant. As if you were just trying to hit the tank in some entirely calm, safe place. You also had to risk as much as you could stand to be sure that you wouldn't miss.

'And there's my shot.' Koskela pulled the igniter and rose to a crouch. He threw on an upwards curve, and the arc was beautiful, like a great toss in a ball game. The charge fell just beside the gun turret, rolled across it onto the fender and went off. The tread broke and the tank stopped, turning onto its side. Koskela couldn't see it any more. He'd been shot by a submachine gun across the road just as the satchel charge left his hand. He tried once to rise up onto his elbows, but his limp body collapsed onto the floor of the ditch, and Quiet Koski was dead.

The other two tanks paused for a moment, but then drove boldly past the wrecked vehicle. When the men in the line saw that Koskela didn't get up, and that the tanks were drawing nearer, they started to run. And everything unraveled from there.

Karjula hadn't left Lammio's command post. He had to block off the road in that direction, or else 'the whole Combined Combat Unit Karjula would go thtraight to hell'. What was holding up that damn anti-tank gun? You'd think the Red Army itthelf wath manning the thing! The ground-attack planeth have nothing to do with the gun tranthport. The main road'th not an air-thtrip. The planeth are in the thky! Yeth, of courthe the main road ith open over there!

The phone rang. Positions lost. Koskela dead. Part of the Third Company in a panic.

Karjula left.

Lammio followed after him, but Karjula ordered him to remain and organize a blockade with the reserve units.

When Karjula reached the battalion, the retreat was in full swing. 'You goddamn flock of thheep! Get into pothition! Not one more thtep! Anyone who keepth on running ith a dead man!'

Panicked men ran down the road, and somebody panted defensively, 'What are we supposed to do? There's no anti-tank guns! Koskela already went and got himself killed.'

'Quiet! Who'th thtill mouthing off over there? Halt! Or I'll thhoot.'

Karjula had a pistol in his hand. The men closest to him stopped hesitatingly and dropped to the ground, taking cover in the ditch. But the men further off just kept on running.

'They're coming, boys! Tanks!'

The shout further exacerbated the panic and even one of the men who had stopped at Karjula's command now shot off again. The Lieutenant Colonel lost his last shred of self-control. The blatant disobedience made his body shake. A thick, blinding rage blurred his brain, in which there was nothing but a vague thought. 'This is the moment. It should be put into action now. This is the situation it's meant for.'

The groping thought was a sign that even he at least hesitated. That was why he formulated the thought: to defend himself against the pressing awareness that he was committing a crime. He spotted a man further off who was walking along unfazed by his shouting, a submachine gun over his shoulder.

'Halt! What are you doing? Halt! For the latht time, halt.'

It was Viirilä. He pretended not to hear and just continued on his way. He wasn't fleeing, he was just walking calmly onward – which was also why he hadn't obeyed. He wasn't actually being defiant, he was just scoffing at fear. The command didn't concern him, because he hadn't been running to begin with. He had abandoned his post just like all the others, but now, with his calm stride, he was demonstrating that he was not afraid, neither of the enemy nor of Karjula. His disobedience was a parody, enacted for the benefit of anyone who might mistake him for one bowing to fear, an emotion he felt not in the least.

'Halt. Where are you going?'

'To bang the wolves in Lapland,' Viirilä blurted out in his signature, all-blaspheming voice. The only thing missing was the snorting guffaw that usually followed it. Karjula flew into a wild, bloodthirsty rage. This feeling that was constantly fermenting in his soul, making him a terrorizing presence to all around him – and he certainly was that – was now purified and distilled into exactly what it really was: a desire to kill and destroy. And this rage that dwelt within him, constantly seeking an outlet, now rose to the surface and all means of controlling it were powerless to hold it back. There he was. That huge-headed ape. Standing right there was the repulsive personification of everything that had turned the army into a flock of deserters. And the man was laughing.

Viirilä lowered his submachine gun into the crook of his elbow, a certainty descending upon him at the last moment that Karjula was going to shoot. The movement gave Karjula the last impetus he needed to turn desire into action. He shot into the middle of the chest. Viirilä fell to his knees, then doubled over and rolled to the ground. His body jerked for a little while, as the bullet didn't kill him right away.

Karjula breathed heavily and pointlessly paced back and forth. Then he got his voice back and screamed hoarsely, 'Men! Calling upon the Code of Military Juthtithe I have condemned thith traitor to death. Men, thith ith a quethtion of Finland. Right here . . . Right now. Thith event . . . ith not itholated, but related to every other ithue. The joking endth here. The thame fate awaitth anyone elthe who wantth to rebel.'

The men looked at one another in a state of shock. The silence was broken by Karjula's hoarse screaming alone. He raved like a madman, destroying what little effect his act had had, which was already pathetically small compared to what it might have been, had he carried it out in a different mental state. The men didn't know what to think, but they immediately sensed that Karjula hadn't performed this act out of unavoidable necessity, but rather out of his own deranged fury. And to top it off, it was Viirilä, their Number One man.

Little by little the men's bewilderment gave way to rage. Jaws clenched and fists squeezed tight around their gunstocks. One of the men further off even took aim at Karjula, but he couldn't bring himself to shoot. Instead, someone else began to scream brokenly in a voice of shock, 'Russians! Come here! Come on over! Come on, finish us off. We're killing people over here! Come on!'

The man was screaming like he'd lost his mind. His screeching was like that of a frantic child, full of shock, hate and fear.

The screeching brought Karjula back to his senses. A beastly roar emerged from his throat. The situation being what it was, there was nothing he could do but continue. Just as a person terrified by the realization that he has done something irreparable inevitably proceeds to compound his error, Karjula flew into a renewed rage at the man's cries. Viirilä was the second man he had shot. The screaming man would certainly have been the third, had the enemy's tanks not come to his rescue. From behind a bend in the road came the whistle of a shell that came crashing down at Karjula's feet, laying him flat on his back in the center of the road.

The flight resumed.

Karjula revived instantly. He tried to stand up, but fell down again, as his leg had been nearly torn off. He lay on his stomach, pressing himself up on his arms and screaming, 'Get in pothition! Damn it! Halt! You goddamn cowardth, help me get into pothition and give me a thubmachine gun . . .'

His cry betrayed not the slightest hint of weakness or pleading. It had just the same commanding fury as before. He was still trying to get up, screaming curses and howling with anger and pain. There was something in that struggle like the fight of a wild, wounded animal in the final throes of self-defense – filled with rage against everything and everybody, and beyond that the untold despair of knowing that it has already lost the power to fight. Later, the machine-gunners came to think that Lehto and Karjula had had something in common. 'Exactly like Lehto would've been if he'd been a lieutenant colonel,' they said.

Maybe somebody would even have seen something admirable in this madman's wild, hopeless rage. But those who watched Karjula's vigorous efforts to rise didn't admire him. They hated him – with an intense and relentless hatred. One of the men running by even yelled, 'We hear you, we just can't help you!'

'Blast a row through that motherfucker!' somebody else called out.

'We aren't nurses . . .'

Rokka arrived in the last group. He hadn't witnessed the event himself, but quickly gathered what had taken place. Just then Karjula fell unconscious a second time. The tank was shooting a machine gun and everyone vanished. Rokka grabbed the heavy man by the waist and ran beside the road to cover. He carried Karjula a little way, but once he was out of immediate danger, he lowered him to the ground. 'Don't feel like goin' much further 'nnat. That fella there's stepped outta the bounds a human ways and far as I'm concerned he can stay there.'

Two officers from the Second Company took him from there and carried him a little way, until they could get him into the hands of a couple of medics. The medics carried him because it was their job, but that didn't prevent them from cursing, officers or no officers.

The battalion retreated without pause. After a small skirmish, the men on Lammio's roadblock joined the others. The entire combat unit was ceding its positions. Their spirits had reached such a point that the battalion might have dissolved completely had the old border not opened up to greet them. Once they were behind it, their spirits seemed to rise all by themselves. They were even put on break. No questioning of any kind was carried out. Actually, the only real infractions connected to the event were the men's shouts and the fact that they had not helped Karjula. And the issue was subject to interpretation, since wounded men had been left behind in panic situations before. It was probably determined that the matter would be best forgotten on both sides.

And when, after their rest, the battalion was pulled into a counterattack, the men pushed back powerfully against the enemy. Their previous slackness had given way to vigor and a will to fight. The men spoke of nothing except that now it was time to start fighting for real. They hardly even noticed the whole thing themselves. 'National defense' just seemed like a self-evident duty as soon as the surface of their own land appeared, authorizing the use of such a term in relation to the war.

The battles over the Uomaa-line began, and even the enemy noticed that it seemed to be banging its head against a brick wall again.

# Chapter Sixteen

## I

Rokka was worried.

He paced back and forth along the length of his platoon, moving from one position to the next. Actually, the platoon was no longer his, as the ensign assigned to lead the Third Platoon had just arrived from the home front that day. Nevertheless, Rokka still felt responsible, as they had a tough situation in front of them. There was a river at their backs. A new line of defense was being set up along the opposite bank, and their assignment was to hold onto the bridgehead, protecting it as long as possible so that the others would have more time to fortify their positions. The bridge over the river was on their left.

Having sunk their machine guns back in the pond, the machine-gunners were now operating as a regular infantry platoon. Only Määttä's machine gun remained. A couple of days earlier, the platoon had received three more new recruits as replacements. Two men were transferred from the utilities staff as well, bringing the total number of new men to eight in all. In Rokka's opinion, that meant the percentage of inexperienced men was too high. The new recruits were not particularly worse than the other men, seeing as a man gets his nature from birth and not from the army, but inexperience would make them more susceptible to panic, and that was exactly the worst thing that could happen in this situation.

Susling was lying in his foxhole, blowing the smoke from his cigarette all around him to disperse the swarming mosquitoes. Rokka walked by and said, 'Suslin', you remember how we use'da go swimmin' in'na Vuoksi down in Kannas as kids?'

'Why wouldn't I? We ain't never gonna see it again, Antti. Nothin' but corpses swimmin' there now. Rumor is water down there is runnin' red.'

'We're gonna be swimmin' 'cross this crick here pretty soon. You believe me?'

'Mm . . . if anybody gits that far.'

They had received several days' dry rations, and the new recruits wrapped up their sugar and put it in their bread bags. Rokka winked at them and said, 'Don't you fellas save that sugar now! It'll git all wet and then it'll be ruined. We're goin' swimmin' soon!'

'Don't be stupid. We'll hop that stream if it comes to it.' One of the new recruits drew manfully on his cigarette, his cap tilted off to the side. The creases pressed into the cap gave a pretty good idea of its owner. The boy had an arrogant, devil-may-care machismo about him. His cap was ostensibly askew out of carelessness, but it was actually set at a carefully considered angle, deliberately selected to convey its carelessness. This new recruit was the same fellow who had turned up at the brook line asking for enemies to kill. His name was Asumaniemi. Back then Rokka had answered his question with mocking contempt, but although he had continued to address the boy in a jocular, offhand sort of way, his contempt had vanished. That very evening, when they had been fending off the counter-attack at Sarastie's command post, the boy had taken down three of the attackers. Bare-headed, as his cap had fallen off in his excite-ment, the boy had risen to his knees and fired, shouting every time he hit his target, 'Missing one, the devil said, counting up his ants!'

When the fighting was over, the others were obliged to endure rather too much carrying-on about these three fallen soldiers, but they granted Asumaniemi his right to boast, as he really had been right at home under fire. And the event was not the last of its kind. Asumaniemi became one of the sturdiest pillars of the platoon. Rokka's voice was good-natured as he shot him a word of warning, 'Damn it, boy! You hush up now, you hear? You're gonna swim just like all'a rest of us. So swallow that sugar and don't leave it to git wet!'

Ensign Jalovaara arrived from the command post.

Rokka went over to greet him, and when they met up, the Ensign said angrily, 'What were you saying about swimming?'

'I ordered the fellas to gulp down that sugar so it don't git wet when we swim across'sa crick.'

'You'll make them all panic talking like that.'

'Lissen here, Ensign! It'ssa enemy causes panic, it ain't me. You can see for yourself we're gonna end up flappin' our way across that crick like a flock a ducks!'

'Well, toss some corn why don't you! What do you think is going to happen when the deputy commander's the first one to start talking about fleeing?' The Ensign was angry, all the more so because Rokka's 'lissen here, Ensign' had offended him.

Rokka had already seen the new ensign and decided on the basis of his speech that the man did not entirely comprehend why the war was different now. Once the Finnish advance had ended, Jalovaara had been sent back to his civilian post on account of its importance, and it was only after the heavy officer losses that he had been ordered back into service. Rokka feared his blue-eyed naïveté, and found the Ensign's speeches all the more irritating for it.

'Lissen, that ain't what we're talkin' 'bout here. We've learned'da take the neighbors seriously, see. They got their plans too, and we ain't always been able to keep 'em from carryin' 'em out, and that's what I'm thinkin' might happen here too. Go watch next time you hear a shot, you'll see how the fellas start peerin' around. That ain't a good sign. I don't like it when fellas start peerin' around like that.'

'We will retreat in an orderly manner over the bridge when we are commanded to do so. And you will carry out your mission and leave the rest for others to take care of.' The Ensign's tone was decisive. On receiving his summons to return to the army, he had decided to conduct himself forcefully and decisively out on the front. On the train he had re-confirmed this decision, as he took stock of his position in relation to the defeat. He still couldn't quite bring himself to believe that the war was lost. That would have been too bitter a pill for him to swallow. But nothing was going to prevent him from fulfilling his duty. That much was clear.

This attitude infuriated Rokka, and he began to eye the Ensign with suspicion, smiling that same smile that Lammio hadn't been able to endure without losing his temper either. It was more taunting than anything he might have said. Congenially, as if he were speaking to a child, Rokka explained, 'Lissen. It'd be real swell if the Third Company could make it over the bridge. Seein' as they're already over there on'na main road. The rest of us's gonna swim. But if you don't quit makin'na racket, it could happen that we don't even make it to the swimmin' part. Neighbors'll hear you and come rushin' straight on over.'

'You will obey the command just like everyone else and that is that. Now, head to the positions and keep your eyes peeled! They told me about you earlier today. In my platoon, there will be no master but discipline and the demands of the situation. Headstrong behavior is not something I am prepared to tolerate. I have no use for empty formalities, and I do not need any kowtowing, but I expect the platoon to carry out its assignments without grumbling about it.'

'It ain't carried out a mission yet without grumblin'. Lissen, you still got a lot'ta learn. But damn it, I ain't gonna start goin' in'na all a that here. You go ahead and take that bridge if you can!' Rokka threw his hands up in anger and left. He went to the positions, sat down and started griping.

'What the hell is it makes those officers so impossible to git on with? Just a word or two and already we're fightin'. Koskela's only one I never fought with. What the hell is wrong with those fellas?'

Rokka's tone of the unjustly accused made Vanhala laugh. 'I dunno. You ever wondered if maybe it might be somethin' wrong with you?'

'With me?' Rokka was genuinely flabbergasted. 'How in'na hell could it be sumpin' wrong with me? I always talk straight about what needs done. And those fellas's like they're bent on startin' a riot! What'd I ever say to git anybody all riled up? It's those fellas that's just like they was lookin' for a fight! Here I am tryin'na do everythin' I can to make this war go best it can do, and they start pickin' fights with me! Like right now, all I want is for everythin'na go smooth so we can retreat right when we gotta. And he's yellin' at me 'bout takin'na bridge! Well goollord! How we gonna do that when'na enemy's already over there? You'd think they wanted'da lose everythin'!'

Rokka stared angrily at the toes of his boots, then shrugged his shoulders and said, 'Well, what the hell do those fellas matter to me now anyway? Karelia's gone. War's lost. There ain't nothin' left for me to lose. I'm just here'da make 'em pay for takin' Kannas now. Nabbed a major day before yesterday. Served 'im right, comin' over here with a patrol! Fellas from the First Company took the shoulder tabs. Missed a chance, Rahikainen.'

'Oh, I'm not collectin' those anymore. To hell with 'em. To hell with the badges, Karelia, the war – and good riddance!'

'Shut up! The guys are puttin' up a tough fight down in Kannas. They've stopped the advance,' Sihvonen said.

'Ain't gonna help nothin', you can be sure 'bout that. They'll git through anyway, sometime or other. War's lost. All that gaddamn work for nothin'.'

*Phi phiew* . . .

'Bullet, boys,' Asumaniemi said.

They all pressed lower into their foxholes. Only Rokka didn't move. He sat right where he was and said, as if to himself, 'There they go, flyin' bullets. Got all the men in'na world takin' their weapons and hot-footin' it through the fields an'na forests. Every one of 'em shootin' his off somewhere. Yeah, I bet there's bullets flyin'.'

'Git in'na pit!' Susling said, his voice slightly worried.

'Even a fella like Koskela,' Rokka continued in the same tone, indifferent to Susling's urging. 'If anybody knew there was no point in dyin' out here for nothin' it was him. And then there he goes, just like he was committin' suicide. There's no way he was gittin' outta there after he'd thrown that satchel charge. I think he knew it, too. Lissen, Priha, what did you say to the chaplain yesterday when he started talkin'na you?'

'Heehee . . . He asked about the watch that guy from the First Company had, the guy shot by the patrol . . . and I said somebody without a watch prob'ly took it . . . This religion thing's started gettin' pretty weird, too. There's men being killed all over like pigs in a slaughterhouse, but that doesn't interest the minister much. Seems like stealin's a sin worse than murder! Heehee. Doesn't seem like such a big deal to me, pinching a watch off a guy like that who doesn't know the time anymore anyway, heehee.'

'Damn it, boy! Now you're startin'na talk sense. How did you git to be so wise?'

'I am an independent-minded forest fighter, not some herd animal who just repeats propaganda, heeheehee . . .' Vanhala erupted into hearty laughter, then sprawled out on his back on the bottom of his hole. Rokka was about to join in as well, but just then heavy shooting started up on the left, from the direction of the main road, accompanied by a call to charge. In the same moment, the men grabbed their weapons and once more the chatter ceased, faces grew serious and, in a state of intense anxiety, they prepared to repel the attack.

## II

Half an hour later the situation was such that a retreat over the bridge would have had to have begun immediately. The enemy wasn't putting any pressure on them, however, and the command was slow in coming. But the Third Company, which was defending the main road, was already retreating at full steam toward the bridge, and there was no doubt that the enemy would follow close on its heels. When the Company Commander then sent word to disengage and retreat, Rokka thought it would be best to swim across the river. He said as much to Jalovaara, but the Ensign thought only of the instructions he had been given. He might also have been resistant to taking up Rokka's suggestion because of their earlier quarrel over the issue. Not that Jalovaara would have done such a thing consciously, but he wasn't able to separate out the various forces influencing him, so the sharpness of his refusal may well have reflected his reluctance to recognize that Rokka had been right.

So, they set off to retreat across the bridge, but were unable to make it that far. They did see the bridge, gruesome sight that it was – with wounded men from the Third Company crawling the length of it while the enemy kept them under constant fire. The new Third Company commander collapsed there as well. Then they heard the sappers scream hoarsely, 'The bridge is gonna blow!'

The scream was like a call of distress. The sappers were obviously aware that there might be somebody out on the bridge who was still alive. But they couldn't save him – all they could do was wait for the wounded to become the deceased. A powerful explosion shook the entire surrounding area, and bodies flew into the air amidst chunks of the bridge.

And so the Third Platoon ended up swimming after all. Wood debris and human body parts were still raining down in front of them when Rokka yelled, 'You young fellas head out first! Määttä, take the machine gun! Rahikainen, Sihvonen and Honkajoki'll help! Rest of us'll hold 'em back from the bank in'na meantime.'

The men waded into the water and started floundering their way across. Only in the very center of the river did the water reach above their heads, but two bounds was enough to get across that bit.

Jalovaara, Rokka, Vanhala, Susling and Asumaniemi remained. They fired as fast as they could to keep the enemy from reaching the bank. Jalovaara ordered Asumaniemi to start swimming immediately, but the boy was too busy blowing through cartridges to listen.

'I got him! Hey, I got him! Look! Over there, by the root of that bush . . .'

'Git in'na crick! Damn it, boy, didn't you hear me?' Rokka yelled angrily.

Even in his panic Jalovaara remembered what Rokka had said about swimming, and said, 'You men go! I'll be right behind you.'

Rokka, however, never let that kind of thing influence him while he was fighting. He understood that the Ensign wanted to make up for what he'd said earlier, but he still didn't think the suggestion made any sense, so he said, 'You come with us, damn it. One man ain't gonna make any difference. Here we go!'

They went. The Ensign figured he had done his duty and followed suit. Just as Susling was stepping into the water, he lurched and fell onto a rock. He said in a low, resigned voice, 'I stay here, Antti. I stay here.'

'What happen'na you?'

'Go! Run! I'll stay here. I can't make it . . . Run . . . I'm hit. Run, you all! They're shootin' from the bridge!'

The bullet had come from somewhere far off, near the bridge, as their position was still protected from the land by a bluff running alongside the river. Just then a whole hail of bullets splashed into the water. They'd been noticed.

The water around Susling turned red. He tried to get up, but slipped on a rock and fell again.

He gave just one gulp of pain as Rokka swung him over his shoulder. Susling was a decent-sized man, but up onto the shoulder he went, and Rokka plunged into the current like a strapping stallion. There was no point in crouching. All that mattered was speed. Vanhala, Jalovaara and Asumaniemi tried to shoot at the enemy as they floundered across. It was no use, however, as they couldn't even see the men shooting. When they were halfway across, Rokka bellowed, 'Keep your head up . . . Keep your head up . . . Here we go, Suslin'!'

And so they all went. Rokka popped up to the water's surface only once, taking a gulp of air and gasping, 'Head up . . .'

The guys manning the opposite bank were also trying to send in some fire to cover the unlucky five. The worst part would be climbing up to the positions, as at that point they would be vulnerable to enemy fire coming from above as well. The high banks protected them as they swam across the river. The bullets were coming from a spot far over by the bridge, from which the river itself was actually visible.

They were already scrambling up the opposite bank. Susling hung across Rokka's shoulders, and Rokka blew water out of his nostrils, asking, 'You git water in your lungs? You git water in your lungs?'

'No,' a weak voice said from over his shoulder. They were already at the edge of the positions when a crash came from the opposite bank. The men dived headlong for the ditch and, just as he leapt, Rokka howled, 'Gaddamn it!'

The others lifted Susling from his shoulders. Susling kept repeating over and over again, 'Antti . . . it hit you . . . I heard . . . you're hit.'

'I know . . . left shoulder . . . Gaddamn it that hurts.'

They huffed and puffed, and sneezed out water. The medics from the Border Patrol Jaeger Company started binding Rokka and Susling's wounds. Susling's wound was bleeding profusely, but it wasn't dangerous. The bullet had torn through his side, but just at the surface. Rokka's shoulder, on the other hand, was worse. The bone had obviously been crushed, and when the medic ripped his shirt and moved his arm, Rokka erupted into a litany of curses and his face twisted into pained contortions.

'Gaddamn it . . . my shoulder, damn it! See, fellas, you see how it's bleedin'?'

Vanhala sneezed and coughed, 'Boys, take a look at this boot! Nearly got me . . .'

'Boot nothin'! Just look at my shoulder!'

'Wouldn't have taken much. Went right there and right there. Look, guys!'

'Naw, see here! Who took it worse here, huh? Boot . . . Just look at my shoulder! Gaddamn it that hurts! If I wasn't in such pain, I'd laugh. I saw Sankia Priha the Great crawl up outta that crick. I even thought, damn, even you ain't laughin' this time!'

'Heeheehee . . . brutal fighting as our boys pull out . . . heeheehee. That'll wipe a smile off your face all right, heeheehee. But you should've seen the glob of snot that came out my nose when I blew it! Heeheehee . . . But I sucked 'im back up in there where he belongs, heeheehee. Oughtta get a Swimming Cup for that. I mean, we earned it all right.'

Then Rokka remembered the Ensign. He had rushed off to organize the men who had crossed the river first so they could offer support for the Jaegers, as he was afraid the enemy might try to take the same route across. But the enemy stayed on its own side, and the Ensign calmed down.

'Lissen, Ensign!' Rokka yelled to him.

'You badly hurt?' Jalovaara asked, coming over.

'Shoulder, damn it. You, you are a curious character.' Rokka looked at the Ensign for a long time waiting to see his expression.

The Ensign smiled perfectly calmly, however, and said, 'I was. But I've learned my lesson.'

'You believe me now that we swam?'

'Can't deny it. At least not until I put on some dry clothes.' The Ensign was so calm that Rokka let up right away. He had just wanted to make sure that the Ensign believed him now. He let the issue drop, and Jalovaara started rounding up the platoon to take them further behind the positions, as they were being put on a break. As they headed back, they carried Rokka and Susling to the side of the road to wait for the ambulances. Rokka cursed away on his stretcher, lecturing the others in between his howls of pain. 'Now, did I really have to live to see the day you fellas'd be carryin' me round like a cripple? I ain't never needed help from nobody! But gaddamn it that shoulder burns like hell. How you doin,' Suslin'?'

'Better when I ain't movin'.'

'You fellas know where Antti Rokka's goin'? To Lydia. I'm gonna have to count the youngsters to see if we got more of 'em now . . . Damn it! I ain't seen'na littlest fella but that one time on leave. The missus' old man had'da take care a gittin'na family all evacuated. I'm gonna make him up a good barrel a home brew . . . Antti's wars's done. Guess we'll just see how things go with the arm here.'

'Shouldn't be too bad,' the medic said. 'It's just the collarbone that's broken. Bullet got it on its way out.'

'Whatever. Hurts like hell, that's for sure. Of all the stupid ways a . . . I was three months out in Taipale when it was rainin' lead and nothin' happen'na me. Now I git it crossin'na gaddamn crick! But ain't that the way it always goes . . . ain't nothin' you can do about it.'

The ambulance arrived. Jalovaara took Rokka's hand and said, frankly and seriously, 'So, see you . . . I hope. I would have liked to hold on to you. It's really only now that we're going to be short of men. I hope you'll forget what we said back there. I was a little green. I don't have to dwell on it, and I guess that kind of thing always happens when you're inexperienced, but I'd feel pretty bad going around thinking I'd offended you. I heard more about the bad side of your reputation on my way out here than I did about the good side. Now I've seen that for myself and I have to say it was pretty stupendous. Well, get well quick, then . . . ! Both of you. Not much chance we'll be seeing one another out here again.'

'Lissen, Ensign, don't you worry 'bout none a that! That was nothin'. You ain't the only officer I had my spats with. Lissen, I don't hang on'na none a that stuff. I'll just tell you a couple a things . . . you got two good fellas in Määttä and Vanhala there. That lil' brat Asumaniemi'll be a real devil once he learns to fight with a little sense about 'im. Honkajoki's a good fella. Just talks like a crazy man. You just ignore that part. Rahikainen's a businessman. When you all git hungry, you just put him in charge, he'll come up with sumpin'. And you're always gonna be hungry. Have been up to now anyway.'

When they had all said goodbye, they lifted Rokka and Susling into the ambulance. 'Well, so long, fellas! Suslin', you better watch out now they don't go tryin'na separate us in'na transport. I'll make a real stink if I notice 'em tryin' anythin'. Gaddamn it! Don't you put me in like that! I ain't headin' out a here feet-first! Uh-huh, well now, that's just fine.'

The ambulance left. A great shouting emerged from it as it started to move. The medics were being lectured on how to handle the wounded.

'Same racket he made when he came,' Vanhala said. He didn't smile. They were all feeling pretty dispirited. Their group had been stripped of so many members in such a short time. Vanhala, Määttä, Honkajoki and Sihvonen felt as if they'd been orphaned. All around them were strange men.

'Hietanen, Koskela, Rokka and Susling. Group shrunk all of a sudden,' Sihvonen said.

'All of 'em leaders of some sort, except Susling,' Vanhala said, looking at Määttä. 'If it keeps on that way, I guess you're up next, heehee . . .'

Määttä didn't answer right away. After a little while he started walking over to another platoon and called back, 'Doubt the Lord'd bother goin' after a guy who just happened to end up corporal . . .'

## III

The morning sun had just risen.

Nervous shooting crackled in the crisp air. A fine mist hovered over the river.

Ensign Jalovaara crawled over to Vanhala. 'Try to run along that low stretch down there. See that body, the one that's a Finn?'

'Yeah.'

'Their light machine gun is right next to it. There are at least two machine guns in that thicket of fallen trees over there, but their fire can't reach into the bottom of the low stretch where you'll be running. Määttä will try to keep them occupied. If you can make it into the trench that way and take the machine guns out of play, the rest is easy.'

Vanhala looked grimly at the hill in front of him. 'Yeah, I can make it into the trench. Makin' it out's another story. Keep that light machine gun quiet.'

'We'll follow right behind you and start clearing them out . . .' The Ensign looked at Vanhala. 'If you'd rather not, I can go alone. You can bring the guys in after. I won't force you to do it.'

'No, I'll try. Best to take Asumaniemi and Honkajoki . . . no more than that. More men won't be anything but trouble . . .'

'All you have to do is take out the machine guns. That'll open everything up. Honkajoki and Asumaniemi!'

The men crawled over.

'So here's the situation. Two or three men need to try to go along that depression and make it to the trench. If we try any other way, it'll cost us too many men. Vanhala's going to give it a shot. You guys go along?'

'I'll go!' Asumaniemi said, shooting up his hand like a schoolboy.

But Honkajoki said, 'You'll have to order me. I would hardly be so bold as to volunteer.'

'Well, I order you then.'

'Well, that's a different story.'

'So, good luck with it! They have to be pushed back now, boys, that's all there is to it. If they manage to widen the breach, we're really going to have our work cut out for us. So, let's give this a try. At least show them that we're not going to let them spit in our faces.'

Jalovaara crawled off to the rest of the platoon, leaving the three men to plan their advance.

'What kind of idiots are they, letting those shitheads get right into the positions! And over the river!' Asumaniemi swore with manful emphasis, but Vanhala and Honkajoki were silent as they carefully surveyed the foreground. Honkajoki did say, however, as if to restrain the boy, 'Whoa there! Whoa there! Hold your horses, little bro.'

'Yeah – you know there are eleven of our guys' bodies lying over there too, right? They didn't let it go without a fight,' Vanhala said.

Since becoming squad leader, Vanhala had started taking things more seriously. To be sure, there was something even in the heavy fighting that stirred his desire to poke fun at it, but responsibility had reined him in somewhat. The corners of his eyes still crinkled with his smile, just as they always had, but his everlasting heeheeing rang out less frequently now.

The enemy had crossed the river during the night, and under cover of darkness it had succeeded in seizing control of two of their strongholds. The machine-gunners who had been in reserve were assigned to retake them, and so Jalovaara's platoon was now preparing to take the first. It was to be a surprise attack, with no artillery barrage to soften things up ahead of time. Launching one would have been difficult anyway, as the targets were so close to their own positions. Vanhala, along with Honkajoki and Asumaniemi, had to get into the end of the communication trench that led to the positions. It looked possible, as in between the positions there lay a deep depression, along which they might be able to make it over, if the

light machine gun guarding it could be taken out of play. Then the
three of them would have to silence the two dangerous machine
guns. After that, Jalovaara would be able to get into the positions
with the rest of the platoon and start clearing out the enemy.

Vanhala looked at the low stretch for a moment and then said,
'There's no telling how it'll go. Let's go. No running, huh? It's too
easy for them to spot. Along that heather there, then.'

'First time in a shock troop.' Honkajoki tried to smile, without
quite succeeding. 'Quite an undertaking.'

'Into the river with those shithead Russkis . . . We'll pounce like
wildcats.' Asumaniemi shoved a hand grenade into each of his
pockets and the others did the same. Vanhala put the drums for the
submachine gun where he would be able to reach them easily.
Asumaniemi aimed his submachine gun at a tree trunk.

'Trrrrrt trrt trrrt . . . trrrt,' he rolled his tongue, playing like a little boy. He had quite an array of gestures and sound effects, mostly
drawn from animated films. He took a hand grenade, pretended to
yank the pull ring, and howled, 'Dist . . . fiew . . . oooo . . . ooo . . .
dong! There she goes and dong! What a sight, boys, neighbors flying through the air!'

The corners of Vanhala's eyes crinkled as he grinned, 'Assuming
we get to the throwing part.'

'And assuming you know how to throw,' said Honkajoki.

'You bums have no idea how far I can hurl 'em. Year before last I
got my teacher right in the forehead with my slingshot at school.
That's my best distance one yet.'

'Heeheehee . . .'

'Oh, I was in for it after that. Well, actually it wasn't exactly for
that. The gum was smuggled from Sweden – the guys bootlegged it.
Well, actually I bootlegged it. But that wasn't the real reason either.
We bought booze with the dough we made and they caught us . . .'

Vanhala looked at Asumaniemi with indulgent interest. The boy
had the makings of just about anything in him. He was troubled by
a sort of aimless restlessness. At no moment were all the parts of his
body still. His eyes were constantly hunting down something new

to look at. He operated on almost no sleep at all, yet he never showed any signs of fatigue. He just craved action and made it clear that he enjoyed danger.

'You'll end up in officer training once you're out of grade school,' Vanhala said.

'I'm not ending up in any school. I'm gonna be promoted straight off. There's no way I'm going to any school any more.'

Vanhala looked at his watch. 'Eight minutes.'

'Couldn't we just go earlier? Why do we hafta wait for the group? The three of us can take care of it ourselves.'

Honkajoki rolled his eyes. 'Let's go home, Priha . . . The boy can take care of the rest.'

'Well, yeah, if you want! I can go on my own.'


# IV

Jalovaara lay behind a tree. Time was passing slowly. The platoon was ready, but they had to wait for the appointed time. The Ensign looked at the low stretch along which the shock troop was supposed to advance. He would have liked to have led it himself, but there was no one he could leave in charge of the platoon. Määttä couldn't manage big groups, as, despite his bravery, he had no ability to get other men moving. He would head out in front himself, but he wouldn't open his mouth, and the others wouldn't follow. How desperately they needed Rokka now. The quality of the men just kept deteriorating. The replacements called out of the reserves were useless, and the new recruits born in '25 were too young and inexperienced. They were often brave, even eager, but it would be weeks before they were fully fledged soldiers.

The past two weeks had changed Jalovaara a great deal. It wasn't just that he had grown thinner and sprouted a beard, his entire attitude had fundamentally altered. He wasn't strict any more, as he had originally intended to be, but he had a quiet strength. He was friendly and unpretentious in his dealings with the men. He treated all members of his platoon as his equals. For the past two weeks they had been fighting tough defensive battles in the positions beside the river, and during that time Jalovaara had matured into an officer that the recently promoted Major Lammio could entrust with the most difficult assignments. The battalion had held steadfast to its position, but the fog and darkness of the previous evening had helped the enemy, enabling them to take control of those two key emplacements. The event, however, did provide some evidence of the men's improved fighting spirit. The Second Company, who had been defending the positions, had only given them up after a bloody, hand-to-hand struggle in the dark. Eleven men from the Second Company's already sparse Third Platoon were lying back at one of the positions.

'We have to take it back. We have to hold on to those positions. Even if it means we die here.' A desperate, bitter defiance surged up in Jalovaara. He knew now that they had lost the war. There could hardly be any doubt about that. But there would be no laughing just yet. Never before had Jalovaara hated the enemy as he did now, with defeat staring him in the face. They were enjoying their victory, making a mockery of everything that was dear to him. No. If everything goes, then we go down with it, fighting like beasts of prey.

Jalovaara got the enemy in the sight of his light machine gun. The men were camouflaged, of course, but they gave themselves away. His shot would announce the attack.

He pressed the trigger.

The clatter of tens of weapons descended in one moment. Määttä's machine gun quickly joined in, its even, constant hammering cutting through the sundry shooting of the others.

The Ensign spotted Vanhala crawling forward. He had to keep firing continually, though, so he could only follow the action out of the corner of his eye. He did manage to catch a glimpse of Asumaniemi blowing by Vanhala, running practically upright with his rifle blasting away under his arm.

The boy had started crawling behind Vanhala, but when the whistling bullets started raining down around his ears, he rose to his feet and started sprinting forward. That was where he lost his cap.

Its showy angle was too steep, and any sudden movement was liable to send it flying.

When Vanhala saw him, he stood up as well. Almost without thinking, he realized that Asumaniemi's bold sprint had made hiding impossible, and that nothing but speed was going to help them now. *Pi phiew. Phiew phiew phiew phiew phiew.*

Holding his breath, Vanhala sprinted the forty yards standing between himself and the end of the communication trench. Angry squeals followed him as he ran, and he was conscious of being in a gun-sight the whole time. He hadn't had time to see where Honka-joki was.

The communication trench began as a low ditch and continued on that way for some distance. The ditch was unmanned, but it was under fire. Vanhala dived to the bottom of it, nearly butting his head up against the heel of Asumaniemi's boot. Then he glanced backwards and saw that Honkajoki hadn't followed at all.

Asumaniemi raised his head and looked forward. The movement provoked an angry shower of bullets into the parapet. The boy was pink with excitement and flushed from his run as he gasped, 'Woo-hoo! We made it! I'm heading in. Follow me and keep your grenades ready! There's a Russki round that bend. I'll kill him first. Now listen, man, now we just gotta get 'em right in the eyes. Let's crawl closer along the bottom of the trench.'

'For Christ's sake, boy! There's two of us!'

'Don't be such a whiner! We hafta act fast . . . I'm going now.'

Asumaniemi set off and Vanhala followed. Just then a hand grenade thudded down in front of them and exploded.

'I'll throw.' Asumaniemi took a grenade and yanked the pull ring. 'Take that, man!'

The grenade sailed from his hand like a ball from a schoolboy's and landed precisely where it needed to. The boy sprinted off, his blond hair blowing in the wind, and Vanhala followed on all fours, huffing and puffing, his rear in the air as he scuttled along in a curious sort of gallop. *Phiew phiew phiew phiew phiew . . .*

The clattering only intensified. Their own men were shooting furiously, as they had seen Vanhala and Asumaniemi make it into the trench. Jalovaara knew, though, that the hardest part was still to come. The hollow itself was almost in a blind spot, so the danger there wasn't the greatest they were going to face. Once they reached the positions, however . . . and that gangly giraffe . . . fuck!

Jalovaara realized that Honkajoki hadn't gone out at all. But what was that? There he goes!

The Ensign witnessed a peculiar sight. The towering Honkajoki was crawling forward on his hands and knees. But he didn't move his hands and legs normally, he moved them in turns, lifting either both hands or both feet at the same time. This made his advance a bizarre sort of hopping procedure. The most amazing thing about the maneuver, however, was its incredible speed. His hands and feet moved jauntily, and he progressed like some outlandish animal straight down the bottom of the hollow. He wrapped up his sprint with a few leaps and disappeared into the communication trench.

Behind the curve in the trench lay a Russian corpse the hand grenade had torn to pieces. Another man was crawling away wounded. Two more were coming down the trench to help him. In the blink of an eye, it was as if they had been frozen in place. They knew that enemy soldiers had made it into this end of the communication trench, but they were still stunned at the sight of this bare-headed boy standing before them with his submachine gun raised.

*Trrrrrrrrrrt trrrt trrrrrrt . . .*

Both died without a sound. Asumaniemi yelled backwards, 'Fork in the trench! Somebody go check the other direction . . .'

'He didn't come,' Vanhala gasped, but then saw Honkajoki flop down into the trench behind them.

'Hurry. Hurry . . . come here!'

Honkajoki came, his eyes round, too out of breath to say a word.

'There's a fork in the trench over there . . . Remember . . . Whoever goes to the second bunker . . . Make sure that we can make it into range to take out the machine guns . . .'

'Bam.'

'Hand grenade.'

456

'I'll answer.' Asumaniemi tossed another grenade. Right after the blast, he took off and made it to the fork in the trench. Three hand grenades in a row sailed toward them, and they leapt a few steps backwards. As they were lying there, Asumaniemi said, 'I'm gonna go kill that wounded guy. So he doesn't get us from behind.'

'He wouldn't be able to,' Vanhala panted.

The grenades having gone off, they tried again. Asumaniemi took Vanhala's grenade too, as Vanhala couldn't throw very far at all. The boy sped up and threw hard. The grenade flew to just about the spot from which the three grenades had emerged.

'What will be will be ... ding ding ding!' Asumaniemi ran to the next turn in the trench and shot from behind the corner.

Over the uninterrupted pounding of his submachine gun came Asumaniemi's shouts of, 'Guys! ... Come here! ... Four! ... No, more!'

Vanhala and Honkajoki ran crouching after Asumaniemi, making it around the curve in the trench just in time to see the boy empty a drum into a heap of a body that was still moving slightly. They were at the fork in the trench. Vanhala threw two grenades, one after the other, in the direction of the second bunker, and commanded Honkajoki to stand at the head of the trench.

'Just don't let 'em through ... keep your grenades ready ... And if they throw, dodge – but don't leave ...' Priha was panting with anxiety from the speed of their exertion. Honkajoki was just as frantic, but he nonetheless feigned an air of propriety and straightened up into shooting stance as he said breathlessly, 'Shock trooper Honkajoki at your service ...'

Then Priha threw his last grenade over Asumaniemi's head, and as soon as it exploded, they headed around the next turn, stepping on the bodies obstructing the trench floor. Soft, limp flesh squished gruesomely underfoot. Asumaniemi was glowing with ecstasy and excitement, and Vanhala was starting to feel some of the same enthusiasm as well. He realized that the operation had succeeded, and this success, combined with his awareness of his own role in it, tickled Priha. He was already smiling.

Just as they both opened fire along the edge of the trench to hold back the enemies manning it, they heard Jalovaara shout from further back on their left. Vanhala glanced over and saw the Ensign running, with Sihvonen and a few of the new men behind him. The other section arrived from behind, coming by way of the same low stretch they had taken.

The two machine guns they had set out to silence sat mute on the bank of the trench. The soldiers manning them had already run by the time Vanhala threw his last grenade. The advancing platoon did encounter some fire from further off, but not enough to halt their attack.

Jalovaara was the first to leap down into the trench. He ordered Vanhala to head back and lead the second section down the trench to the second bunker. The men had received these instructions earlier, of course, but the Ensign still wanted to make sure. He also ordered Vanhala to remind Honkajoki that he was to wait at the fork until Määttä brought the machine gun. It had to be positioned so as to prevent the enemy soldiers from climbing out of the trench and escaping as they evacuated the positions.

'All right, boys! Now we're in and we are not letting go. Get to it! Guys in the back, make sure that not one nose peeps out over the edge of this trench. Men in the back, keep the hand grenades coming to the fellows up front. Asumaniemi ... OK, here we go.' Jalovaara was whipped up into a real battle rage. He stepped out in front, hoping to do his part in the whole mission. Watching Vanhala, Asumaniemi and Honkajoki carry out their hand-grenade operation, he had begun to wish he had gone himself and left the platoon to Määttä. He felt a bit ashamed of having sent the others out first – hence his desire to take part in the fighting personally.

They started clearing out the trench. The Ensign walked in front with his submachine gun tucked under his arm, and Asumaniemi threw hand grenades over his head. Some came flying at them from the opposite direction as well, but Asumaniemi easily overwhelmed them. The length and precision of his throws guaranteed that the men could move forward practically unobstructed.

Then the trench joined up with the main artery running along the riverbank. An intense exchange of hand grenades halted them there for a moment, until Jalovaara put a swift end to the skirmish by running boldly up to the turn in the trench and mowing down everything behind it. He brought down a Russian captain along with his three men. That cued the flight.

Then things began to clear up elsewhere too. They were able to retake the other stronghold position the enemy had seized by putting it under heavy fire from the position they'd attained. Jalovaara ordered Määttä and his machine gun to be brought to him as soon as they arrived with the second section, and as soon as they came, they started sending machine-gun and submachine-gun fire over to the neighboring position, over which some intense close-range combat was underway. A large percentage of that stronghold's posts were practically laid out on a platter before them, and once Määttä got going they could watch the enemy soldiers abandoning the trench. The position had been lost for the very same reason. Once the invaders had taken over the hill that controlled it, they could just shoot their opponents out of their posts and force them to abandon the stronghold, just as the enemy soldiers were now compelled to do themselves, as Määttä shot belt after belt into the trench and the gun-nests.

The others immediately resumed pushing out the enemy. Then came the moment Jalovaara had been waiting for. Their opponents had to climb out of the trench and abandon the position. Hand grenades were still crashing down constantly over by the second bunker, but in front of them the first fugitive was already climbing up onto the parapet. He was trying to make it to the riverbank, but went down after a couple of strides.

Vanhala was behind Asumaniemi and yelled, 'They're leaving . . . Hey . . . at least ten . . .' Several soldiers were climbing from the trench about thirty yards out in front of them. Their plight was hopeless, however.

Jalovaara's men rushed to the nests and opened fire. Even the more timid men were in a wild frenzy, as the danger was not great and the targets were all the better for it. Enemy soldiers died all along the riverbank. A few made it to the river, but no sooner did they reach the water than it splashed up around them.

'Aim sharp, boys . . . time to settle the score, boys . . . they asked for it . . .' Jalovaara's voice was hoarse as he yelled out brokenly, panting with fury and the rage of battle. Asumaniemi rose up carelessly and said, 'Hey . . . I put a stop to that butterfly stroke . . . did all you bums see that?'

'Me, too . . . we came that way too . . . there . . . for my bootleg . . .' Priha was settling old accounts.

The one who killed fugitives with the greatest panache, however, was Honkajoki, who had joined in late in the game. Actually, it would be false to say that he killed fugitives. That is, he didn't actually hit anyone, because he didn't aim – he just shot in the same general direction as the others, looking very splendid and calling to Vanhala, 'Shock trooper Vanhala, brilliant execution. The homeland will not forget you.'

Honkajoki figured he had pulled his weight in the whole ordeal, if only by the seat of his pants. Although, indeed, he had been a little tardy setting out. But one does have to assess a situation first. Understandably.

Not one enemy soldier made it across the river. Those on the opposite bank were firing intensely, however. A thud came from the direction of the second bunker, and the men could instantly guess what had happened. Blown up with a satchel charge.

'Guys, I'm out of ammo. Any of you bums got extra?' Asumaniemi turned slightly to the side in the nest and simultaneously rose so that his head and shoulders popped into view through the opening in the nest. Just then, he tumbled over, grabbing his chest.

The others saw him take a few steps as if he were drunk. Then they heard him say quickly a couple of times, 'It's on the left . . . the heart is on the left . . .'

Then he fell to the floor of the trench, and when Jalovaara and Vanhala turned him onto his back, they saw that the boy was dead. The bullet had actually struck quite close to his heart.

Jalovaara suddenly turned away. He took a few violent steps, but then got himself under control and said, 'Always the best . . .'

The shooting ceased. Everyone was stunned. The easy slaughter of a moment ago and the success of the counter-attack, with no casualties, had lifted their spirits almost to the point of exultation. Asumaniemi's death thudded down like a sledgehammer in the middle of the elated atmosphere. The final expression on the boy's face was one of astonishment. No doubt his bravery had been connected to a perfect certainty that danger did not actually exist. He had had one, brief moment in which to realize that playing with one's life can lead to losing it.

He was, incidentally, one of the most beautiful corpses they had seen. That slightly childish expression of amazement still beamed from his face. Otherwise it was perfectly calm, untroubled by any of the warped contortions that usually made the features of the dead so horrible to look at.

Jalovaara left a few men to secure the riverbank, then set off toward the second bunker's communication trench with Vanhala, Honkajoki, Sihvonen and one of the new recruits. Six enemy soldiers surrendered there, seeing that they had no hope of escape. They had been retreating down the road the second section had come along when they saw that their escape route was blocked. The last man raised his hands like the others, but then suddenly grabbed the submachine gun he had dropped, stuck the barrel under his jaw, and shot himself. He had the shoulder tabs of a second lieutenant.

The position had been retaken. Two men from the second section had been wounded – one by shrapnel from a hand grenade and the other by a piece of wood that had sailed from the doorpost of the bunker after he threw the satchel charge through its opening. They had taken three prisoners from the bunker, making eight in all. Jalovaara sent them away immediately and hurried to man the positions. As soon as the enemy was sure their own men were all out of the stronghold, they would launch a terrible barrage in revenge. There was no doubt about that.

Things were already quiet in the neighboring stronghold as well.

The enemy soldiers over there who had tried to make it to the river ended up dying helplessly, as Määttä's machine gun was situated at a particularly opportune angle. When Jalovaara reached the machine-gun position, the new recruit who had been assisting Määttä was bursting with excitement. This many and that many men we shot! They dropped like frogs!

Määttä himself was smoking a cigarette and looking indifferent. When Jalovaara congratulated him, he paid the Ensign no attention, then said, as if he hadn't heard him at all, 'Might want to pull the team back into the foxholes for cover. Iron's gonna start comin' down pretty soon.'

Jalovaara could see that Määttä took no interest in anything but the strictly practical side of things. The Ensign set off down the trench toward the others. They had gathered around Asumaniemi's body, which the medics had lifted onto a stretcher.

'He was good at gymnastics,' a voice said. 'He was always practicing at the training center 'cause they had bars there.'

'He was always dangling from the tree branches here, too, whenever he had any time.'

Jalovaara ordered the body to be taken away so that it wouldn't end up in the barrage.

When the medics had left, he said to Vanhala, 'This means another stripe for you, Priha. It's . . . just . . . too bad.' Jalovaara's voice trembled. 'What a horrible reward for Asumaniemi.'

Then the Ensign looked at Honkajoki. 'Well, you did quite all right too.'

The Ensign smiled. He was remembering Honkajoki's hop-crawl. Honkajoki raised his eyes with a look of respectful earnestness, removed his cap and bowed.

Then they all laughed. A little too much, perhaps. The joy felt slightly hysterical as their anxiety began to wear off. Only Vanhala's heehee-ing was just as it had been as he said, 'So we're gonna have a real live officer on our hands! Lots of blood, sweat and tears goes into a rise in the ranks. But a man's rewarded in the end! Hee-heehee . . .'

Then they ducked into the foxholes without being commanded. Back-clapping and heehee-ing stopped in a second. Booms sounded from the other side of the river, like potatoes dropping onto the floor. Stalin's organs.

## V

They lay curled up in the shelters dug into the walls of the trench. Fire, dirt, iron and smoke swirled up over the positions. Their terror was just the same as before. It hadn't changed at all. Eyes closed, hearts thumping, bodies trembling, they tried to sink themselves into the very earth.

They might have been even more scared today than they had been before, though. They knew that the firing would end soon.

'Stop, just stop.'

They had finished with the war the day before, but the enemy had yet to do so. It was as if might was flaunting its divinity, taunting them, even in these final moments.

Watchful, exhausted and beyond worn out, they waited for the blasts to cease. What use had their dogged stint by this river been? What use had the counter-attack a few days ago been? They were going to have to relinquish the positions.

Right. They had lost. Received their punishment. Why had it happened this way? Well, there would be many answers to that, no doubt. There was, at least, one consolation in it all. In handing them this whipping, fate had released them from all responsibility. What would victory have meant? Responsibility. Responsibility for deeds they would have been obliged to account for, sooner or later. Because as long as the history of humanity marches on, the cause of what follows will be what came before. And in cause lies responsibility. He who presides over the cause must answer for the consequences. And maybe it was just these exhausted men's good fortune that neither they nor their descendants would be the ones obliged to answer. They had already atoned for their sins – paid for them with their own hides. They had but one hope left: to pull the shreds of their lives through these final minutes.

And after that, they would stand free, cleared, blameless. Happy.

The thunder continued. It roared in fantastic crashes far through the clear, autumn air. It churned on even in these final seconds, as if it were declaring, intoxicated by its own greatness: Woe to the vanquished!

But at least they did not have to fear the voice resounding in its echo: Woe to the victors!

Määttä opened his eyes. He saw dirt falling to the trench floor. A man appeared around the corner of the trench. It was some older guy who'd been called out of the reserves and who had seemed a bit off for a while now. He was bare-headed, and in the middle of his filthy face the whites of his eyes bulged out, round, wild and frightened.

'Get under cover!'

The man heard Määttä yell, but instead of obeying, he remained standing in front of his shelter.

'Get down!'

'Would if it was any use.' The man stared straight ahead as he spoke, paying no attention to Määttä. The latter emerged from his shelter and said, 'Get down. Peace is coming.'

The man gazed wide-eyed at Määttä, and then, without further ado, started climbing up to the parapet. Määttä grabbed hold of him. The man started to wrench himself free, but Määttä yanked him to the trench floor, where a tough wrestling match ensued. Just then, the cannon fire ceased, and once it had fallen silent, the stillness was broken only by Määttä's grunting and the shouts of the madman. 'Get off! Goddamn parachutists! Lemme go! I'll dictate . . . Land and peace for everybody . . . And I'll give power to everybody . . . But lemme go for Christssake . . .'

Vanhala, Sihvonen, Rahikainen and Honkajoki hurried over to help. The man struggled and howled as he thrashed about beneath Määttä, who was trying to hold him still. They didn't manage to get him under control until there was a man on each of his arms and each of his legs, in addition to Määttä, who was sitting on his chest. The man screamed and cursed, his teeth clenched and his mouth foaming. He muttered senseless words and phrases between wild howls.

Men emerged from the shelters. With tired faces, they followed in silence as the madman was led away.

The Finnish War was over.

Tins of ersatz coffee dangled from the ends of sticks. Mielonen walked along the road, calling out, 'If anybody wants to hear, you can come listen to the rrradio at the command post. Some Secretary spoutin' off.'

The men were lying about by the roadside, some sleeping, others making coffee.

'We can hear it from here. Anyway, we know what's coming. Old as the alphabet.'

'Them and their goddamn speeches. Speeches won't help anything. When you're all out of gunpowder, you're better off just keepin' your trap shut. Now they're gonna go dronin' on about the rights of small nations. Dog's cue to piss.'

It was Rahikainen.

'Yup. That's for sure. Losers get the shit kicked out of them. And that's that.'

It was Sihvonen. Angry and exhausted, but somehow not quite certain who it was he was angry at.

'. . . the establishment of good relations with our neighbors. May friendship and cooperation with other nations be our aim henceforth.'

It was the Secretary.

Honkajoki fished some bread out of his pack and came across a couple of pieces of wood carved into bizarre shapes. He tossed them to Vanhala and said, 'Into the fire with them, Priha! I've lost my inspiration.'

Priha was on his knees beside the campfire. He blew into it and got a light flurry of ash in the eyes. He rubbed them with his fists. Then he looked at Honkajoki. Dirt and grime covered his face, which had lost much of its previous roundness. But the red, puffy corners of his eyes still crinkled with his smile as he shook with laughter and said, 'If only we still had your bow . . . heeheehee!'

'Alas. If only that damn Bushki, excuse me, that Soviet in the shrubbery, hadn't made it into the position from the side . . . making me suffer the most distressing loss of this war.'

Priha turned toward the campfire again and said, blowing on the flames, 'The Union of Soviet Socialist Republics won, but racing to the line for a strong second place came feisty little Finland.'

The ash swirled up. Heeheeheeheehee.

Soon, even the last of them had dropped off to sleep. A lone horse-cart made its way along the road, its rattle echoing through the forest. Tent tarps covered its load. A stiff hand clenched into a fist dangled down beneath one of the edges. The last of the casualties were heading home.

Ensign Jalovaara sat far off in the forest. He had made his way there gradually, as if he had no idea where he was going. When he saw that no one was around, he sat on a mound of grass and let his head drop between his hands. He sat motionless for a long time, staring at the ground. From far down the road, the clatter of the cart receded further and further into the distance.

His eyes were damp. Jalovaara clenched his jaw for a long time, trying to steel himself against what was coming. But eventually his shoulders began to quiver, and his whole body shook with the bitter, violent convulsions of a man brought to tears. Between sobs and clenched teeth, he repeated over and over, 'We heard . . . they let us know . . . that Finland's dead . . . her tombs already deep beneath the snow . . . snow . . .'

The autumn sun had climbed to midday, warming the ground and the men sprawled out over it. Clusters of lingonberries glistened in their low-lying bushes. The cart rattled faintly off into the distance and silence fell, swallowing everything up into the stillness of the dry pine forest. The tired men slept. The sun smiled down on them. It wasn't angry – no, not by any means. Maybe it even felt some sort of sympathy for them.

Rather dear, those boys.

# Note on the Translation

'Some Secretary spoutin' off,' Mielonen calls out through the camp, unofficially signaling to the men that the Finnish authorities are conceding defeat. His tone in these final pages of the book is as flippant as it was at the start, when he made his rounds with a similar announcement portending the declaration of war. So perhaps it is not surprising to learn that the gentleman 'spoutin' off', whose historic words are quoted verbatim, was not 'some Secretary', but Risto Ryti, President of Finland.* Mielonen's misattribution could be a joke – or perhaps he just didn't know who was going to speak before the voice came over the radio. Just after the decisive words are delivered, however, the narrator affirms Mielonen's account with a gravity that would be difficult to construe as jocular. 'It was the Secretary,' we read, in the final installment of a parallel structure aligning the Secretary with Rahikainen and Sihvonen (p. 465).

I like to think of this closing gesture on Väinö Linna's part as a cautionary one: a reminder that the story you have just read is not history, but fiction. I'm not sure how else to make sense of the blatant and irresolvable incompatibility between narratorial assertion and historical fact. It certainly seems implausible that the author simply forgot that the words he was quoting verbatim were spoken by the president of his country. More convincing, I think, is the reading by which the deliberate violation of history seeks to clarify the distinction between testimonial truth and the kind of truth the novel pursues. The historical elements that have appeared here, the author seems to imply – the school songs, the propaganda, the President's speech – are no more real than the imagined exclamations of

* See Jyrki Nummi, *Jalon kansan parhaat voimat* [*The Finest Forces in the Noble Nation*] (Helsinki: Werner Söderström Osakeyhtiö [WSOY], 1993), pp. 48–9.

Sihvonen and Rahikainen. Reality and the use I have made of it belong to separate worlds.

The distinction between these two worlds was a matter of crucial importance for Väinö Linna. It is for this reason, above all, that I have refrained from annotating my translation of his text with historical references, maps, timelines or other textual supports. To gloss unfamiliar items with information drawn from history seemed to me to suggest an unwarranted equivalence between Linna's fictional world and the one we live in. Some readers will no doubt protest that some such information is necessary to a full understanding of the book. I would argue that, for the most part, this is not the case. One might turn to any number of examples, for instance: 'Around Christmas time, the German battleship *Scharnhorst* sank in the Arctic Sea' (p. 361). Should contemporary English readers be alerted to the fact that the *Scharnhorst* was a real German battleship that sank in the Arctic on 26 December 1943? Finns reading the novel in 1954 would have known, one could argue, and the information would have enabled them to recognize the reference as an ominous chronological signpost. But then, one might also note Linna's introductory appositive, 'the German battleship'. Had the author been confident that all his readers knew of the event, such an appositive would have been unintuitive. Surely 'the *Scharnhorst*' alone would have been more natural. Whatever its intention, the gesture bears two immediate consequences: it ensures the inclusion of readers situated slightly beyond the novel's immediate frame of reference, and it creates a closed world whose logic relies on nothing outside of itself.

Given Linna's own tendency to make explicit whatever tacit information he deemed necessary to understanding his text, I decided that this would be the most appropriate way of incorporating such information into the translation as well. So, on the rare occasions in which implicit information available to the Finnish reader needed to be explained to the English one, I have incorporated it into the translation following Linna's own style. When the brawny Hietanen starts shouting out instructions 'in his amusingly

staccato Turku accent', for example, the 'amusing' aspect of the dialect as well as its place of origin are implicit in the Finnish, explicit
in the English (p. 7). I thought it important to retain the foreign, or
semi-foreign, words Linna uses – undefined – throughout the Finnish text, which often meant inserting appositives for the English
reader: '*tshasovna*, one of those Karelian Orthodox chapels'; 'kolkhoz ... collective farm,' etc. (pp. 311, 129). The appositive 'the
women's auxiliary' beside the name 'Lotta Svärd' is also my addition, as is 'the Friday Fishing Club' beside 'Rajamäki Regiment' (pp.
21, 135). I chose to double these last two references rather than
replace them with English equivalents because each presents a literary reference I wanted to retain. The women's auxiliary 'Lotta
Svärd' takes its name from a poem by the Swedish-speaking Finn
Johan Ludvig Runeberg (*Tales of Ensign Stål*, 1860), and the 'Rajamäki
Regiment' refers to a rather unruly crew in the first major novel
written in Finnish, Aleksis Kivi's *Seven Brothers* (1870). I privileged
the sense of each reference in the appositives, as that was what com-
prehensibility in the English text required, but I left in the Swedish
and Finnish names as well, so that the literary reader would have
the means to recognize them.

I italicized the two attempted quotations from Runeberg's *Tales
of Ensign Stål* in Chapter Three (pp. 88–9, 102), though, as Hietanen
remembers both sections from Paavo Cajander's Finnish translation
a bit erroneously, I improvised verse versions of his Finnish rather
than quoting Clement Burbank Shaw's translations from the Swedish.* Similarly, I tried to indicate, through English meter and rhyme,
the versified origins of Ensign Jalovaara's closing lines, which recall
Eino Leino's Finnish translation of Heinrich Heine's 'Die Grenadiere'
['The Two Grenadiers']: 'We heard ... they let us know ... that
Finland's dead ... her tombs already deep beneath the snow ...' (p.
466). Because Jalovaara's invocation of the lines relies so heavily

---

* Johan Ludvig Runeberg, *Fänrik Ståls Sägner* (Helsingfors: Sederholm, 1860); *Vän-
rikki Stoolin tarinat*, trans. Paavo Cajander (Helsinki: Kansanvalistus-seura, 1889);
*The Songs of Ensign Stål*, trans. Clement Burbank Shaw (New York: G. E. Stechert,
1925).

upon the particular structure of Leino's translation, adapting a published English translation of the Heine seemed wide of the mark.*
Songs quoted in the text, like the poems, I have kept in verse measured to the tunes in question, and I have italicized or inset all sung
lines to indicate their status as quotations. Though these lines are
pulled from some of the best-known songs in Finland, I was unable
to locate English verse translations for any of them, and so must
answer for all such lyrics myself.

I am also responsible for all the speech patterns of the characters,
which the reader will have noticed are often quite marked. In the
Finnish text, the characters' speech is rendered in more or less phonetic orthography, corresponding to regional variants of Finnish
pronunciation. Evoking the tribal stereotypes of centuries, the
Finnish dialects contribute to the creation of immediately identifi-
able characters, whose distinctive voices allow the author to omit
such cumbersome attributions as 'said Rokka' or 'said Hietanen'.
The pronounced presence of the dialects also reflects the particular
historical circumstance of the Continuation War in Finland, during
which platoons were geographically integrated (during the earlier
Winter War, they had been organized by hometown, as we glimpse
through Rokka and Susling). Finally, and perhaps most significantly,
the dialects in the book carve out a particular socio-political position in relation to the verbal class distinctions of wartime Finland,
as well as to the politics of the war itself.

Because the dialects function in so many different ways at different moments in the text – asserting class, authority, defiance,
belonging, comedic intent – I felt that it would have been impossible, or at least irresponsible, to translate them in a single, formally
systematic way. To substitute English dialects for Finnish ones
would have been to reduce the many functions of a character's dialectical speech into a flat, totalizing equivalence on the basis of one

* See Yrjö Varpio, *Pentinkulma ja maailma* [*Pentti's Corner and the World*] (Helsinki:
WSOY, 1979), pp. 35–6; Heinrich Heine, *Buch der Lieder* [*Book of Songs*] (Hamburg:
Hoffmann und Campe, 1844), p. 73; and Eino Leino, *Maailman kannel* [*The World's
Lyre*] (Helsinki: Kustannusosakeyhtiö Kosonen, 1908), p. 98.

aspect like class, and it would also have created jarring confusions of geographical and national identity. So, stripped of the Finnish dialects, I developed an array of compensatory maneuvers, which I will endeavor to outline here.

The identificatory burden carried by the dialects in the Finnish was transferred onto a number of pronounced idiolects: particularly distinctive, individual voices crafted partly through speech patterns, rhythm and word choice, but also partly through systematic misspellings. Hence Hietanen's signature 'pre-tty strange', Salo's 'purty good', Rokka's 'Lissen!' and so on. The stand-off between Riitaoja's vulnerable dialectical Finnish and Lehto's cold, impersonal standard Finnish was transposed into Riitaoja's stutter on the word-initial /k/ and Lehto's mockery of it. The Savo dialect posed a particular challenge because it appears explicitly in the text three times, in association with three different individuals: the Master Sergeant on the motorbike leading the truck transport (p. 35), Corporal Mielonen (p. 175), and finally Vanhala – who is not actually from Savo, but affects the dialect for comedic effect (pp. 307–8). Though the comedy (and distinction) of the Savo accent lies, to my ear, primarily in its prosody, marked prosody is a difficult thing to convey in the space of a line, so after much experimenting with risible effects in English, I finally went with the word-initial rolled /r/, transcribed *rrr*, which, like the Savo prosody, lies just far enough beyond the limits of the standard language to be striking. And it was precisely because the rolled /r/ does not fall within the limits of the English language that I transposed Lieutenant Colonel Karjula's speech impediment – in Finnish, an inability to roll his /r/s – into an English lisp, or inability to pronounce the letter /s/.

One character's dialect did compel anomalous treatment in the English, and that character is, of course, Antero Rokka. Even within the world of the text, Rokka's dialect borders on incomprehensibility (recall the failed communication with the neighboring guard in the trench on p. 347), and it has only become more incomprehensible with time, having died out with the generation of Finns that saw the Karelian Isthmus ceded to the Soviet Union in 1944. Nevertheless,

Rokka's voice is still unmistakably sharp, lively and irreverent – and charged, precisely because of its lost place of origin. To create such a voice in English was obviously an impossible task, but just as inconceivable was the prospect of letting it fall flat. So, I fashioned an Antero Rokka in English, calling upon the sharpest, cleverest, mythically proportioned voices in my memory. If Rokka's dialect sounds American, which of course it does, that is because the voices in my memory do, too. I could not really have written him any other way.

Finally, the 'vicious verbal volley' between Lammio's stilted, standard Finnish and Rokka's rapid-fire Karelian chatter was mostly transposed into a difference of register, though the textual reference of Lammio's 'pretentiously crossed "t"s' on p. 71 (known to the specialist as aspirated /t/s, roughly equivalent to Finnish /d/s) did prompt me to drop several 't's from Rokka's speech ('listen' became 'lissen'; 'winter' 'winner', etc.). That these dropped 't's resulted in the transformation of 'Winter War' into the comical commentary 'Winner War' (which, as we know, 'both sides won') was sheer luck.

The aspect of the dialects that proved most elusive was not their class hierarchies, which could be transposed into register and non-standard spelling with a little work, nor their geographical specificity, which is stated explicitly in the text. Even the dialects' identificatory function could be carried by idiolect and orthography. The elusive element, in the end, was the particular distrust of the written word that *Unknown Soldiers* paradoxically enacts. For the Finnish dialects, in their phonetic transcription, exercise a peculiar effect on Finnish readers, and one that is not quite replicable in English. Calling upon a powerful Finnish metaphor by which phonetic spelling is equated with equality of access, transparency of representation, and even democracy, phonetic spellings in Finnish stage an unequivocal claim to truth. Pitted against the newly standardized, written Finnish of the nascent state, the phonetically transcribed dialects in Linna's book lay bare the artifice of that state's 'paper language', calling into question the entire national project and undercutting its proud wartime propaganda. (It is perhaps worth mentioning, for those rusty on their Finnish history, that when the Second World War broke out, the Finnish tongue as a written language was scarcely a century old, and the Finnish state, not yet a quarter-century.)

*Unknown Soldiers* is a national classic if ever there was one, but it is a national classic that rejects a single, national language in favor of a multiplicity of idioms. I am not entirely certain that the translation succeeds in embodying that profound act. In searching for ways of making the English language perform such a feat, I have to admit that I came up short, contenting myself with the most minute of gestures scattered throughout the text.

By way of conclusion, I will mention only one, which appears in the passage with which I began. The war has ended; the men are sitting, dazed, beside the road; and Mielonen has just invited them to come and hear the Secretary's speech. Apathetic, one of the men replies, 'We can hear it from here. Anyway, we know what's coming. Old as the alphabet'(p. 465). *'Vanha kun aapinen'* – 'Old as the ABCs' – is a Finnish saying, which in most instances one would replace with the English idiom 'as old as the hills'. But such a formulation would run counter to the accusation staged through all of the dialects. 'What's coming' – the entirely disingenuous speech of the Finnish Secretary, or indeed, the Finnish President – is not as old as the hills. On the contrary: it is as old as the alphabet.